SERIES OMNIBUS

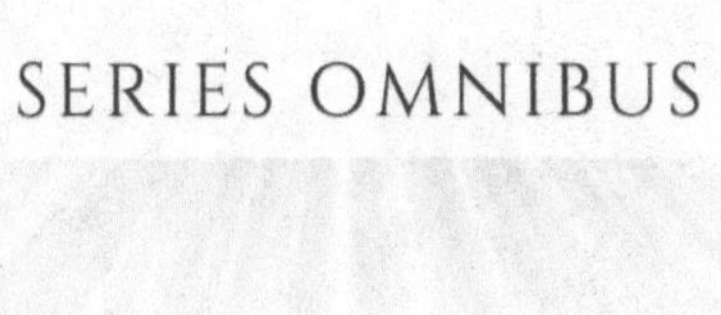

THE URBAN UNDERWORLD

SERVING UP BITE-SIZED COZY FANTASY BASED IN GREEK MYTHOLOGY

GWYNETH LESLEY

OUTSPOKEN INK PRESS

First published in New Zealand in 2024 by Outspoken Ink Press

Text copyright © Gwyneth Lesley, 2024

Cover image copyright © Gwyneth Lesley

Editor for The Signature Dish & Taking Orders: Machediting

Editor for Drinking Wine, Let Them Eat Cake, You Are What You Eat and The Restaurateur: Erin Driessen

Character art: Alex Durand @drnd_art

A catalogue record for this book is available from the New Zealand Library.

EBOOK ISBN: 978-1-7385837-6-8

PAPERBACK ISBN: 978-0-473-70703-3

HARDBACK ISBN: 978-0-473-70704-0

To the waitresses working forty six hour weeks
The bartenders on their feet
And the chefs constantly in the kitchen heat.

OTHER BOOKS BY GWYNETH LESLEY

The Femme Fatale Series

(Modern-day mythology retellings with heartbreaking romances)

Prometheus' Priestess

A Lifetime Kind of Love

Madonna: Medusa's retelling

PRAISE FOR THE FEMME FATALE SERIES

"Gwyneth Lesley is back with another heart-wrenching story (in a good way)! So well-written, so much raw emotion. I am in love with how the author can ... not 'retell' Greek myths ... but she 'continues' the classic stories in a modern-day setting. I cannot understand how she does this so well, but it works! Beautiful. Inspiring. Emotional. Challenging." – *Taylor*

"Continuously so impressed at the way that Gwyneth can make her books so relatable. So much sadness, hope, and inspiration in these pages. Beautifully written and a genius blending with the myths. It's truly amazing the way that the Femme Fatale series books have each taught me something about self-growth or acceptance." – *Monica*

"Third book in the Femme Fatale series and Gwyneth Lesley's writing and storytelling still leaves me awed. Harrowing, passionate, vengeance, and the ultimate vindication."

– *Steffy Smith, Historical Romance Author*

"The author has a wonderful way of building the story and the characters." – *Sandra*

"I always read her books so quickly because they're so easy to read and so captivating that I don't want to put them down. I love a myth-based retelling that doesn't feel like I'm reading something written hundreds of years ago." – *Rene*

GREEK GLOSSARY & TERMS IT MAY HELP TO KNOW

THE UNDERWORLD

Made up of three neighbourhoods: Asphodel Meadows, Elysium, and Tartarus

THE RIVERS BORDERING THE UNDERWORLD

Styx – the river of hate, on which everyone travels from the mortal realms to the Underworld

Lethe – the river of forgetfulness, for those who wish to forget their mortal life

Acheron – the river of pain and woe, where Souls go to wash away these things and heal

Cocytus – the river of lamentation, frozen over on traitors and those who committed terrible acts of fraud

Phlegethon – the river of fire that flows into Tartarus and boils violent criminals

THE INHABITANTS OF THE UNDERWORLD YOU WILL MEET THIS TIME

Royals:

Hades – God of the Underworld

Queen Persephone – Goddess of Spring & Queen of the Underworld

Aphrodite - Goddess of Love and Fertility

Asteria – Goddess of Falling Stars

Ate – Goddess of mischief, delusion, ruin, and blind folly, rash action, and reckless impulse, who led men down the path of ruin

Atropos – one of the three Moirai, goddesses of fate and destiny. The oldest of the three, also known as "the Inflexible One." She chooses the manner of death and ends the lives of mortals by cutting their threads

Charon – the ferryman that takes Souls over the river Styx and into the Underworld

Demeter – Mother of Persephone and Goddess of the Harvest and Agriculture.

Dionysus – God of winemaking (also orchards and fruit, vegetation, fertility, festivity, insanity, ritual madness, religious ecstasy, and theatre)

Erebus – Personification of darkness and lover of Nyx (as well as one of the primordial deities)

Eros - God of Carnal Love (and Aphrodite's assistant)

Gaia - primordial deity who personifies the Earth

Hecate/Hekate – Goddess of Magic, Witchcraft, the Night, Ghosts, Necromancy, and the Moon. She is also the protector of the oikos (family unit), and entranceways

Helios – the personification of the Sun, a Titan

Hera – Goddess of marriage, women, and family, and the protector of women during childbirth, Queen of the twelve Olympians and Mount Olympus, sister and wife of Zeus

Hermes – the messenger of the gods, who also plays the role of the psychopomp or "soul guide"; a conductor of Souls into the afterlife

Hephaestus – Greek god of Blacksmiths and Craftsmen

Hymenaeus – God of Marriage

Hypnos – the personification of sleep

The Judges of the Dead – Minos, Rhadamanthus, and Aeacus judge the deeds of the deceased, decide where they will reside in the Underworld as a result, and create the laws that governed the Underworld

Nyx – Goddess of Night and the personification of it (one of the primordial deities)

Poseidon – God of the Sea (and water in general), Earthquakes, and Horses

Selene – goddess and personification of the Moon

Thanatos – the personification of death

Tisiphone – One of the original three Furies (or Erinyes) that punished crimes of murder: parricide, fratricide and homicide. In this retelling, the Furies are the aunties of Araes

Zeus – God of Thunder (and who likes to think of himself as the God of Gods)

WELL KNOWN AMONGST THE DEAD

Cyclops – a giant one-eyed creature, the most famous of which is a skilled blacksmith

Eurydice – an oak nymph, and Orpheus' wife before her untimely death

Homer – a Greek poet credited as the author of the *Iliad* and the *Odyssey*, two epic poems that are foundational works of ancient Greek literature.

Oneiroi – the dark-winged spirits of dreams which emerged each night like a flock of bats from their cavernous home in Erebos; the first of these, made of horn, was the source of the prophetic god-sent dreams, while the other, constructed of ivory, was the source of dreams which were false and without meaning

Orpheus – The son of a muse and a king, Orpheus is our ancient Greek legendary hero endowed with superhuman musical skills

Phantasos – the personification of unreal, deceptive dreams

Theseus – the legendary Greek hero who navigated the labyrinth and slew the Minotaur

The Witches of Thessaly [Thessilian Witches]: In legend and myth, a group of witches from ancient Thessaly, a region in ancient Greece. Sometimes considered a number of female astrologers regarded as sorcerers connected with the Aglaonice in the third to first centuries BCE. They are often associated with magical practices and their stories are sometimes intertwined with the adventures of legendary heroes like Jason and the Argonauts.

COMMONERS

Araes [Rae and Nika] – female spirits, oath-bound to curse the newly-dead who have sworn false oaths in the mortal realm

Agathodaemon [Garth] – serpent-like daemon with scales along his body

Keres – female death spirits

Lamia [Lexie] – a vampiric daemon

Nymphs: personifications of nature

Meliae [Melamene]– ash-tree nymphs

Dryad [Tomas] – oak-tree nymphs

Oread [Irid] – mountain nymphs

Nereids [Yani] – sea nymphs

Naiads – freshwater nymphs

Satyrs [Savvas] – a male nature spirit with ears and a tail resembling those of a horse

Souls – newly-dead mortal souls

ITEMS YOU'LL FIND IN THE UNDERWORLD

Éos – a cash register of sorts

Fire stick – herbs wrapped in a tube of rice paper and smoked, most commonly traded between the tree nymphs

Ibrik – Rae's coffee pot

Kylix – a drinking cup that was a broad shallow bowl with two handles

Véa – the parchment with the Underworlds daily announcements

Liquid palladium – mined from Tartarus, this replaces all mortal metal in the Underworld

AUTHOR'S NOTE ON THE MYTHS

As an omnibus, this book is a collection of short novellas following a team of creatures in the Underworld, all just trying to get by. Each one of them has been pulled from an original Greek myth and placed in a new urban setting, which means these events are definitely NOT mythological fact. Where necessary, I will explain any relevant myths before each story begins. Beyond that, I encourage you to treat this as a whimsical trip to the Underworld you are yet to inhabit.

Now for a little bit about each story you will read.
(Feel free to skip this if you don't want any spoilers!)

THE SIGNATURE DISH OF THE UNDERWORLD

In the annual Hades cook-off held at the Asphodel Meadows, Rae has repeatedly lost to the formidable libation daemon, Garth, a four-time champion. However, this year, when Garth offers Rae a job in his kitchen, she faces a dilemma: is it a ploy to undermine her chances of winning, or does he truly recognise her culinary talent and seek her assistance? As both chefs grapple with the complexities of competition, their reputations are on the line, and only one can emerge victorious.

TAKING ORDERS IN THE UNDERWORLD

After the results of the last cook-off, Garth decides to break away from the restaurant's libations agreement with Zeus, which results in a rapid decline of business. When Garth suggests Nika go trolling for customers on the cobbled streets of Asphodel Meadows, Nika has had enough. She leaves in search of something that she believes can save the team from ruin, but her quest takes her deep into the heart of Tartarus, the neighbourhood Nika escaped from long ago, and for good reason.

DRINKING WINE IN THE UNDERWORLD

Ampelos Savvas Boötes has only ever had one love. That love ended disastrously, and with Ampelos' death. Given the chance to start afresh in the Underworld as Savvas, he makes a name for himself as the winemaker in town working at The Watering Hole. Until one day, when his old lover, Dionysus, walks through the doors and offers him a once-in-a-lifetime opportunity. But after his last lifetime was ripped away from him so cruelly, can Savvas really risk letting Dionysus back into his life?

LET THEM EAT CAKE IN THE UNDERWORLD

In a world where witchcraft is a fading art, Irid, the manager of Hecate's Herbs Apothecary, decides it's time for a new adventure, expressing this desire to her partner, Melamene. The couple has navigated change before, with Melamene pursuing her patisserie chef aspirations. But the fear of failure and the potential loss of everything they've worked for looms large. As the couple grapples with these uncertainties, their journey unfolds into a heartwarming tale of support, the importance of seeking help, and the unwavering faith in one's dreams.

YOU ARE WHAT YOU EAT IN THE UNDERWORLD

The origin story of Lexie and Yani: Both fleeing from familial threats, they forge a deep bond in the unfamiliar world of Asphodel Meadows. Taking jobs at The Watering Hole, Lexie becomes Yani's anchor on land, and he, her closest friend. Yet, as two beings from vastly different worlds, can they truly rely on each other in this uncharted territory?

THE RESTAURATEUR IN THE UNDERWORLD

Garth's origin story: Part male, part snake – Garth is a creature others have always inherently distrusted ever since his great-great grandma encouraged some woman named Eve to eat an apple. When Garth finds him and his family condemned to the Underworld, he is tasked with navigating the complex dynamics of Hades' realm. Then she comes along. His little Rae-of-Sunshine. Suddenly, Garth finds himself putting more than just his heart on the line to see if she could ever love him in return.

Welcome to the Underworld...

CONTENTS

LET THEM EAT CAKE IN THE UNDERWORLD

YOU ARE WHAT YOU EAT IN THE UNDERWORLD

THE RESTAURATEUR IN THE UNDERWORLD

RECIPES FROM THE UNDERWORLD

THE SIGNATURE DISH OF THE UNDERWORLD

1

A WATCHED POT

The first Soul to walk through the doors was Simon: a flabby flat-nosed phantom of a being that came to the bistro every day, at eleven every morning.

Rae already had a pot of warmed coffee waiting for him, served in Simon's favourite kylix; which was why he kept coming back day after day. She had different kylix's – you mortals might know them better as cups – for each of the regulars she saw every day. It was the little things like that which made a difference to this place.

Simon sat at the table underneath the one domed window in the bistro, where he read the latest from the νέα; the parchment with the Underworlds daily announcements. Rae watched as he smiled at something he read and lifted the cup to his mouth. The very act transformed the kylix into a mask; the painted eyes under the rim became Simon's, the handles his ears, and the round base became an open mouth. That way, those drinking were always conversing and looking at who they were dining with. It was a sign of polite society that separated the Meadows from *other* places, like the drinking holes in Tartarus.

"Anything good in the νέα today?" Rae asked when he was finished, refilling his kylix, this time with warmed spiced wine. Simon didn't have to ask – it was custom for him on the fifth day of every week to have a glass of spiced wine, and it had been for the five decades he'd been coming here.

"Just the usual. It's all about how Greeks and Trojans keep on coming to the Underworld. Apparently, Charon is overworked and the river Styx is still swamped, even with the new housing developments. Plus, there's turf wars in the suburbs about who gets to live where."

"You'd think they'd have realised that petty squabbles don't matter now they're dead."

"Ah, Hades will come sort them out. No one wants to face the wrath of a god, much less one they have to spend the rest of eternity with."

"If they don't sort it out, they can expect him to make them drink from the Lethe and forget," Rae warned.

"Apparently there are already hundreds of soldiers that are lining up at that river."

"I'm not surprised," she said. "I'd want the Lethe to take my memories of war too."

"I wouldn't." Simon surprised her by saying. "I'd want to remember what I'd done. A life without memories would be an ache in your chest that would never leave once you were here."

"Perhaps you'd forget that too."

"I don't think so. A life without a story – some part of your soul would remember that."

Rae pursed her lips, nodded, and moved on to serve a nymph that had wandered in and headed for the counter.

By midday a steady stream of customers had trickled in, and the lunch hour rush had begun. Despite being an Arae,

Rae's reputation for some of the most delicious food in the realm preceded her, and even the pious creatures that tried to avoid even being *close* to her kind – for fear that she was one of the ancient originals evils not to be approached – came in for some of her baked goods.

The food cabinet was filled with many items that had been adapted from the mortal recipes Rae had collected from Souls that had accidentally strolled into the bistro. They didn't know why they ended up in this area of Asphodel Meadows, only that they had a compulsion to travel there, to see her. It was an invisible thread that tugged them to her – the Souls that had broken an oath, a promise, a vow, always sought one of her kind out; for redemption.

Endless, incessant, redemption.

When they asked what they could do, she asked them for a recipe.

Over time, she had gathered as many recipes as she could. Many of them had to be adapted to work with the ingredients she could gather from the Underworld and its Meadows. The cabinet was now stocked with the product of these half-earthside, half-underworld recipes. There was fig and spikenard leaf salad freshly tucked into homemade wraps that soothed fears, corn fritters served with a pomegranate and vinegar glaze that immediately filled the consumer with positive thoughts. Rae's filo pastries with fig and creamy goat cheese warmed the cold blood of Souls, while the pan-fried fish caught from the Lethe were stuffed with lotus flowers, dill and lemon, and made anyone eating it temporarily forget everything other than their latest task.

The meat that the mortals sacrificed earthside ended up down at the meat market in the Meadows; cows, lambs and pigs all made for juicy sausage rolls wrapped in the thinnest layer of pastry Rae could manage to make. Not that Rae often managed to get any meat from the market – many of the vendors wouldn't sell to her for the same reason the pious ones tried to avoid her. It was one of those old urban legends that had spread, and Rae had become tired of trying to correct people. She figured if she could just *show* them what she could do then maybe she could change the narrative that Araes were to be avoided at all costs.

Not that everyone down here believed that, of course. When Rae did manage to get an Underworld butcher to agree to sell her the burnt bits that were so charred that no one else wanted them, Rae caramelised them in such a way that everyone came in to try her 'sweet and savoury' sausage rolls.

This was why Rae focused her energy not on her pre-disposed destiny of haranguing oathbreakers, or correcting those of the old beliefs, but on her dream. She diverted all her energy to her beloved copper pots and pans in the kitchen at Geras' Grub.

The sweet section of her cabinet was just as impressive. Lemon and pomegranate seed muffins cleansed the palette. Apple ice, a fudge-like substance made from the juice of an apple and frozen in the depths of hell, was also a popular choice among the patrons. Big billowy lavender meringues gave a Soul courage before a speaking event, grapefruit and pomegranate bliss balls gave them a healthy glow and complexion, and ambrosia gave ... an orgasm.

Rae's ambrosia that had become the signature dish for "Geras' Grub: the little lunchtime bistro that's not to be missed." That was what the νέα had called her dish in Rae's first food critic review, four centuries ago now. It was not the traditional honeyed version the gods up on Olympus drank. Instead, it was a cake slice made of yoghurt from goats milk, her homemade marshmallows, honey and biscuits all mixed together.

It wasn't often that there were any ambrosia slices left at the end of a lunchtime shift. That review had turned Geras' Grub from an old, dingy tavern that no one would be caught dead in, to a bustling lunchtime corner bistro that had a steady stream of customers. It was why the owner, Geras, kept her around. Well that and the fact he didn't actually *like* doing any of the work. He just liked the fruits of Rae's labour.

But today had been slower than most.

"Three ambrosias to finish off, Keres?" Rae asked the final lunch table of ladies, who had been gossiping and cackling increasingly loudly throughout the lunch service.

The three female death spirits nodded and made general noises of agreement with one another.

"I should think we want three ambrosias and a bottle of golden wine," one of them said to another, refusing to look Rae in the eye. They wouldn't look, no matter what she did. But they would eat the food – and that was what mattered more to Rae.

"Of course," Rae nodded and headed back behind the counter to collect the wine kylix's and the golden liquid that Rae bought privately from one of Dionysus' acolytes.

"You know we're supposed to be locking up in an hour," Geras grumbled. "Not serving those Keres more wine and waiting around here."

"I'll wait for them and then lock up, Geras." Rae rolled her eyes when her back was turned while she grabbed the cold ambrosia slices. "You can go home to your wife."

"Too right," Geras grumbled, opening the éos, a cash register of sorts, which was filled with slips of parchment – tokens they were called – and pilfering through the ones collected for the day. As the owner, he got his pick of tokens first.

The coins that the dead travelled into the Underworld with only paid the ferryman, Charon, to carry them across to the Underworld. Once they were here, Souls had to settle on what tokens they would like to trade. That way, rich mortals did not necessarily make rich Souls. It was a clean slate, of sorts. Something their Queen Persephone had introduced after her time in the mortal realm.

On each token was a favour, or an offering, that the recipient gave in reasonable exchange for the food, drink and service of the bistro. Some daemons offered to guide the recipient to their dream jobs, others could make it rain on your patch of land (or that of an enemy). Some tokens offered love potions, success, windfalls, luck.

Just because it was the Underworld didn't mean creatures didn't still crave all the things they always had before.

Rae watched Geras with displeasure. His long, gnarled fingers and nails that looked like talons flicked through each token. When it got to a token Geras liked the look of, he would laugh wheezily to himself and pocket it. Rae had collected over two dozen tokens today, stocked the kitchen, and ran most – if not all – of the tables.

Geras, meanwhile, had spent the entire time interrupting the guests with tales of his own life and occasionally clearing a stack of plates. Rae couldn't figure out if he was lonely and his wife had stopped listening to him back home, or if he was just unaware that the customers did not want to talk to him.

But this was Geras' bistro, and he got to decide who he talked to and which tokens he wanted to take. Rae was left with the rest. That was the deal they had made way back when she'd started here, desperate for a chance to be taken seriously as a cook. Desperate to make her dream come true.

Geras grinned at her. "I'll leave you with these. I'm sure there will be something useful in here for a cursed one like you."

Rae's smile was tight. "Thank you, Geras."

The fact was, she couldn't afford to piss him off. He was one of the only daemon-run eateries in Asphodel that would have her. She had to have tokens to survive. Sure, no one would starve to 'death' in a place where death was the constant, but survival of the spirit was a different beast. Survival of the spirit meant you actually had to enjoy the existence you lived.

So Rae sat on the stool, while the Keres cackled and gossiped, occasionally throwing her scorned looks when they thought she wasn't looking, and painted a new scene onto one of the cracked kylix cups that needed a bit of love and attention. Rae was painting it sea-foam green — the colour of the ocean Aphrodite walked out of. Looking up every so often to check on the table and make sure they didn't need anything from her, Rae continued her task dutifully and in painstaking detail until the ladies finally got up to leave without so much as a goodbye, throwing their tokens on the table as if they were used serviettes.

The door squeaked shut behind the last of them and the bistro — who Rae had come to consider a good friend over the last four centuries — gave a visible sigh.

"I know," Rae smiled, stroking the wooden countertop. "Another day done. Tomorrow we begin festival preparations though, so you should get some rest. It's going to be a busy next couple of weeks."

The door opened in agreement.

"Yes," Rae agreed. "I'll go home and get some rest too."

2

VRAVEÍO ASTÉRI
(THE GREEK PRIZE STAR)

Every century in the Asphodel Meadows, there was the Vraveío Astéri festival, otherwise known to the locals as the Hades cook-off.

Asphodel Meadows was like any other city earthside, with suburbs and shops, roads and roadkill. Rae was always amused when she saw a screech-owl lying in the road. They lay there for a moment, then sat up dazed, before they went to hunt down whatever idiot had run them over.

Rae's suburb was a leafy district, home to more ash-tree nymph Meliae than anything else, but she loved it for its quiet understatedness. Her home was a cavern under one of the roots of the largest ash tree in the area. She merely had to take one right turn at the end of her cobblestone street, carry on straight for three hundred metres or so under-neath the awnings of ash tree leaves, cross the road, and then she was at the bistro.

Unlocking the tree stump door, Rae got to work setting up the kitchens for the day. This would be the year she would win the cook-off.

The rules were simple: the festival was held in the first

year of every new century and ran for twelve days. During that time the contestants had to produce a festival dish – the ultimate showcase of the best produce and chef talent Asphodel Meadows had to offer to their queen, Persephone. Hades then presented the winning dish to his bride, their queen. Hence why they all called it Hades cook-off instead of its fancy festival title.

Each century there was a theme and the dish had to include a key ingredient. This year's theme was The Kallistē Clash; the key ingredient – apples.

The clash was still all anyone could talk about, even though it felt like it had been millenia since it had occurred. Hera, the Goddess of Marriage, Athena the Goddess of Wisdom, and Aphrodite, the Goddess of Love and Beauty, had all been attending a wedding, when Eris – the Goddess of Discord – had thrown a beautiful golden apple inscribed with the words "for the most beautiful" onto the wedding buffet. According to the Greek gossip mill, the goddesses had squabbled over it so incessantly, Zeus had let a young mortal prince decide who the apple belonged to.

To this day, a whole host of starving Greek and Trojan soldiers continued walking along the river Styx and through the doors of the bistro as a result. All because Paris had chosen Aphrodite, and Aphrodie had promised him the love of the world's most beautiful woman. It was a pity then that the woman in question, Helen of Sparta, was already married to King Menelaus. And so, when Paris had stolen her away on the ships, war had ensued.

The majority of the Underworld was happy about a good bloody war – it meant new customers. Business was good, the Underworld economy thriving. The only ones who didn't particularly appreciate it were those of Rae's kind – the Arae that were hounded by the newly-dead who had sworn false oaths in the mortal realm. The new arrivals – simply known as Souls to the locals – thought they would find absolution with an Arae, unknowing it was the deities job to take vengeance on them, however they saw fit.

Rae turned on Ibrik - a small brass pot with its long spout whistling as it heated Rae's coffee blend on a small spherical gas element that the Souls always commented looked like a camp stove. Whatever that was.

The counter stocked, the coffee brewing, Rae moved to checking the table set ups were perfect. She'd done them yesterday afternoon, but sometimes, when the bistro was being playful, it rearranged things. It was a little game they played together.

Just because she was only the supervisor did not mean she did not hold Geras' Grub to the same standards as other restaurants in the area.

Each table was made of a dark wood, so brown as to be black. The cutlery was freshly polished palladium mined from deep within Tartarus, laid on brown linen napkins. In the centre of the tables were small plant cuttings that she had taken from her own garden over time, nourished with Asphodel soil, and encased in glass bowls. Watering each plant, straightening each piece of cutlery until it was perfect, Rae surveyed the place and nodded to herself. Yes, this would do for the day.

One day, Rae wouldn't just be the supervisor of this place – she'd own it. That was the dream. Perhaps with the prize tokens Hades offered with the festival, this would be the century it would finally come true.

Ibrik whistled.

"Yes, I know." Rae chuckled, turning to her brass companion. "You're my biggest cheerleader."

The brass pot rattled – an indignant protest.

"Oh? You aren't my biggest fan?" Rae widened her eyes at the pot in mock surprise.

At that moment, the door tinkled. There was no bell above the entrance, the greeting itself came from the door as it opened, its voice singing through the air at whoever had walked through.

Rae turned towards it, and her surprise was immediately replaced with a scowl.

"What are you doing here?"

The agathodaemon slithered in, a cocky smile on his face. He reached the edge of the counter, opposite Rae, and grabbed a handful of pomegranate seeds from the offering bowl in front of the éos where the tokens were held. The offering bowl was similar to what the mortals called a 'tip jar', though there was no need for tip jars in the Underworld, given that mortal currency didn't work.

Instead, the offering was for their queen – the goddess, Persephone. The queen to their lord Hades, and the love of his immortal life. It was thanks to her that the plants in Asphodel Meadows now thrived as the mortal realms vegetation did. Before that, the flowers had been in eternal death. Beautiful, but with no hope.

Now, there was hope.

The agathodaemon opened that wide mouth of his and poured the pomegranate seeds down his throat.

"Are you drunk?!"

Taking from an offering bowl was as good as insulting the goddess herself.

"This early in the day? You think so little of me, my Rae of Sunshine?"

"I think nothing of you, Garth." Rae pinned him with a stare, one hand on her hip.

A look like that on a Soul would have worked, especially

coming from an Arae. Instead, Garth laughed. Loudly.

"Liar. Besides, Persephone won't miss a few. Not when she sees what I'm making in her honour for the cook-off."

He was no mere mortal Soul. He was a daemon. Worse than that he was *the* daemon that people in the earthly realm paid libations to after a meal. They would smash their drinks on the ground, singing his praises and thanking him for the food on their plates.

"So," Garth niggled at her. "What are you making for the cook-off?"

"None of your gods-damned business," she grumbled.

"Of course it's my business, Sunshine. You're my competition."

Rae tried not to smile at that, because for the last four centuries Garth and his restaurant just down the road from her – Zeus' Watering Hole – had won the cook-off. Rae had never been to his restaurant but she knew why he was winning. It wasn't based on talent. Garth won because of the libations. Every time a mortal ritually poured water, wine, oil, milk, or honey in honour of the gods – Garth grew in popularity. The more popular he was, the more powerful he grew down here in Asphodel.

The fact that he considered her actual competition this century was a good sign.

"Why are you here?"

Garth let out a breath, his wavy dark hair blowing up before settling again around his oval face. The light hanging from the bistro highlighted the jade green tints in his otherwise black hair, making it look like snakes were hugging his skull.

Rae was about to tell Garth to forget the question, she was busy, and that he should leave when Ibrik let out a low whistling howl in warning.

"Fine," she muttered under her breath, turning and taking her friend off the element.

"Can I have a cup?"

"No."

"I'll tell you why I'm here if you'll give me one."

"I suspect you'll tell me anyway." Rae threw a shrewd look over her shoulder as she began to pour the coffee into a kylix.

It wasn't that she disliked Garth. It was just … unfair. It was unfair that the mortals paid him libations without knowing what it meant. It was unfair that he grew more powerful simply because people believed in him. It was unfair that he won the competition every century, and the prize token from Hades, when he didn't even need it. Not like she did.

"I need a favour."

Now he was just messing with her.

"What could a good daemon like you possibly need from me, a cursed one?"

"I need you to work in my kitchen tonight."

Rae almost dropped the kylix holding the molten hot liquid. Ibrik let out a high-pitch squeal in protest until she put the pair of them down.

"Excuse me?"

She turned to face Garth leaning against one of the tables. His corded forearms bulged as he leaned his weight back onto it, but Rae's eyes zeroed in on the fact that one of his wide hands had skewed the napkin just twenty or so degrees.

That was annoying.

"I need you to work in my kitchens tonight," Garth repeated, a smile in his tone.

Rae roamed her eyes over him, eyes still narrowed, as

she watched his body language for an explanation. Garth was not a young daemon. He'd been in Asphodel since Rae was a new deity almost a millennium ago, but that grin on his face and the way his dark eyes twinkled gave him a permanent youth. The muscles in his neck were thick, which translated to a wide torso, a dark sprinkling of coarse black hair on his chest that was just visible from the short chiton tied over one shoulder. But it was his skin beneath his chiton that gave away he was an agath-odaemon.

Every inch of him from the head down was made of snake skin rather than human flesh. It almost looked like a tattoo, and as he leaned back on the table further crossing one leg over the other, the scales shimmered.

"Why?" Rae asked.

"Because my sous chef is ... unavailable."

"Unavailable?"

Garth shrugged. "We had a disagreement."

"What kind of disagreement?"

"He lost his head over something silly. It doesn't matter."

"That depends. Did he lose his head figuratively or literally?"

Garth grinned. "He had three. He could afford to lose one."

Rae laughed. "And people think I'll be the one to curse them if they don't like my food."

Garth continued to smile at her, his scales glistening under the swinging bistro light. Rae looked up and scowled at the playful chandelier.

"Cut it out," she told it.

The bulbs simply glowed brighter. Rae knew what it was getting at, the glow showering Garth in angel light.

"I know you've always wanted to work in a real kitchen. This would be your chance. Come play in mine."

When Rae didn't reply, he continued. "At the very least, you might get to see what I'm preparing for the festival tomorrow." Garth wiggled his eyebrows suggestively.

"If I'm your competition, why would you give me that advantage?" Nothing in this place was done without calling in a favour later down the line. Not even from a good daemon.

Garth shrugged. "Like I said, Sunshine. I'm short staffed. I need your help."

At that moment the door opened, this time on a groan.

"Good morning Geras," Rae said without even glancing towards the bistro entryway. It only ever groaned for its old, tired owner.

"Think about it," Garth told her. He rose up off the table to his full height again, knocking the table setting even further askew, and turned towards the door.

"Geras," he nodded at the other old daemon, who was hunched over, his bald head shining underneath the light.

"Garth," Geras grumbled.

Then he was gone.

"Why," Geras grumbled again, "have you not put the baked goods in the cabinet yet, Arae?" His pointed nose and chin drooped naturally towards the floor, until it looked like someone had attempted to melt his flesh off and had only half finished the job. It left him with a permanently displeased look on his face, often directed at Rae.

"Sorry Geras. I'll do that now."

"And why isn't this table set like the others?"

"I'll get on that too."

Ibrik whistled out a sad song.

"Tell me about it," Rae muttered.

AN APPLE A DAY …

It was four in the afternoon by the time Rae headed home, an hour later than usual. Along the way, she stopped as she always did, at one of Hecate's stores, run by one of her witchy devotees.

Like all potions and trinket stores that honoured their allegiance to Hecate, the walls were lined with bottles and potions of all shapes, colours and sizes. Herbs and dried flowers hung from the rafters, and the stones on the floor were warmed, leaving a beautiful – yet heady – aroma as the heat rose. Rae found she could never stay in one of these stores for long without developing a migraine. Despite that, she often visited as they had the only things that would take her dishes to the next level.

"Ah Rae," the kind Oread, a mountain nymph as pale as snow with jagged cheekbones, smiled as she walked into the shop. "You all ready for tomorrow?"

"I'm hoping you're about to tell me I am, Irid."

Irid remained smiling, those grooves around her eyes reminders of her mountain lineage. They looked like permanent wrinkles. But she otherwise gave no further answer.

"Well? Do you have it?" Rae asked impatiently.

"You have to know I do."

Irid smiled further, then reached underneath her counter and produced a crumpled brown paper bag.

Rae's face lit up with excitement before she looked either side of her, making sure no one else was in the shop.

As Irid rolled down the paper bag, a golden apple began to shine on the dark marble countertop.

"Where did you get it from?" Rae breathed in awe, staring at it.

"From the Garden of Hesperides."

Rae shook her head. "That's not possible."

The garden was, according to rumour, in a spot near the edge of the world under the power of the Olympians and inaccessible to anyone else. Hercules had been the only one to get in, and even then he'd tricked a Titan into helping him. These apples – in the mortal realm – would be worth a fortune.

Down here, it was the thrill of getting one that had Irid agreeing to find it for Rae. That and the fact she also didn't like Garth winning the festival every century.

"It is, and I did," Irid said in that no-nonsense way of hers. "Well," she continued. "Hercules did – and after that whole palava of giving them to King Eurytheus, only for Athena to return them to the garden again, it seemed fitting that one or two went missing …"

"Thank you, Irid. Really." Rae gently scrunched up the brown paper bag again to hide the apple from view.

"What are you going to do with it?" Irid asked, leaning forward slightly. Usually, Rae would let her in on her recipes, but not this one. Not this time.

"I'm going to eat it."

BACK HOME, Rae let herself in through the only tree door painted red in the Meadows.

She dropped the keys on the wooden side table and rubbed the vines that had begun to curl up and around the mirror.

"Hello, girl. Good to see you."

The vine purred in agreement.

Rae sighed and padded down the hallway, turning right towards a small kitchen. There was only enough room for a dining table that doubled as a desk under the window, where Rae sat doing the sums of how many tokens it would take to buy the bistro off Geras night after night, and the kitchen island she loved to cook at which overlooked the dining table desk. With only a little cupboard space behind her to store ingredients and crockery that had been chipped and repaired too many times to count, everything in this room had its place.

Rae took the golden apple out of the brown paper bag and set it in the middle of the table. Then, she took a seat at the table and stared at it.

She had practised the dish for the festival a dozen times in the last week alone. It worked. The only thing she needed to check was that the consistency of the filling and the colouring would be a perfect match to the original apple.

But, what if, when she ate this apple, it invoked some sort of state of mind? What if she forgot what she was supposed to be doing? It would help if she had someone else here, someone who could keep her on track if something was to happen.

Rae had no one. She hadn't had anyone to help her for a long time.

She glanced up at the clock on the wall that hung above the concave arch to the hallway. It blinked at her with the eyes of old Chronus, keeper of time. Five o'clock in the late afternoon. She should spend the evening here, understanding the composition of the Hesperidian apple. The cook-off, after all, began tomorrow.

But the temptation to work in Garth's kitchen ... *that* was the stuff of legends. The fact that he considered her good enough to even offer work in his kitchens meant she might finally be getting somewhere. And, she might get a sneak peek at what his festival dish was, and be able to get her head around what she needed to do to beat him this century.

If she was going to go, she had to get ready and change now. It's likely he'd expect her to work until well into the night – dining hours tended to run on a little longer down here. So she'd only get a few hours sleep between the end of the shift and getting this apple recipe exactly right. She could get it all done.

Couldn't she?

Shaking her head clear of self-doubt, Rae got up and padded across the hallway and into the other rooms in the house. The first was a bedroom just large enough to fit a double bed shoved against the wall and a chest of drawers, both made of ash-tree oak. The latter was shoved against the end of the bed.

On the opposite end, by the headboard, was a door that led to the equally small bathroom. It had nothing more than the basic essentials that dealt with waste – toilet, shower, sink. Just because it was the Underworld didn't mean they didn't have plumbing.

Sewerage was a real issue when you had Souls trying to drink from the rivers.

Turning the shower to scalding hot, Rae waited for the hornwort plants on the shower floor – all trimmed so as not to be prickly but exfoliating – to freshen up. Once they had turned from a dull to bright green, Rae knew it was the right temperature to step into.

She washed quickly. She was an Arae. That didn't mean she had some weird form, another common misconception by the Souls. The humans forgot – they had been made in the gods image. She was, technically, one of the "originals". She had what the mainstream called a mortal body.

Ok, so her's was slightly curvier than most of her kind. Most Arae were tall and lithe. Others would suspect that Rae would be too but – surprisingly – staying on your feet all day did not help you shift the weight. Instead, Rae found she under-ate when she was working in the bistro all day then gorged on her own creations as she tested over and over again at night. Besides, she just didn't generally have the disposition the others of her cursed kind seemed to have. Perhaps it was because she didn't hound those who broke their oaths by literally chasing them across the Asphodel plains.

Instead, Rae soaped heavy breasts, a stomach that still carried the angry red marks where her chiton cinched at the waist, over wide hips and thick thighs. So, she was slightly on the thicker side – that didn't make her slow. She was in and out of the shower within five minutes and redressed in a fresh white chiton.

She grabbed a jacket, the keys, and her purse carrying a few tokens (the rest she hid in a cookie jar in the kitchen for when she knew she needed them), assuming Garth was going to pay her for this favour tonight. Then Rae locked her red door, headed down her street and turned right ... towards Geras' Grub. At the crossing, she took a left, turning her back on the only job she'd ever loved, and walked the five hundred metres to *the* place to eat in town: Zeus' Watering Hole.

The legend, no doubt started by Garth, was that the name had come from the fact that Zeus himself had been spotted dining here when he travelled down from Olympus, on one of his rare visits. It made sense. After all, the two deities that got drinks smashed on the floor in their honour were Zeus and Garth. Perhaps the two had made a pact of some kind.

Rae took a deep breath as she looked up at the mauve neon sign.

She could do this ... she could do this ... she could do this.

She couldn't do this.

About to turn on her heel and go, a voice to her right stopped her in her tracks. "Hello, my Rae of Sunshine."

"Garth."

There he was, leaning against the doorway to the right, which was clearly the staff entrance. The other door, the one Rae had been facing when she was looking up at the sign, was the customer entrance. With its big, black foreboding double doors, decorated with metal studs, the place screamed 'best place in town'.

Black and purple were the chosen colours of their Lord and Lady, Hades and Persephone, and this *was* the place that had won the festival every century since its inception. It was intimidating. Rae had half expected she would have been turned away by the maître d' if she had entered through that door, even though she had an invitation here tonight – albeit to work. It's why she'd turned away to leave.

But there was Garth looking at her, *leaning* in that lazy way of his against the door frame, that cocky smile on his face as he watched her.

"You came."

"Well – what were you going to do without a sous chef?" Rae grumbled.

Garth's grin widened further. "I do so like when you're grouchy. Come on, Sunshine, come and meet the team."

4

KITCHEN ... NIGHTMARES?

G arth's kitchen was the stuff of dreams.

Rae watched as pots and pans flew overhead into chefs hands when they reached up for them, knives did the dicing themselves, even the dishes in the sink washed themselves – though there was a big, burly nymph of some kind overseeing the latter.

"Long before the mortals adopted AI, we figured out a way for it to translate down here," Garth told her. "AI and gods-given powers are a heady combination."

Rae was so busy staring at all the moving pieces that she would love to have in her kitchen as they moved around that when Garth stopped, she almost bumped into him.

"Careful there, Sunshine. Can't have you being clumsy in my kitchen."

Rae flinched at her first mistake.

Garth pretended not to notice and put one hand on her shoulder, gesturing to the chef in front of them. "This is Lexie. She's on the grill tonight."

"I'm on the grill every night," the voluptuous creature

sent Garth a sharp look, her long canines glistening as she did so.

"You're a Lamia – a vampiric daemon," Rae blurted out. The minute the words left her mouth, Rae had to physically stop herself from flinching again at her faux pas. Of course, Lexie knew what she was. If it wasn't for Garth's hand still resting heavily on her shoulder, Rae might have physically tried to recoil into herself.

"Don't worry, *Sunshine*," Lexie threw a smirk at Garth, "You aren't my type. I prefer them ... young. And male. Preferably warm-blooded."

"And bleeding," Garth muttered under his breath.

"I heard that," Lexie quipped.

"I meant you to. Come on, *Rae*, let's introduce you to the rest of our crew."

The chef on fish duty was a tall and lanky male water nymph, named Yani. The other water nymphs – Nereids – in the team were also males. You could tell because their hair was always permanently wet. There was the big burly one Rae had seen supervising the dishes – Ross – and apparently the other one was out front as a bartender, called Savvas.

The pastry chef was a dainty ash-tree nymph named Melamene. Like Rae, her name was indicative of her kind. Rae watched as Melamene loaded some sort of cream that seemed to shimmer into a piping bag that wriggled in her hand until it was full, and then moved on to placing berries into a dark sauce.

"I've never seen a compote that dark before," Rae noted.

Melamene looked up from her hunched over position and smiled at her. "You wouldn't have. This one is a special blend. Right, Garth?"

"Right."

Before Rae could ask more, Garth ushered her through the kitchen and out into the front of the pub.

"And this is where they all come to feast."

The front of the pub, Rae suddenly realised, made this place look deceptively small. Because, before her eyes were four separate dining areas. The one immediately to her right was a lavish indoor garden, like a greenhouse room, thriving with the same plants that coated her shower floor, except here it was a feature wall. With the plants hanging overhead, it felt like you were dining in a lush forest garden.

"Most of our nymph customers prefer to dine in there," Garth told her.

Opposite the garden room was another section with two feature walls. One wall was a floor to ceiling wine rack, with every kind and type of wine the gods and deities enjoyed imaginable. It was a statement of an establishment doing very well to have that many bottles on display. Then the perpendicular wall confirmed who drank from those bottles, the area littered with carvings of who had come and dined here over the years. Rae couldn't see them all in detail from where she stood, but she'd put a prized token on the fact that all of the current twelve Olympians were on it.

Adjacent to what Rae called the 'wealth corner' in her mind, was a section that reminded Rae most of the bistro. Where she was standing was a machine for the serving staff to put through orders, benches for the customers to sit along, a total of twelve tables, and a coffee machine at the other end. Which was where a tall female deity was scolding an even taller, gangly young dryad as he attempted to make coffee.

Before Rae could look around and explore the fourth and final section of the restaurant, Garth called out.

"Nika, get over here. There's someone I'd like you to meet."

The Arae that walked towards her was the definition of perfection for her species. Lithe and elegant, where Rae was stout, the only thing she shared with the female Garth called Nika was the same hair and eye colour. Both were a pearl white, which was often why the mortals thought Araes haunted them. Though they did have other, cuter, features – like their little pointed pixie ears that stuck out beyond their hair. Rae's hair was usually tied in a low plait, so it didn't get in her way in the kitchen.

Nika's, by contrast, was a short sharp bob that accentuated her sharp cheekbones and perfect heart-shaped face.

"Nice to meet you," Rae said as confidently as she could.

Nika's thin lips thinned further and her eyes – pearl white with the lightest blue pupils, they were barely noticeable – narrowed.

"For the record, I don't think you belong here." Nika looked her up and down. "But Garth thinks you're worth a trial run for some reason, and he always gets what he wants." Nika shrugged.

"Nika," Garth warned.

Nika smiled at him saccharinely before turning to Rae. "Let's see if you really can play with the big dogs."

With that, she sauntered off.

"Don't mind her," Garth muttered before she was out of earshot. "Nika can be a little ... prickly."

"You don't say."

He grinned at Rae. "Come on, let me show you the rest of the place."

The final section of the restaurant was a cosy little nook of four tables and then a long galley bar.

"We use The Nook for guests looking for a little more

privacy," Garth explained. "Then the tables that you find in the galley are bar service only, but customers can still order food at the bar."

"The bar tables are numbered I take it?"

"Yeah, it will come through on the ticket. Don't worry, I run a tight ship here. Easy enough to follow once you find the rhythm of the place."

At that moment, a fireball exploded from a cauldron on the bar that was being manned by the bartender.

"Savvas!"

"Sorry, sorry. Just trying out something new for the festival, boss!"

"You want to try something new *now*?!" Garth groaned.

"Well I thought of it this morning, you see. Instead of dipping the apple …"

"Ah, ah, ah! Don't reveal trade secrets just yet, Savvas. I want our little Rae here to experience the dish first. Get her to give me her feedback."

"You do?" Rae looked up at him, puzzled. This place was turning out more unusual than she expected. She'd *expected* them all to be hoity-toity, up themselves, winners. Not a team that seemed at ease with one another. It made her hesitate slightly. Particularly when Nika had mentioned this was a job trial.

Surely, she'd been joking?

"Of course." Garth grinned, as if sensing her hesitation – a crack in her hardened exterior. "But for now, we have a dinner service to prepare for."

Heading back to the kitchen, Garth clapped his hands together and everyone snapped to attention.

"Listen up, team. I know you're putting your finishing touches on your preparations for tonight but seeing as we have a new team member joining us for the evening, I want to remind everyone of how tonight is going to go."

Rae gulped. She hoped it was inaudible.

"It's going to be a slower night than usual. The festival kicks off tomorrow, so everyone is saving themselves for that. Slower does not mean sloppy, you hear me? You send a sloppy dish up to my pass and I will gut you myself, am I clear?" Garth smiled as he said it.

"Yes, Chef." They all chorused.

"Now, because she doesn't know how this is going to go, Rae here is going to be on the pass, plating for me. Help her out. Don't waste her time letting her plate something that you know isn't up to the standard I'd expect. Don't let me down, and don't think you can let it slide just because she's a newbie. Got it?"

"Yes, Chef."

"Well, then. Let's have some fun."

5

A HELPING HAND

If this was Garth's idea of slow, Rae was definitely out of her depth. This was why he'd recruited her, she realised. To prove she couldn't compete with him.

Sure, a few tickets had trickled in at the beginning, but the minute it hit seven o'clock – BAM – it was like everyone and their dog wanted to come in here.

"Don't worry," Garth chuckled as he saw Rae stare wide-eyed as the ticket machine spat out a flurry of three more tickets.

"We only have one seating tonight. Tomorrow it will be double this, maybe even triple if Nika can flip the tables like she usually does. You just have to ride the wave for the next hour and a half. You think you can do that?"

"Do I have a choice?"

Garth chuckled again. "No, you don't."

With his sleeves rolled up, Garth took the time to show her how he wanted each plate dished at the pass. One run through was all she got. Then Rae had to commit it to memory and replicate it to perfection for every other ticket. Essentially, it was copying and replicating how a dish was put together – something anyone could do if they were good with precision and paying attention. You didn't need professional training to do it, which was good, because Rae didn't have any qualifications beyond her own experience.

Side by side, they worked together in silence while surrounded by a crashing symphony of a kitchen team stretching its legs. Occasionally, Garth would yell out a ticket, the team would chorus "Yes, Chef!" and then he'd shout instructions or timings when he needed certain things sent up to Rae on the pass. Pots and pans whizzed and clattered overhead, while plates came back carried by the lanky waiter, Tomas, who Rae learnt was on his first training shift too.

"Here," Garth said quietly to her, as Rae hesitated to place a crab claw in between the three oysters that finished off the Styx seafood chowder. His hand covered hers as he guided her to pinch the tongs that squealed in protest and placed the claw square in the centre.

"Oh hush, you like it." Garth said to the tongs before going back to his place on the pass and turning to Rae. "You have to do it with confidence, like you do for the dishes at Geras'. Don't worry, you're not going to mess it up."

"In theory, I know that. In reality, these aren't my dishes. It's nerve wracking," Rae muttered as she attempted to try again with the next chowder on the ticket.

Garth quirked an eyebrow at her as he realised what she meant. "You made all those dishes at the bistro? No one else helps you back in the kitchen?"

"Nope. I've never had help in my life. Not sure what to do with it if I was offered it." Rae laughed, but the laughter quickly died when she saw that Garth was looking at her like she was a lost little deity looking for her place in the world.

"You're doing great. Just ... trust yourself."

Rae nodded and focused on the new plate that had zoomed in front of her, her jaw still clenched. A ticket waved its corner at her to remind her what dish she was supposed to be focusing on next.

"Right. Trust myself."

It was hard, though. While Rae was used to sandwiches and baked goods, taking decadent ingredients and turning them into mouth watering home comforts, Garth's food was just ... Decadent, deserving of the capital D.

The Styx seafood chowder that was made with squid ink to look like the river itself, managed to mix the smoky illusion with the fresh seawater flavours, as Rae discovered when Garth asked her to sample it to check its salt levels were right. There were warm hot loaves of bread that were so soft, Rae just wanted to dunk her head on them like a pillow. Those loaves came with self-buttering knives but in place of butter, there was a saffron rouille that made Rae actually moan out loud.

Garth had grinned again at her for that reaction.

It was hard to choose a favourite main dish that Rae saw come and go from the pass. The goat's curry invoked feelings of wet, rainy days in the meadow. Plus it was one of the easiest dishes to plate in a deep bowl that had a large rounded white edge. Though there was something to be said for the fish that was the length of a table for six and stuffed with lemons, bunches of herbs and vegetables that looked like mini trees, bright red cherry tomatoes, and delightfully sharp capers, drizzled over with warmed olive oil. Although the meats that Lexie had sourced — Rae didn't recognise the cuts or which animal the Lamia had taken them from and she wasn't about to ask — was served on an *actual* mini crackling fire, where the customer got to cook their meat to their liking.

"Fire's a waste of time," Lexie had winked at her, grabbing an additional piece of meat that wasn't up to Garth's standards on the pass and dangling it into her mouth before swallowing it whole.

"If you say so," Rae had replied wide-eyed, scared to make a move.

Lexie had just smirked and moved back to her station.

By the time dinner service had begun winding down, Rae had a pretty good idea of which of the desserts was her favourite. The fig σορμπέ was light and creamy, it melted only when it came into contact with a creature's tongue, meaning it could be shaped on the plate into any form.

Garth told her to have fun with it – to create whatever shape she wanted. So at first she made a simple pink pyramid and balanced the fig beside it. Garth had merely raised his eyebrows and said, "Come on Sunshine, you can do better than that."

Letting out a little "hmph," Rae set about getting a little more *creative*. She decided to mould the frozen treat into the shape of a small horse and had the horse bending down to eat from the fig itself.

This time Garth laughed. "Now *that's* more like it! Service!"

The other two signature desserts weren't as fun, but they were just as delicious when Rae sampled them. One was a pomegranate tart that was both tart in its nature and description with the perfect golden crust. The other was a walnut souffle – the biggest souffles Rae had ever seen.

The skill and complexity in flavour palettes and techniques in this kitchen had shown Rae exactly what she was up against. And though the time in the kitchen had flown, that she'd survived a whole shift and held her own, she knew her one-Arae bistro couldn't compete with the likes of this place.

Perhaps, she considered, Garth did deserve his reputation. Or perhaps this was simply what libations and belief got you. Power.

"You did well," he said, as they all began to pitch in with the washing and cleaning of the kitchen once service was over. Large buckets of soapy water and thick bristle brushes had begun busying themselves, but it was a rule of thumb that chefs were meticulous about their clean kitchens. They wouldn't allow sentient objects to take on that responsibility. Which was why everyone was on their knees, or balancing on benches, as they scrubbed the life out of the kitchen surfaces until they shimmered back at them; radiant.

"Thanks."

"When we're finished up here, there's something I want to talk to you about."

Probably to tell her she should drop out of the competition and stop wasting her time.

Instead Rae said, "You're not leaving us to do the cleaning ourselves?"

Garth grabbed a fresh bucket. That sad look was back in his eyes. "Your boss isn't very decent to you, is he?"

Rae snapped her mouth shut at that, but Garth wasn't budging. "Is he?"

"He gave me a job. I've got nothing but gratitude," Rae managed to get out between clenched teeth. Her tone, thankfully, remained neutral, though she began scrubbing her 'patch' on the pass more aggressively.

Garth obviously sensed she needed space. Moving to another area of the kitchen, he left her to it after that. By the time the team was finished, Rae was so exhausted that she just grabbed her belongings that she'd put in the staff locker room before service had begun, and headed out the staff entrance.

"Where do you think you're going?"

Rae turned around, her shoulders slumped, her body exhausted from two back to back demanding jobs. "Home. I'm going home," she told Garth.

"You didn't think I was going to ask you for a favour and then not pay you, did you?"

He stepped forward, a token in hand.

"Oh, right. Yeah. Thanks."

"Well, aren't you going to read it?"

Rae glanced down at the parchment. "Dinner at Zeus' Watering Hole."

"It was the least I could do seeing as you helped us out tonight. And you held your own – just like I thought you would." Garth crossed his arms and gave her a dashing smile.

"I don't know about that. It's too ... busy. I felt like I was barely getting the dishes ready in time. I was surprised you didn't bark at me to hurry up, to be honest."

It was a brush off, an intentional one. If Rae admitted she wasn't cut out for his world, then Garth couldn't beat her to it.

"It's not as scary as it seems."

Rae raised an eyebrow at him as she scoffed. "You're kidding, right? That place is the stuff foodies like me can only dream about. It was fun, but I'm better suited to the bistro."

Another brush off. Another attempt to get him to admit that tonight had been a test she'd failed.

"But you didn't dream about it tonight. You lived it. You

survived it. Why do you insist on playing small? On down-playing your own natural skills and talent? What are you afraid of?"

"Why are you trying to push me into something I'm not cut out for? Are you deliberately trying to psych me out, is that it?!"

Before Garth had a chance to reply, someone else stepped out into the cool, dark air.

"Not bad for a first time, Sunshine. Not great, but not bad," Nika acknowledged as she brushed past both of them.

"Thanks."

And with that, Nika walked off into the twilight streets.

"Look," Garth said, drawing Rae's attention back to him and not Nika's receding form. "Don't listen to Nika. Use the token tomorrow night. I've got a special table set up. You could come and actually enjoy the first night of the festival, experience the other side of our place. I'd like to show you what you were a part of tonight. We can talk."

Rae offered a tight smile before she turned and walked the same route home.

6

LATE FOR A VERY IMPORTANT DATE

The clock on the wall of her kitchen told Rae it was midnight, which meant she had five hours until she had to get up and start the baking for the bistro. That meant she could either spend five hours nailing her golden apple recipe or she could spend just two on it, and then get three hours of rest before the day began.

Rae shrugged off her coat, threw it over the single chair, grabbed the apple from the table and went to work.

She woke up, seven hours later, with her face smooshed against goat's cream.

"Oh no, oh no, oh no, oh no."

Wiping her palm against her face, she stood from the table where there were two dishes – one the original apple with a bite taken out of it, the other her replica that she'd broken with her face – and hurried to the sink to wash off the remnants of food from her cheek. Pots and pans littered Rae's small kitchen. The wooden spoon was making a garbled noise, stuck in the honey glaze now firmly attached to the bottom of the pan. The remaining cream was gloopy when she needed it to be set, which wouldn't happen if she didn't get it in the fridge ASAP. She went to grab the pot and sling it in the fridge, but there was no space.

Usually Rae's fridge *always* had space, there were days where she would have gone hungry if she didn't have the leftovers from the bistro to rely on. But with the festival coming up, Rae's fridge was – for once – packed.

"URGH!"

Desperately trying to rearrange things, she wedged the pot between a bowl of goat's cream and an unidentifiable block of something that Rae vaguely believed was once cheese. Slamming the fridge door shut, she looked around, trying to get her bearings.

There was dried lotus leaf ... *everywhere*, Rae realised. It was sprinkled across her bench, over her face, in her hair. She looked like someone had sneezed on her with glitter. Except it was a well-known fact that lotus leaves could drive you to lose your mind.

"Bugger it."

She showered quickly, removing as much of the lotus leaf as she could, and ran out the door to work.

Of course the one and only time Rae would be late to open the bistro was the one and only time that Geras would already be there early.

"I'm sorry, Geras. It won't happen again."

"It better not." He began to walk away to the backroom now that Rae was here, muttering something under his breath about how females walking out on him would get their comeuppance.

The day went from bad to worse from there.

Because Rae hadn't had a chance to do the fresh baking, she only had the baked goods that had been kept in the stock cupboards. Luckily, she had enough ingredients prepared to also make up the wraps between the few early-morning coffee stragglers. And the signature dish – ambrosia – was easy enough to whip up too, though it would need to go into the freezer to set in time.

Still, by the mid-morning rush, Rae felt like the wind deities had spun her into a tizzy this morning for fun.

"Not much of a selection here today, Rae. Trying to make us all hungry for the festival are you?" Simon asked.

Rae looked at Simon, her head cocked to one side, puzzled, wondering why he was standing at the counter, in his slumped clothing that was one size too big for him. Simon never stood at the counter. He always just came in and took his seat under the window, then settled up his tokens when he was ready to leave.

Then Rae realised she hadn't served him Ibrik this morning.

"Simon, I'm so sorry. I'll be right over with your kylix of coffee."

"Take your time. You seem a little out of sorts."

Rae offered a tight smile. "Festival jitters."

"Mmm," Simon offered half-heartedly, clearly not interested in anything other than his usual as he toddled back to his seat.

The complaints kept on coming. By midday, Rae had run out of the wraps that soothed fears, she only had two corn fritters with their positive pomegranate glaze left. There'd been no chance to make more filo pastries, and the fish dish was always her hardest sell. There was no end of grumbles that the sweet and savoury sausage rolls were out, and apparently daemons, nymphs and other deities in the area simply didn't want apple-ice or meringues today. Which left four slices of ambrosia and a handful of bliss balls, given that Rae hadn't had a chance to make a batch of fresh muffins today either.

It was a long time until two o'clock rocked around and Rae could shut up shop.

Dragging her feet home, Rae barely managed to shut her little red door before she was sliding her back down it and collapsing onto the floor in a flood of tears. Today had been an utter failure, and she was exhausted.

When the sobs eventually began to subside to hiccups, the vine wrapped itself around a box of tissues and handed them to her.

"T-th-thank you," she stuttered between sniffles.

A gentle tug.

"I know, I know, I'll get up. I always do."

A more insistent tug that hauled Rae to her feet. Then a push in the direction of the kitchen. Her home knew her better than she did – knew she would feel better after she got herself back to work. But returning to the bombsite she had left this morning almost deflated her back to her knees again.

"No," she scolded herself. "Shake it off. Get it together, Rae."

Drowning out the thoughts in her head by only focusing on the task in front of her, she scrubbed the kitchen until it was sparkling again. Benches were wiped, then washed and scrubbed with a soap and brush, before being rinsed with water. The palladium appliances were next, with an extra sheen of sparkle given to them with one of those tinctures Rae had gotten from Irid at the Hecate store. The fridge was tackled last.

She was not one to waste food, but the festival period was a strange time. She separated her food into edible and 'not-sure-what-in-the-Underworld-that-is' and then washed, soaped, scrubbed and wiped the fridge shelves and dirty dishes too.

Restacking the remaining food in containers and layering them according to purpose – fuel, bistro new recipes (?), festival prep – Rae was done. Then, only when it was clean, and Rae herself was freshly showered, did she mess it all up again.

The Vraveío Astéri festival officially kicked off tonight at six o'clock. Originally, the competition had only been for restaurants across Asphodel. With the population continuing to grow, and the festival popularity too, the offer had been extended to bakeries, bistros and cafes in the last four centuries. It gave Rae an extra day to prepare – which, this time, was a blessing in disguise. Usually, however, it gave restaurants the advantage: getting to wow with their show-stoppers on the first night.

Rae glanced at the token peeking out of her bag on the dining table across the counter. It fluttered at her, flirting.

"I'm not going to Garth's. Look how today turned out after yesterday. No, I need to stay here and prep my entry for tomorrow anyway."

The rules were clear: you had to meet the brief, impress with your flavour and food combinations, *and* you had to have enough for whenever the secret judge came to visit.

In her first entrance to the competition, Rae's ambrosia had been her entry but she hadn't known about the secret judge. She had just *assumed* they'd turn up on the first day.

She'd been incorrect.

They'd turned up on the sixth day, according to the score card she'd later seen in the νέα and cringed at. The judge hadn't had a chance to sample it at all. "A pity," the report had read, "because a loyal customer told me the bistro had sold out of them by day three. If only the chef had been more prepared."

Rae had been prepared the next time. But she'd *still* come second to Garth. And the time after that. The time after that.

This time would be different.

The competition ran for twelve days, which meant there was no way Rae was going to be able to prep every individual entry tonight. Even between her own home and Geras' place, she wouldn't have enough space to store all the ingredients that made up her dish. Instead, she'd make the first batch of apples today. Enough to get through the first three days of the festival, then reload at three more intervals. Due to the ingredients she was using, the only thing she could completely make now was the apple moulds anyway, which meant tonight's workload would be the heaviest.

Her entry dish had to be bistro appropriate and still hit the brief, so Rae had settled on an apple casing that she would first make in a caramelised honey mould before filling with a cream she had whipped herself from the goat milk provided from the same mountain it was rumoured Zeus was raised on.

The milk was heavier, making it easier to whip, but the process of separating the milk and cream took far longer than usual, meaning Rae had gallons of the stuff in containers by the fridge that kept the cold in.

Finally, two lotus leafs, cut to look like apple leaves, would sit on top of the apple.

That's what Rae had been deciding last night – whether to sprinkle the lotus leaf within the golden moulds, the cream itself, or have them resting on top. So, she'd taken a bite of the golden apple she was trying to replicate.

Last night's memories reappeared in Rae's mind like an old dream shaken awake.

The first bite had made her realise that the caramelised honey moulds she was thinking of using would be too delicate. To get that crisp consistency she was looking for, she would have to dip the moulds in an extra layer of warm honey right before serving so they didn't turn out brittle.

With the second crunch, Rae had realised that if the lotus leafs were placed either inside the cold filling or the warmed honey, they'd lose their primary nutrient: which held the ability to make the eater lose their minds. So that had determined the lotus leaf position as leaves that would balance on top.

Finally, as the juice of the apple seeped onto her tongue and into her bloodstream, Rae's eyes widened as she realised exactly how to make her competition entry a winner. She remembered feeling euphoric, as if she'd just been told the secrets of the gods. The sweet juices from the original apple had penetrated Rae's cerebral fluid, shot up into her brain, and swept away the fog of her subconsciousness. She knew exactly what it would take to win the cook-off. She simply had to trust the process.

Which was why Rae decided to do one final thing to her entry dish. She took the Hesperides apple that she had taken a bite out of the previous night and began to press the rest of the juice out of it.

She would store the juice in a vial and add just one drop to each apple as she piped the cream in. Whether it would replicate the effects or not, it was worth a try. Some part of her synapses zinged in agreement, as if they remembered what the knowledge in the apple had revealed to them.

It felt like a hunch, a knowing, an 'aha', a tug on the thread of life from one of the Fates themselves. Rae followed the tug and got to work.

SHE WAS JUST ABOUT to turn the lights on in the bistro's kitchen for the day when there was a knock on the door.

"Who would be here at five in the morning?" she asked the walls.

They seemed to give her a little sigh, as if they, too, were still sleepy.

Rae padded to the door. Only to open it and find Garth there, hands in his pockets, on the street.

"What are you doing here?"

"You didn't come, last night to dinner, you didn't come. And after what you said, I was worried." He ran a scaly hand through dishevelled hair.

"I was busy," Rae chose to reply, keeping both arms wrapped tightly around herself. It was chilly in the early morning hours. "That's why I didn't come."

"Too busy to eat?"

Rae scoffed. "I barely had time to breathe between doing a shift at yours and going back to the bistro. I was exhausted yesterday."

"I heard."

"You heard what?"

"News travels fast down our little road. Everyone was

coming in for lunch for a change, complaining you were out of everything. What happened?"

"I overslept," Rae grumbled, staring at her feet.

"You overslept?"

"I was working on my festival entry, alright?! Then I fell asleep in a mound of goat mush, and then I had to get that to set, so there wasn't time to bake, which meant I was late, and—"

Garth laughed, a loud, good-natured rumble. "Goat mush? What on the Asphodel-green-Meadows are you making, Sunshine?"

"None of your business."

"Well ... that's what I was here about actually."

Rae stared at him a moment. "Huh?"

Garth smiled. "To be honest with you, we don't usually get such a busy lunch. Ever since you started at Geras' Grub, you put us out of the lunch service. I thought the least I could do was help you out for your cook-off prep, seeing as you helped me out too."

Rae went to open her mouth, but Garth held a hand up and stopped her. "I know, you don't need my help. But please. I'm starting to feel bad here, and I don't want people thinking I *deliberately* sabotaged a cursed one's efforts. It would be bad for my reputation. So, let me help? Let me prove I'm not trying to 'psych you out'. It'll put my conscience at ease."

She knew he was deliberately baiting her, but for the life of her she couldn't think of a single reason to justify saying no to him. She *could* use the help.

"You have a conscience?" Rae muttered sarcastically, though she didn't really mean it, so she stood aside and let him enter.

"I do. And I haven't seen the bistro this quiet in ... a

couple centuries at least." He looked around, then threw a smile over his shoulder at her.

"Yeah, well, you might see it quieter later after the disaster that was yesterday."

"I wouldn't be too worried about that," Garth continued as he stepped behind the counter and began rolling his sleeves up as they entered the kitchen. "Everyone's allowed an off day. They'll be back today to see how you fare. They'll especially want to see what you've created for the festival, if it's anything like your ambrosia."

"How do you know about my ambrosia?"

"Sunshine, *everyone* in Asphodel knows about your ambrosia. It's the stuff of legends."

The kitchen lights flickered to life in agreement.

Across every available surface was a golden bauble in the shape of an apple that sparkled to life under the lights.

Garth stopped in his tracks.

"Holy gods," he eventually said.

"These are just for today," Rae explained, trying to scoot around him and then busying herself in the kitchen, attempting to organise chaos. "They still need to be piped, then kept chilled, the honey warmed and the lotus leaves plucked and ready for presentation. Not to mention the usual dishes."

"Well then," Garth looked at her, eyebrows raised. "Where do you want me?"

Rae couldn't help but grin back. "How are your baking skills?"

SHE'D SET Garth in charge of the sweets. Sure, it would have been easier to have him whip and set the goats cream, but Rae wasn't entrusting her entry dish to anyone. So, while she laboured over each individual apple; carefully piping the cream into the edges and then adding the apple juice drop, Garth was covered in flour.

Every so often he would turn to ask her how exactly she wanted something done when it came to the flavour combinations, and Rae would answer him without looking up from her work.

When she was done with the final apple for the day, she looked up from the dropper to find Garth staring at her, his arms crossed in front of a flour-bombed apron.

"What is *that*?"

Rae narrowed her eyes slightly, her lips quirked to one side, considering something. "You want to try it?"

Garth surveyed the apples in front of him. "Well, you can't be wanting to poison the whole Meadow so ... sure."

Rae tried not to break out in a grin. This was the perfect way to test if just a drop of the apple was enough to induce the effects she'd experienced from taking a bite.

"Hold out your tongue then."

Garth took two steps towards Rae and then stooped down so that he was the right height for her to place a drop on his tongue, their eyes perfectly aligned. The eye contact made the act seem more intimate – uncomfortable – and Rae tried not to squirm away by focusing her attention on the dropper, on the pale golden drop forming perfectly on the end of it, then heavily dropping onto Garth's forked tongue. She watched his eyes dilate, black pupils meeting shards of palest green, before returning to their normal sizes a minute later.

Garth took a moment to stand to his full height and cleared his throat. "Well."

"Well?"

Garth looked around, looked anywhere but at Rae. "Do you still need me? I think I've done about as much as I can do to help you here. I should really get to the restaurant."

Rae frowned. She'd expected him to comment on the flavour, or the reaction – because he'd definitely had *a* reaction – not ignore it completely.

"Uh, yeah, sure. I'll be fine. Thanks."

"Good."

And with that, Garth strode from the kitchen. The lights dimmed ever so slightly.

"Oh, stop it."

AN ODE TO THE MOST BEAUTIFUL

The first official day of the festival would, to anyone else, have been a roaring success.

To Rae, it was adequate.

Sure, all of the apples sold. Customers had smiles on their faces. She even received compliments. But she'd spent the entire day so on edge, looking for the secret judge – even though she *knew* how unlikely it was that they would turn up on the first day – that by the time the doors of the bistro were shut, Rae felt deflated.

Plus, she admitted to herself now that she wasn't busy, Garth's reaction this morning had been bugging her all day. What had the clarity of the apple revealed to him?

Sighing, she took off her apron and got on with her closing tasks: washing Ibrik until he was squeaky clean, literally squeaking at her, the floors the same. Polishing the cutlery in blistering hot water and vinegar, putting away what little of the cabinet food was leftover, and now piping day two's apples.

And so the days continued. Rae, constantly on the look-out, was exhausted by the day's end of going through the motions on high alert. Yet still, in the back of her mind was the knowledge from the apple that promised the cook-off would end in her favour, though not – the thought continued to niggle at her – the way she wanted it to.

How could it end in any other way but victory?

If her story wasn't going to be one of success, then surely that meant the theme of her life was failure, and that was unacceptable. There could be no other option, not that her mind could piece together. If she didn't have a story worth sharing, well that was worse than having a life without a story at all!

The fourth and eighth days were the worst, where she had to spend extra time prepping the remaining apple casings. The caramelised honey was so delicate, peeling them out of each individual casing was a painstakingly slow task. But everything else ran smoothly, until Rae found herself finishing up the eleventh day of the festival with time on her hands for a change.

Finally, too exhausted to battle her mind, she accepted defeat and decided to go and see the dish that she knew was her main competition: Garth's.

His restaurant was as packed as ever as patrons stumbled past her and into the pub that was so packed, condensation had begun to form on the inside of the windows. Rae dithered by the door, bracing herself from the chill by stuffing her hands in the pockets of her jacket. Something curled into the palm of her hand.

Rae pulled it out, curious, only to see Garth's token fluttering in her hand.

"How did you get there?"

The token curled into her palm again, snuggling.

"Alright, alright, I'm going in."

She took a deep breath and marched up to the door.

"I have a token." She told the door that was twice as tall and wide as her. Its knocker morphed into a smile before it threw itself open. The minute Rae was inside, she was accosted by the one deity she'd been hoping to avoid.

"Well, well. Miss Sunshine is back. Did you think Garth was going to hold a table for you every night this week? How presumptuous of you." Nika bit, rising to her full height and looking disdainfully down her nose at Rae.

Rae was about to apologise before she took a breath and said the only thing that was going to garner any level of respect with the Arae in front of her.

"I'm happy to take a seat at the bar if there's one going and order myself. If not, I'm happy to come back another night. There was no expiration date on the token."

Nika sniffed. "And piss Garth off? I'd rather be hounded by neanderthals. Come with me."

Turning on her heel, Nika led Rae to a small corner table in The Nook that seemed to have been left deliberately empty.

"You'll obviously be having the chef special; Styx seafood chowder, slain and marinated goat's curry, and Garth's theïkós for dessert – the crowning glory and our festival entrance this century – An Ode to the Most Beautiful." Nika informed her, as if she was rattling off specials to someone who hadn't worked here just last week.

Rae had no idea what would constitute a theïkós, but she knew if it was anything like the rest, it would be exquisite.

"Sounds great."

Nika smirked at her again. "Oh, just you wait and see."

With that, Nika sauntered off leaving Rae sitting by herself.

Usually, she would bring a book with her, sit and read

in silence – at least the creatures in books didn't seem to mind her company. But, she'd forgotten her book in the post-cook-off haze; had to now settle for people watching without seeming intrusive. Having a cursed ones gaze on you, after all, could be … unnerving. It was the pale blue iris' that did it.

No wonder Nika could turn tables so fast.

Luckily, Savvas came over at that moment with a large glass of golden wine and set it down on the table in front of Rae.

"Hello, Sunshine."

"Savvas," Rae smiled as she picked up the wine and saluted him. For some reason, the water nymph with his neatly trimmed white and grey beard, didn't annoy her by using a monika she hadn't chosen. Instead, there was something melodic about the name on his lips – like the ebbing and flow of an ocean wave – that made Rae relax into her chair.

Well, that and the first sip of golden wine.

It was thick in flavour, though it held the consistency of any other wine. Hints of butter, honey, walnuts and apples crept through, until Rae finished savouring her sip and placed the glass back down on the table with a sigh.

"You like my homemade blend then." Savaas, his arms folded, held a delighted smile on his long face that made his eyes twinkle.

"This is homemade?" Rae stared at the glass, then at Savvas in turn, shocked. "This could rival Dionysus' acolytes."

That had Savvas breaking out in a full on grin before he bent down to conspiratorially whisper in Rae's ear. "Perhaps, one day, I'll tell you of my time in Dionysus' vineyards."

Before Rae could so much as utter a word of protest, Savvas straightened, winked at her, and then made his way back to the galley bar.

Rae sat there, sipping her wine, watching the other patrons from her corner in The Nook. There was only one other couple with her in this section of the restaurant – they looked like two lovers that had been reunited after death had torn them apart. There were crystallised tears falling down the old woman's cheeks, as her lover cupped her wrinkled cheeks and wiped them away.

The age you left the mortal realm was the age you remained down here. It used to be that death would rejuvenate a Soul's form into youthfulness, but – surprisingly – it had been Queen Persephone that had insisted that rule be changed, according to the νέα reports. She said that there was beauty to be found in the age of all things, that those who resided in the Underworld should not forget it.

Watching the old lovers, Rae had to agree. There was something beautiful about it.

The young waiter, Tomas, interrupted Rae's thoughts by presenting her with the Styx seafood chowder. He wavered slightly, as if his arms were not strong enough to hold up the plate the dish was balanced on, and for a moment Rae was convinced she was going to end up wearing the chowder as it began to wobble and slosh precariously. After what felt like forever, he managed to place it down – his arms shaking as he held two other dishes to deliver to another table – with only a splash on the outside rim.

Rae wasn't going to complain about that. Instead she said, "Still enjoying working here?"

"Oh, uh, yes. It's just- it's a lot to learn. I don't think

Nika is very happy with me." Tomas winced as he said her name.

"I don't think she's ever very happy with anyone."

Tomas let out a nervous chuckle. "No, I suppose you're right."

"Though don't let her catch you agreeing with me," Rae replied, deadpan.

Tomas gave her another nervous chuckle at that, out of politeness more than anything Rae suspected, and then left her with some mumbled reasoning that he needed to get the other dishes to their guests.

Rae nodded and turned to the chowder in front of her.

The dish was as delicious as she remembered.

When her chowder was finished, Rae turned her attention to other guests in the establishment, not wanting to intrude further on the lovers in their corner. From her table, she could also see the galley bar clearly, and watched Savvas talk to a middle-aged male Soul who was perched on a bar stool across from him. They appeared to be friends, Savvas laughing good-naturedly at a joke the male Soul had said.

Wherever he had hailed from in the mortal lands must have been hot, because even as a shade of his lookalike human form, he was still darker than most other patrons in the bar. Though race was less-so a factor when you were dead in these parts. Much more prejudice was put on what *type* of deity you were.

Nika chose that moment to interrupt Rae's dark thoughts with the goat curry.

"You know, I can't think why Garth calls you sunshine with a scowl like that."

"Well," Rae said, picking up the spoon ready to dive in,

"how often do you get told to smile for the morons hounding *you*?!"

Nika gave her a hard stare and then laughed. Actually laughed. It was a shrill shriek that had Rae tensing in place.

"Point conceded, Sunshine. Enjoy."

Pleasantly surprised with herself, Rae let her shoulders relax as the warmth of the curry and something else invaded her insides. She continued to watch the patrons come and go, all with smiles on their faces that said they were leaving with full bellies and happy with themselves.

Of course, that warmth in her belly turned to anticipation when it was not Nika, but Garth, who bought out the final dish for her to try.

"I wanted to see what you thought of my festival entry yourself," he said, as he placed not one but *two* plates in front of her. One was a clean white plate that held a single, bright green apple. The other, Rae discovered as Garth lifted the lid, was a small black cauldron, the size of a coffee kylix.

"What do I do with it?"

Garth pointed to the folded piece of paper that sat in front of the apple.

Rae picked it up, flicked it open, and began to read.

An Ode to the Most Beautiful: Queen Persephone
Pomegranate: Latin translation: an apple with many seeds

Dip this apple in the cauldron, as our Queen dipped her toe into the Underworld, and fall in love with our world all over again.

. . .

RAISING AN EYEBROW, Rae took the apple by its stalk and dipped it in the miniature cauldron. A gasp fell from her lips as she pulled it back out again.

The apple was a stunning, gleaming, ruby red.

"How did you...?"

"Keep going," Garth told her, his chin now propped up on his palm, his elbow on the table as he took a seat and watched her.

Rae took the sharp knife that accompanied the dessert and went to slice a section of the apple. The skin of it was hot to the touch, so she balanced her nails delicately against it as the knife cut through the apple like butter, smoke beginning to curl out of the apple in a wonderful show of culinary skill, and ....

Pomegranate seeds spilt out.

Taking the spoon, Rae scooped up a collection of them and brought them to her lips. Flavour exploded on her tongue. The darkest compote – probably the one she had seen Garth's pastry chef perfecting when she'd been in the kitchen – held levels and depths of taste that made it feel like Rae was travelling down into the Underworld for the first time. Each pomegranate seed was a step further down into the abyss, but as light as a woman's – Persephone's – footsteps. It was the perfect combination of heavy and sweet, the smokiness of whatever Garth had trapped inside the apple before you cut it releasing this velvet-like sauce that complemented both the compote and the seeds, the flesh of the apple, and the coating on the skin from the cauldron.

It was ... a masterpiece.

"What is the sauce?" Rae asked, a small frown between her eyebrows as she tried to place it.

"Think of it as dried ice meets goat's milk that was creamed."

"Goat's milk that was creamed?" Rae slowly said, realisation dawning on her as she sat back in her chair and folded her arms. "I wonder where you got that idea from."

"I confess," Garth braced his arms on the table and leaned forward in a whisper, "you gave me the inspiration for that. In fact, your take for this century's cook-off was excellent. I had one of the waitresses grab us a collection of your apples and bring them back here for us to sample the day your dish came out. What you did with that lotus leaf was genius. And whatever was in that vial ... I don't know what it is or how you got it ... but it's what told me to make this version of the sauce." He nodded at the sauce still spooling out of Rae's apple. "So, I have to thank you for that. In fact, I'd like to thank you by offering you the position of sous chef here, permanently."

He looked at her like the offer was genuine. The *audacity* of the agathodaemon!

"You stole part of my idea, and now you want to offer me a permanent job?!"

"I didn't steal. I was inspired."

"And you think that will make me want to work for you?"

"Well, you can't want to work for that old, gnarled, Geras for the rest of your immortality. I thought you wanted the job when you agreed to the trial run the other night."

"You're unbelievable. You didn't even tell me it was a job trial!"

Garth frowned. "I don't understand why you're getting upset. Okay, so I didn't tell you it was a trial run. You still did great work, though. You inspired me to do great work.

And now I'm offering you a job where we could do great work together. No one would even come *close* to touching us in the cook-off if we were creating on the same team. I know you're not usually one to look for help, hell even teamwork, but cutting off that pretty nose of yours just to spite your face seems awfully silly, Sunshine."

"STOP calling me that!"

Now people were looking.

Garth cocked his head at her. "I still don't understand why you're upset."

Rae nudged her chair back. "No, well, Mr-wins-this-every-century, you wouldn't. Excuse me."

She rose from her chair and walked towards the bathroom, barely managing to keep one foot in front of the other.

8

EARLY MORNING MARKETS

Each step caused another tear to fall. Rae blinked rapidly in an effort to keep them at bay as best she could until she was in the bathroom stall, all alone.

There, she collapsed onto the toilet lid and wept.

Garth was going to win the cook-off. Again. There was no doubt about it, that dish was the best thing she'd ever eaten *and* it was the cleverest homage to Persephone that anyone could have come up with while staying on the brief. As much as she wanted to say that Garth had sabotaged her cook-off efforts, she knew that was a lie. Never could she have hoped to pull something like his dish off.

So why had the apple made her feel like she could win?

That was the real kicker. She'd been so sure that this time she had *it*. If she hadn't been so foolish as to test the apple essence out on Garth, to make sure it worked, he wouldn't have got the idea to create that sauce. Because it was that sauce that pulled it all together. The individual components were amazing in their own right, but it was that piece of magic that had really sealed the deal, as well as the flavour in. No pun intended.

Perhaps Rae had been lying to herself all along. Perhaps she had convinced herself of something, and used the juice from the apple as an excuse. An excuse to justify herself not working *harder, smarter*. Losing, *once again*.

Eventually, she managed to concede to herself that sitting on the toilet seat wasn't going to change that. Garth was going to win this century's festival, and she was going to have to spend another hundred years scraping by working for Geras. She could either mope about it or just crack on with it.

She chose the latter.

Wiping her face clear of snot and tears, Rae exited the stall and splashed her face with ice cold water from the taps that sang as they let the water run through them. When the splotches on her skin returned to their normal pale colour, and Rae was confident no one would be able to tell she'd been crying, she turned the taps off and headed back out to the restaurant.

Her table had been cleared, and her jacket was no longer hanging over the back of her chair. Turning towards the bar, she caught Savvas' eye. In return, he gave her a look that was both sad and expectant.

"Nika put your coat away. You'll have to go and find her for it."

Rae nodded, for some reason feeling chastised. "Thanks."

She wandered about the sections of the restaurant, checked the area where deities dragged on fire sticks outside, before figuring Nika must be in the staff section. She was about to enter through the staff entrance when she heard raised voices.

"You can't forfeit the competition!" That sounded like Nika's voice, Rae was fairly certain of it.

"I can and I will." That was definitely Garth's.

"What, for her? You just want to hand it all over to *her*? After everything all of us have stuck with you for. Why, Garth? Tell me why," Nika demanded.

"Because she deserves it."

"She deserves it?" Nika laughed, but it was a cold sound. "You've basically given her a free pass to come and join the team, and now you're going to let her win the cook-off. You know how hard all of us work to make sure that you win that every time. You know why we *have* to. You're willing to throw all that away, throw all of the team's hard work away, because she ... deserves it? Or because you want to sleep with your little Rae of Sunshine?"

Rae's eyes bulged wide. Slamming herself against the outside wall of the restaurant, she continued eavesdropping, trying to keep her laboured breathing as quiet as possible, even though she was freezing without her jacket.

"You'll watch the way you speak to me, Nika. This is still my restaurant. It's my call. I've made my decision."

"You'll ruin us, for her."

"We'll find a way through this, we always do."

"Not this time, Garth. This time you're about to spit in our faces and ask us to smile while you do so."

"I've helped each and every one of you when you asked me. Now, there's a talented Arae out there who is barely getting by, who deserves a break like the rest of us got, and I'm damn well going to make sure she gets it. Surely, you of all deities should understand that, Nika."

"You know what I understand, Garth? I understand the books. I look at them, just like you, every night when we close. I see how many tokens you send off to Zeus. Fifty percent of them! All because your *stupid* great-great grand-father agreed to that ridiculous libation tax with him! Who the hell agrees for libation power in exchange for fifty percent of their profits?! And *don't* even get me started on the fact that Zeus never pays his bill when he's down here. The cook-off token prize is the *only* thing that has kept this place afloat the last five centuries. You know it, I know it, the whole team knows it. It's why we work so hard for you. You're willing to throw all of that away, just for her to catch her break?"

"Yes, I am."

Nika sighed. "You can't help the poor by getting poorer, Garth."

Before she could hear any more, Rae forced herself to head back inside and ask Tomas to fetch her jacket instead.

RAE WRIGGLED around in an uncomfortable silver dress. The awards show envelope that had spat through her house door yesterday was welcome, it meant she was a finalist, but unfortunately that meant she had to go to the show.

"Can you believe we're at one of these things again?" Geras said, as he handed her a glass of bubbly golden wine. "You might actually have a chance of winning this silly little thing you insist on competing in!"

"Can we just go in and get it over with?" Rae muttered, putting the untouched glass back on one of the moving side tables that was going round, collecting and disbursing drinks. Accolades – while wanted – Rae realised, were not something she was comfortable with.

If she won.

"Come now, Sunshine. You should be celebrating! It's

an awards night!" Garth appeared in front of Rae and Geras, smiling that suave smile of his, his hair slicked back and a tux sharpening his look. If he was here that meant he hadn't pulled out of the competition, and Rae's chances had just plummeted.

Rae was about to berate Garth – wondering where he'd come from and why he'd been eavesdropping – when another tall, white daemon schmuck waddled up to the group.

"Geras, of Geras' Grub?" he said.

"Yes," Geras smiled, the smile taking up his whole face in a maniacal way.

"My name is Plutus, I'm an Olympic investor. If you and your—" a glance at Rae, "cook win tonight, I'd like to discuss making you an offer." He handed Geras a card, a vigorous handshake passed between them, and that was that as Plutus wandered off to go schmooze another schmuck.

"Well then," Garth clapped his hands. "Shall we head on into the awards?"

Geras nodded, striding ahead of them. Garth went to follow, until Rae grabbed his elbow and tugged him back towards hers – hard.

"What the hell was that?"

"What the hell was what?" Garth feigned an innocent look.

"Why is an Olympic investor getting Geras' hopes up?"

"Is he?" Garth raised an eyebrow at her. Then he shrugged her off, and headed into the awards show.

"AND THE WINNER IS ... Rae from Geras' Grub!"

Rae barely remembered being pulled up from her seat by an ecstatic Geras. Or being pushed towards the stage by an over-enthusiastic Garth. She didn't remember the judge handing her a sack of tokens, so heavy it felt like a sack of potatoes, or the delight on Queen Persephone's face when Hades presented her with Rae's dish to try.

It all felt like a surreal, slow-motion, dream.

One which was announced in bold lettering across the top of the νέα the next morning: GERAS' GRUB TAKES TOP SPOT IN Vraveío Astéri! There was a brief paragraph talking about the "smart hire" Geras had made in bringing Rae into the fold "to bake out back", and how he had generously – out of the kindness of his heart and not his pocket – backed Rae to win every century.

The picture was one of Geras standing outside the bistro, arms raised triumphantly. Rae wondered when the photo had been taken.

Of course, there was also a paragraph dedicated to the dish that had won it all. Rather surprisingly, there was a sentence or two from Geras about how he had come up with the inspiration for the winning dish and, with the help of Rae, perfected it.

But there was no mention of the grand-champion daemon, or why he had chosen to pull out of the cook-off. It hadn't even mentioned that he *had* pulled out of the cook-off.

"I see you went and won this thing!" Simon

commented, as normal business resumed and Rae served him his morning kylix.

"It would seem so." Rae offered him a tight smile. The feeling of winning wasn't quite what she had expected, Garth's overheard confession from nights ago still sitting heavily on her conscience.

"They given you your prize tokens yet?"

Rae nodded.

"They've already spoken to Geras by the looks of things, too! I mean I practically saw him skip out the building when I went by on my walk earlier. I swear that old boss of yours looked like a frog, he was leaping so high!" Simon kept talking.

Rae couldn't imagine Geras as anything but hunched over, but sure enough, an hour later when the door groaned open, he was practically skipping on long legs that seemed to have grown several inches overnight.

"You're not going to believe it! That investor signed with me! ME!" Geras blurted out to no one in particular, as he headed to where Rae was pouring the cold coffee out of Ibrik to replace with a fresh batch.

"Excuse me?"

"You heard me, Arae! Thanks to my ingenious bet on you, and that marketing with the interview in the νέα, the Olympic investor signed with me this morning!"

"As in, to franchise the place?"

"What?" Geras looked around at Simon, then the few other occupied tables, then back at Rae. "No! He bought me out! I'm free!! Can you believe it? With enough tokens to last me ... well, I don't know how long!"

"But, Geras, remember our original agreement? You said if I ever won, you would let *me* buy you out of this place and take it over," Rae stressed, that heavy feeling on her chest suddenly coming back to settle like a doom cloud.

"Oh, poosh. Even with those winnings, you wouldn't have been able to offer me as much as this fellow. Besides, now you can keep those winnings for yourself and still work here. I told them you would stay on."

"You did?"

"Well, where else are you going to go? This place made you famous! You have a name for yourself. Now, people will actually *want* to come and see you. Buck up!" Geras boomed as heartily as he could, offering Rae a clap on her shoulder that had her bones shaking.

She was surprised at the strength of him.

"This is everything you've dreamed of."

"Yeah," Rae agreed softly.

Geras let out another whoop of delight, as he moved back around the counter. "I've got to get my things. Time to go off exploring, before my dreaded ex-wife comes and tries to score some of these investor tokens off me. If she comes round looking, you tell her I no longer own this place and you have no idea where I've gone. You hear me?"

"Geras, I have no idea where you're going or exactly what is going on right now."

Geras chuckled. "Atta Arae."

The door tinkled when he left.

"So?"

Rae looked at Simon, sitting under the domed window, at the table he sat at every morning at eleven. As he had been every day for the past five decades. "So?"

"What now?" he asked.

Rae sighed, flipping an unruly tea towel over her shoulder. "Now, we crack on with the lunchtime rush."

As PER USUAL, Rae's stomach growled the minute the last customer left the bistro.

Geras had decided to leave right before the *height* of the lunch rush, which meant she'd had another day where she'd been behind the tidal wave of customers. With Geras gone, and no sign of the Olympian investor yet, there was once again no one to help her.

Not that Geras had been much help anyway, she supposed.

Now ... now she was so tired she could barely stand. Her feet ached and she felt faint as she went about cleaning the place down. The bistro helped as much as it could, knowing how exhausted she was, but Rae found herself missing the sentience of Garth's cleaning equipment. In fact, she found herself resentful to even be in this position.

Who worked for something their whole lives, only to feel like a failure, a fraud, a cheat, when they got it?

Barely managing to drag her feet around, Rae somehow found it in her reserves to carry herself home, shut the door, and make it to her fridge. Where there was one of her perfect, golden apples waiting for her.

"I'm not sure I can face eating you right now."

The fridge pushed the shelf out to greet her, the apple sliding with it.

"Alright, alright – I'll eat."

She took the apple, placed it on a small side plate, and stood there in her small kitchen while she cracked the honeyed casing of the apple with the side of her teaspoon, and wondered what she was going to do with the winnings now that her plan for them had fallen through.

The crack of the golden edge was exactly how she wanted it, even though she hadn't dipped it in warm honey like the festival entries. The goat's cream was the perfect consistency. Rae moaned in agreement at her own flavour combinations before her pupils dilated as the final drop of Hesperides apples landed on her tongue.

And, right then and there, she knew why everything had unfolded as it had.

And, right then and there, came a knock on the door.

As Rae walked back out into her small hallway, her house opened the door for her to see Garth standing on the other side of her doorstep, on the cobbled street under the awning of ash trees.

Rae stood there a moment, her mouth hanging open, a half-finished mouthful of cream still on her tongue ... just. She closed her mouth, swallowed, and tried to think of the words she wanted to say.

What she came up with was, "How did you know where I lived?"

"I've seen you walk back from the bistro once or twice," Garth shrugged.

"You've been following me?"

"No, I was making sure you got home safe," Garth scoffed. "Anyway, that doesn't matter. I came to congratulate you on your big win, Sunshine."

The vine from her hallway table gently reached out beyond the doorway and took the plate and teaspoon away from Rae, which was when she began to wring her hands nervously. The vine gently pushed her toward the street.

Before she could get a word in, Garth continued. "Look, you won it fair and square. You were right, I should have done my original dish off its own merit, not used the influence of yours to change it. But you had to know – I need you to know – that I thought I was doing the right thing."

Finally, Rae had the words. "Like you thought you were doing the right thing by pulling yourself from the cook-off so I could win?"

For the first time ever, Garth narrowed his eyes at her. "Who told you that?"

Rae shrugged. "I have my ways."

Garth shook his head. "Nika," he muttered under his breath, the wind nymphs barely just carrying his words to Rae's ears.

"It wasn't her. I just ... I know."

"You ... *know*."

"I do. And I know you need the winnings to keep your place open. So I want you to take them."

"I can't take those from you." Garth shook his head incredulously, causing his hair to fly around his head like a dog drying themselves off. "I won't."

"You didn't let me finish. I want you to take them, and then I want to take you up on your job offer as a sous chef too."

Garth turned back towards her. "You ... want the job? The sous chef job?!"

Rae smiled at him. "Yeah. My plan for what I was going to do with the winning tokens fell through, and I've been thinking about it all day. I may as well use the tokens to keep a place I *actually* want to work in open."

"They're your winnings. I can't take them."

"Well, if you don't I'll have to stay working at Geras' Grub for some ruddy Olympian investor who probably doesn't know the difference between a baster and a basting brush, so you may as well..."

"You're hired," Garth interrupted her.

Rae snapped her mouth shut then immediately opened it again.

"Wait ... I am? And you'll take the tokens? Hold on a minute, that was far too easy to get you to agree. What's the catch? If you think-"

Garth grinned. "Get some sleep, Sunshine. You and I have an early morning at the markets."

TAKING ORDERS IN THE UNDERWORLD

1

___

WELCOME BACK TO ZEUS'
WATERING HOLE

Nika dropped four seafood chowder bowls with a spectacular crash. Pieces of ceramic and chowder flew in all directions. One giant shard flew across the wooden floor and embedded itself in the leg of the chair and – thankfully – not in the occupier of said chair. Another piece bounced and jumped across the other side of the floor of the bar area and landed in a sleeping dogs' fur. The dog's owner, whose feet the dog was lying over, looked perturbed, to say the least, but his scowl quickly faded and was replaced with a look of fear when he saw that it was an Arae who had dropped the dishes.

The definition of perfection of her species, that was what Nika's mother had called her when she was born. Tall and lithe, with pearl white hair, eyes and skin, she had been born to chase and curse the Souls who came to the Underworld after they had made statements under oath and broken them, deliberately deceiving others.

A pity then that she hadn't wanted to do that job. Instead, she'd found a love for putting all that chasing energy into something she found productive – serving the finest food in all of Asphodel Meadows as the lead maître d'. That was, when she wasn't dropping said food.

"*Gods dammit!*"

"Are you okay?" Tomas, a lanky dryad Nika had been training as a waiter for the past three months, asked as he appeared in front of her.

"Do I look okay?" Nika muttered, as she began to carry the remaining plates towards the back. As soon as she rounded the corner that separated the staff from the diners, Garth rounded on her.

"I'm trying to run a dinner service here, and here you are throwing my food all over the floor," he drawled.

"Yes, well, perhaps if you'd put enough staff on tonight, I wouldn't have to run myself ragged and make such clumsy mistakes," Nika bit back, letting the ruined plates clatter into one of the dishwashing caddies.

"I know you're stressed but I'd watch your tone, Nika. I'm still your boss."

"You *watch it*," she hissed back. "We've had two hundred covers tonight, Garth, and you've only given me three waiters! Three! Half the amount we need!" Nika's voice went up an octave, until it was an uncomfortable screech to anyone who was eavesdropping, which was the entire kitchen team. "You ask too much of us, Garth!"

"We all knew forgoing the libations agreement was going to be a bit tight on the way we run things around here, that we were all going to have to make sacrifices. This is that sacrifice."

Nika rolled her eyes. She wasn't going to get into this argument with Garth again, not here. Not now.

In the aftermath of the cook-off festival last year, when Garth had offered to sacrifice the prize tokens for his new hire Rae, he had also somehow got it in his proud head that they no longer needed the libation deal with Zeus. The libation deal, where for fifty percent of their profits, Zeus made sure that half of the drinks and food sacrificed to the gods in the earthly realm were offered to Garth. As a result, mortals often sought out Garth's pub first when they travelled to the Underworld, thinking they'd find favour with him after half a lifetime's worth of offerings.

It had made the pub quite popular.

It had been a costly brand deal, essentially. One set up by Garth's great-great granddaddy. But after centuries of winning Hades cook-off, Garth had obviously assumed his work – *their work*, Nika reminded herself – and the pub's reputation stood well enough on its own merit, and ended the agreement in order to claw back some more of the profits.

He hadn't foreseen that Zeus would take the split so badly. Or that their reputation would change seemingly overnight.

Perhaps, Nika thought for the millionth time, he shouldn't have told the petulant God of Gods to also settle up his tab. As a result, Olympus was going out of their way to make Zeus' Watering Hole the place for the obsolete. No more libations now meant fewer new Souls knew of them. Human Souls had *very* short attention spans, it turned out. Like goldfish. The ones that did know of Garth's place liked to go to the places Olympians were seen dining in, and the other members of the Olympic Twelve had been making their way down to the Underworld and – very deliberately – visiting other eateries in the area.

The dead liked to gossip and the gossip was that this place was losing its touch, *fast*.

For now, the team were just managing to hang on to the

post cook-off momentum, but Garth had already started cutting corners – like the number of staff on shift.

"This isn't sacrifice, this is slave labour," Nika said.

Garth stepped forward until they were standing toe to toe. "I'd be very careful about the next words that come out of your mouth."

Nika opened her mouth when a quiet voice cut in.

"That's enough, both of you. The guests can hear you." Rae's voice was all the more powerful for its quietness, as her head nodded towards the part of the restaurant they could all see.

"Fine," Nika said, blowing out a breath, causing her pale blonde hair to flutter in the air before settling around her harsh cheekbones.

"Fine," Garth agreed, running one of his scaled hands through his slick black hair, a curl of it falling over his forehead as he did so. "You're off for the rest of the night, Nika. You clearly need the rest."

"You can't—"

"I just did."

Nika crossed her arms over a flat chest. "We're already short-staffed and struggling, and you want to take me off the shift? You're out of your mind!"

At that moment, tall and gangly Tomas stepped into the archway of the small area between the guests tables and the kitchen, a dustpan and brush enchantingly sweeping up alongside him. Inside the dustpan; the rest of Nika's broken bowls.

"Tomas can take on your tables. There's only an hour left, it's only a few extra tables and dessert orders. You can handle that, can't you Tomas? Nika's definitely trained you well enough for that?"

"Yes, sir. Not a problem."

Garth smiled wide and slyly at Nika. "That's settled then."

She wanted to slap the smile off his smug face. She debated doing it too, until she felt a little touch on her elbow.

At first she thought it was Rae. Rae who had been the catalyst for all this change in the first place. Garth's soft spot for the other Arae had led to him jeopardising the *one* place and the *only* job that Nika had ever loved. On top of that, Rae had the nerve to have a perfectly-imperfect demeanour, where nothing was ever too much trouble for her to take on, which grated against Nika, who had always been taught that perfection was the standard to attain.

Luckily, it wasn't her who touched Nika, but Lexie – the grill chef – instead.

"Want to take a fire stick break with me?"

Nika released a breath, rolling her shoulders and cracking her neck. "Sure."

Before she turned to leave, she pointed a long, pale finger at Tomas. "You better not screw it up."

Tomas gulped and nodded.

"The boy will be fine, Nika," Garth drawled.

She sent him a glower and made her way back through the kitchen to the service entrance outside, where Lexie was waiting for her, fire stick in hand. The tall, voluptuous vampiric daemon, whose dark red hair was currently wickedly spiked and short, gave Nika a look that suggested Nika had been out of line back inside. Nika scowled back at her.

"What?" she said, as she snatched the fire stick Lexie offered her, lit it, and took a long drag.

Lexie shrugged. "Seems like you're going out of your way to make sure you aren't Garth's favourite anymore."

"Oh please, I haven't been Garth's favourite ever since his little right-hand Rae in there showed up."

"She's been good for business. You, on the other hand, I hear almost just decapitated a dog with a plate shard."

"Hardly on purpose."

"That's not the point, is it? You're making mistakes, noticeable ones."

"Isn't everyone allowed to make mistakes?" Nika snapped.

Lexie snorted out a laugh, smoke billowing out her nostrils. "For anyone else, yes. But I've known you since we were five, running around in Tartarus. *You* don't make mistakes. You make, what is it you call them? That's right – calculated moves."

"So?"

"So? What's the game plan here, Nika?"

Nika was about to open her mouth and tell her long-time friend exactly what she planned to do about Garth's newfound independence, when Yani poked his head out of the service entrance, a loose curl of his wet hair bouncing around his forehead from under his chef's cap.

"Lexie, someone's just put through an order for oxen steaks – and I know you'll kill me if I grill them like a fish."

"Damn straight I'll kill you. Those cost a fortune to trade for, and that's once you find them," Lexie muttered. "I'll be right there."

Then she turned back to Nika. "Are you going to be okay?"

Nika waved her off. "I'll be fine."

"Okay, I'll see you tomorrow."

"Yeah, see you."

Enjoying the fresh night air on her skin, Nika spent the next five minutes listening to the clattering sounds of the kitchen behind her. The sounds felt just far enough removed to not feel like her problem, especially when she was looking out at a quiet cobbled street. Firebugs danced in the air above her, the trees rustled and swayed as the wind nymphs danced through them. Occasionally the odd deity, daemon, or Soul would wander past.

Nika didn't feel like going home. She felt like a drink.

"ANOTHER ONE, BAR KEEP."

Savvas refilled her glass with golden wine for the fourth time, that delightful glugging noise that came out of the bottle making Nika sigh.

"*Thank* you."

"You're going to regret this in the morning, you know."

"I have no regrets, Savvas," Nika said, swirling the liquid while looking him square in the eye. "I only have calculated moves and consequences. And my calculated move right now is to continue to drink this delicious nectar you brewed."

"Suit yourself. A warning though, boss man is heading back this way." Savvas nodded behind him as he went back to drying glasses.

The bar was almost empty, there was only one straggler at the other end of it. Garth had sent the chefs home, the only one still in the kitchen was Melamene. Being the pastry chef really did suck when it came to being the last one to get to clock off. All the wait staff had clocked off too, all that was apart from Tomas, who was cleaning the coffee machine and waiting for the final table to pay their tab.

Nika watched as Ross – their water nymph in charge of the dishwasher – delivered a caddie full of clean crockery to place on the coffee shelves above Tomas' head; a collection of terracotta kylix's with different designs on them that made the shelves as decorative as they were storage.

"What are you still doing here, Nika? I told you to go home," Garth said behind her.

"This is my home."

"Don't be glib."

"I'm not." Nika hiccuped.

"How much have you had to drink?"

"I'm *fine*."

"Really?"

"*Reeeeeally*."

"I'm about to walk Rae home. You want me to walk you, too? Or are you going to let Savvas here take you home once he's closed up tonight?"

"I don't need walking home like your precious Rae. Where is she, anyway?"

"Doing your job of making sure all the tables are set up for tomorrow."

"Well," – another hiccup – "if you'd have let me stay on, that wouldn't be a problem now, would it?"

Garth let out a sigh and took the bar stool next to her. "Look, Nika, I know you're not happy about my decision to step away from the libation agreement. But it's not like it was going to last forever anyway. You and I both know more and more mortals choose to believe in different gods these days. Hell, some of them choose to do away with all of us altogether. I *know* now is the time for us to strike out on our own. You have to trust me on that, because I can't have you going around causing fissures in the team with your insubordination."

"Insubordination? When have I ever been … subordinate?"

The only indication that she'd managed to get under Garth's skin was a brief clench of his fist that was resting on the bar.

"You know what I mean. You know the sway you have on the team. I'm just asking you to trust me, to back me."

"Trust is a tricky commodity. Slippery as one of those eels in the Cocytus river."

Garth rose from his chair, and tapped with his fist briefly on the bar when he saw Rae coming round the corner, coat in hand. "Yeah, well Nika, have I ever let you down before?"

Nika threw her head back and tipped the rest of the golden liquid down her elongated throat. When she looked forward again, Garth and Rae were gone.

"No," Nika said, staring at her now-empty glass. "But that's not to say you won't."

2

NEEDS MUST

S he needed a tar-black coffee and a freshly-baked bagel, in that order.

Nika groaned as she locked up her house – just one of the many rooms underneath this particular tree cavern – and stumbled out into daylight. Making her way through the alleyway and out onto the main road, Nika headed straight for the only place that could sort her out.

It was a tiny hole in the wall place really. It was one of those spots in the Meadows where those who didn't know it existed walked right past it, but those who *did* know of it would always stop by. The sign overhead was old and battered, covered in cobwebs, and in desperate need in a lick of fresh black paint. But Nika could still make out what it said; KNEADS MUST.

"Needs must alright," Nika scoffed as she knocked on the open window-frame that connected the customers with the store. There was a door to Nika's right, but no one ever came in or out of it. The owner – a big, burly, bald daemon – was the only one in his shop, and he operated right out onto the street.

He appeared at the window and smiled at Nika. "What will it be today, darling?" Christos grinned at her, as he looked her up and down.

"Don't even think about saying whatever it was that was about to come out of your mouth next," Nika warned.

Christos' grin widened further. "Rough night, huh?"

"It's about to be a rough day if I don't get that delicious coffee you make."

"Coming right up." Christos turned his back to her for a moment and flicked the coffee machine on, the mechanism yawning through the steam wand and getting to work.

Christos turned back to Nika. "Another early morning shift for you? I'd have thought Garth would just keep you on the lates."

"Oh, Garth is quite happy to put me on double shifts lately. Courtesy of his new favourite Arae, Rae, aka Sunshine."

"She can't be that bad. It's been, what? Three months of busy lunchtime shifts? She's got to be bringing something good to the team if your Sunday lunch service has picked up."

Nika scowled at Christos, who was clearly baiting her. They'd had this discussion several times over the last few months. Nika grumbled about how well Rae was fitting into the team, and Christos gave her a hard time about it – and then usually gave her a coffee for free.

"That's exactly my point. She's far *too* good. There's a whole new bloody lunch menu – as if I needed any more dishes to memorise and sell. Garth says it'll help profit margins, but right now all it's doing is adding to my workload and lack of sleep."

"Someone's grumpy this morning."

"At least when I had three pm lie-ins I had a chance to sleep off dreaded headaches like this one."

"A headache, huh?"

"You know what? Why don't you throw in one of those bagels too, huh? Maybe I want to be taken pity on and taken care of. You ever thought of that?"

Christos laughed. "You don't need anyone taking care of you. You do just fine for yourself."

"Does that mean I don't get my bagel?"

Christos turned again, Nika assumed just to grab her rich, double-shot coffee with three sugars – but when he came back, he presented her with a brown paper bag, the grease stain on it growing by the second.

"Here you go. Something sharp and something sweet, just like you."

Nika didn't particularly care what was on the bagel, only that she desperately needed something to soak up the rest of the alcohol in her system. It took a *lot* to get a spirit like Nika drunk.

Gods, had she opened the spiced liquor when she got home? The memory of it was fuzzy, but now Nika thought about it – definitely there.

"What do I owe you, Christos?"

"Put in a good word for me with your mother? I'd like to go home to visit my folks."

"You want to go back to Tartarus? Why in Hades hell hounds would you want to do that? Why not just get your folks to come out here?" Nika began shaking her head even as she finished her sentence. "You know what? Never mind. I don't want to know. Sure, I'll put in a good word for you, next time I speak to her."

Christos nodded. "Appreciate it, Nik."

She nodded, waving her goodbye, before taking a sip of

deliciously hot coffee and opening the bag. The smell of sharp chilli jam and roasted onion with garlic cream cheese on a warm bagel wafted to her thin nostrils. She sighed, and ripped a chunk out of it with her teeth.

"Oooh, did you get that from Christos'? Go on, give me some!" Lexie beseeched her from across the room, as Nika wandered into the team meeting and took one of the remaining restaurant chairs that had been pulled out from neatly-set tables for lunch.

"Get your own!" Nika said, tearing off a small chunk and throwing it at Lexie's head.

The Lamia cricked her neck and managed to catch the piece in her mouth. Swallowing, she moaned. "No fair. Christos always gives you the best bagel combos."

"What can I say? I'm a charm-and-disarm kind of Arae."

Lexie snorted at that before a cough interrupted them.

"If you two are quite done, can I get on with the briefing for the team? Or are you going to be interrupting us the whole time just because you were late again, Nika?" Garth asked.

Lexie and Nika threw a pointed look between them before Nika smiled saccharinely at Garth and mimicked zipping her mouth. When he went to turn back to the team, she deliberately mimicked unzipping her thin lips and turned to Rae beside her.

"Well, Sunshine, whatever you're doing when you take him home at night clearly isn't working ..."

A blush spread across Rae's cheeks. "I haven't, we

haven't, he just walks me home. We're friends!" she hissed, stressing the last word.

Nika raised an eyebrow. "If you're sure."

She could feel Garth glowering at her. They'd had their ups and downs over the years, and the team knew them to butt heads on occasion. But this rift between them was opening up into a chasm. Nika just couldn't reconcile herself with Garth's decision to forgo the libations. Sure, she saw his point, they *would* be better off in the long run. But to risk losing the place that had become her home because he'd been so bullish and headstrong, forging ahead with the plan with no fall-back in place, that she couldn't forgive him for, and he knew why.

This had been the first place she had found happiness when she left Tartarus all those years ago.

At first, she regretted her decision to leave. The small cramped room she had rented in the Meadows had black mould instead of the black veins of marble she had grown up with in her parents' palace. She'd been able to hear her neighbours through the walls, as if the crinkled wallpaper was deckle-edged cotton paper in its place. In an effort to get away from the four walls she'd locked up what few possessions she had in the room, and gone to explore the leafy suburb around her.

Nika had never seen trees like it – they didn't grow in Tartarus. The nature she had known had been mining, the constant burring of a drill somewhere in the distance, the clang of metal on metal.

Here ... the trees had space to whisper to each other.

Then she'd seen it. The pub on the corner glowed internally with fire. It was the first thing Nika had seen that reminded her of Tartarus – that inner glowing fire.

Desperate for a taste of home, but not ready to head back and admit defeat, she'd walked in ... and never really left.

Zeus' Watering Hole had changed over the centuries, of course. They'd had a few makeovers. Then there was the fire of 250 BC that had cost them for the following decade in tokens; the pieces of parchment with favours and offerings that all Souls and creatures were willing to barter and trade with as currency here in the Underworld.

Nika had never expected to become a waitress, let alone stay in one place long enough to be considered part of its history now. Her mother had birthed and raised her to be a true Arae, cursing those who deserved it. That had been the lesson drilled into her over and over as a child; she was to be of service. She was born for a purpose.

She just hadn't wanted to do that, not after she'd seen what happened to those who were cursed. After she had visited the caves where they were kept, and heard them scream at her, begging to be put out of their misery, clawing at her skirts as they crawled along the ground like worms.

Instead, after that first night she had wandered into the Watering Hole, she had fallen in love with the hustle and bustle of the place. She watched the family of servers dart in and out and around tables, delivering drinks and food, and hounded Garth until he'd offered her a trial run, despite the fact she had no experience.

She'd been a natural at it, working her way up until she was the best in the team, until this place had become her home. Gone were the large cold floors with high ceilings and cold draughts from her childhood. Gone were the screams from the caves far below. Instead, her days were now spent in the restaurant with warm hearth fires, cosy armchairs by the windows, the smells of rich foods, and the busy sounds of happy people.

She didn't want to lose that.

Nika was pulled from her reverie when she heard her name mentioned by Garth.

"Nika and Tomas, in between the lunch and dinner service tonight, I want you to go out into the streets and see if you can corral some of the Souls to come and join us for dinner this week. Tell them they will get a bottle of Savvas' homemade wine on the house should they order two courses from us."

"You can't be serious," Nika butted in.

"Of course, I'm serious. We're moving into a quieter season," – and what a convenient excuse *that* was, Nika thought – "so we may as well put an offer out there."

"I'm not walking around the streets like a common harpy to try and drum up business just because you made a rash call with our Olympic Investor."

There, she'd said it.

The entire team went silent, waiting for the tension of the room to dissipate and see what wreckage was left behind from Nika's words.

"Oh come on, Nika. It'll be fun!" Tomas tried to break the tension – tried and failed.

He was sent a scathing look for his efforts.

Garth's words, on the other hand, found their mark.

"You can either help the team drum up new business, or you can leave."

3

THE RETURN TO TARTARUS

Nika had stormed out.

Her worst fear had come to pass – she was losing the only place she'd ever loved. Even if Garth didn't fire her, he'd drive that place into the ground trying to prove that he'd made the right decision.

She had to find a way to save it.

Overnight, a plan had begun to formulate in her mind. Something in her reminiscing recently must have jogged her memory, for when she was brainstorming Orpheus had popped into her mind. She recalled seeing him in the caves when she was a youngling. The once great musician who was now a recluse. If the rumours were true, he stayed in the caves voluntarily to avoid Hades, whom he had slighted, making a mockery of the god by trying to take his wife out of the Underworld and back to the world of the living.

If Nika could find a way to get the recluse maestro to come out and play, specifically at Zeus' Watering Hole, they could charge their patrons double, triple the tokens they usually did. And if they could get the musician to *only* play for them ... well, that would be the ticket that would have them back to turning a profit comfortably without cutting corners or relying on another investor. Perhaps then Garth would forgive her for storming out, too.

Not that he didn't share some, if not *all*, of the blame.

There was only one problem. If she was to go to the caves to find Orpheus, that would mean she'd have to return to Tartarus, and she hadn't exactly left her family on good terms all those centuries ago.

She also hadn't been back since.

Young Nika hadn't had the nerve to tell her mother she didn't want to do the job she'd been born for. Instead, she'd waited until her parents were both sleeping and then snuck away in the bright light of day. For Nika's mother was none other than the Goddess and personification of night itself, Nyx. And her father, the personification of darkness, Erebus.

If she was to go to Tartarus to look for Orpheus, there would be no way to avoid them. They were the deities that presided over the neighbourhood itself. They'd likely know the minute she stepped foot over the border again.

But, with no better plan in mind, Nika began packing a small, black, leather-skin bag etched with one of Hephaestus' stamps that said the bag had been crafted in Mount Olympus and shipped down here on one of the freight canoes that Charon ran, now that he'd expanded his boating business.

The bag was only big enough to fit enough items that would get her across the Tartarus border: distilled water from the rivers, a loaf of bread that Rae had baked that Nika begrudgingly admitted was pretty good with its rosemary and olive oil glazed crust, and a couple of extra layers of clothes. Definitely an extra pair of boots. Finally, cramming a thick chequered scarf that would help her withstand the icy wind nymphs of Tartarus into her bag, Nika slung it over her shoulder and strode out of her house – making sure to lock the door behind her.

On the northern side of Styx's border, closer to the river Lethe than anywhere else in the Underworld, it would take almost a day to cross the Asphodel rolling hills and plains, where green hills gave way to large stretches of dense forests and ploughed farming fields.

Nika had left the Meadows early enough that it was late afternoon by the time she heard the tell-tale sign that she was getting close to Tartarus – the wailing.

A thousand broken-hearted cries from Souls that had spent their mortal lives pursuing the love of another who did not love them back rose up to greet her, and as she walked closer they rose up over the horizon, a throng of phantom forms with desperation draped around them, so dense Nika could almost see it. As she got closer, they began to swarm her.

"Please, miss, just tell me where my Henry is. Is he beyond the flame-filled river? Tell me where to find him."

"Miss, have you seen my Penelope?"

"Where is Crantor?!"

"I'm looking for Arrian. Arrian! Arrian!"

"Selene? Is she with you?"

"Get off me," Nika muttered, swatting away grey, cold hands that reached and clawed at her. "You are wasting your time, just like you did in the mortal realm. Leave. Me. Alone!"

Nika hated the Vale of Mourning, that was what this stretch of land was known for. But she hadn't had much choice. She'd either had to pass through here or the Plains of Judgement and Nika didn't particularly want to cross the three judges of the dead and be mistaken for one who had come for judgement of her deeds and deciding on her placement. *Hades knew* what they would hold over her for the rest of her immortal life.

No, far better to move through the heartbroken. They were a nuisance, but once she got to Phlegethon – the flame-filled river – they would leave her alone. These Souls weren't brave enough to cross it, though not many were, Nika supposed.

Ironically, if the heartbroken *did* find the courage to cross the flames, they'd find their heartbreak eradicated, free from the spell of sleeping Eros and cruel Aphrodite. But the thing that made these Souls such a scourge was the fact they would rather remain lamenting their plight on others than find the courage to choose better for themselves. It's why the judges sent them here.

Then, Nika heard the most interesting request.

"Is Orpheus in the place you come from or where you go?"

Her head snapped around to see the bearer of such a question. Surely, Eurydice, Orpheus' wife, would not be found amongst the broken-hearted. Everyone in the mortal realm and the Underworld knew their tragic tale. Eurydice had died during her wedding celebrations, and Orpheus had travelled all the way to the Underworld to get her back. On hearing his tale through song, Hades and Persephone had decided to let Eurydice return with Orpheus to the mortal realm on one condition: that he should walk in front of her and not look back until they both had reached the upper world. But he'd – famously – turned the minute he was in the mortal realm. His wife, however, had only had one foot in the upper world. One remained in the Underworld ... and so she vanished back to Hades to serve her time amongst the dead.

No, it wasn't Eurydice who asked the question of her. Instead, it was a young male Soul, who couldn't have been more than twenty mortal years when he died if he remained looking so young. With blonde curls cropped close to his head and cherub cheeks, Nika regarded him.

"No. Why do you ask such a question when you are not his great love?"

"He was my first," the young Soul answered in turn. Then his eyes went cloudy, as if pulled into the infatuated memory of the Orpheus he had created in his mind. "He would sing me the great stories of love, though, and I knew I was special. He did not sing them for anyone. It was rumoured amongst us that he only used to sing them for his wife, so when he chose me, I knew ... I knew he loved me too."

Nika waved a hand in his face to silence him. "I've heard enough."

But the young man continued now, waxing lyrical about his love for Orpheus and Nika knew she had lost him to the longing. Pressing through the remaining horde of lamenters, Nika eventually made it to the river.

Beyond it lay Tartarus, a colossal mountainous deity ingrained into the rock face, casting an ominous shadow over everything beneath, and yet, it still paled in comparison to Nika's parents. She shuddered.

Beneath Tartarus lay The Caves, a stormy abyss that — it was rumoured — no one could ever leave. It was true that those sentenced to The Caves were not allowed to leave; an agreement bound between Tartarus and Hades. Those Souls were ... tortured. They suffered, there was no other word for it. But not every inhabitant was condemned to eternal residence in Tartarus. Nika, Lexie, and even Christos from the hole-in-the-wall bakery had managed to escape.

The gigantic form of Tartarus and the intricate caverns beneath him channelled the Phlegethon river and ran downstream towards Styx. Where the two rivers met marked sacred ground, and Nika knew better than to disrupt the uninterrupted meeting place of the two lovers. Between them, the hot pools bubbled, emitting a metallic, sulphur-like scent from the mingling mud.

There was, however, somewhere here along the river of blood that boiled Souls where Nika could cross.

She ventured upstream.

Everyone expected Phlegethon to be deeper the higher up the river went, but that wasn't strictly true. Like every mountainous range, Tartarus had peaks and valleys. One just had to stumble into a valley to find where the flames barely licked at their feet rather than the peaks where those with the greatest misdeeds in the mortal realm continued to stand, up to their eyebrows in flames.

For Phlegathon raged, but it did not consume those who stood in it. It would not kill a Soul, but it would flow hot blood through their veins. The more violent the deeds they had committed, the deeper they would sink into the river's depths.

Nika was immune, due to her nature as an Arae, but that didn't mean she wanted to turn up in Tartarus looking like a scorched mess. There were *standards* to be observed in Tartarus, especially in her family, and if she showed up covered in burns and soot marks, she was bound to be a laughing stock. Something no one wanted to be in the most merciless place in the whole Underworld.

After climbing a particularly deceptively rocky hill, she came across a section of the river that was patrolled by centaurs. She nodded her head in a slight bow, a sign of respect demanded to the intelligent race, as she approached one.

"Darthyria," she greeted.

The centaur frowned for a minute, his thick eyebrows knotting together before a look of surprise shot across his face.

"My, my, Nika. I haven't seen you here since you were a wiry young spirit, leaping over the river ditch."

Nika grinned. "Ready to watch me do it again?"

He chuckled, a deep echo that bounced off the river's edge.

"Do you even remember where the low point is?"

Nika scowled. "How far away am I from it?"

Darthyria smiled gently. "Not too far, actually. There was a rumble between one of the prisoners and Tarturus – caused a slip a few years back and shifted Phlegethon slightly. Follow me."

The two of them continued in silence, Darthyria occasionally raising a bow and arrow at those in the river who were trying to secure a more advantageous position by wading to more shallow spots where the flames didn't lick nearly as high. They quickly returned to their rightful level when they saw the spearhead aimed at them.

Meanwhile, Nika's mind began to nibble at her with worry about the reception she could expect from her family on the other side of the river.

After another five hundred metres or so, they reached the crossing where Phlegethon gently pulsed under volcanic ash.

"There you go."

"Hades! There's barely any fire at all. Why aren't more leaving Tartarus?"

Darthyria smiled down at her. "So young, still, Nika."

She scowled. "I've been around for thousands of years."

"And yet you still think to leave is to escape."

"Don't speak to me in riddles," Nika grumbled.

"Very well." Darthyria inclined his head. "Then this is where I leave you." And with that, he began trotting back downstream to his post.

Nika took a deep breath, steeling herself, knowing that while there was no fire this was still likely to hurt. She marked out the easiest path, memorising where she would put her feet so she could move swiftly across, and went for it.

The whole process probably took no more than thirty seconds, but on the other side of the river Nika had to bite back a small scream of pain. Raising her heels, she saw that they were indeed blackened – the soles of her shoes having disintegrated.

Luckily, she'd packed a spare pair of everything with her layers. She had just finished fishing on her boots, and tucking the scarf into her leather jacket, when she heard another sound that had her head whipping around.

A cackle.

There, snapping her wings shut and walking towards her in a blood-wet dress, was Tisiphone, a serpent wrapped around her waist in place of a belt, and a whip in one hand that dangled down to her boots and kissed the ground as she walked towards Nika.

"Hello, Aunty."

"Nika."

"I should have known you'd still be here, guarding the gate to the entrance of Tartarus." A small smile played on Nika's lips.

She accepted the open arms of Tisiphone for the

briefest of hugs, though her own arms were practically limp in their return, before stepping back.

"Are you going to let me through?"

"Is that any way to speak to the blood of your blood?"

Nika shoved her hands back into her jacket. "I can imagine what's been said about me behind my back."

It was Tisiphone's turn to tsk her. "Just because some of us don't understand why you felt the need to leave doesn't mean we don't still love you. You still perform your duties as an Arae when called upon, I suppose?"

"Of course," Nika lied smoothly.

As one of the original three Erinyes, Tisiphone had taught Nika everything she needed to know as an Arae when it came to cursing the Souls who broke their oaths. Of her three aunties, Tisiphone's speciality as the guardian of the gate was inflicting madness that would haunt the Soul — a little voice at the back of their heads, which got louder the more they tried to ignore it.

Sometimes Nika swore she could hear a little voice like that in the back of her own head and wondered if her aunt had placed it there as she'd left Tartarus the first time.

"Well then, welcome home." Tisiphone held out one long arm and gestured to the black iron gate behind her at the mouth of Tartarus.

It had been too easy.

"You're really just going to let me through?"

The unspoken words sat thick in Nika's throat: after she had run away in the bright light of day all those years ago.

"I'll have to tell your mother you're here."

"I'd really rather tell her myself."

Tisiphone shrugged. "That's my price of entry. You of all spirits know that nothing goes without consequence, particularly in this land."

"Fine," Nika said, rolling her shoulders back and squaring them beneath her leather jacket. "I can handle Nyx."

Tisiphone cackled again. "Don't let her catch you calling her that, or there will be much more than consequences you'll be facing, child."

But Nika was already heading through the mouth of the mountain.

4

AS NIGHT FALLS

N o sooner had Nika entered through the gates than night descended.

"Hello, mother."

Nyx appeared before Nika in her traditional black robes, while the dark mist surrounding her settled as a crown on her head and wings at her back.

The angel of the night. That's what Nika's father called her mother. But there was a reason other creatures in the realm feared the things that happened at night. Her mother could be *unforgiving*.

That was one of Nika's most vivid memories as a young spirit, her mother cursing at her older siblings for not doing their duties, for shirking them off, for not being a good reflection on her. Nika had more siblings than she knew what to do with. Luckily, most were off living their own lives, for their mother had tasked them all with *something* to do. To be a child of Nyx was to be born with an immediate responsibility. Your life was not your own, but to be given in service for the good of the realms.

Nika had always gotten the impression that to do something other than your chosen task was to spit on the gift of life their mother – primordial that she was – had given them. She had been the last Arae Nyx had birthed herself. After the disappointment Nika had become, the Eriynes – like her aunty, Tisiphone – had been tasked with birthing future curse children. Apparently, Nyx did not want that burden any more.

"My child, you return." Nyx opened her arms wide, the shadows of the night parting to make way for Nika to step into her mother's embrace.

Unnerved at the show of affection, Nika stepped tentatively forward, her arms remaining at her sides, as Nyx's shadows enveloped her. Her mother kissed her temple and sniffed her hair, then pulled back, a pinched look on her face.

"You smell like fire."

"Well, I did have to walk through Phlegethon to get here."

"Come, let us return home together. You can bathe. I have some of Hecate's tinctures that will take that foul smell right out."

That was how Nika came to find herself in her old bedroom, one plush charcoal towel wrapped around her body, the other wrapped around her hair like a turban. She sat on the edge of her old bed and stared at the stone walls that had been replastered over – the carvings of days Nika had left behind in her childhood smoothed away. She had scratched in a line every day she had to wait until Nyx had deemed her 'old enough' to wander around the Underworld unsupervised during the sunlight hours. It had caused Nika's now long nails to turn to stubs, her fingers a bleeding mess, to carve in all those lines day in and day out … but it had kept her sane.

She'd escaped to Asphodel Meadows the first chance she got.

Sighing, Nika rolled back onto the bed and stared at the ceiling. She had forgotten this familiar weight that sat on her chest, the heaviness of expectation and disappointment that she was not the dutiful daughter Nyx had wanted.

She was not enthusiastic.

She was not proactive.

She was not what she should be.

Never words her mother had said to her, of course. And not faults that Nika *owned*, in fact. For she was all of those things — it was just that she was all of those things for a profession that was considered *distasteful* to her family.

Ironic, really. Given that everyone had to eat.

But now she felt that disappointment shroud her once again.

"Nika! Supper!" her mother called.

She wasn't even hungry.

"Coming."

Sighing, Nika rolled back up to a seated position on the bed.

"I said, supper! Now, young lady!" came the screeched reply.

"I said I'm coming!" she screamed back. Punctuality was important in this house. As if Nika could forget.

Quickly dressing and combing out her towel-dried hair, Nika walked down the turret that led to the main dining hall, in the underground palace that her father had built for her mother, as legend had it, when Tartarus was formed in the rock. She found both of them waiting for her at the long dining table. It was a piece of polished rock that looked like it erupted from the floor itself, another thing Erebus had done for Nyx as a sign of his devotion.

Even the way he looked at her now, like he would do anything for her and her alone, made something in Nika's chest curl uncomfortably tight. Another reminder that she was nothing compared to the greatness that was her mother.

"Is no one else in the family joining us for dinner?"

"The twins will be with us shortly," Nyx said.

Nika raised an eyebrow. So she'd been screamed at to arrive to supper on time, but the boys were allowed to come and go as they pleased?

Her father shot her a warning look, his thick black eyebrows furrowing as he gave her an almost imperceptible shake of his head.

Sighing, Nika knew now was not the time to push the matter and took a seat opposite her father, and directly to the right of her mother.

Nyx clicked her fingers and in front of them, sparkling palladium plates were suddenly filled with all manner of foods. Blackened fish and roasted marrow dripping with melted cheeses, savoury curd sprinkled with mint and a dash of citrus juice, sheets of floppy laganon pasta topped with a tomato sauce and more grated mizithra cheese, spanakorizo rice and spinach, and—at the centre of it all—a small, roasted goat.

"Do you think we have enough food?" Nika asked.

"Why don't you tell me? Apparently you work in an establishment that would know. One which we still haven't been invited to," Nyx admonished her.

Nika stiffened. She'd known this was coming, that someone would have reported back to her parents what she was doing. But she'd expected them to berate her about it, not show an interest or ask for an invitation.

"I didn't think you'd want to go somewhere that was

named after Zeus. Especially after you called him an upstart."

Her mother sniffed. "Well, he is one."

"Ergo, why there's been no invite," Nika said curtly, wanting to move away from the subject as quickly as possible as she reached for the tongs to the fish.

"You will watch your tone, young lady." The words spoken by her father were quiet, but when he spoke, Nika listened. So did Nyx. So did everyone in the family, for he was the only one who knew how to broker peace amongst them. Erebus, who the world knew as the help-meet to Nyx, was actually the glue that kept the family from tearing one another's throats out.

Breeding children to be duty-bound deities and spirits tended to make for a lot of headstrong, independent, right-eous personalities.

Nika was about to apologise for her brusque response when footsteps sounded.

"Well, well, well, who do we have here? Why is that our little, long-lost sister?" a voice boomed into the depths of the dining hall, as one broad-shouldered male walked into the room, followed by one who looked identical to him. Both strode over to Nika before she so much as had a chance to stand to avoid them, one coming either side of her, lifting her from her chair, and squeezing her between them.

"Put me down!"

"Oh, but sister, how we've missed you."

"Look! Your hair is back to its lovely colour. Whatever happened to that bubblegum blue we last saw you have?"

"Oh yes! Right before she left when she was trying to prove a point."

"What point was that again?" one of them asked the other.

Nika wriggled. "I said, Put. Me. Down!"

At once Nika's two brothers released their arms and she dropped into her chair like a ragdoll, bruising her tailbone with the force at which she collapsed.

"Ow!"

"Missed us?" Thanatos grinned at Nika, as he placed a peck on their mothers cheek and took a seat beside their father.

"Not even slightly." Nika scowled, as Hypnos too placed a kiss on their mother's cheek, ruffled Nika's hair, and then took the seat beside her.

Both brothers immediately helped themselves to large portions of each dish in front of them, piling up their plates until there was a small mountain of food on each of them.

"See? There is only just enough food," Nyx smartly reprimanded Nika.

"That's because these two are monstrous," Nika pointed at both her brothers, whose muscular frames were three times the size of any muscle-bound Soul that turned up in the Underworld.

"Hey! It's not our fault you're stick-thin."

"Don't body-shame me," Nika bit back.

"How is it body-shaming when you're tiny?"

"It works both ways, pea brain."

"If you were just going to come back and insult us, why bother coming back at all Nikita?"

The use of her nickname had Nika grinding her teeth. She hadn't realised when she was younger that Nikita and Nika did not mean the same thing. She'd been perfectly happy being called Nikita, until her mother had pointed out that the former meant 'unconquered' and her actual birth name meant 'victory'.

Which, in her family's world, meant her brother had just called her a loser.

But — if she were to rise to the jib, she would only encourage them further.

"Yes, why are you back here, *Nika*?" her mother asked, taking small, dainty bites from her food.

Meanwhile her brothers were shovelling it in like they were starving. It was hard to imagine such a boney, slim goddess giving birth to two of the largest presences down here in Tartarus.

Nika shoved a large forkful of rice in her mouth to buy herself time from answering. She didn't want to tell her family that the place she forsook them for was in trouble. She didn't want to look like a failure who had come home with her tail between her legs. In particular, she didn't want her failure to suggest that she wished for a job back here because she *didn't*, and she most certainly did not want to have that conversation with her mother. It's why she'd run away in the first place.

She swallowed the mouthful of rice and reached for her glass of wine, immediately taking a large gulp.

Coward, the little voice in her head whispered at her.

Shut. Up.

"I'm looking for someone," she eventually said.

"Who?" her mother demanded.

"Just someone, it doesn't matter who."

"Well, if you tell us, perhaps we can help you find them," her mother pointed out.

"Yeah, go on, tell us," her brother Hypnos added. "Perhaps I could whisper something in their ear for you as I send them off to sleep tonight and get them to come to you.

Would save you having to run around this place trying to find them."

That uncomfortable feeling was coiling itself around Nika's throat again. Even if she logically knew that accepting help didn't make her weak, she was wholly adverse to the idea of letting her family help her. Because she knew that help now meant something called in as a favour later. There were no actions without consequences, just like there was no day without night.

But she could see no way of getting around the question without causing an argument. Given that they appeared to be making an effort to cultivate a tentative peace now that she was home, it would be impudent if Nika did not try to do the same.

"Fine, if you must know, Orpheus."

A hush fluttered between those at the table.

"And why," Nyx muttered, "are you looking for the famous Orpheus?"

"We want him to play at our restaurant." Nika kept her eyes on her plate, now pushing around the sad tail end of the goat on her plate, in case her mother saw the lie in her eyes. In case she realised there was no 'we' to speak of.

"And why are you seeking out a recluse musician for your place of work? I thought you were a waitress," her mother asked.

"I am. I'm the maître d', in fact." Nika swallowed the lump in her throat, not allowing herself to think about how Garth had told her to leave, not allowing herself to think about if that meant she'd been officially fired or not.

"Then why were you given this task?" Nyx pressed on.

"Because it was my idea, and Garth – the owner – respects my ideas. He lets me take the lead where I wish.

Seeing as I had ties to Tartarus, we thought it best that I come and do the visit."

Nyx let out a little sound of approval.

But, surprisingly, her father wasn't buying it. "Is everything alright where you work, Nika?"

"Of course. Why wouldn't it be?"

"Well, you could have any number of talented musicians. To seek out one who gave up his gift a long time ago seems like a punt ... and to punt, to gamble like this, usually means someone, or something, is in trouble."

"I'm not in trouble, father," Nika lied again, using her napkin to wipe at her mouth. "We're the best restaurant in the Underworld, and we want the best to play for us. That's all."

A MAESTRO BY MORNING

It was agreed that Nyx would escort Nika to Orpheus' dwelling the following nightfall, as her mother's schedule for tonight had already been set. Nika, for once, was more than happy to accept the offer. She did not want to go to The Caves alone.

The memories of the screams of insanity down there still haunted her.

The Caves were where those the gods wanted to make an example of were found. King Sisyphus, after cheating death twice, was forced to push a boulder up a hill never quite reaching the top before it rolled back down to the bottom of the hill, only for the king to start pushing it all over again. Tantalus was imprisoned in a cave with a pool of water and a fruit tree, neither of which he could eat or drink from – thereby being eternally hungry and thirsty. Then there were the Danaïdes who had murdered their husbands. They were all forced to carry water in a jug to fill the bath that would wash off their sins. A shame then that the jugs were filled with cracks, and the water never made it to the bath.

Nika had experienced her first tour of The Caves beside her mother when she was a brand-new, fresh-eyed deity, believing that her role was to restore good in the world. But to learn that these were the curses put upon Souls … no, she had not wanted to play in the land of madness. Her mother had always tried to tell her that madness was essential. Without it, one couldn't appreciate logic – 'logos', she'd called it, still fluently speaking the language of the ancients – or reasoning. Nika disagreed. She'd not wanted to become the curse lackey that placed such a burden just because some god felt slighted.

So, after a surprisingly sound sleep in her childhood bed, Nika decided to spend the day in her old neighbourhood while she waited for nightfall.

Her parents home, a castle really, sat on top of one of the crags that overlooked the spider-like district of Tartarus, each road leading out from the centre of the mountainous rock. The palace cast a shadow across the tarred streets, which was appropriate for her mother and father, given their titles. They were treated like royalty here. Even Hades tended to leave Tartarus to them, not wanting to piss off the primordials who had been around even longer than his existence.

Making her way down the jagged footpath, Nika went exploring in all her old local haunts. There was the old carriageworks building, where craftsmen welded the palladium that was mined out of the depths of Tartarus. Then there were the mining market stalls behind the carriageworks, where said items were traded on the blackmarket. There were the mines themselves, though those were no fun. And, of course, there were the usual shops, cafes and eateries that Nika had grown up with; Asclepius' Apothecary, Hecate's Witchcraft Herbs & Tinctures, and Aristaeus' Butchery to name a few.

By the time she returned to the family home, her mother was ready and waiting for her, as dusk had begun to fall around them. As was Nyx's way, she would not leave the home before another of her daughters – Hemera, Goddess of Day – returned.

As such, Nika hadn't met her much older sister until she'd left Tartarus in the bright daylight. Hemera, like Nika, had a ... complicated relationship with their mother. Being given a task that literally kept you apart forever from the one who was supposed to love you unconditionally could do that, Nika supposed.

"Nika, there you are. Come, we must go," Nyx declared.

"Now? It's still dusk."

"Your father's gone to cover the land in darkness. Surely you saw him on your way back in? By the time you tidy yourself up, I'll be ready to take my leave on the Under-world. Now go, hurry."

"Mother, I'm ready. We can leave now."

"You are windswept and have little-to-no face on. Is that how you wish to make an impression on a Soul whose business you wish to gain? Go and make yourself presentable. I will not tell you twice, Nika."

Nika clenched her jaw shut and marched back up the spiral staircase.

Five minutes later, for Nika hadn't truly needed to do anything other than reapply kohl to her eyes and red lipstick to her thin lips to plump them – a female's armour, her mother called it – Nyx swept them out the front door and into a weightless smog in the darkness. Night incar-nate, that was her mother. A primordial who could take any form she pleased, because she had been one of the originals birthed from Chaos itself. As such, Nika and her mother did not have to climb down the rockface of Tartarus that sat above The Caves, but rather swept into a cavern where Orpheus lived.

There was no door to the cavern, just a deep chamber of space. In the middle sat a small square table, just large enough to seat four at a push, where Opheus sat with – to Nika's surprise – Eurydice. On the left side of the cavern there was a small double bed pressed up against the wall with a quilted blanket and pillows neatly fluffed. To the right, where the rock seemed to have formed a half-wall, was a chamber pot and washing features.

There was no modern plumbing in this part of Tartarus. Nika had forgotten that.

On the table where Orpheus and his wife sat were strewn papers Oprheus had been scribbling on when Nika and her mother had arrived. Only the glow of the flickering oil lamp allowed Nika a glimpse at what was on those papers; music notes.

Upon Nyx materialising in the entranceway of their cavern in her 'mortal' form, both Orpheus and Eurydice had stood from their chairs and dropped into such deep bows, their faces were no more than inches from the cavern floor.

"My Goddess of the Night, to what do we owe the pleasure?" Orpheus said, his deep voice more gravelly than Nika had expected.

"My daughter seeks to ask a favour of you."

Both sets of eyes landed on Nika.

"Perhaps we could discuss it over refreshments?" Nika asked.

"Of course," Orpheus nodded, while Eurydice was already walking to a small cavern shelf to grab fresh cups.

"I have duties to perform. I take it this will not take long to sort?" Nyx turned and looked down at Nika as she asked. The fact that she even had to look down at Nika, who stood over six feet tall, said a lot about the space her mother inhabited. Not just physically, either. She soaked up the air of the place her presence was in until it made it difficult to breathe.

Nika shook her head.

"Good, then I shall return for you before day breaks."

With that, Nyx swept out of there, leaving Nika to deal with two puzzled faces.

"I suppose I have some explaining to do."

WHEN ALL WAS SAID and done, it only took Nika twenty minutes to explain everything that had happened in the past year. From her pub losing the Hades cook-off, Rae joining the team with the prize tokens, Garth deciding he no longer wanted to pay the libation tax he'd always done and rely on the cook-off again as he always had, and why they were now in desperate need of help.

"And this pub, this is your pub?" Orpheus asked her.

"No, well, yes. I don't own it ... but it's just as much mine. At least it feels like mine. I've put my blood, sweat and tears into that place. I don't want to see it go into ruin."

"It's a beautifully sad story, Nika," Orpheus said, having learnt her name when they first sat, "but I fail to see how I can be of assistance."

"Well, I thought, perhaps if you were willing to come

and play at the Watering Hole? It would be the event of the millenia, greater even than the festival last year ..."

Already, Orpheus was shaking his head.

"I will not leave here."

Nika barely stopped her heart from free-falling into her stomach, her one plan, her one hope, disappearing right in front of her.

"Why not?" she demanded.

A gentle hand rested on hers, and Nika turned to face Eurydice. "Because we are not supposed to be together. I am supposed to be in the fields of Elysium and Orpheus was sent here."

"I *thought* you were supposed to be in Elysium. Why *are* you here?" Nika gestured to the space around them, her scowl clearly indicating that the cavern was little better than squalor.

Eurydice smiled at her, as if Nika was still a newborn who had much to learn about the world, just as that damn centaur had. "Because I love my Orpheus, and I have already lost one lifetime with him. I would not choose to lose another one. Besides ... I'm not that fond of fields anymore. Grass snakes," Eurydice shrugged.

"You crossed the Phlegethon to get here?" Nika was stunned.

Eurydice smiled that soft smile of hers again. "There is not much I would not do for my Orpheus."

"And so, you see, we cannot risk leaving," Orpheus said as he took Eurydice's hand across the table. "For I would not have my Eurydice taken from me a third time if Hades remained mad at me. That is a fate worse than torture or squalor." He sent Nika a rue smile.

Nika bit her lip thinking. "What if playing at the Watering Hole would allow you to roam freely again, wherever you wished, in the Underworld? Would you consider it then?"

The two lovers looked at one another – a shared look that held an entire conversation without saying a word aloud.

Eventually, Orpheus answered her.

"We would," said Orpheus carefully, "but again young one, it is no use. The golden lyre Apollo gifted me with and taught me to play, has long since been cast in the stars by the Muses."

"If I were to get you another lyre?"

Orpheus shook his head again. "There is no lyre like that one."

When Nika scoffed, he continued.

"How do you think I – a mortal – gained such a reputation for my sound and song?"

"Talent?"

"Talent will get you so far, yes. But being gifted by the gods ... well, the gifts they give you become part of the story that makes it legendary. I'm afraid you've rather wasted your time in coming all this way. You could get any musician to play as well as me without it."

Still, Nika would not be thwarted.

"If I get you your lyre, the one the Muses cast in the stars, and I could find a way to make sure that you were allowed to roam freely thereafter together ... would you come and play for us?"

"Yes," Orpheus agreed. "For someone who clearly would do anything for that which she loves, as my Eurydice did for me, I would."

YESTERDAY'S SORROW AND A
PROMISE OF TOMORROW

Nyx had come for Nika at precisely the dawn hour she had promised, only for Nika to get home and find an unwelcome visitor on her family's doorstep.

"What in the Underworld are *you* doing here?" she asked Tomas, who was waiting beside her father on the paved stone staircase that led up to the giant black doors of the family home.

"This young man says he knows you, Nika?" Erebus answered, blocking the doorway with his arms folded across his chest.

Before Nika had a chance to think of a story off the top of her head, Tomas butted in.

"I've been looking for you everywhere. Garth wants you back, Nika. You have to know the restaurant isn't the same without you there."

Nika narrowed her eyes at him. "You shouldn't have come here. I can't believe Garth would be stupid enough to send you out here looking for me."

A faint blush formed on Tomas' cheekbones, his skin a shade of oak she could still make out the blush.

"He didn't send you, did he?"

Tomas rubbed the back of his neck.

"Nika, is this guest unwanted?" her father interrupted.

She waved him off. "No, no, it's fine. Just Tomas telling me something I already knew."

She stared at him, her lips pursed, willing him to be smart enough to read her mind and *walk away* before …

"Well then, why doesn't he join us for dinner?" Nyx suggested.

Tomas swivelled on his heel and faced them. "I'd be delighted, Mr and Mrs, uh, Lord and Lady, uh …"

No one offered Tomas an answer until the uncomfortable silence engulfed them all.

"Just get inside," Nika pushed at his shoulder blades and marched him past her parents.

For some reason her parents decided to hang back, undoubtedly to figure out who the weed-like dryad was to her. No matter, it gave Nika enough time to pull him aside in the long foyer with the high ceilings and into a broom closet.

"You need to leave. *Now*."

"Why? Your parents are perfectly happy to——"

"Because you're going to ruin everything."

"Ruin what?!"

"My parents don't know that the restaurant is suffering," Nika hissed. "They think I'm here on some kind of, *marketing* meeting. And you've already dropped me in it by saying that Garth wants me back!"

"Wait, what?"

"Don't question me, that's all you need to know. And now I need you to leave."

"No."

"Excuse me?"

"You heard me," Tomas said, puffing out his chest slightly. "You're not the boss of me, right now. I came here of my own free will to find you, and I'll be damned if I don't go back to the others with news of you. And I'll tell you another thing—"

The door to the broom closet swung open of its own volition, her parents both standing there, their arms folded and their heads cocked.

"Nika, what in Hades playground is going on?" they asked in unison.

"Tomas was just leaving."

"Oh, no, no, no," her father said, taking a step forward. "I think it's time you told us everything, young lady, including why this boy has turned up looking for you. And I think having him stay will help us determine if you're telling the truth or not. He stays. Come."

Nika sighed and stepped out of the broom closet, Tomas following close behind as her parents escorted them to the small office Erebus had claimed as his own. Deep leather chairs sat either side of a gothic fireplace that was lit, which both her parents sunk into while she and Tomas stood before them.

"Explain from the beginning."

Knowing that her parents would be able to break Tomas if she was caught out in so much as a hairsbreadth of a lie, Nika sighed again feeling the weight of imminent condemnation settle on her shoulders, and began telling them the whole sorry story from the beginning; the festival, the prize tokens, the libations tax, everything. Eventually, she came to the present moment and revealed what Orpheus' demands were.

"So, in order to make this plan of yours work, you need his lyre." Her mother looked down her sharp nose with those never-ending dark eyes of hers at Nika.

Nika felt like she was being chastised.

"Yes."

"You need my help."

"Well, I can—"

"You need my help."

"I never said—"

"The lyre was placed in the constellations by the Muses, yes? So the one who can collect it for us is Asteria, being that she is the Goddess of Falling Stars. And the last time I checked, you did not have a working relationship with the Titaness as I do."

Nika was sure her mother hadn't meant to make that statement of fact sound condescending, but somehow Nyx's statement always came with an air of condescension. Nika didn't think it was intentional ... simply a byproduct of the age of her mother.

She opened her mouth to respond, but Nyx waved her delicate hand in the air, effectively shushing her, before continuing. "Besides, how exactly were you planning on making sure Orpheus and Eurydice were allowed to roam freely thereafter? Do you think Hades would listen to *you*?"

That had definitely been intentionally condescending.

"How are *you* going to get him to agree to it?" Nika retorted.

Nyx sniffed. "If Hades wants to go ahead and call himself the king, god, underlord of the realm, he is welcome to. But he will not stop those that wish to be together from being so. To be torn apart from someone you love is ... not something I would wish on anyone." Nyx's features took on a sadness as she looked at Nika, before Nyx shook her head and whatever thought had flitted across her face was wiped away.

"So, you're going to help me get this lyre and find a way for Orpheus and Eurydice to roam freely? Why would you help me do that when this isn't exactly a career you had in mind for me? What's the catch?" Nika narrowed her eyes at her parents, in particular at her mother.

Nyx's eyes bored into her, but it was Erebus who answered her. "Your mother and I just want to be part of your lives again, Nika. We want to help."

There was that uncomfortable sensation wrapping around Nika's throat again, making her eyes water. Then, thankfully, Tomas interrupted.

"I was there that day. The day Eurydice died."

Nika turned to silently thank him with a look of gratitude on her face when she saw a forlorn expression across his.

"What happened that day, boy?" Erebus asked.

"There were plenty of us nymphs there to celebrate their wedding festivities, Orpheus' and Eurydice's. It went on for days and days. People from all over came to see the happy couple. They were so in love, it was obvious to see. The way he would smile at her, and she would dance and dance and *dance* to his music until she had worn through the grass. No one believed Hymenaeus when he said their marriage would not last. Of course, we should have. He was the God of Marriage, after all. If we had, perhaps we'd have looked out for her in the gardens when..."

"Was it truly a snake that bit her? I always thought that shepherd Aristaeus murdered her when she refused his advances, personally," Nika butted in.

Tomas threw her a scornful look. "Other people's misery should not be your gossip."

Erebus chuckled. "Unfortunate trait of the family, I'm afraid."

Nika noticed a slight tick in Tomas' clenched jaw, clearly unhappy with the answer, but he continued with his tale anyway.

"To answer your question, yes, it was a snake. Venomous, as we all know now. When she dropped to the ground, we all thought it a joke, for she kept saying that dancing to Orpheus' music would be the death of her. She even said that was what Hymenaeus was apparently alluding to. It was as if she knew. This small, graceful creature, truly the beauty among us all, and none of us immediately ran to her when she fell."

A single tear ran down Tomas' face. He impatiently wiped it away.

"By the time we got to her, it was too late. The poison had travelled to her heart and she was on her way to meet with Hades."

Tomas felt guilty, Nika realised.

"You couldn't have known," she said, in that no-nonsense way of hers. "And you likely couldn't have stopped the poison anyway."

He continued as if he hadn't heard her. "Afterwards, we all listened to Orpheus lament. When he played ... it was as if the air stopped moving, as if we were all dead with her. As if we were in that pit of unfathomable, unending grief with him. The only thing that has bought those of us who were there any comfort was the thought that they had been reunited again in the Underworld."

Tomas turned towards Nyx. "So, thank you, Goddess of

Night, for your offer of help. Even if your stubbornly foolish daughter can't seem to accept it. Those two deserve a lifetime of happiness after being ripped away from each other so cruelly, not once, but twice."

Nyx inclined her head. "You're very welcome, young one."

"While I agree my daughter can be stubborn," Erebus added, "she is not, and has never been, a fool. I would urge you to think more carefully about the labels you attach to her, Tomas. She is not one you do not want on your side, trust us on that. And I would urge *her* to rethink preconceived notions that may have been embedded in a young mind erroneously."

Nika pursed her lips again. It appeared she was getting reprimanded on all fronts, a situation she neither liked nor was she familiar with.

Gods damn you, Tomas. Why did you have to be here to interfere?

"Come, we will make up a room for you to stay in while I sort this business with Asteria. I should still be able to catch her before the next dawn." Nyx rose fluidly from her seat, her black robes sweeping across the stone floors.

"How do you plan on getting Asteria to assist you?" Nika asked, for the first time in centuries curious enough to want to tag along on one of her mother's outings. Perhaps it was because she'd just been reprimanded as a child and wanted to soothe old wounds with old habits.

Nyx turned and pinned her with a stare. "You do not need to concern yourself with my work, daughter. Us ancients like to keep our secrets between us, too. Perhaps, instead, you can see to it that your friend is taken care of. I hear you are rather good at that."

And so, as her mother left, Nika followed, kissing her father goodnight on the cheek out of habit and childhood ritual more than anything, before walking back up the spiral staircase. Tomas followed along behind her, to one of the many spare rooms in the sprawling mansion.

"You know, this really isn't what I would have expected your family to be like."

"What's that supposed to mean?" Nika grumbled, as she pulled linens and silks aside in the bedside trunk and found what she was looking for: an ugly, orange knitted blanket.

"It gets cold here," Nika said, thrusting the blanket into Tomas' flat chest. No muscle, no definition, just flat. It was a wonder he didn't fall over at the force with which she'd thrust the blanket at him, but Tomas stood fast.

It seemed that was his talent.

"I didn't expect them to be nicer than you."

"Charming. Is that why you travelled all the way to Tartarus to find me? Why did you come looking for me if Garth didn't send you?"

"Because, you didn't just leave Garth in the lurch. You left all of us in the lurch."

Tomas turned to the small wooden bed – the only thing in the room except the side table and trunk, both of which groaned with age whenever they were opened – and began making his bed. An uncomfortable silence filled the rest of the space.

"I'm sorry. I didn't mean to. I'm just used to doing

everything on my own, figuring it out on my own," Nika eventually said.

"Yeah, well, you don't have to."

"Is that the other thing you were going to tell me?"

"Huh?" Tomas gave her a quizzical look over his shoulder as he finished making up the bed.

"In the broom closet? You said 'And I'll tell you another thing'."

"Oh, that. It doesn't matter."

Nika narrowed her oval eyes to slits at him. "What?"

"I've already called you stubborn and foolish this evening, I don't want to push my luck."

"The fact you think you have any luck to push in the first place is quite frankly a testament to how stupid you are."

Tomas sighed. "There you go again, being classically cruel Nika." He turned to face her fully. "You know why I really came here? Because I figured you needed someone to show you they cared about you, Nika. I don't know, maybe I thought you had a cruel family, or brothers or something. Maybe that was why you were so mean. I came to show you we weren't all like that. But it turns out they're not cruel, you're just cold. I came to tell you, you were a good teacher for me. Did you know that? You made me a damn good waiter, so much so, I bet I could even replace you!" Tomas laughed. "Imagine that, the great Nika, usurped at the Watering Hole! I could replace you, you trained me that well. And now I think you deserve to know that we did just fine without you, in fact. So, actually, maybe you should be grateful I came looking for you at all."

Nika stood there, stunned. Tomas had never stood up to her like that. She'd always teased him about his long-fuse, that she was going to break him in, but here he was – in

Tartarus – at his limit, because she couldn't seem to accept care and concern in place of scheming and self-defensive smart remarks.

Or, perhaps — if she was going to be honest with herself — because she'd turned more into her mothers daughter than she'd like to admit.

Nika cleared her throat. "I'll, um, leave you to it. See you tomorrow."

REMAINING up all night with her thoughts, Tomas' and her parents' words circling through her mind, Nika had come to the uncomfortable decision by the time her mother had returned to the house that she would attempt to take everyone at their word that their offers of help were genuine.

First, she tried making eye contact with Tomas at the breakfast table across from her, to apologise for what she'd said in the late hours last night.

His eyes remained firmly on his plate.

"Are you still angry at me?" she hissed at him.

Tomas looked up. "What? No. I was angry last night, now I'm not."

"Then why won't you look at me?"

"Because now I'm hungry." He sent her a dashing smile, and she realised his anger from last night truly had gone. If only she could let her suspicion of others slip away so easily.

Mentally resolving herself to try again, she kept eating

her own breakfast – a delicious dish of barley bread, wine to dip it in, and figs – when her mother entered.

In her hand, the lyre.

Nika pushed her chair back immediately, her mouth still full of food she quickly swallowed, as she walked towards Nyx and the most beautiful, golden lyre, covered in stardust. Bending down to examine it more closely, the lyre sneezed, covering Nika in a spattering of stardust.

Tomas laughed.

Nika wiped it off, casted a scornful look at Tomas, and looked at her mother. "Thank you for this."

"I did not realise that our lessons when you were younger had affected you so. The trips to The Caves, their purpose, it was not to beat you into submission," her mother stated.

"Okay..."

Nika hadn't mentioned anything, to either of her parents or any of her siblings. *How had they known?*

"My mother was Chaos. When Chaos is all that exists ... it is not a world any others have known. It is not what I would have our world descend into again. Duty, rules, the way things are done – these are the things that I was trying to teach you. A way to stop Chaos reigning again. But I fear I made you loathe me as I loathed my mother. I can see now that there are more than enough creatures on this earth that someone will inevitably come to take the role of another."

At this, Nyx cast a pointed look at Tomas before turning back to Nika.

"Your happiness, dear daughter, is just as important as the duty you decide to undertake."

Tears threatened to spill out of Nika's eyes. She tried to viciously blink them away, but one heavy droplet escaped.

Nyx stepped forward and wiped it away with her long, elegant finger.

"I do, however, ask for one more request."

Nika half hiccuped, half laughed. "Oh yes? And what is that, Mother?"

"A visit to this Watering Hole of yours."

7

FOR NIGHT ONLY

The journey back to Asphodel Meadows seemed to take half the amount of time with Tomas as company, though watching him attempt to cross Phlegethon's fires had taken up quite a bit of it. Mainly because Nika was curious as to how he had crossed the first time and was quite content to watch him balance precariously on rocks on the way back, until she'd had to save him from falling in.

Eventually, he'd made it across, and together they continued their journey. This time they went through the Plains of Judgement (for they were coming in the opposite direction of those that were there to be judged and would not be confused with the others), and crossed in front of the palace of Hades and Persephone, which sat on a sprawling acreage of land hidden behind black bars that were decorated in growing vines and blood-red roses. Then, they simply passed the border and they were back in the Meadows.

Tar and sand and grass gave way to the smooth, worn cobbled streets Nika had become accustomed to, and she caught herself breathing a deep sigh of relief at being back.

Tomas sent her a grin, which she ignored – he couldn't expect her to suddenly become some happy-go-lucky-skipping-spirit – and together they headed straight for the pub.

Of course, given that the time they got back was mid-afternoon, most of the team were on their break between the rush hours, leaving only Savvas to greet them as they entered the restaurant.

"Well, well, well ... What do we have here? Where did you find this bedraggled monster, Tomas?"

Nika scowled. "Call me bedraggled again, and I'll drown you in your own vat of wine."

Savvas laughed goodnaturedly, before coming around the bar and squeezing Nika into a hug. She hugged him in return.

"It's good to see you," she muttered in his ear, his beard scratching against her cheek.

"It's good to see you, too. I take it you've got a plan to get us out of this mess?"

Nika pulled back and looked around at the empty place she called home. "How bad is it? Truly?"

"Everyone's been offered three hours off, one person dropped from the lunch rota, another from the dinner service. It's been like this ever since you left."

"Garth up in his office?"

"Yup."

"Well then, let's go and sort this mess out, shall we?"

At the end of the galley bar, to the right of The Nook, there was a staircase that led to the second story where all patrons could find the plumbing. It was also where the staff could find their lockers, and where Nika found Garth, in a tiny shoebox of a back office, crunching token ticket numbers at his desk.

"Going well for you, is it?" Nika asked, leaning against the door jam.

Garth pulled his thick strands of black hair back from his hands and regarded her. A heavy uneasiness fell between them.

"You're back."

"I am."

"Here to officially tender your resignation?" Garth crossed his arms, those scales rippling with the effort. Defensive.

"You really think I'd do that? After all this time? After all the things we've been through over the years working here?"

"No," Garth eventually said.

It was Garth who had been the one to see Nika was just a lost little spirit from Tartarus who hadn't known what she'd wanted, only what she *didn't* want. Unbeknownst to Nika at the time, Garth had known what the pressures of family obligation and expectation could do to a Soul: how it could crush them under the weight of responsibility. His great-great grandfather, after all, had been the one to set the libation agreement with Zeus, for no other reason than he was a greedy bastard who wanted more fame, more attention, and more accolades.

When Garth had agreed to give her a trial, despite the fact she had no experience, he had pulled Nika from the crumbling wreckage of expectations she had always believed herself destined for.

"Well then," Nika cleared her throat, blinking back tears for the second time in two days – *whatever had gotten into her?* – "you'll be pleased to hear the news I bring."

"Oh?"

"Orpheus is coming to play here, tomorrow night."

Garth blinked at her once, slowly. Then again.

"Repeat that for me."

"Orpheus, the recluse legend, the one and only, is coming to play here tomorrow night. That should draw us in quite a crowd, don't you think?"

Garth blew out a breath. "You're serious?"

"And you thought I was leaving for good."

"Well, fuck. How in Hades did you manage to do that?!"

"I'll tell you all about that later. Right now, we've got a hell of a lot of work to do if we're going to make this place ready in time. Are you game?"

Garth grinned at her. "Let's show them all what we can do."

THE TEAM, more than happy and willing to be put back to work, had pulled out all the stops.

Rae, genius baker that she was – though Nika was still loath to admit it – had created canapes that practically leapt off the trays, they were so moreish. Juicy prawns wrapped in bacon and dipped in honey, pistachio scoops of sorbet on mini sterling palladium teaspoons, and curry bombs that exploded in your mouth when they made contact with a tongue, had all the creatures of the Underworld moaning in delight as they gathered in the pub.

The rest of the kitchen staff were busy preparing the food for those who had chosen to dine with them tonight; their usual three-course menu, perfectly cooked, impeccably presented, all with complimentary bottles of Savvas' homebrewed wine.

When Savvas and Tomas had gone to spread the word earlier, the voice in Nika's head said that no one would believe them. But, the two had charmed the pants off of any creature who would listen to them, it seemed, for all the tables were full. Even those who didn't choose to dine milled around the bar – a line now six creatures deep – craning their necks, hoping to get a view of the maestro that they'd heard of but never heard play.

Thankfully, Rae's canapes were keeping them quiet while they all waited.

"You're sure he's coming?" Garth muttered out of the corner of his mouth as he slithered up to Nika at the hosting station.

Together, they looked towards the wealth corner, where a small platform had been set up as a stage in place of the tables. Those had been moved into the bar now crammed with Souls. The lights that illuminated the small platform caused the rows of wine bottles on the back wall to glow and sent flirting flickers to the audience that waited. The other side of the wall, where the carvings of all who had come to dine with them, appeared to be watching the empty stage too.

"They'll be here," Nika said.

"They?"

"Oh, didn't I tell you? My mother's escorting them. It was only under the cover and protection of night they could travel out of Tartarus without Hades throwing a hissy fit. My mother's words."

"Your mo—? Well," Garth said, cutting himself off, "We're in for quite a time."

As if she had heard them, Nyx appeared in her corporal form and whispered in Nika's ear. "We are here. Where would you like me to escort Orpheus and his wife?"

Nika cleared her throat and muttered under her breath, "On the stage. Over there."

Without confirmation, the wisp of power that was her mother skirted past her. Nika couldn't help it; she shivered. To be close to something that was so powerful yet unseen caused a biological reaction even a daughter could not control.

Then, as if by magic, Orpheus and Eurydice appeared in a plume of black smoke on the stage, the golden lyre in hand. A hush rippled through the crowd, as if they couldn't quite believe their eyes, before a roar of cheers and applause rippled back.

"Well..." Orpheus chuckled, squinting out into the audience, "I wasn't quite expecting to be so popular after all these years."

A chorus of laughter and cheers rang out amongst the crowd again.

"I see some of you are eating," Orpheus continued, "and I don't want to disturb your meal, so let's start with a soft melody I played to call my Eurydice, here, back to me when we were finally both in the Underworld, shall we?"

The crowd cheered again, even those with their mouths half full, as Orpheus pulled a couple of the barstools on stage up to the microphone, only to offer it to his wife, before he took the other one and sat beside her.

His fingers began to pluck over the strings so quickly, it didn't even look like he was touching them, as a sharp, sweet melody began to play out. Orpheus' mouth opened and he began to sing, looking at no one but Eurydice.

Nika couldn't hear the words. All she could hear, all she could feel, was the sharp sting of bitterness at being torn away from one she loved, a trickle of hope that tickled that back of her eyes and throat, and the long, mournful longing of the low notes that carried the song – like waves – through the atmosphere. Looking around, she saw that same melancholy she felt on the faces of those around her. A few were crying. A few were smiling. All the lovers were holding each other, as if scared the song was a prophecy they, too, would have to endure.

Her gaze settled on Tomas, who was standing behind the bar with Savvas, the glass in his hand almost forgotten as he absentmindedly polished it.

He caught her eye.

She narrowed her gaze at him and he began furiously polishing the glass in his hands again. *Good.*

Nika leaned her head towards Garth and spoke quietly to him underneath the thrum of music.

"Savvas isn't teaching my protégé his lazy habits is he?"

"Give the kid a break, Nika. There's a show on," Garth whispered back, his arms folded across his chest as he leaned against the host stand, his eyes still on the stage.

"I just don't want him thinking he can get away with anything now that he feels he can stand on his own two feet."

Garth looked across at her. "You care about the boy."

Nika snorted. "In the same way a sister cares about her annoying little brother, sure."

"Well then, you should be proud of him."

"Why?"

"A couple of night's back, Tomas stood up to a couple of rude patrons that Savvas was tired of dealing with. After that, they proceeded to get very, *very* drunk together. If anything, he handled it exactly like you would. I think Savvas wants to steal your protégé for himself, not teach him bad habits."

Nika scoffed quietly but inside something uncomfortable stirred inside of her. For some reason, she found herself protective over Tomas. She wanted to keep an eye on him, to make sure he was reaching his full potential.

Nika had to wonder if that hadn't been what her mother was trying to do for her all along.

The song ended and she snapped back to the sound of clapping all around her.

"Thank you, thank you," Orpheus chuckled, still casting long glances at his wife. "I must admit, I said to my love on the way over here that I wasn't sure I could still play this thing," he held up the lyre for all to behold, "but she still sings true."

Another round of applause broke out until Orpheus held up a hand to quiet the crowd.

"Now, I would like to offer you all something I have never shared with the living or the dead world before."

Feverish whispers broke out.

Orpheus chuckled again. "Fear not, I shall put you out of your misery. You see, it is not I who is truly the maestro of music, but my wife, who can sing and dance in a way that will entrance all the male Souls – and a few of the women, I should imagine – like no other. And, she has agreed to sing and dance for us tonight. So, if you wouldn't mind obliging an old Soul?"

The crowd whooped, some rising from their chairs to clap insistently.

Eurydice smiled in that demure way of hers at them, as if both grateful for the attention and unneeding of it. It was an alluring sort of star-quality. Of course, she only had eyes for her husband as she went to stand at the microphone and began to sing.

Not wanting to be caught up in the music again – or alone

with her intrusive thoughts – Nika began sweeping the tables. She moved swiftly and deftly between them, clearing as she went, refilling glasses where she could, taking whispered orders with no need for a notepad and accompanying pencil, and delivering the food from a kitchen doing their best not to crash about. Even the pots were trying their best to be silent.

By the time Eurydice was done with her song, all the sections had been taken care of again. Yes, Nika was very good at her job.

Happy that everything was dealt with, Nika stepped out the back of the staff entrance to take a breather in the cool, night air where twilight had descended.

Her mother appeared beside her a moment later.

"You run this place."

It was a statement, not a question.

"Well, Garth owns it."

"Yes, but you run it."

"I do."

"You're good at it."

Another statement.

"I am."

Nyx looked down, gave Nika a prudent look, and then turned to face the purple sky in front of them.

"I shall speak to Zeus and Hades regarding your little place here."

"About what?"

An arched eyebrow from her mother.

"I mean, excuse me?"

"It is clear you love this work, and no daughter of mine is going to work herself into the ground only for that upstart, Zeus, to take what he wants. I will tell both him and Hades that I am to be the new investor of—" Nyx looked at the sign hanging over them, "Zeus' Watering Hole," she said, distastefully.

Nika was still caught on the first part. "You want to be our investor?"

"More of a silent partner. I have already spoken to Orpheus and Eurydice. They have agreed to play once a fortnight at this place, under my protection in the cover of night, and within the walls of this establishment. By day, I've suggested they stay out of the way of anywhere Hades might be publicly, but I'm sure he will not cause trouble knowing that I have a personally vested interest in them now. You and your team will be able to assist with such matters such as accommodation for them too. Am I correct?"

Nika nodded. "Yes. We can find them safe harbour during the day."

"Well then, I shall go inside and talk with this Garth, ensure he has enough tokens to keep this place you love so much still running. Away with this silly libations nonsense. I certainly didn't need it, and I did just fine. So will you, especially with the pull having Orpheus here will give this place."

"Thank you, Mother."

"There is one last thing."

"Yes?" Nika laughed. She should have known.

"Your father and I would like to dine here, sometime soon I should expect. The food looked rather good, and it seems a shame our likings are not on that wall."

"Yes," Nika found herself agreeing, "it does."

"Then it's settled. First thing on the agenda is to change the ridiculous name of this place."

Nika smiled to herself, as her mother stepped back

inside. No doubt *that* would be an interesting conversation to be a part of.

"There you are."

Nika glanced behind her to see Tomas' head poking out from the doorway. "We're turning tables for the next round of guests to see Orpheus perform. You're needed."

Nika glanced at her watch, coiled around her in a snake-like fashion. It blinked, then showed her that the evening was almost halfway through.

"Well then," she said, turning towards Tomas. "Let's get on with it."

DRINKING WINE IN THE UNDERWORLD

AUTHOR'S NOTE

As with all myths, there are many tales about the Greek God of Wine (and many more things). I've pulled most of the history in this novella from the Dionysiaca by the poet Nonnus, though I have taken some creative licence. Well, the characters did.

This tale revolves around Dionysus' supposed first love, Ampelos. Ampelos was a handsome, young man (or Satyr, in some cases) who was loved by Dionysus. There are at least two accounts of his death. In one, he is slain by a wild bull due to other interfering gods and goddesses. In the other, he fell while picking grapes on a vine and was set amongst the stars by his love, Dionysus, as the constellation Vindemitor or Vindiatrix (better known as Boötes).

We're about to see what happened after Ampelos died and remade himself as Savvas – the winemaker of our story.

1

SAVVAS AND HIS BARTENDER'S CHARM

It was a busy night on the bar. Of course, it always was when Orpheus and Eurydice came to play at The Watering Hole.

Nika's mother, Night herself, had arranged for the two famous lovers to play at the pub fortnightly, and every fortnight the bar was packed six rows deep with Souls, deities, and creatures of all kinds, hoping to catch a glimpse of the lovers. Tonight was no exception.

Music thrummed through the air, a lively folky upbeat number that told the tale of Orpheus and Eurydice reuniting. Savvas could feel the happiness seeping into his bones as the melody swam across him, but he knew what would happen once this song ended and the next began. Eurydice would sing a hauntingly sad melody that shared how the couple had to go into hiding, to keep out of sight of Hades should he still harbour a grudge against them for trying to defy him. That was always the next song in this particular set. Savvas had been listening to them alternate their tales for over a year now.

They were clever, he'd give them that. If a Soul came to

listen to one set, they'd get the lovers' mortal story. If they came on a different night, they might hear Orpheus' descent into the Underworld to find his beloved wife. Other nights, like tonight, they got the reunited tale. And very seldomly, Orpheus and Eurydice would throw in a new ballad about their lives now that would have the crowd in an uproar. Gossip would spread through the Meadows like wildfire, and sure enough, Souls who had visited two weeks ago would be back at the bar hoping for a chance to hear the new ballad.

The current song ended and applause erupted, so loud that Savvas could not hear what the cute spritely nymph in front of him, with leaves weaved into her curly blonde locks and a blush spread across her apple-like cheeks, was asking for. He waited for the clapping to stop, and when the cue for the next song began, Savvas threw himself forward and into his work.

He did not like Eurydice's heartbreaking solo. He did not like to listen to how one mortal man would risk his life to save the woman he loved in the Underworld, even if it meant eternal damnation and the wrath of Hades forever. He did not like to hear how cherished and loved she felt, knowing that Orpheus had come for her.

Savvas did not like to listen because the man who had walked the mortal earth with him, who had promised to love him like that, had not done the same.

So, Savvas blocked out the tune, smiling at the pretty deities who fluttered their eyelashes at him in the hope they would get a little something extra in their drink, or perhaps get to go home with him at the end of the night. When it came to who he went home with, he did not discriminate. They were all lithe, willing participants. Everyone always had a good time.

And none of them were … him.

The cute spritely young nymph was a good option for tonight. Savvas flicked a glance her way and caught her watching him with her friends. The group exploded into a fit of giggles and Savvas grinned back. Oh yes, tonight held promise.

Working through the next line of patrons, leaving those who pounded impatiently on the polished oak bar until last, Savvas made his way down to the end of a long galley where a male Soul sat patiently waiting on one of the bar stools. His arms were crossed and resting on the bar, his head bowed, his brown hair tied up in a bun. As Savvas approached, he raised his head and offered a lazy smile, his eyes sparkling with mischief.

"Hello, Ampelos."

Savvas stilled. Not a Soul; a god.

He would know that melodic voice anywhere, let alone that face. The chiselled jaw, always freshly shaven. Golden skin that used to glisten in the sun-soaked vineyard. Those supple biceps that looked like they had been carved from marble, and those eyes … no. Savvas did not want to look into those eyes.

Besides, no one else down here would know that name: Ampelos.

"It would seem you, like myself, have developed a penchant for collecting wild feminine devotees," Dionysus chuckled, casting a glance behind his left shoulder at the group of Meliae who were still giggling.

"You shouldn't presume to know a thing about me anymore," Savvas snapped.

There was the merest flicker of surprise in Dionysus' eyebrow twitch, before a suave grin masked it.

"Oh? What should I know about you now, Ampelos?"

"Savvas, can you pull your finger out and pour those three glasses of wine I need for table twelve? I asked for them like half an hour ago!" Nika swanned past, her hands full of plates piled high with food steaming with heady aromas.

"Three glasses? Didn't you tell them it would have been cheaper to just get the bottle? Why do you insist on making my job harder, Nika?" Savvas yelled back.

Nika turned on her heel and stared at him. "Wow! Someone's about as charming as a three-headed dog this evening."

"*Someone* shouldn't exaggerate when they say they've been waiting for half an hour when they've been waiting ten minutes. I saw the ticket come through. If you can't tell, I've been a little busy." Savvas gestured to the bar around him.

"Then why are you still talking to me?" She flounced off.

The bar was, indeed, getting busier. But, try as he might, Savvas could not pull his feet away from the spot on the wooden floors where he stood, desperate to know why Dionysus was here and yet loathe to ask.

"You don't go by Ampelos anymore?" Dionysus cocked his head.

"I found I didn't like the attention it garnered." Savvas took a deep breath and willed himself to look at his old lover, his eyes hardened as he regarded the god.

He hasn't changed, Savvas reminded himself. *He's still the same reckless god he always has been. The same reckless god that could get a young man killed.*

"I suppose a lot of things have changed now," Dionysus smiled.

And there it was, that crooked grin, where the left side quirked slightly higher than the right. Dionysus had only ever smiled like that when he was nervous about what Savvas might think. It made something low and painful swoop down in Savvas' belly and back up into his throat.

Savvas coughed, trying to clear the lump in his throat, but that only made it worse, until tears threatened to spring in the corner of his eyes.

"Do you want something to drink? I have other customers," he eventually managed to get out, gesturing to the line of Souls who were all actually being taken care of by the other bartenders.

"I wouldn't say no to a glass of wine."

"Red? White?"

"Bartender's choice."

"You should ask him for some of that golden wine of his," Nika butted in, as she walked back past the bar, her hands now empty.

"Oh?" Dionysus glanced at Savvas.

Savvas scowled at Nika, but she simply smiled sharply at the pair of them and wandered off around the corner back towards the kitchens. The bell that chimed for service rang out every few minutes, the place heaving with hungry patrons.

"Fine," Savvas grumbled, turning back to Dionysus.

He did his best to hide his trembling hands as he picked up the heavy, green-glass bottle, and tried to soothe himself by rubbing his thumb over the luxury embossed label.

On the label was an image of two bull horns, but instead of expanding outwards, the two horns crossed, and at their juncture was a perfectly rounded, weighted golden drop of liquid. The name read: *Effulgence, Savvas' Edition*. It was a label *he'd* designed, the wine *he'd* taken time to carefully curate, down to finding the perfect patch of land in the

Underworld to grow his small selection of grape vines over the decades.

Which only made him more nervous.

Uncorking the top and waiting for that first 'glug' to hit as he began pouring the golden liquid into a pristine full-bodied glass, Savvas willed his hands to steady. But, he was pouring his wine for the very first time to *the* god of wine and pleasure. Even when the aromatic notes of honey, apricots, walnuts, and butter began to hit his nose, Savvas still kept holding his breath in an effort to control at least one of his body's reactions.

Sliding the glass over to Dionysus, Savvas busied himself putting away the bottle and going to take orders from the next round of Souls who had stepped up to the bar. When he could no longer take the anticipation bubbling up through his body like champagne, he risked a glance at Dionysus.

He had his head thrown back, the thick column of his throat flexing as he swallowed another mouthful of wine. Savvas couldn't tear his gaze away, until Dionysus' lilac eyes slammed into his. Savvas found his feet moving without volition towards him.

"Well?"

"You made the wine of old. Our wine."

"Have you come to claim it as your own?"

Before the words were even falling off Savvas' tongue, Dionysus was already shaking his head.

"No, I haven't come to claim it. But – I would have this wine at events I host. What does it cost you to produce it down here?"

Savvas whipped up one of the tea towels that was hanging limply off the bench and picked up a wine glass to polish. Something, anything, to distract him from those eyes.

"It costs what it costs."

"You use whatever you're paid at this place to fund it, I take it?" Dionysus said, looking around.

Savvas nodded, not trusting himself to reply to that. *Why bother asking if you already knew the answer? What game was the god of pleasure playing?*

Dionysus reached into his pocket and placed a matte black business card on the bar, a gold swirl resembling a wine glass the only indication it was his.

"I would match whatever token amount they are paying you here. I'd give you access to the finest vineyard in all the realms. In exchange, I'd ask you to export your wine to me – and only to me."

Savvas stilled the wine glass he was polishing.

"Why?" It was as much a question for himself as for the god in front of him.

"I just told you – so I can use it at my events. Events like you've never seen before, Ampelos. Such extravagance, such grandeur. I don't think you realise what people would pay to get a wine of old again. I can bet you're not charging enough for it here."

Savvas resumed his polishing.

"Well, what do you say?"

Savvas shook his head. "I don't think so."

Another flicker of surprise crossed Dionysus' face. "It would make you very rich, Ampelos."

This time, Savvas did not have to think about his response.

"Some things are not worth the price, Dionysus."

2

WATCH AND SEE

"**W**hat's this?" Nika picked up the card that Savvas had left untouched on the bar, long after Dionysus and the rest of the patrons had left.

"Nothing," Savvas said, snatching the card out of her nimble fingers and pocketing it in the short brown apron around his thighs. He had told himself he was going to throw it in the bin, but when he saw it in her hands, knowing Nika would throw it out immediately, he'd acted without conscious thought.

"Oh? Doesn't seem like nothing," Nika said, moving around to the back of the bar and going to the fridge to grab the bottle of golden wine that Savvas had opened earlier. Reaching up above her, she made a grabbing motion, and one of the clean wine glasses whizzed into her hand. Righting the glass, she poured herself a generous measure before heading back around to the other side of the bar.

"So? Are you going to tell me what that card is about or not?"

"What card?" Rae, the short and curvy Arae who Savvas had developed a soft spot for, came and joined them. As was custom after the busiest nights, the staff would all gather around the bar for a drink on the house. Rae, too, came and helped herself to a glass of the golden wine, and for the first time ever, Savvas found himself irked by it.

Didn't they know how much time and energy it cost him to produce that? Did they really have to pick the most expensive and valuable drink on his bar to consume as their freebie? Did they not see the value in him? In his work?

Of course they did, Savvas thought, shaking the snake of the thought that had slithered into his head. Gods damn Dionysus and his ability to turn Savvas' world on its head with just one visit. These were his friends, his family, who loved him, who worked hard with him. Of course they valued him.

"Underworld to Savvas calling ... "

Savvas shook his head clear and sent Rae a dazzling smile.

"What was that, Sunshine?"

"Are you okay? You haven't seemed yourself all night." There was a genuine look of concern on her face as she regarded him. In just under a year, she had become his favourite of the team. The nickname the rest of them gave her, Sunshine, was an apt description. She always had a smile on her face, nothing was too much trouble or effort, and Savvas could tell she genuinely cared about people when she asked after them. There were many times now that Savvas had confided in her when he'd been having a rough day, and she'd either done something to acknowledge it, make him smile, or he'd find some sweet treat waiting for him on the bar the next morning. His favourite were her warmed caramel slices made with the darkest of chocolate and the butteriest of biscuit bases. The secret, she'd told him last time, was the thin layer of honeycomb that gave an added layer of texture that ensured the gooey, rich caramel did not drench the senses.

"I'm fine, it was just a hard night on the bar."

"Who was that you were talking with for ages? The handsome one who was giving you the eyes all night?"

Savvas' eyebrows shot up in surprise. How had they not recognised Dionysus?

Then Savvas remembered: Dionysus did not come to the Underworld. He had only visited once according to the Greek gossip mill ... and that had been a long time ago.

It was Nika who asked the question. If Rae was sunshine, then Nika was starlight, a sharpness and a darkness surrounding her all at once. Hauntingly tall, all sharp cheekbones and elbows, with pale hair and eyes just like Rae's, Nika took the form of an Arae most were scared would hound them. But, she had good intentions. She and Savvas had been good friends for a long time. He knew she had a good heart. It was just encased in a block of unmelting ice. The only one who seemed to manage to get under it was the dryad who joined them now, Tomas. Though it was more like he niggled at her with a pickaxe by simply breathing that seemed to drive Nika wild. It was amusing to watch.

"What can I get you, Tomas?" Savvas asked, avoiding Nika's question for as long as he could.

"A glass of your finest dark pomegranate ale, sir."

Savvas grinned at the kid and obliged, stepping forward to the beer tap and slowly pulling the ale through to the glass below. Tomas, of course, could have come and got the beer for himself. He was a natural on the bar and the floor – a rare hybrid, but he had a certain flair when it came to making the complicated drinks. It helped that his dark-blonde hair flopped over his eyes, and those eyes sparkled when they caught the attention of the nymphs lined up along the bar.

He would have done well with that curly-haired Meliae Savvas had been eyeing up earlier. She had approached Savvas towards the end of the night, when it was only the stragglers left, but he'd had nothing more to offer her than a brief smile and a small shake of his head. He was in no fit state to entertain after his run-in with Dionysus.

Eventually, a thick foam settled on top of the beer Savvas was pouring and he handed the glass over to Tomas.

"Well? You still haven't answered my question," Nika badgered.

"Oh, I'm aware."

"How do you put up with him?" Nika turned and asked Tomas, a scowl on her face.

"It's more a question of how *he* puts up with *you*. How do any of us?" Tomas smiled as he sipped at his beer.

"Careful now, Tomas, or Nika will drag you back to her cave and do gods-know-what to you," Garth added as he came down from the office upstairs and took a seat next to Rae, while Nika pinned her scowl on him.

"All done for the night, boss?" Savvas asked.

"All done. The books are all balanced. Your mother makes my job significantly easier, Nika." Garth tipped his head in mock salute, the scales on his arm shimmering, as he raised the amber beer Savvas had just passed him, his drink of choice always the same.

"Perhaps she won't, after she hears your quips."

"Ah, but would you really tell her?"

Night – Nyx – Nika's mother, was the team's new silent partner. She had renamed the pub after she had taken it out from Zeus' demanding clutches and saved them from beggary over nine months ago. Her only terms had been to visit her daughter, the pub's maître d', whenever she pleased. When Savvas had asked Nika why a primordial, known for the fear she could arouse in others, had been so lenient with them, she had muttered something about her "wanting to be an involved parent."

Savvas had laughed at that, loudly. He laughed again now with the rest of the team as Nika poked her pointy tongue out at Garth. The chefs and the younger waiting staff had already finished earlier in the night, had their drinks, and gone home. There were only the five seniors left.

"Can we get back to more important matters, please?" she said. "Who was the handsome stranger eyeing you up all night, Savvas?"

As if noticing his immediate discomfort at the question with the tensing of his muscles, Rae jumped to his defence in that gentle way of hers.

"Savvas always has handsome strangers eyeing him up all night. Look at him. Our handsome silver-haired barkeep."

"Yes, but this stranger left him a card, and our dear Savvas here couldn't seem to prize himself away. Snatched the card right out of my hand."

Four sets of eyes bored into him at that.

"It doesn't matter."

"Is there something I need to be worried about, Savvas? Has someone come to poach you out from under us?" Joking, Garth tried to keep his tone lighthearted, but Savvas could sense the genuine worry rumbling underneath it. After all, things had just started to get good for the pub – and the team – again.

"No, there's nothing you need to worry about. It was just an old friend. Nothing more."

As was tradition, the drinks never finished with just one. But, rather than raid their own stocks, they locked up and all headed onward.

Together, they walked down two cobbled pavestone alleyways that twisted and turned like serpents, until the paths made way for a small outdoor courtyard, heated by firepits, and lit by firefly lanterns hanging from the tree branches above: Mahogany's, the only bar open later than The Watering Hole.

Garth went with Tomas to the small wooden bar that curved around the tree stump to order a round of drinks, while Savvas sat with Nika and Rae, who secured a small cherrywood table by one of the firepits, the seats coated with extra red wool blankets should the air have a particular cold bite to it.

Other Souls and deities, those also known to operate in the night of the Underworld, eyed them up as they passed the table. A couple of Oreads – large, boulder-like mountain nymphs – eyed shy Rae up like a piece of candy and subsequently flinched at Nika's glare. There was also a tall, stringy sea nymph, with green hair that cascaded down her back in a long plait, who batted her eyelashes at Savvas. And all Savvas could think was, she must be freezing in that barely-there scaled dress that started in a dip above her breasts and travelled down to her belly button before tailing off just beneath her ass.

Rae's hand reached out to softly sit on top of his.

"Why, my friend, do you have such sadness painted on

your face? You haven't been able to shake it all evening."

"It's about him, isn't it? The stranger you won't talk about." Nika surveyed him.

Savvas ran a hand through his hair. "Fine, if you must know, yes."

"Who is he to you?" Rae asked.

For a moment, he considered not telling them. But, the female creatures in front of him were literally born to harass — even if these two didn't take on their traditional Underworld roles. It still seemed foolish to tell them, but Savvas knew they would eventually tease it out of him if he didn't.

He stared down at the table and said quietly, "An old lover."

"Not one you wanted to see again, I take it?"

"No. Yes. I don't know."

"He hurt you," Rae guessed.

"Yes."

Savvas didn't know if Rae or Nika heard him. He'd barely been able to confess it to himself above a whisper. But, he felt the squeeze of Rae's smaller hand comforting his own. Nika's hand, too, rested on his forearm in a show of solidarity.

Perhaps if he told them the whole sorry story, this pressure that had his chest caving in and his heart cracking would disappear.

Savvas sighed. "Do you remember when I said I would tell you about my time on Dionysus' vineyards?"

Rae nodded. Nika leaned in.

"Well, that was him. That was Dionysus."

At their sharp inhales, Savvas hesitated, but the floodgates had opened now, and the words began pouring out.

"He was the one who got me killed."

3

___

THE FIELDS OF PHRYGIA

"**I** grew up in the fields of Phrygia. One day, a new boy appeared in our village ...

"In those days, Phrygia was simply fields of long golden grass, as far as the eye could see. To the north and the west there were dense forests made of dark trees, and on the northwest border was a river where we would play as younglings. The rest was never-ending, unrelenting land. The summers were harsh, the winters even more brutal. Not much grew there, but our families managed to use it for livestock and growing barley.

"I'll never forget the day I saw him. He just wandered over the horizon and down one of the roads between the farms, whistling a tune to himself, using a long branch he'd found like a walking stick after he stuck a pine cone on the end of it. It looked like he'd come from nowhere and had nowhere else in the world to be. No one came to Phrygia — there was nothing there. But here he was, the prettiest boy I had ever seen."

"Knew you liked males even then?" Rae teased.

"I didn't know anything about myself then," Savvas

offered a wry smile. "But there he was, and there I was, and that was the first summer I remember feeling truly happy."

"So what happened?" Nika asked.

"I ran right over to him and asked him what he was doing in Phrygia, as if this wasn't a perfect stranger. He told me he'd come to visit family, but I knew that was a lie, and he soon caught on that I knew every family in the village. I knew no one was waiting for a visitor, because if that was the case, it would have been all anyone could talk about. That was when he confessed he had run away from home and was seeking sanctuary."

"So the rumours were true? Hera really had him hunted down because he was a child of Zeus?" Rae asked.

"Oh, she did much more than hunt him down; she hounded him. There was nowhere safe for him to go, nowhere she couldn't find him, until he assumed a new identity and went to hide with his grandmother, Rheia. But he didn't tell me that at first, and I can see why. This was a *boy* being hunted down by a queen threatening to throw him down to the Titans in Tartarus and have them tear him limb from limb."

"He must have been scared for his life," Rae said.

"If he was, he didn't show it. He acted like any other our age. We swam in the river together, hunted with crossbows for the fat, fast fish. He even helped me gather the cattle."

"Did you know then that he was a god? Did you suspect?"

"For the most part, no. He looked like any other mortal boy. A little on the skinny side, and he had these long brown locks he used to hold back with a headband. His robe looked like it had been nice once, but with all the travelling he did, it ended up looking as tatty as the rest of ours on the farm," Savvas shrugged.

"The only time I ever got an inkling that he was a god was when he was angry. His eyes would flash this brilliant lilac. It would only be an instant, one blink and it would disappear. I would convince myself it was a trick of the light. But I think deep down within myself I always knew; I just didn't want it to be true. I'd grown up around the mortals, I'd heard the stories. I knew how gods treated them. I didn't want my best friend to turn into one of them."

Savvas took a breath before continuing.

"When I saw him today, his eyes were a brilliant, unending lilac. I had always wondered, when I'd heard the stories that he'd finally joined the ranks of Olympus, if they would change permanently ... I guess I was right."

"Well, you must have been quite a catch yourself if a god was interested in you when you were just a gremlin of a youngling," Nika said, her attempt at trying to lighten the mood dry, and welcome.

"I did alright." Savvas grinned.

"Wait – you said you grew up around the mortals and that there was only a river nearby in your hometown. But aren't you a sea nymph?" Rae asked.

Savvas let out a booming, good-natured laugh. "Whatever made you think that?"

"Your hair is always wet! Just like the others!"

Savvas laughed again. "It's oil. I use it to cover my horns, see?" He flicked back a curled lock to show her.

"Oh!"

Savvas chuckled.

"So, if you don't identify as a Nereid, may I ask what you do identify as?"

"There's a tail tucked between his thighs, if you know what I mean." Nika joked crassly.

A blush spread across Rae's cheeks. "Nika! That's rude!"

"Well, she's technically not wrong," Savvas told her. "I do have a tail. I'm a Satyr."

Rae looked at him, puzzled. "I thought Satyrs were supposed to have long ears, too."

"I'm not a donkey."

Nika snorted at that, while Rae's blush deepened.

"And anyway, the tail gets wrapped around ... never mind."

"I can't believe all this time I thought you were a Nereid. I'm so sorry."

"Don't be," Nika cut in before Savvas could say it. "He sleeps around like one of those fish fiends, anyway."

"Nika!" Rae admonished again.

"Oh, come on! He's about to tell us why the God of Wine and Pleasure was making googly lilac eyes at him all night!"

"You can't go around calling them 'fish fiends'."

"Well, they are."

"Well, you're a bitch sometimes. We don't go calling you that behind your back."

Savvas scoffed. "Speak for yourself, Sunshine."

Nika shrugged. "I don't care what you call me. What I want to know is what our *fiendishly* good-looking friend here did to get the God of Wine after him."

"Where are those drinks?" Savvas muttered.

Nika turned and checked over her shoulder. "Oh, looks like they'll be a while yet. Garth and Tomas are *bonding*."

Savvas groaned. Garth could really talk the hind legs off a donkey, Satyr, *and* nymph if he was in the mood for it. Which, looking over, he most certainly was.

Tomas caught his eye and sent back an apologetic grin.

Savvas looked towards Nika and Rae again.

"Very well. If you must know, he didn't come here to find me. If he'd wanted to do that, he could have done that a long time ago. He didn't."

"You said he was responsible for your death. Surely he came to make amends with you?" Rae asked.

"Apparently not."

"Oh, come on, Savvas. Stop being so cryptic. Spit it out."

Rae sent Nika a scathing look that could flambé a fresh lamb.

"I mean, what happened?" Nika tried again.

Savvas muddled the words over in his head, unsure of how to explain what had happened between him and Dionysus. In the end, he settled for the thing that had changed it all between them.

"You have to understand, I spent the summers of my youth with him. Three years of glorious summers under the stars and winters warmed by the fire together. He was my *best friend*. When it naturally progressed into something more ... it felt right, it felt natural. There was no one I loved more on the mortal plane than Dionysus, and I knew he felt the same way about me. To get him to be all mine—" Savvas shuddered, remembering the feeling. "There was nothing else like it."

He could still remember the feel of Dionysus' sure and steady hand cupping the back of his neck, the feel of his soft lips crashing into his own when he'd taunted the god to 'do his worst.' When his tongue had plunged into Savvas' mouth, in the back of that old barn they'd been rough-and-tumbling in, it was like a line of fire had travelled straight down Savvas' torso. His cock had ached with the need to return the favour. Instead, he'd pressed himself against Dionysus, who had groaned, reaching under Savvas' shirt to pull it over his head. Somehow, eventually, they'd made it to the barn floor, covered in hay.

The rest ... the rest was a memory Savvas slammed the door in his mind shut on.

"It was like that for a while, just me and him, enjoying what it meant to be young men under the golden sun. Down by the creek, Dionysus had started cultivating a grape vine. He'd found a trunk with a shoot sprouting off it, trailing along the ground. He showed me how to graft it with the scion, and explained why the soil was perfect. The margins, the depth, the right terrain for drainage and the eight hours of sunlight, even if the winters were brutal. He was right. I watched the leaves and the flowers grow over time. I watched the flowers mature into grapes over seasons. He showed me how to press them, the fermenting process, everything it took to get the grape into the most delicious drink. Everything he taught me is still the basis of the way I make the wine today.

"Those were the best summers of my life. We had to work day in and day out in the summer of course, to bottle it all and sell it at the local market, but it was worth it. Every moment with him was worth it.

"Then, one day, Dionysus came storming down the track that led from the fields to the river. For some reason, I remember it so vividly because he tripped on one of the sharp rocks as he stomped down the bank. I remember thinking how the rock must have hurt because he had this angry look carved into his face. When I asked him what was wrong, he told me to leave it, that it was nothing. Of course, I pushed back. I asked if he was hurt, if he needed to sit, that I could handle the grapes without him that day, but that only made him madder. He told me I didn't know what I was doing, that I wouldn't be able to spot the dragons for what they were until it was too late. That I needed him more than he needed me. I had no idea what he was talking about, but it pissed me off. To prove him wrong, I stormed off into the northern woods."

"And then?" both Rae and Nika asked in unison.

"He followed me."

4

___

BULLHEADED

"At first, I didn't realise he was following. My plan was just to cool off. Dionysus could get nasty when he was in one of his moods. It may have been the first time he'd taken it out on me, but I knew what to expect. He could sulk for days. I didn't want to be around that energy, not when it was targeted at me this time, so I was just going to walk until he gave up waiting and went home for the day.

"But after I'd walked a good way into the forest, I heard rustling in the bushes. Then, when I turned around, there he was, glowering at me."

"What do you want?"

"I want to know why you're trying to leave me."

"Leave you? I'm going for a walk because you're being an ass."

"No, you're running from me. I want to know why."

"Because you told me I needed you more than you needed me. Perhaps I wanted to prove you wrong. Look! Here I am! Perfectly fine without your help."

"Prove it. If you're so perfectly fine without me, I dare you to

ride one of the wildest creatures on earth. Go ride a bull and tame it."

"You can't be serious."

"Of course, I'm serious. Ride a bull without needing me to intervene and then I'll know you're right. Then I'll know that you'll be just fine without me when I'm gone."

"Why are you saying this? Where are you going?"

"It doesn't matter. Do you want to prove it or not?"

"Fine. Find me a bull and I'll ride it!"

As if the words he uttered had conjured the creature himself, an impressive bull came charging through the forest. Its strong, muscular body was covered in a fine black coat of hair. With broad shoulders and a thick neck, it was easily over two thousand pounds of pure muscle and raw power. But, the part that had Savvas worried, was the prominent set of formidable horns that curved out from either side of its head, the ends sharp enough to spear a man.

He gulped. But, backing out wasn't an option ...

"If I hadn't admitted to myself before then that Dionysus was a god, I certainly did in that moment. The bull appearing felt like a test from the gods to prove my words *and* my worth."

"You didn't seriously ride the bull, did you?" Nika scoffed.

Savvas glanced at her sheepishly.

"Oh, for Hades' sake."

"I was young! I was foolish. Weren't we all when we were young? I didn't know about actions and consequences. I knew in-the-moments, proving others wrong in a desperate attempt to understand the truth of who I was, falling in love with a man who would, who had, hurt me. Can you really say you've never done the same?"

Nika didn't have an answer to that.

"Go on, Savvas," Rae said.

"There's not much more of the story left to tell. I managed to jump onto the bull by climbing one of the nearby trees and dropping onto its back when it got close enough. Of course, the minute I landed, the beast started bucking like crazy. Still, I held fast, squeezing my thighs together. As a Satyr, I had strong legs – strong enough to stay on.

"I looked around for Dionysus, to make sure he could see, but he wasn't where he'd been before. I turned to look in the other direction, and that was when I lost my grip. I went flying over the bull's horns. My neck snapped as I hit the ground, and that was that. I opened my eyes and there was Hermes, telling me he was taking me to Charon."

A tear rolled down Savvas' cheek.

"That wasn't all, was it?"

To Savvas' surprise, it was Nika who asked the gentle question, Rae remaining silent, tears falling down her cheeks.

"No, it wasn't. When I looked down at my body ... when I could look ... I saw the bull had torn my head clean off. His horns had gored their way through my chest. I'd been turned into mincemeat. My only saving grace was the two coins in my pocket. They got me past Charon, and I've had a lifetime to forge myself into someone who wasn't the broken boy the tales sung about.

"Poor Ampelos, his body beaten, battered, and bruised.

But none more so than his heart, which cunning Dionysus used."

. . .

"THEY SANG THAT? So what on Hades' fertile ground is he even thinking about doing here, coming to see you?" This time it was Rae who took him by surprise with her angry outburst.

"Well, apparently he wants me to supply him with my wines at his infamous parties. That's what the card was about. He told me to think about it."

"The man who dared you to do something that he knew could hurt you, who inadvertently got you killed, wants *you* to supply *him* with wine? You should have told him where to shove that wine bottle immediately ... and painfully," Nika sniffed.

"I agree," Rae said.

Savvas was about to explain his reasoning for keeping the card, from what little he'd managed to figure out in the muddle that was his head, when Nika interrupted again.

"Who the hell does Dionysus think he is, anyway? He's married to Ariadne. Imagine if she found out that he'd popped down to the Underworld to meet up with his first love. I can't imagine she'd be too impressed. On second thought, maybe I should get someone to tell her ... "

Savvas slammed his hand down on the table, causing both females to jump.

"No. No one will be interfering. I don't want this all dragged up again for everyone to hear and speculate on. Do you understand me? I've built a life for myself, a name for myself now. Everyone knows me as Savvas, the winemaker. I don't want them thinking of me as Ampelos. You know the stories they'll tell if they catch wind of my past. Please, keep this between us, won't you?"

Garth and Tomas were finally heading over to the table, their hands filled with drinks. With each step they took closer, Savvas felt the pressure building. He clenched his jaw in an effort to not lean across the table and shake both Rae and Nika into giving him an answer.

Luckily, he didn't have to.

"Don't worry, Savvas. We won't tell a Soul. We swear on Styx, don't we, Nika?"

Nika sighed. "We swear it."

5

HEARTBREAK AND LIES

Swearing on Styx was an oath no one could break, unless they wanted the river to come and swallow them whole. No one was particularly keen on being devoured by the inky black river whose cold could make them want to scream, and sucked all the air from their lungs simultaneously.

However, given that the god standing in front of Nika knew the whole sorry story, she felt no compunction whatsoever in revealing what she knew.

"You're not welcome here."

Nika was tall, but Dionysus was taller still – he was a god, after all. His brown hair was worn down today, a golden laurel wreath weaved through his hair as a headband, keeping the stray locks out of his lilac eyes. The wreath was decorated with tiny amethysts that looked like grapes. Oh, there was no mistaking it this time – this was Dionysus in full regalia.

This time he'd come not as a scout, but as a god demanding answers. And Nika would be damned back to Tartarus with her family before she let that happen.

"Oh?" Dionysus leaned against the doorjamb and flashed her a suave smile.

Nika remained stony faced.

"We know who you are. Savvas told us all about you."

"Ampelos."

"His name is Savvas. That's his choice, and you will choose to respect it."

"And if I don't?"

"You don't scare me," Nika challenged.

Dionysus leaned forward until their faces were mere inches apart.

"I should," he smiled.

He clearly had no idea who she was.

"And you should know when you're not welcome," Nika hissed.

"Nika, who is it?" Garth asked as he rounded the corner, stopping in his tracks when he saw who stood in the doorway.

"Why, Dionysus; what can we do for you?"

Dionysus looked past Nika and sent Garth a dazzling smile. "I've come to speak to your winemaker."

Garth came to stand shoulder to shoulder with Nika.

"Ah, so you're the one who's come to try and tempt Savvas away from us."

"Oh, I don't know about that." Dionysus sent a small smirk to Nika. "I get the impression that it would be a difficult task."

"Damn straight," Nika muttered.

Garth shoved a pointed elbow into her ribs.

"Don't mind our hostess here. Ironically, she's not known for her hospitality. Please, come in. I'll see if our chefs can't whip you up a little something to break your fast, while I find Savvas for you."

Garth turned and gestured for Dionysus to follow him to one of the corner bar tables nestled between the windowsill and the firepit. Nika remained unmoving in the doorway, causing Dionysus to have to turn side-on to slip past her. Her eyes followed him as he took a seat at the table the staff all knew as the 'lovers corner', and narrowed to slits as he leaned back and cocked one ankle over his knee so nonchalantly she wanted to slap him.

Conjuring that iron will so as to avoid physical violence, she made her way out towards the kitchens, Garth following closely behind her.

"What the hell was that, Nika? Since when do you refuse entry to one of the Olympic Twelve?"

"Since he's an ass."

"They're all asses. You're going to have to come up with a better excuse than that."

Nika pursed her lips. "I can't."

"Well, then you're going to go out there with a smile on your face and serve him."

"Yeah, no, that's not going to happen."

"Yes, it is, Nika. Do we have to have this argument *again*?"

"Rae will back me up on this one."

Garth's eyebrows shot up. "You think Sunshine is going to defend you? Really? Oh this I have to see," he laughed. "Rae!"

The sous chef, her porcelain skin further whitened by the dusting of flour on her cheeks, poked her head around from the kitchens.

"Yes?"

"Nika here thinks you're going to support her in not serving a customer."

"It's 10 a.m. Who's the VIP that needs serving before the

lunch rush?" Rae frowned, wiping her cheeks with the back of her forearm.

"Dionysus," Nika said.

Rae didn't even skip a beat before replying.

"Oh, Nika's right. We should *not* be serving him."

Garth cocked his head, puzzled. "Why not?"

Rae's mouth formed a little 'o' as she realised she couldn't reveal exactly why she'd just made such a statement. Her eyes darted between Garth and Nika while she searched for her answer.

"We just shouldn't," she shrugged. "After all, he's trying to steal Savvas away from us."

"He's hardly stealing Savvas away from us. Besides, if we block Savvas from the opportunity, we risk losing him sooner. Trust me on this — it's not the first time it's happened to me."

Both Araes turned on Garth and fixed him with a look.

He pointed at both of them in turn. "No, no, no, you're not pinning this on me. Rae, whip something up for our guest. And make it good!"

Rae grumbled, but she turned back to her kitchen bench. Nika watched from the service station where the plating happened as Rae moved about the kitchen, grabbing seemingly random ingredients from drawers as knives magically chopped and prepped for the lunch service of their own accord, and pots and pans whizzed about overhead.

Twenty minutes later, Rae placed a small black disc of meat on a dainty white plate, topped it with a quail's egg, and sprinkled shards of bacon so crispy they looked burnt. It made the whole plate look like one giant quail's egg shell, as Rae sprinkled the charred remains randomly around the plate.

"So, what do you call this creation?" Nika asked.

"Heartbreak," Rae smiled across at her.

It earned her a rare, true smile back from Nika.

"What's that black thing?"

"Black pudding. It's made from the blood of a pig, or in this case, a cow. If I could have got the blood of a bull I would have, to really make a point, but we make do with what we've got."

Nika held a hand to her chest in feigned shock.

"Who are you and what have you done with our Sunshine?"

"Some things are more important than playing nice. Come on, let's go and serve this."

"Both of us?" Nika arched a pale eyebrow.

"Unless you don't want to present him with a scorching hot coffee that is going to scald his throat?"

"Ohhh, you are playing mean."

Dionysus echoed those exact sentiments when he cut into the quail egg and the yolk bled red rather than orange.

"Neat trick," he muttered, his eyebrows knitted together as he gathered all the elements on his fork before popping the morsel into his mouth. "Yet, delicious. You've got a real talent." He nodded at Rae.

She crossed her arms in front of her chest, accidentally pushing her breasts up.

Dionysus' eyes zeroed in on her cleavage. Rae snorted.

"So do you, it seems."

Dionysus' fork clattered to his plate. "Alright then, why don't you two tell me exactly what he told you? A blood red yolk, the snarky comments. You clearly have an opinion, and no respect for your lives if you insult one of the Olympic Twelve so freely."

"We live in the Underworld, it's not like you can kill us.

Besides, you don't get the say on who ends up in Tartarus," Nika smirked saccharinely at him.

"I can still make your life a misery."

"Like you made Savvas'?" Rae asked, her head cocked, her gaze questioning.

The first real flash of anger crossed over Dionysus' face. "I actively made sure not to make his life awful, even with my presence in it."

Rae scoffed. "Apart from getting him killed."

Dionysus' eyes narrowed. "Excuse me?"

"Come now, you can't be that obtuse. Savvas told us the things they sing of him – of Ampelos and Dionysus," Rae said, her arms still crossed.

"Not to mention, you did just threaten *our* lives," Nika added.

"Yes, well, you two I don't particularly like. Ampelos – *Savvas* – was my friend."

"He was more than your friend," Rae said.

There was a moment where none of them said anything.

"Yes, he was."

"So, why did you do it?" Nika asked.

"Do what?"

"Encourage him to get on that bull. You had to have known it was going to kill him."

"You really think I got him killed?"

Both Araes nodded.

"Then I suggest you get Savvas here immediately."

"Why should we do that?" Rae asked.

"Because it's clear our *friend* didn't tell you the whole story. In fact, he lied."

6

___

INTOXICATING

Savvas was already on his way to work when he got the call from Rae asking him to come in early. She hadn't said why, but given that he'd just finished perfecting another small barrel of his golden wine, he was heading in early to bottle it, anyway.

Carrying the small barrel across his back like a sack, while he held the ropes that fastened it to him, Savvas walked up to the side door of The Watering Hole. Transferring the ropes to one hand, he fished out the old iron key from his pocket before realising that Rae was inside and it would already be unlocked, and then headed up the two steps into the galley bar.

There, he found Dionysus, Rae, and Nika waiting for him.

"Well, this looks cosy. What are *you* doing here?" Savvas directed his question at Dionysus, before he walked behind the bar, unlaced the ropes, and heaved his precious cargo onto the oiled surface of the back bar. He continued busying himself, beginning set-up for the day, as if to prove having Dionysus here – again – was no big deal. As if it didn't make his heart thump loudly in his chest.

"Why don't you come and take a seat, Savvas?" Dionysus asked.

"I would, but I have work to do. Don't you two?" Savvas pointed at Nika and Rae.

"I said, take a seat, Savvas. There are things that need clearing up." Dionysus' tone was unyielding, in this moment one of the Olympic Twelve. Certainly not his friend, and not the man who had tried to charm him the other night.

Trying to hide what he assumed was an audible gulp, Savvas moved around the bar and pulled out a bar stool, facing the corner where they all sat. Dionysus was opposite him, his eyes boring into Savvas' skin while Savvas looked to Nika and Rae, each on his left and right respectively. The four of them made a diamond-like-shaped cluster in the corner of the bar area closest to the firepit.

"What is this about, then?"

"Well, let's start with the obvious, shall we? Why are you going around telling people I got you killed?" Dionysus leaned back in his chair and folded his arms, while continuing to stare relentlessly at Savvas.

He may as well have poured freezing cold water over Savvas.

"I don't want to talk about that."

"No? You seemed plenty happy to talk about it with these two," Dionysus gestured either side of him. "And you were more than happy to leave a few details out."

"I left nothing of consequence out."

"Oh? You didn't tell them that the reason you were bucked off that bull was because you decided to yell out to

Selene, the Moon herself. What was it you said again? Oh that's right, you said, 'Give me best, Selene, horned drive of cattle! Now I am both; I have horns and I ride a bull!' I see those horns of yours are no longer present. I wonder why, Ampelos."

"I was young, foolish – I don't deny it," Savvas murmured.

"Foolish enough to invoke a jealous goddess to send a cattle-chasing gadfly to prick the beast you were on. *You* got yourself killed. You think I wanted to see you thrown from that beast and gouged to death?"

"I would not have been on that bull if it was not for you."

"Not for *me*? I didn't tell you to get on the bloody thing!"

"Yes, you did! You dared me!"

Dionysus stared at him, his eyes growing wide with shock. "I wasn't there, Savvas. You stormed off into the forest ... "

"And you followed me."

"No, I didn't."

There was a beat of silence.

"Then who encouraged me to get on the bull, hmm?"

Dionysus closed his eyes, sighed, and pinched the bridge of his nose. "Ate, that little mischief-maker," he muttered.

"Ate?"

"It wasn't me you saw that day, Ampelos. It would have looked like me, but ... Ate is known to blind the men who cross her path with her illusions. Why do you think they call it 'blind folly'?"

"Why was Ate there?" Nika butted in.

"I don't know. I can only assume she was trying to gain

favour with Hera, and obviously word had gotten back that I was in Phrygia with someone. They must have learnt what Ampelos meant to me, and Ate took her opportunity when she saw it. She was the dragon I saw in my dream." Dionysus murmured that last thought to himself so quietly that Savvas didn't hear it as he interjected.

"But you knew what I said to Selene. You must have been there."

"So, you admit you did say it? Don't you think that might have had an effect on the *consequences* of your actions?"

As if swatting away the imaginary gadfly even now, Dionysus waved his hand in front of his face. "Never mind, I wasn't there. She told me afterwards, when I was standing over you, weeping like a little boy who'd had his favourite toy taken away from him. She came and told me what you'd said, what you'd done. She was more than happy to tell me how foolish I was for indulging a mortal friendship."

"It wasn't you?" Savvas said, realisation slowly dawning.

Dionysus shook his head. "It wasn't me, Ampelos."

The pointed tips of Savvas' ears turned a blush pink as embarrassment flooded his body. All these years he'd thought ... Savvas shook his head, unwilling to let the new belief take root.

"It doesn't matter; all you gods are the same. Look at how you just spoke of mortal friendships being foolish. You all learn to stop caring for the rest of us eventually."

Dionysus flinched. "How can you say that after our time together?"

Savvas shrugged. "I knew you didn't care about me the minute I heard you'd come down to the Underworld in search of your beloved mother. If you ever cared for me at all, you would have sought me out. I didn't expect you to take me back with you like you did with her, but not even a visit to see how I was … ?" Savvas shook his head. "That's when I knew you truly didn't care about me."

"Amp–, Savvas, I didn't know you were here. Did you not hear the tale they tell of us when they sing of Ampelos and his Dionysus?"

His Dionysus … that was nice. But, it was an illusion, just like the one that had got him killed.

"I didn't care to listen to the rest of the songs," he said.

Dionysus shifted his elbows until they were resting on his knees, his hands clasped and his head bowed as if in prayer.

"You died … and there was no hope left in the world anymore. There was no laughter, no sunshine, no warm earth to walk through with you, no clear waters to swim in. There was no life without you in it."

Dionysus looked up, a shimmer in eyes that had not cried over Savvas, ever.

"Oceans did not have the capacity to hold the depth of my grief for you. If I'd have begun crying, the world would have flooded. As it was, my howls of despair caught the ears of The Fates. Those batty three, they always speak in riddles." Dionysus wiped at his cheek angrily, reliving the memory.

"The eldest, Atropos, told me that my display on 'just *this* occasion'," Dionysus held up one crooked finger as if to mimic what the withered crone had done, "would 'undo the inflexible threads of unturning Fate, turning back the irrevocable.'"

"Come again?"

"She told me she would undo your death, and then your body sank beneath the earth."

"Pretty hard to see that as anything but death," Savvas said.

"Yes," Dionysus agreed, "but, then you rose. Except you weren't *you*. Where your hooves had been, roots began to form. From the fingers I had just been holding sprung small outstretched branches, and from your elbows and neck grew bunches of plump grapes. The vines just kept growing and growing in the direction your horns had been facing when you'd fallen. You grew into the most magnificent vineyard the world had ever seen. So you see, I thought you lived on. I visited you every day. I still have that vineyard. It's the one I want to offer you."

Finally, Rae leaned forward on her chair, the creaking sound of her shifting weight interrupting the moment.

"If you assumed he lived on, why are you here now?"

"I was in Zeus' office when Nyx visited last month. Apparently, now that you are all doing so well, he wants back in on the investor front. Don't worry," Dionysus added in response to the looks of alarm that fell on their faces, "Nyx told him in no uncertain terms where to go. When she did, she said something that caught my attention."

Dionysus looked at each one of them in turn expectantly, until, eventually, Savvas took the bait.

"What did she say?"

"She said she was surprised Zeus hadn't seen the true potential in the place given that the winemaker made wine of old." Dionysus' eyes slammed back into Savvas'.

"So, I did some digging. Well, more specifically, I got Hermes to go back through the records and find out who you were, where you came from. After all, I'd only ever taught one how to make the wine of old – and I thought him remade into a vineyard. When Hermes confirmed that you did indeed make the wine of old, I had to come and see for myself. Then, the minute I saw you, I knew exactly who you were. Ampelos. Even if you have grown a beard and hidden your horns from the world."

"What's so special about wine of old?" Savvas frowned.

"Of course, you don't know," Dionysus grinned. "When the vines grew in place of your body, the grapes they produced were *different*. They made a wine that didn't just burst with flavour on your tongue, but brought with it that sense of delusion Ate offers. It made the drinker deliriously intoxicated the more they drank. It's the only wine that both those in the mortal and Olympic realms know."

"If they already have wine that can do that, why does Nyx think wine of old is so special?" Rae asked.

"With intoxication and delusion comes consequence. Hours after the wine is drunk, it brings with it the most horrible ailments for all those not of an Olympic constitution. Wine of old, however, offers a more mellow joy ... still enough to let go of your cares, but without the ailment afterwards. Haven't you ever noticed that?"

"I don't drink that much," Rae said.

"I only sample my own product, not drink it like everyone else," Savvas said.

They both turned to Nika.

"What?"

"You like a drink – didn't you ever notice it?" Savvas asked.

"No, because I always end up on the spiced liquors, which *do* make you regret your mornings," Nika scowled. "Why haven't we heard about this from our patrons? Why aren't they telling us that our wine has different properties?"

Dionysus shrugged. "Perhaps they think the wine down here can't get you drunk. Only the stronger spirits."

Savvas shook his head. "There are other winemakers in the Underworld."

"Ah, but have any of them been trained by the God of Wine?" Dionysus grinned.

7

___

PURPLE REIGN

"No one down here knows I was trained by you," Savvas shook his head. "I never told anyone my history."

"How'd you end up a winemaker then?"

"I worked my way from place to place as a bartender once I crossed over Styx's border. I ended up here, eventually, and one night I was brave enough to ask Garth to try my wine I'd been harvesting in a little patch of land I'd found down here. The rest is history." Savvas shrugged.

"Well then, your reputation precedes you not just because you make wine of old, but because it's the best wine they've tasted. You remembered what I taught you." Dionysus sounded smug.

"I tinkered with the methods a little bit," Savvas said, enjoying the way Dionysus scrunched up his nose in displeasure, as if there was no better way. But of course, methods changed over time, as well as location and soil. Grapes fared better the older the vines were, producing more elegant and complex flavour profiles, giving an intensity like no other. Savvas had found ways to make the most of where he was, streamline his processes, and get the chemical balance to the exact ratios that produced the most exquisite wines. He wasn't going to hide that.

"But yes, it appears my wine is popular," Savvas eventually conceded.

"It could be even more popular if you were willing to take me up on my offer ... "

Savvas took a breath and looked at Rae and Nika.

"It is tempting, but—"

"Ampelos," Dionysus rashly interrupted. "Let me make it up to you. Though I did nothing wrong, *technically*, you *were* put in danger because of your relationship with me. Let me make your life here a little easier. I owe you that."

Savvas thought about it for a minute. "Well, I can't disagree with you there."

"Neither can we," Nika muttered.

Dionysus clapped his hands together. "Well then, I shall host one of my soirées! And you can come and see exactly *who* would be sipping your wine, and just how successful we – *you* – could be if we were reunited once again."

"No." Savvas shuffled in his seat.

"But you just—"

"No, I don't want to go with you to one of your parties, Dionysus. You can host your festivities here at The Watering Hole, or not at all."

"Here?" Dionysus looked around. "I suppose we could."

Savvas nodded and stood abruptly. "I'll leave you with Nika to sort out the details, while the rest of us get back to work. Not all of us can lounge around all day."

GET to work the team most certainly did. Dionysus had been very particular about the guest list, the decor, the food, and most importantly, the drinks. In the past week, he'd had a say over everything down to the place settings, overseeing Nika's every decision. It had wound her up no end, which the team had taken quite a bit of pleasure in.

"Bets on when she loses it and chases him across the Asphodel Plains like a banshee?" Savvas asked the crew in the kitchen, as he came back up from the basement after checking the beer kegs were all set up. Just because they were showcasing his wine this evening didn't mean Souls and creatures wouldn't want other things to drink, and Savvas wanted to be prepared.

Garth let out a throaty laugh, the rest of the kitchen team laughing along with him. They were all there tonight, ready for the event. Garth and Rae as head and sous chefs, Lexie on the grill, Yani on the fish station, Melamene getting ready at the patisserie station, and Ross already cleaning up the dishes from the prep time earlier.

"We ready to do this?" Garth asked the team, though his eyes were trained on Savvas. A round of nods and "yes, chef" followed.

"Good! Let's show that god's groupies that we know exactly what we're doing," Garth clapped his hands together with glee.

Everyone agreed with a hearty cheer and went to their stations.

Savvas wandered back through the restaurant,

admiring how the whole place had come alive. Lilac and white flowers adorned the walls like bunting, while the tables were laid with thick cream tablecloths and decorated with gold cutlery and wine goblets that had a band of gold across the top. Vines, of course, were the centrepieces running along the tables, occasionally broken up with clusters of long-stemmed candles. Finally, gauze in white and all hues of purple hung from the rafters, transforming the restaurant into an intimate chrysalis of celebration.

The air was thick with anticipation as the sun began its descent and revellers began flooding through the restaurant. There would be no walk-in guests tonight; only the ones who'd been invited by Dionysus. There was a chalkboard outside with a beautifully calligraphed message telling their usual patrons that they'd be back in business tomorrow.

Not that they were losing out tonight. Dionysus had paid handsomely for the privilege of hosting the party here – Nika had made sure of that, and that was before all the running around he had put her through. As she'd said to Savvas, it wasn't as if he was strapped for barters or boons of any kind, given how often he threw festivals where people paid homage to him with all manner of gifts.

A symphony of laughter, music, and the clinking of glasses filled the air, as Dionysus personally welcomed his guests one by one and introduced them to Savvas. He suavely led each one of them to the complimentary glass of golden wine on the bar, a hand on the small of each deity's and nymph's back, nodding encouragingly as they gushed about how delightful it was to sample a wine of old again. Then, Dionysus made the same joke about how much they'd enjoy it the next morning with no regrets, the small thing in his arms would laugh, and then he'd let them drift into the crowd.

Savvas watched with an amused look on his face, as he busied himself as much as he could on the bar. He had been right — others had wanted beers and cocktails, many of them curious to see what else was served in the Underworld. Seeing as it was a private party, there was only himself on the bar, and there was only just enough interest in the other types of drinks to keep him busy.

An hour into the festivities, the team began to bring out the food. They had outdone themselves. An array of exotic food was displayed along the tables to tantalise the guests. There was Styx's smoky seafood chowder featuring succulent morsels from the depths of the River Styx. Garth had played with the recipe some, and now it featured smoked eel and charred squid tentacles. There were the charcuterie platters made up of an assortment of cured meats, including venison salami, smoked duck breast, and aged boar prosciutto. Accompanying those was a harvest salad of roasted blood-red beets, charred corn, and black garlic, tossed in a pomegranate molasses vinaigrette and topped with shards of fiery goat cheese. There was also the cauldron soup: a velvety broth infused with flavours of roasted pumpkin, nutmeg, and truffle oil, garnished with crispy sage leaves. Finally, there were juicy slices of succulent prime beef, slow-roasted to perfection and served with a reduction of pomegranate and blackberry, accompanied by truffle mashed potatoes and braised bone marrow.

"My friends," Dionysus, dressed in his revelry robes, boomed from the centre of the room. He looked ever the royal, his robe a dark grape purple, the golden wreath in his hair, and ivy vines adorning his arms in a way that made them appear alive and moving, as if they too were infused with the spirit of the god.

He was balanced precariously on a chair, surveying them all as he said, "As you can see, tonight we shall feast! And tomorrow, thanks to this glorious wine we have rediscovered, we shall remember it all!"

A chorus of cheers went up, while an ensemble of musicians burst forth. Dionysus had asked for Orpheus and Eurydice of course, but it was not their night to play, and Nyx had vetoed the request for an additional night of work. As she put it, they were not "show ponies for young upstart gods to use for their own gain, but working Souls deserving of their airtime."

Dionysus hadn't had a clever repartee for that.

Regardless, the musicians he'd hired were still talented as they weaved their melodies through the air, and beckoned those who were not hungry enough to take their seats to join them in dance. The rhythm pulsated between the guests as they swayed and twirled, their voices merging with the music and echoing off the walls, and their faces already flush with merriment as the staff watched on.

The food, the drink, the music, the dancing – it was all an intoxicating mix.

"This is why they call him the God of Ecstasy," Savvas muttered to himself, watching the show in front of him. And a show it was; Savvas knew that. He knew what Dionysus was doing, showing him a world where the boundaries of ordinary life no longer existed; where passion and pleasure danced in unison; where life would become an endless tapestry of laughter, music, and celebration.

It was a fleeting glimpse into a whirlwind of unadulterated bliss, and Savvas would be lying to himself if he didn't admit he was a little tempted.

8

___

ALL GOOD THINGS MUST COME TO AN END

"Well?"

"Well, what?" Savvas glanced over at Garth, who had come to join him on the bar (not that Savvas needed help). The tea towels could polish the glasses themselves. He only did it manually to give him something to keep his hands busy.

The main food had now been cleared from the long banquet tables. In its place were bowls of Rae's Ambrosia Crème Brûlée – she and Garth had worked together to tinker that recipe, too, and get it up to Watering Hole standards. It was now served not as a parfait, but as a velvety vanilla custard infused with the ambrosia nectar, caramelised on top to form the golden crust, and decorated with three candied ambrosia fruits. Alongside it were dainty teaspoons of Pomegranate Delight – a refreshingly tangy pomegranate sorbet, garnished with a sprig of mint.

"What have you decided about Dionysus' offer? You could be part of all this, travelling the realms, seeing new cultures enjoy the fruits of your labour every night."

"I already do that here."

"You know what I mean. This would really be getting your name out there."

"And leave the Underworld?"

"You wouldn't be the first one a god has taken from the Underworld and made immortal. Hell, Dionysus already did that for his mother," Garth said.

Savvas didn't reply.

"Ah. You're worried about returning to the mortal realm?" Garth guessed.

Savvas nodded and continued polishing, not trusting himself to speak.

Garth leaned in and conspiratorially whispered, "We're all scared of our dreams, Savvas, even when we're living them. I'm scared every day that I'm going to screw this up – with the patrons, with my staff, for myself. Sometimes you've just got to take the risk anyway, you know? To see if it holds promise."

Garth knocked on the bar with his fist, as if his words were now decreed, and left Savvas to his thoughts. He watched the boss follow Rae outside.

A little while later, as the night deepened and the party raged on, Melamene approached the bar.

"Well, that's me officially all done and cleaned up. I'll see you tomorrow, Savvas."

"You're not staying for the party? Dionysus said the staff were welcome to join once they finished – and you work so hard every night."

Mel offered him a small smile that caused her small eyes to shrink even further and little tiny crinkles to burst around the corners of them. Dainty as she was, with a small pointed face, almond eyes, and a pixie cut – Savvas always had to crush the urge just to hug Mel, she was such a slight, cute ash-tree nymph. In fact, the only reason he hadn't tried his charms on her was because he refused to get involved with anyone at work.

"Parties aren't really my thing."

"No?" Savvas smiled back. "What is your thing, then?"

"I like the quiet life, Savvas. I like going home to my girlfriend in our little tiny cottage. I like being greeted at the door by my cat who weaves himself through my legs. I like spending my mornings cooking a slow savoury breakfast over my heated stove, steeping tea, and then getting to go out into my garden and tend to my plants."

"This," she gestured to the party around her, "this hustle and bustle is great in small doses, but when it becomes your life, it gets tiring. To be constantly on, with a smile on your face, where all the interactions are shallow at best. No, that's not for me."

And with that, she, too, left Savvas with his thoughts.

Eventually, Dionysus approached him.

"Come, let's take a walk outside. I want to talk to you."

Savvas, with nothing left to do on the bar except wait for the last few stragglers to leave, agreed. From her post at the hostess stand, Nika watched with narrowed eyes as they walked out the door.

Dionysus waited until they'd stepped into a secluded courtyard out the front of the pub before turning excitedly to Savvas.

"So? Now that you've seen what it's all about, what do you think?"

The way Dionysus' eyes lit up, so big and round, like an excited puppy dog, reminded Savvas of a younger time. The feelings of those summers came back and flooded Savvas' system, and right then – in that moment – he could feel that same promise of excitement. It made him want to grab onto it, run with the opportunity for as long as he could, and devour whole all the experiences it brought with it.

"I think it's very tempting," Savvas whispered.

Dionysus grabbed his forearms and pressed his forehead to Savvas', their noses touching.

"We would get the lifetime we never got to have together, and it would be as magical as it was before."

Savvas breathed it all in, basking in how good it felt to be wanted after all this time, before the sting of reality had him pulling back.

Dionysus refused to let go of his arms.

"But I can't leave the team here in the lurch."

"Why not? They're holding you back by staying here. Can't you see that?" Dionysus scowled.

"They're my family. Even if I go with you, I don't want them to suffer in my absence. You should know a little something about that."

Dionysus dropped his arms. "So, you would choose them over me? Really? You're still going to hold a grudge, even though I'm offering you the world?"

"No," Savvas said slowly, holding out his hands like one might to calm a horse. He could see that stubborn, sulky streak of Dionysus' rising in him like the tide. "I just don't want to abandon them completely. So, I was thinking I would leave with you, but the wine would not be exclusive to the festivals. I would ship some back to the team here, too. That way it has a home, a place where people can come and see where it was originally made, and others get to experience it. It's what's best for everyone, don't you see?"

"Half measures? You know I don't do half measures, Savvas. You're either all in, or you're out."

"It's called compromise."

"I'm a god, I don't have to compromise, Savvas."

"Well, you do if you want to have me come along with you."

"Gods, you're a stubborn mule," Dionysus muttered.

"And you're being an entitled brat."

Dionysus' eyes flared with anger, but Savvas wasn't going to take being called a mule – it was an insult of the lowest kind.

Suddenly the illusion burst, and Savvas could see what this 'opportunity' would be. It was not to give them the chance they never had, even if Dionysus did believe that. Instead, it was a chance for the god Dionysus had grown into to show himself as both the god of old and the god of new. He had always been treated like a mortal. The νέα – the parchment that reported the daily comings and goings in the Underworld – still called him 'The youngest of the Olympic Twelve'. Wine of old would give him the gravitas he sought, and the safety that would bring as it solidified his position – a position Hera would not be able to take away from him if he proved he had belonged there all along. Savvas wondered if Dionysus even realised that was what drove him.

"If you are unwilling to compromise, then I'm afraid I'll have to decline your kind offer. These festivals aren't my world – they're yours, and I remember what being a pawn in your world did to me. I need something real, something tangible, something that can anchor me, something that's *mine*. If you loved me, you would respect that," Savvas said.

"And what about us?" Dionysus asked. "You would throw away our chance to know each other again, too?"

The thought stung Savvas, but the thought of being used was worse.

"You were my best friend once, but we had our time. Just because our story was short doesn't mean it wasn't an important part of my life. It just can't become *the* most important part of my life again. *You* can't become the most important part of my life again."

"You would make me a memory," Dionysus accused.

Savvas searched for a way to soften the blow, but there was nothing he could say that would undo the damage of choosing to walk away this time. He couldn't even say he was sorry, because he wasn't. His life had been a series of cautious what-ifs, never allowing anyone to get too close, and constantly trying to prove himself against the backdrop of a past that had determined his fate. Now, with a clear head, he could see a life of choice – not to rectify the past, but to embrace the unknown of the future. *His* future. And that excited him more than the prospect of any reconciliation could.

9

GRAPE-FUL

Nika found Savvas with his face in the dirt. The sun was warming his back as he knelt in the soil and carefully assessed the leaves on his grape vines. Dew shimmered on his fingers as he pulled away and turned to see who approached him.

"What are you doing?" she asked.

"Checking for signs of vitality and disease."

"And?"

Taking a pair of small pruning shears, Savvas meticulously snipped away at the three select branches he'd identified as problematic. It was important to guide the growth of the vine — a well-pruned vine would yield the best-quality grapes.

"That should do it. Here, come," he gestured to Nika.

She grumbled something about new boots that she did not want to get dirty, but she obliged.

Savvas took her hand and held it out, gently lifting a cluster of grapes into her palm.

"See how plump and heavy the berries are?"

"Yes."

"I'd say they're ready. Go on, try one."

"You're sure?" Nika looked at him apprehensively.

Savvas nodded. "You won't spoil the cluster by plucking a grape."

He showed her, plucking one and then testing its firmness by squeezing it between his fingers. She followed suit. They 'cheersed' the grapes together, laughed, and then popped them in their mouths.

Savvas assessed the flavour profile, letting the juices coat every area of his mouth before he swallowed. There were both sweet and tart notes dancing on his palate, giving him insights into the vine's process. Nodding, he stood, and again Nika followed suit.

"Well?" Nika asked.

"They're definitely ready," Savvas said, carefully plucking each cluster on this particular vine and gently placing it into the basket he'd brought with him. "It should be a good vintage this year."

Nika rolled her eyes. "You make a good vintage every year."

Savvas felt something warm spread through his chest. It was true, he did make a good vintage every year. The journey from vine to bottle was a delicate dance, a harmonious symphony of nature and craftsmanship that required acute patience and attention to detail. He had always given the grapes the care and nurture they required to meet their full potential.

But this year, after Dionysus and his merry band of travellers had left with a sharp goodbye, Savvas was finally going to start taking some risks again. He would blend two varieties of grape the winemaking world had never before seen successfully put together.

The result, Savvas thought to himself based on the

flavour profile he'd just tested, was going to be his best wine yet.

"Come on, they'll probably be needing our help in the kitchen," Savvas said, dusting off his knees.

Nika snorted. "The only thing those two need our help with is eating everything they've made."

Together, they walked back into Savvas' home, a small nook not five minutes from The Watering Hole that had an unobstructed view of one of the golden fields of Asphodel that reminded him of the Phrygian hills.

Entering through the back door that led straight into the kitchen, Savvas and Nika found that both Melamene and Rae had covered every available surface in food.

"What's all this?"

"Well," Rae said, turning around to face them, her hands on thick hips before she began pointing at each individual dish. "Right in front of you is a grape and goat cheese crostini."

Savvas reached forward and grabbed the toasted baguette slice, biting into goat cheese, a sweet grape compote, and a drizzle of honey that had him groaning.

"That beside it," Rae continued, "is an arugula and grape salad with roasted walnuts. Careful, it's quite peppery. We haven't quite got the blend of the lemon vinaigrette right yet."

"What are these?" Nika asked, popping one in her mouth before Rae even had a chance to answer her.

"Those are roasted grape tarts with creamy brie, fresh thyme, and a touch of balsamic reduction. They're Mel's new speciality."

Mel, who had just slid another tray of tarts into the oven, brushed her hands together. "Yup, those are going on the menu alright. Garth is going to die when he tastes those."

"And this?" Savvas asked, pointing to the dish in front of him.

"Oh, that's my grape and gorgonzola risotto, with a hint of your golden wine, pine nuts, and fresh basil. What do you think?" Rae asked, her eyes wide with anticipation.

Savvas picked up the spoon next to the pan, heaved a great big dollop of the creamy rice onto it, and shoved it in his mouth. He groaned again on his swallow.

"Sunshine, if Garth doesn't put that on our new menu, then I'll open up my own winery just so you can come and run the cafe within it."

Rae smiled a smile so dazzling, Savvas couldn't help but return the favour.

"Ah, none of us are going anywhere without the other. We're family, you know that."

LET THEM EAT CAKE IN THE UNDERWORLD

AUTHOR'S NOTE

The phrase "let them eat cake" is most notably attributed to Marie-Antoinette. However, it can actually be traced back to Jean-Jacques Rousseau's *The Confessions* from 1765, in which an unidentified princess says, "Qu'ils mangent de la brioche," which translates to, "Let them eat brioche."

It's believed the princess said this in response to finding out the peasants had no bread, so the anecdote is meant to illustrate the disconnect between the extravagant lifestyle of the nobility and the hardships faced by the common people. It's since become a symbolic expression of perceived indifference and insensitivity, which is the inspiration for the lessons in this tale.

We not only follow our patisserie chef, Melamene (who makes a mean brioche), but also her girlfriend, Irid, and Irid's connection to the witches of Hecate. While nobility does not get involved, when Irid finds herself starting from scratch when everyone else around her has established lives, and she comes up against various attitudes and perceptions, we see how small moments of disconnection can brew perceived indifference and insensitivity.

The chapters alternate between Melamene's and Irid's perspectives.

1

IRID
BREAKING BRIOCHE

The only living thing in the store, apart from Irid herself, was the damn ginger cat who insisted on going to work with her every day. That wasn't to say things weren't *moving* in Hecate's Herbs.

The herbs and dried flowers swung playfully from the rafters, though there was no wind to push them, seeing as no one walked through the door. The lavender bunches, belladonnas, and dittanies simply enjoyed playfully bashing into one another. The walls were lined with bottles and potions of all shapes, colours, and sizes that remained still, though if one watched closely, they would see the occasional bubble ooze from the surface of different liquids. Out the back of the store, there were numerous half-potted plants of mandrakes, a chopping board with half a crushed garlic bulb on it, and a large mortar and pestle filled with the dried root of wolfsbane – now in a powdered form that Irid poured into a wooden bucket of boiling water.

Flicking her wrist in an upward motion, the mop stirred once, twice, and then heaved itself from the bucket and plopped itself onto the warm stone floor. Irid made a side to side motion with her hand and the mop got to work.

Irid watched her stupid ginger cat crouch on its front legs, wiggle its big behind up in the air, and then pounce on the mop.

"Haymitch, cut it out."

The cat threw Irid a look over his shoulder like he knew what he was doing, before sniffing, seeming to shrug, and then jumping up on the chair by the table where the mortar and pestle sat. Curling into a ball, he cast one last evil eye at Irid before pretending to go to sleep.

"Oh, stop sulking, you know I do it so you don't end up licking the damn floor."

The mop used a mixture of one part wolfsbane and two parts sage and rosemary – a common recipe among Hecate's witches to keep thieves at bay. Washing the stone floors with it, while Irid muttered the incantation under her breath, ensured that any Soul or deity who walked into the store with the intent to steal would find themselves breaking out in an incredibly poisonous rash that would spread from their head to their toes in a matter of minutes.

Then, it would be at the discretion of Irid, as to whether she allowed them to purchase the tonic that would cure such a strange occurrence.

However, should Haymitch be stupid enough to lick the concoction off the floor ... Well, if the reversal tonic didn't work on animals, Irid didn't know how she would explain to her girlfriend Melamene that the damn cat had ended up poisoned. And while Irid would happily test the theory, Mel had become attached to the stray cat who'd made his way into their lives one day and then simply refused to leave.

When the mop was finished with the final task of the

day, Irid looked once more at Haymitch, still deliberately pretending to be asleep on the chair.

"Well, are you coming home to see her or not?"

A twitch of his ear was the only indication he'd heard her.

"Very well," Irid sighed. "I suppose I'll leave you here with the plants then, shall I?"

Immediately, Haymitch yawned and stretched before jumping off the chair and moseying towards the door, nose in the air, as if it was his own decision to leave and he had all the time in the world.

Irid rolled her eyes from the open doorway. "Come on, then."

Shutting the heavy door behind them and weaving an enchanted vine through the handle to lock it, Irid turned and walked down the small row of shops on her street. Most had closed early for the day. The weaver, who spun the most fabulous organic cotton clothes, had waved Irid goodbye that afternoon after her last client, so her door was dark. The hole-in-the-wall baker would be back in the early hours of the morning. The newsstand was empty, the ravens that delivered the morning papers tucked up in the branches that hung over the stand, sleeping.

Irid couldn't help but feel a sense of deflation at the sight of all the empty storefronts – like it was a warning. A chill crept down her spine and settled there.

As one of Hecate's devotees, she knew all too well that the spine-tingling chill was no mere biological reaction. After all, Irid was a mountain nymph by heritage. Her skin was pale as snow, her cheekbones jagged. She was used to the coldest of temperatures. Not many knew it, but at the Cumaean entrance to the Underworld were the mountain ranges, under which Grief, Anxiety, Diseases, Old Age, Fear,

Hunger, and Agony slept. What use did they have in the Underworld, where all the residents were permanent? Instead, they came to the boundary of death to rest before going back out into the mortal realm. It had been an eerie place to grow up.

Irid was much happier here ... *wasn't she*?

She frowned at Haymitch, the grooves around her eyes a permanent reminder of her mountain lineage.

He stalked, tail high, in the middle of the road as if one of Hades' horses couldn't come and trample him. She may not like the animal, but she didn't want Mel's beloved pet to get hurt, and Pain still enjoyed a perusal around the Underworld every once in a while.

"Get out of the road, you idiot," she said fondly.

Haymitch, as always, decided to ignore her.

Eventually, they turned at the corner stump that created a three-way split in the cobblestone streets. They headed down the left lane towards the cottage with the overgrown honeysuckle bushes that looked like they were trying to escape the low brick fence perimeter, and the climbing rose that engulfed the front of the house. Then the only thing they could see was the white front door and the bay window beside it, in which sat Melamene, reading.

"What's the bet that's a cookbook in her hands?" Irid said to Haymitch, who finally responded to her with a low, knowing 'meow'.

Pressing down on the wrought-iron latch and releasing the lock, Irid stepped into the small alcove, let a long breath out and ... sniffed.

"Raspberry tarts and custard!"

It was a tradition that whenever Melamene was home, she would have dinner on the stove before she had to go to The Watering Hole for the evening shift. Irid would have to guess what was cooking. If she guessed correctly, Irid would be given the chance to cook the following night. It had become their compromise when they'd moved in together here – Irid feeling bad about not cooking when it was Melamene's day job, and Mel having to convince her that she really did enjoy cooking when she was home. Eventually, it had turned into a running joke, and Mel could often tell Irid's moods by what response she offered when she walked in the door.

Popping her head around from the living room, Mel smiled.

"Bad day, huh?"

Irid sighed, letting the door close behind her, but not before Haymitch bolted past her and immediately entwined himself through Mel's legs, purring. "Not the best."

Mel bent down to scratch behind his left ear just the way he liked it, before she looked back up at Irid.

"Any customers?"

"Nope."

"I'm sorry, honey."

Irid shrugged. "What can you do about it? Witchcraft is a dying art form."

"I suppose that's true," Mel sighed as she scooped Haymitch into her arms. "It's just a shame, you know? You have that beautiful shop with all those useful remedies. Those Souls could really fall back in love with the apothecary life they didn't get to have in the mortal realm with all their modern medicine."

Irid made a non-committal hum in the back of her throat.

"What's for dinner, anyway?" Irid asked, deliberately changing the topic, as she followed Mel into the kitchen.

"Brioche burgers with mushroom patties," Mel said, as

she bent to place Haymitch back on the ground and check whatever it was she was baking in the oven. Giving a nod, she stood again and turned to the sink where she began washing a crisp, fresh head of lettuce.

Irid plonked down at the small dining table behind Mel and watched her petite girlfriend as she moved around the kitchen.

She had a darker complexion than most other ash-tree nymphs, something Mel always claimed had happened because she'd lived in a tree so close to the Phlegethon fire-river. She was joking, of course.

Her dark skin was a beautiful contrast to Irid's own, her other features as complementary. Where Irid was all sharp, straight lines and angles (things she had always disliked about her body, but had eventually come to terms with), Mel was the opposite in all regards. Everything about Melamene flowed and curved as she moved around the kitchen, clearly in her element. Even her dark hair, now growing out of the pixie cut she'd tried last year, curled cutely around her ears. She tucked a few stray strands back as she continued to pull apart the lettuce.

Once Mel was done with that, she wiped her hands on a nearby blue-and-white chequered tea towel before leaning down to check the oven once again. Satisfied with what she saw, Mel grabbed her oven mitts – designed and shaped in the style of bear claw pastries, a Solstice joke present from Irid – and opened the oven door, sliding out a tray of perfectly baked, golden brioche buns, and placing them on the wooden chopping board.

Irid watched as Melamene spread a thin layer of mayonnaise on the base bun before carefully placing the patties, topping them with slices of blue cheese, which Mel then torched until they melted slightly. She followed that by precisely sliding on two perfect circles of bright red beet-root, a crack of black pepper, a curled leaf of lettuce, and finally a small dollop of caramelised red onions, before placing the top bun with a slight crunch.

Carrying the burger on a turquoise plate over to Irid, Mel went back to grab her own before taking a seat opposite.

"Bon appetit."

They had watched an old French film on the projector on their last day off together, and Mel had been delighted with the sayings, parroting them wherever she could.

Irid smiled in acknowledgement, wrapped her hands around the burger, and brought it to her mouth, savouring the combination of the sweet bun, the flavoursome juices from the patty, and the tangy fresh vegetables. Despite that, after just one mouthful, she put it down again.

"What's wrong?"

"Nothing … I just realised I'm not particularly hungry."

Mel continued eating, not one to waste food, as Irid knew. Growing up along the forestry edge of that river, where food could scarcely grow, and raised by a mother who believed food was a luxury and not necessary to survival, Mel was passionate about zero food waste. Everything in their pantry was used, and their fridge emptied every week. Mel even took any of their leftovers and food about to go out of date to a local sustenance spot for those in the Underworld who didn't have enough tokens to indulge in fresh ingredients and finer cuisine.

So, she continued to eat, but that didn't mean she wasn't concerned. Irid knew that.

"What's going on?"

A few minutes passed in silence. Mel continued to eat

her burger, while Irid got up the courage to turn their life on its head.

Irid took a deep breath. "I don't think I want to run Hecate's Herbs anymore."

Mel paused mid-chew, her eyes growing wide before she swallowed her last bite.

"Okay. So ... what do you want to do?"

"I have an idea, but it's stupid. Nothing, really," Irid muttered, dismantling her burger and picking apart the lettuce with her fingertips.

"Mmm, it looks like nothing," Mel said knowingly, eyeing up the small pile of shredded lettuce in front of Irid.

"I was thinking of branching out into floristry instead," Irid blurted.

Mel didn't say anything for a moment. When she did, the only thing that came out of her mouth was, "Huh."

"'Huh?' That's all you have to say about it?" Irid watched as Mel stood and took her empty plate to the sink, turned on the tap, and let the playful bubbles do their thing as they got to work with the scrubbing brush to clean the plate for her.

"Well, I know flowers and their properties were always your favourite part of the job; you've always loved flowers – it's why our home is literally crawling with them. I just think ... maybe it's not a good idea for you to turn your hobby into a full-time gig."

"You think I can't?"

"That's not what I'm saying. You have a gift with flowers. It's just that—"

"What?" Irid uncharacteristically snapped, hurt that Mel's immediate response hadn't been one of unwavering encouragement.

Mel was clearly struggling to find the right words.

"It … *changes* the way you view your gifts, when you put a price against them. Trust me."

Irid glowered under thin eyebrows. She wasn't concerned that she was going to ruin a hobby – she was concerned that changing her job was going to put more pressure on Melamene. Truthfully, she was feeling guilty and selfish for wanting such a thing, and now she realised she'd been seeking validation for that desire. She just didn't know how to voice it.

"But, if it's what you really want, then you're just going to have to go and get started with it, aren't you?"

The way Mel said the words – so flippantly – made it seem as if she didn't care what Irid did. But, Irid recognised the words for what they were: a challenge.

2

MEL

MELAMENE'S MUSINGS

Mel watched Irid wriggle in place uncomfortably at her words, while she took Irid's plate and replaced it with a small glass jar of warmed rice pudding that had been waiting in a pot on the stove. She topped it with a dollop of raspberry jam, made from the raspberries Mel had grown in their vege patch this past season.

"It would be difficult for both of us," Irid warned, as if she was trying to get Mel to see her point, to get the permission she so clearly sought. Mel wondered if Irid knew that the permission she sought was actually from herself. Mel knew exactly what Irid was like – she only took calculated risks when she knew there was a safety net beneath her.

This was her way of figuring out if she had one.

It was convoluted, but this is what Irid did when she wanted something, because she equally didn't want to assume Mel would take on something that Irid herself deemed 'too much pressure' on their relationship. Mel had learnt to find Irid's need to be painfully independent endearing enough that she smiled through it now when Irid came to her with a request.

"I would have to step away from the store. We'd be down to one source of trading for tokens. I think you forget how hard it was the last time we had to do that," Irid continued.

Mel felt a pang of guilt. Hecate's Herbs had been their sole source of income while Mel was completing her official culinary training at The Underworld Institute For Creatures of All Kind (UIFCAK for short), just to get her in the door at The Watering Hole.

Prior to her training, she had been completely self-taught, so Garth – as the owner – had insisted on Mel doing a six-month crash course to determine she was ready for the pace of such a kitchen. He'd been right; she'd needed it. Cooking at home was very different to running a service.

He'd paid for her training upfront and guaranteed her a job at the end of it, so Mel had started in the kitchen to pay it back. Between the classes and the extra hours she picked up at The Watering Hole, there had been no spare time for any actual paid work. There had barely been enough time to sleep.

Back then, they lived in a small shoebox of an apartment. It had been part of a large red-brick building, rapidly assembled after a flood of Underworld inhabitants had arrived unexpectedly. Poseidon had had one of his hissy fits and caused an earthquake along the oceanic plates, and apparently Hades hadn't been given the memo from his brother that he was to expect such a shipment of Souls. It had called for some quick infrastructure.

The Underworld, after all, was not so very different from the mortal realm. Souls and deities still needed a roof over their heads and a place to rest at night. Wind and fire energy still powered the electrical grid and metals were still mined out of Tartarus. The whole place had a rhythm that kept everyone functioning.

Of course, some Souls chose not to work in the Underworld. There were some who simply wandered the Plains of Judgement, or clung to the desperation of the Vale of Mourning. Some chose to forgo it all and languish along the river Lethe, just to be parted from their dreadful mortal memories. But, for the most part, most citizens of the Underworld chose to participate in some form of work, if only to keep themselves busy.

That was how Mel and Irid had met, when Mel was nothing more than a maid at a local inn – a place new nymphs of the neighbourhood often visited when they were debating moving to Asphodel Meadows. New Souls to the Underworld were given temporary housing until they found their feet (or didn't, as the case may be). But, nymphs who came from the other neighbourhoods – Elysium and Tartarus – often stayed at the inn.

Irid had appeared like a breath of fresh air on a cold winter's day, the wind whipping through the doorway with her. Mel had been about to berate the nymph who had allowed a flurry of snowfall to blow across the threshold she'd just swept, when she'd stopped in her tracks at the solitary figure standing in the doorway.

Her skin was like rice paper, and a cascade of silver hair framed a sharp chin and even sharper cheekbones, before falling bluntly to her thin shoulders. She was dressed in a tapestry of fabrics that were ruggedly practical and yet subtly elegant – a fur-lined cloak and some well-worn leathers, the bulk of which only served to highlight how slim she was underneath. A dark satchel hung at her side, delicately embroidered with a snow-capped mountain range. She seemed as enigmatic as the unpredictable snow she ushered in with her.

Melamene didn't remember the last time it had snowed in Asphodel Meadows, but she did know she had never seen a more beautiful sight in her life than that of the nymph in the doorway, who hadn't seen her yet. Mel had hurried away to continue her cleaning duties.

That night, in an attempt to distract herself from her thoughts, Mel had gone and made her very first Snowball: a spherical coconut marshmallow sweet, coated in a layer of white icing. She was trying to capture the essence of the nymph she'd seen, of what she'd felt just by being in her presence, in the flavours; the pristine white exterior with the rich, dark hue of licorice underneath – like the flavour of an attitude she imagined was hiding inside the mysterious stranger. The result had been a complete disaster, but Mel's love of the process – from methodically measuring out the ingredients, to the giant mess left behind, and having to test recipe batches over and over – appeased both her analytical mind that loved routine and her need for creativity.

It was another month before Melamene got up the courage to approach Irid when she sat at one of the inn tables, reading the latest collection of books donated by Homer upon his arrival to the Underworld. By this time, Mel had tweaked her Snowball recipe to include a hidden surprise of pomegranate coulis to add a burst of tangy natural sweetness to complement the licorice and the marshmallow. Of course, the additional element had made the consistency of the marshmallow turn to a big old pile of goo again, and Mel had no idea how she was going to fix that ... yet.

She was far too concerned about what to say to Irid to focus on that, anyway.

Months later, her love had finally told Mel that apparently on meeting, she'd babbled on to Irid about her recipe for the Snowball and how she couldn't get it right, and Irid had in turn mercilessly teased her about how chefs were supposed to keep their recipes a secret until they were perfected.

Mel couldn't recall the conversation at all. She only remembered afterwards that their chat had naturally turned to their jobs, and Irid had said something about coming to take over the apothecary store – the one that had been declared haunted.

Of course, being haunted wasn't the problem. There were plenty of Souls of all ethnicities who practised magic and could bless or sage the place. It was the fact that no one ever stayed in the job long enough for the store to thrive. More often than not, when Mel had wandered past, it was closed for business.

Everyone in Asphodel Meadows knew why. If you wanted to run the apothecary store, you had to get Hecate's blessing. She was the Power when it came to all things witchcraft and magic.

And to get her blessing? Irid would have to enrapt the attention of the witches of Thessaly.

They were Hecate's most devoted followers. All of them specialised in different areas of magic; some could communicate with the spirit world, others performed rituals, some cast spells. Others were herbalists, or divination experts; some even just helped a female with her time of the month and birthing babies. Anything to do with life, and death, was considered magic of their remit.

Anyone could find them at every new or full moon at

one of the crossroads in the Underworld. They moved about according to the moon cycle and the needs of the crops, but it was easy enough to spot them. There would be a collection of torches or lanterns floating above them, and the incantations would rise and fall in song like the waves of an ocean. This would occasionally be accompanied by the smells of herbs or meats that they continued to sacrifice in offering to Hecate, who resided somewhere down here in the Underworld, though no one knew exactly where.

Apart from Hades and Persephone, who lived in the Palace of Hades on the border of the Elysian Fields, no Soul, deity, or nymph knew where the other gods and goddesses lived.

The Crossroad Ritual had been the perfect place for new witches to come and find the coven of Thessaly, to cross over from the mortal realm and join one of the most ancient sisterhoods in witchcraft. There were others, of course, but *that* was the coven everyone wanted to be a part of.

Until the witches stopped coming from the mortal realm.

The ones who appeared in the Underworld between the fourteenth and seventeenth centuries had been ... broken. Most came with blackened skin, like meat left over the fire for too long. Some of their necks still held the marks of the noose that sent them to the Underworld. Others never quite lost the cough that said they'd drowned.

Over time, fewer and fewer of them sought out the Crossroad Ritual; until, to most, the witches of Thessaly became more legend than reality, and seemed to sink into the ether like their devoted Hecate.

But, Mel had seen them. She knew that someone just needed to show some staying power with that shop in order to get their attention. And Irid – strong, stoic, stubborn Irid, as unmoving in her convictions as the mountains she'd been born under – was made for the role.

It had taken just shy of four centuries for the shop to gain enough notoriety that the witches of Thessaly came to visit. In the meantime, Mel and Irid had spent every spare moment together, exploring all the hidden nooks of Asphodel Meadows and travelling beyond to the other neighbourhoods when they tired of their own. Somewhere along the way, Irid had started unpacking Mel's overnight bags into drawers and spaces in the one-bed, red-brick apartment she had rented after leaving the inn.

A short while after that, she'd spent a year refusing to do anything fun with Mel, only to turn around at the end of it with a stockpile of saved tokens and offer to support the pair of them, so Mel could pursue her dream of completing her chef training and becoming a pastry chef.

That had been a long time ago, though, and they were in a better position now. Even though witchcraft was still considered a dying art form, at least the witches of Thessaly kept Irid's store in business.

"The last time we had one source of trading for tokens, we weren't in the same position we're in now," Mel reminded Irid. "We hadn't purchased this lot of land yet, so we were paying someone else rent tokens, and we had to save a lot more to get this place on top of that. Besides, with the shop not exactly pulling in a lot of customers at the moment, it wouldn't really be so different to what we bring home now."

The thunderous look on Irid's face told her immediately that she'd said the wrong thing.

"I just meant, now is as good a time as any to try. You're not going to know how this will play out unless you go for it."

"And what if the coven shun me when I close the doors of the apothecary?" Irid snapped back. "They helped us out more than you know when you were in culinary school."

"Hey, that's not fair. Their help was freely given, don't make out like I should be indebted to your coven for their goodwill. We made the decision together that I would go back to school, just like we'll make this one." Mel pointed her tiny sterling silver teaspoon at Irid, and a smidge of jam and creamy rice pudding went flying through the air. It landed with a splat on Irid's face.

There was a pause between them, where even Haymitch watched to see what would happen, before both females burst into fits of laughter.

Irid sighed.

"I'm sorry, you're right," she conceded. "They did help of their own accord. I'm just worried it will all go wrong."

"I know you are. And I also know that if I don't push you, you'll convince yourself that it's better to keep us safe and content than go after what you want. I'm just telling you, you have all the support you want. We can do this."

"This is the kind of support I can expect?" Irid's clear silver eyes crinkled in humour as she wiped the cream from her cheek.

Haymitch wandered over to her chair and began licking at her outstretched fingers.

"Oh, *now* I get affection from you," Irid said playfully, looking down at the cat.

Haymitch let out a 'meow' and continued licking clean Irid's long, piano-like fingers.

"I know the coven helped us out," Mel continued. "And I'm not saying it's going to be easy. It won't be. Everything worth having comes with hard work, but if this is your dream then we are going to make it happen. Together."

"And if it doesn't work?" Irid asked, her eyes swimming with trepidation as she looked from Haymitch to Mel again.

Mel shrugged. "Then we go back to the way things are now. It just seems awfully silly to me, to be living your plan 'B' life if you have a plan 'A' in mind."

Haymitch took one final lick and meowed in agreement.

3

MEL

BALANCE – LIKE BAKING – IS A DELICATE ART FORM

"I just don't understand why she won't let me help her get started," Mel said to Rae while they were rolling out ribbons of galette dough that would then be cut into delicate casing shapes for a new dessert going on the menu tonight: Grape Galettes. They were the roasted grape tarts with creamy brie and fresh thyme that Mel had perfected when Savvas, the winemaker, had finally agreed to give her some of the grapes from his vineyard.

After all that hoopla with Dionysus last year, Savvas had certainly become less uptight about his precious 'process'. Now, when the bartender smiled, there was no pain behind his eyes. Mel no longer felt like he was watching her with his walls up. It had warmed up their friendship considerably, from her end at least.

At least some of her relationships were thriving.

It had been several weeks since Irid had voiced her dream of wanting to step away from Hecate's store and strike out on her own. And as far as Melamene could tell, her stubborn mountain nymph had done absolutely nothing about it.

Rae replied, "I remember when I thought Garth was trying to push me into working here before I was ready; I got very defensive. Perhaps not letting you help is her way of defending herself?"

"Why would she feel the need to defend herself to me? I'm her partner," Mel countered.

"I don't know. I've always found Irid to be kind, but very no-nonsense when it comes to business. Perhaps it's not defence. Maybe she doesn't want your help. Maybe she just needs to know that if it all turns to shit, you're not going to leave her," Rae offered.

Mel stopped what she was doing and turned to her friend. "Of course I'm not going to leave her! That was what my whole big speech was about! Wait, do you think she didn't get that?"

Rae shrugged. "Some think if they're not providing, then they're a burden to others, regardless of what you tell them. It's about how they feel, not about the facts."

Mel turned back to the dough and began rolling it out more aggressively.

"Uh, any thinner and your filling is going to split right through those," Rae raised an eyebrow.

Mel continued rolling.

"Sunshine, you did tell her that pastry isn't going to hold, right? You two told me you had made these before."

Mel looked up to see that Garth, Head Chef and Restaurateur of The Watering Hole, had strolled into the kitchen and was standing over Rae – who stood at a measly five feet one inch to his six-foot-two frame – watching her work.

"Of course I told her," Rae swatted at him. "She's angry, leave her be."

Mel watched the pair as if everything was happening in slow motion. First, Rae swatted Garth away. He playfully sidestepped at the last moment – almost colliding with an overhead pan that was whizzing overhead – and reached around her to grab one of the sliced grapes they had prepped earlier. He threw it in the air, his large snake-like tongue catching it as he swallowed and winked at Rae.

Who *blushed*.

It had actually all happened so fast that when both their faces turned to her expectantly, Mel realised she'd entirely missed what one of them had said to her.

"Huh?"

Garth smiled lazily. "I said, were you planning on serving holey food today, Mel?" He pointed to the pastry dough in front of her, which was now so delicate it had torn.

"Gods dammit." Mel scraped the pastry back together into a ball. She only had one more chance to get this right before the pastry would be overworked. She had to concentrate.

"See, Sunshine? This is why I'm the boss around here. Because they actually listen to me."

He was clearly playing with Rae. She had led the kitchen a handful of times now, at Garth's insistence, and the whole team had all jokingly agreed in front of him that they preferred taking instruction from Rae because she was nice about it, after all.

Mel would have gone to Rae's defence anyway, but something in her clicked at his words: Irid thought she needed Mel's permission to feel safe enough to pursue this opportunity, but she didn't.

She needed the coven's.

MELAMENE HAD BEEN on the periphery of enough coven meetings to know that they loved three things: candles, sage, and old leather-bound books. Luckily for her, their cottage living room space had all three.

Her and Irid's living room was circular, with books lining one wall, a bay window in the other, and a long plush green velvet sofa along the far wall, before the doorway opened back out into the hallway.

In the middle of the room was a large, black chest on which Melamene now placed a jug of fresh homemade lemonade garnished with mint, and the accompanying four glasses for the three witches she was expecting, plus Irid. The ice cubes chatted amongst themselves as she did so, like excited children whispering to one another. Then she lit the sage stick, smudging it around the room before leaving it in an abalone shell at the opposite end of the chest table and beside the old leather books stacked artfully in a curve, one on top of the other.

Finally, Mel lit the three candles sitting in the middle of the chest tabletop. They were encased in stained orange glass she'd picked up at the local market one year.

"There. Perfect, don't you think?"

Mel looked down at Haymitch who meowed in approval and rubbed his face against her legs.

"What's all this?" Irid asked when she came home not even five minutes after Melamene was finished setting up.

Mel turned to her with a small smile. "You're home

early!" She greeted Irid with a hug before turning back and surveying the living room.

"I heard from the coven and they said you were due to host the next book club meeting. I know how rarely you all meet now, so I said 'yes' on your behalf. I was sure you wouldn't mind; I know how you love these nights. And it's perfect timing, too. You can tell them about what you want to do – with the shop, I mean. I figured somewhere you felt comfortable, in our home, would be ...," Mel's voice trailed off as she watched Irid's face fall in despair.

Before Mel had so much of a chance to undo what she had done, the doorbell rang.

Irid's pale eyes flashed in alarm.

"Come on, it'll be fun! You always tell me how much you enjoy these evenings afterwards," Mel tried, forcing a larger smile on her face as she walked towards the doorway. But, there was no time to turn back and convince Irid, not properly, before Mel was at the door to greet their guests, who breezed into the house like a storm about to break.

"Melamene! How good to see you! Now where is our Irid? Ah, there you are!" The most gregarious of the Thessaly witches – Eupheme – always talked a mile a minute, but Mel had learnt that you did not interrupt the spellcaster whose words always seemed to come to fruition. No one wanted Eupheme to say anything bad about them.

Behind her were the two others who Mel knew Irid was particularly close to. Isolde was the quiet one with her raven-like head of hair bowed beneath a hooded cloak. She tended to avoid eye contact, but she nodded at Melamene as she passed over the threshold and entered the living room. Mel took no offence to it. Isolde had an uncanny ability to look right through you and know exactly what you were feeling. Her abilities as a natural empath, able to feel the emotions of those she watched, meant her affinity for elemental magic was unmatched. In fact, given the situation Mel found herself in just moments ago, she was rather glad to not be looking at Isolde at all.

The final witch to join them was Phillis, whose small almond eyes were fully engulfed by her dark pupils. Appropriate, given that she was the coven's resident oracle with a penchant for divination. One couldn't help but think that staring into the abyss of her eyes would bring no good news of the future of any kind. Still, she was lovely, to everyone. Except Haymitch. The last time he'd tried to jump on her lap, she'd threatened to skin him alive.

Not a cat witch, ironically.

Each of them greeted Mel and hugged Irid, who – after a brief moment of giving a good impression of an ironing board – returned the favour. One by one they took their seats: Irid and Isolde on the velvet green couch, Phillis in the bay window, and Eupheme in the armchair. Mel had pushed it rather forcefully from its neat corner in the hallway under the mirror, as it protested against the hardwood floor.

Apparently, it had not wanted Eupheme's rather large bottom on it.

Still, at least it didn't groan when she sat in it, Mel thought. Haymitch meowed at her knowingly, and the two excused themselves to the kitchen. Neither of them liked to be in the presence of the witches while they gathered together – there was something unsettling in the air around them, and Haymitch now took particular care to avoid Phillis at all costs.

No, it was much better to leave them to it. Hopefully, the delight of the evening would wash over Irid and she would come and find Melamene later, and thank her for the push.

Especially seeing as tonight's book club selection was a guilty pleasure among them. Mel knew, because in all the centuries she'd known Irid, she'd heard them pick this book at least three times before. Without fail, every quadricentennial, someone suggested the club read *Macbeth* by that scandalous Soul, Shakespeare.

Sure enough, a cackle rose from the front room and Mel let out a sigh of relief. This would be good for Irid. A bit of time with her friends and she would feel safe to let her guard down and open up to them. Mel was sure of it.

However, when the witches left at their typical hour, and Irid made her way up the stairs and into the ensuite bathroom without so much as looking at Melamene – who was sitting up in their bed, a new recipe book in her hands – that sinking feeling, like the perfect souffle deflating, began to gnaw at Mel's insides.

"Did you have fun?" she tried, internally wincing as she did so.

When Irid got mad, she didn't get angry. She got … stony. Silent and broody, until Mel was sure nothing would melt her defences. Irid often told her that was just her mountain nymph way; to leave her be and she would eventually come around. But surprisingly, for a pastry chef, Mel had little patience for that. Instead, she often sought out humour to break Irid's stoic shell. But, to do that she firstly had to chip away at it, which was never a pleasant experience for either of them.

"You shouldn't have done it," Irid grumbled, making her way back from the bathroom in old, worn cotton pyjamas (so worn that the baby-blue they once were now looked white), and pulling back the red bedspread with accompanying white top sheet.

"Done what? Invited your friends over?" Mel tried again, lightly.

"Pushed me to tell them before I was ready!"

"*Did* you tell them?"

Irid clenched her jaw. Oh, she was furious. She wouldn't even look Mel in the eye – instead choosing to stare at the curved bedroom window and short, cherry-red curtains spotted with white flowers. The curtains weren't shut, of course, because Mel knew how Irid liked to watch Selene balance in the sky at night, or the occasional purple thunderstorm that Zeus would spread across the skies when he came to visit.

Unfortunately, there was no such display to calm her mood tonight.

So, Mel continued sitting upright in their bed, one pillow between her back and the gold-tinted palladium bars of their headboard, until Irid was ready to speak.

"That's not the point! I'm not one of your baking recipes. You can't just add a dash of this and a dash of that and expect my life to rise like one of your three-tiered cakes!"

"Because you're such sugar and spice and all things nice?"

Irid rolled her eyes at Mel, but she finally looked at her.

That was Mel's opening. She reached out to grab Irid's hand, her smaller one slipping into the palm of Irid's long, elegant one. Irid didn't squeeze it in return, like she usually did, but she didn't pull away either. A small victory.

"I just want you to be happy. I thought if you'd shared your ideas with them, if you had support from them, it would encourage you to finally go after what you wanted.

Because none of us can do that for you, but we *can* support you."

Irid sighed.

Rae had been right, Mel realised. Irid was being far more emotional about this decision than she had been about any other before. This wasn't just something she wanted to do; this was as if the very essence of her being depended on it.

As Mel continued to simply stroke her girlfriend's hand, Irid eventually spoke into the silence echoing between them. "You're right – I did tell them, and they were supportive. It just feels like, no matter how I justify it, I'm going backwards in my career. I'm just not ready."

"Sometimes things moving forward in really fast motion appear to be going backwards, because the light tricks us. Perhaps that is what's happening to you now," Mel offered.

Irid mumbled something incoherent as she let go of Mel's hand and shuffled her way under the covers, growing obviously more frustrated at Mel just not 'getting it'.

Mel followed, and after a moment turned and cuddled into her. "We'll take it at your pace, okay?"

Irid let out a short, sharp breath through her nose, as she was prone to do when she was right. She eventually grabbed Mel's arm again and tucked it under her own.

As they drifted off to sleep, Mel could only hope that Irid would see what she saw: that with all the support in the world, Irid could do anything, if only she believed in herself.

4

IRID

BEFORE THE BLOOM ...

What Mel didn't understand, Irid had thought to herself in bed that night, was how disappointing it would be to have everyone's support and still fail. For some reason, it felt – to Irid – that if she did so, she would have wasted everyone else's precious time, love, and care. They'd realise they only loved her because of what she had provided them. With that gone, they would all disappear from her life, one by one.

That was why her Dryad mother had left her Oread father, when he'd stopped working in the mountain ranges. Irid had tried to help them. With her father's leg mangled in a logging accident, her mother had gone to find whatever work she could, while Irid had stayed home and helped take care of her invalid father. But, no matter what herbal remedy the local herbalist gave her, no matter the things she tried to concoct for him herself, nothing seemed to take. Her father resigned himself to his fate and never seemed to move again from the three-seater sofa in their lounge. It seemed to swallow him whole.

And so, Irid's obsession with finding a herbal cure for

him had developed into a life-long devotion to the craft, despite the bad memories it held.

Irid had never felt like such a failure before her mother left, and she never wanted to feel that way again. She certainly didn't want Mel screaming at her that *she had to "do something" or she was going to leave and never come back to that cold, dreadful house.*

Irid shook her mother's words from her mind. No, it was much better for her to try this on her own. That was why she was here, at the farmers' market – alone – setting up her very first stall. She'd resolved to herself that if she was going to try, no one else must know. If it didn't work, she could just keep telling Mel she wasn't ready until the ridiculous notion that she could be a florist of some kind faded from their lives entirely.

In truth, pursuing something that held no real value felt incredibly selfish, and Irid had been wrestling with feelings of guilt as much as fear of failure. Perhaps the farmers' market would be busy enough today that both would fade from her mind and offer her respite.

She looked around. The cobblestone square hosted two groups of vendors: those bordering the square provided goods and wares; the vendors in the middle provided food. In the centre burned a large, smoky woodfire they could use between themselves as required. At each corner of the square, a busker had taken root. Luckily, the space was big enough to accommodate all the different melodies – and the escalating chatter from the early visitors drowned out the worst of it. One could only really hear each busker when they were in that particular corner. Irid had checked earlier, when she'd done a loop of the market.

That was when she'd also spotted two other florists showcasing their flower arrangements today.

One was from Persephone's chain, run by one of her maidens (Irid didn't know her name). The booth boasted huge bouquets with the most vibrant colours: the whitest of lilies, and roses of the deepest crimson. There were sunny-yellow tulips, delicate blush-pink magnolias, and even bushels of deep-purple hyacinths. Every individual flower was bursting with colour and the vitality of life, as if they had been touched by their queen, the Goddess of Spring herself.

The other florist, Mari, dabbled in rare plants difficult to find in the Underworld. Naturally then, her stall had a smaller selection, but it was still larger than Irid's. She'd dotted little mason jars with fireflies around each display to bulk it out and make it look more magical, but if anyone had asked Irid, she would have said Mari didn't need it. The flowers spoke for themselves. There were Jade Vines, with their turquoise-coloured, claw-shaped flowers; Ghost Orchids with their ethereal, spectre-like appearance; and a few other species Irid recognised. Plenty she didn't.

Irid's stall by comparison was ... pitiful, she decided. Her heart sank into her stomach as she looked at her stall face-on, having now done her walkabout of the others. It didn't look particularly glamorous. She hadn't thought to bring any fresh linen to cover the birch trestle table she'd spontaneously booked the night Mel had invited the coven round and she hadn't been able to sleep, Mel's words going round in her head.

That night, Irid had crept out of bed, down the small spiral staircase, to the small two-drawer desk next to the armchair in the hallway, and written a letter asking for a market stall later that month – if there was still one going, of course. She had tucked the cream envelope into her old brown leather satchel and dropped it into the red postbox at the crossroads on her way to the apothecary the next morning.

Now, here she was, feeling completely unprepared.

At least I made a sign, she thought. Although, re-reading it now, it didn't seem that clever.

"Feeling Flowers" was written in purple chalk and decorated with white and green chalk flowers Irid had enchanted to move around the board. It hung off the front of the table and seemed equally as pathetic as the display across the top.

Over the past week in the apothecary, Irid had carefully chosen each of the flowers and meticulously trimmed and pruned them. She had placed them in a variety of small, shallow water bowls. The flowers floated on top of the water, and due to a nifty spell Eupheme had gifted Irid, would continue to do so in full bloom forever. The real uniqueness, though, was that Irid had mixed a series of aromatherapy concoctions and added them to the carpel – the female reproductive part of each flower – infusing it with the ability to pollinate any room with the ambience the potions had been mixed for.

A flower on its own, while its essence held certain properties, could not infuse a room with the empathetic qualities it held. Flowers in the Underworld, after all, held no true fragrance anymore. Having the Goddess of Spring perpetually here as their Queen meant that flowers were either always on the cusp of blooming, or buried beneath the soil when she went earthside. Taking their nectar, on the other hand, and mixing it to allow the chemical components to react with one another, created ... an effect.

The effect depended on exactly which chemicals and nectars Irid had mixed. She'd been practising for a long time in the back room of the apothecary on empty storefront days. Mixing the practicality of lemongrass for blood flow with the femininity in rose oil almost always resulted in increased romantic tension. Everyone knew lavender calmed nerves, but few knew that sandalwood and patchouli would ground someone having a panic attack. Different Souls responded to different smells for a reason, their brains all wired differently based on their experiences. Except for those who had drunk from the river Lethe – those were truly blank slates who cared for nothing more than the prettiness of flowers.

That was why, when she finally figured it out, Irid had thought she'd been on to something. She'd really thought her achievement met a gap in the market for a fragrance that would permeate the air and have the desired emotional effect (which she may or may not have tested on unsuspecting visitors to the store), especially after she'd overheard some Souls moan about how they missed the smell of flowers. Queen Persephone might have been able to bring flowers back from eternal death, but she hadn't been able to replicate *all* their earthly aspects. Irid also knew of those, like her father, who did not take kindly to necessary medicines but could benefit from even an uplifting mood enhancer, such as her sunflower citrus blend.

But now, seeing the competition, Irid wondered if perhaps she needed a more impressive display to convince anyone to visit her. She hadn't used the full space of the stall like Persephone's maiden had, where the whole front table and two standing wall displays with little shelves for flowers were full to the brim. At Irid's stall, there was only Irid, the trestle table in front of her, and the Souls beyond, perusing the market.

There were so many Souls wandering around – more than she'd expected.

Irid had been to the markets before, when she and Mel had one of their rare weekend days off together that rocked around at least once in a blue moon. Literally, their last day off together had been a year ago on the Blue Harvest Moon. But, she didn't remember the markets being anywhere near as big as this – so full of lively conversations, boisterous haggling, and aromatics that seemed to cling to the air around them.

The market was bustling, the stalls either side of Irid swarming with curious customers. Small nymph children intermingled with the recent mortal Soul children who had come to the Underworld. They were playing with a clown who blew a giant bubble of see-through gold liquid for the children to float in. The bubble would burst before it took them too high, the children would laugh, and demand to go again. The clown continued to helpfully oblige, much to the relief of nearby parents.

It made Irid smile sadly, to think of how the Soul children had come to be here, where they would remain forever young – both a blessing and a curse. It was why the clown continued to play with them, to ease their hardships; for children had them, too.

Irid's attention flickered to the tent that a few of the children had just run into. From the large dramatic curtains draped around it and the mystical incense spouting out the top (as if there was a chimney), she could see it was a fortune teller's. It definitely wasn't one of the Thessaly witches. They wouldn't be caught dead here. The thought further fed Irid's fear that this was a terrible mistake.

For not a single Soul, nor nymph, approached her. No one marvelled at her magic, no one even seemed curious, or to notice her existence at all. They simply averted their eyes from her stall and continued walking.

Irid tried to hide her disappointment, offering friendly smiles to passersby, but it was disheartening to see their gazes linger seemingly everywhere but on her or her enchanted flowers.

Just as she was beginning to lose hope, a figure walked towards her. Irid couldn't believe it, the smile bursting across her face at the fellow Oread mountain nymph who approached. She was smaller and older, hunched over a cane. Irid tried to hide the impatient jiggle of her leg as she waited for the silver-haired female nymph to finish her journey to the stall. Eventually, she stopped at the trestle table and frowned.

"'Feeling flowers'? What are those?" she asked.

"Well, they're flowers that can evoke different states of emotion," Irid answered.

"What, by looking at them?"

"No – I've mixed their properties with those of different oils and medicines that allow the flowers to, to ..."

"To what?" The Oread eyed her sceptically.

"Make you feel things in the air around you." Irid cringed even as she said it. She knew she wasn't explaining it well, but between making sure all the flowers and the sign were ready, and dealing with her fraying nerves, Irid hadn't much thought about her elevator pitch.

"Sounds stupid," the old Oread muttered before continuing on to survey another stall.

Irid wanted to curl up into a ball and hide from the Underworld, shut everything down and not show her face – or her *stupid* flower idea – ever again. But, before she could do that, another appeared to be walking towards her stall. The feeling of disappointment swept through Irid's stomach as she braced herself for someone else to tell her how foolish she was for coming here.

Especially when she realised the daemon walking towards her wasn't one she was particularly fond of.

Half daemon and half serpent, Garth's top half from his neck down to his arms and who-knew-what below the clothing, was scaled. He walked on normal legs, like hers, but Irid had always been creeped out by snakes, so she shuddered as he seemed to slink across the terrain towards her. Irid wondered which one of his parents had been the daemon, and which had been the snake.

"Hello, Irid. What a pleasant surprise."

Irid crossed her arms. "What are you doing here?"

Garth chuckled. "Well, you certainly know how to sell yourself."

"What is that supposed to mean?"

"Well, here I am." He gestured to the table between them. "Come to see your goods, and you're practically scolding me to leave already. Scowl any harder at me and I just might."

Irid made a conscious effort to try and drop the grooves in her face and smile, but it came out more like a grimace.

"Well, that's a little better," Garth jested.

Defeat finally enveloping her, Irid sighed. "I'm sorry. It's been a long, disappointing day. And truth be told, I never much liked you anyway."

"Oh?"

Irid winced. Mel was always telling her that she had to work on being slightly less truthful. She didn't mean to make others feel bad; she just liked bullshitting them less.

"Don't stop now, Irid. You're on a roll."

"Well, you ran Melamene into the ground with that job when she started working for you, and really, you haven't stopped since. I tried to help Rae with her plate the other year for the cook-off – I was the one who got her those damn apples. I was hoping that if she won, you'd ease up on your staff."

Garth shrugged. "That's the nature of the job and the place in which she chose to work. That was Mel's choice. She knew when she was making it – I was very clear about it."

"How would she truly know if she hadn't experienced it?"

"We all have to start somewhere."

Irid sighed again as she looked around. Still, no one showed any sign of approaching and interrupting a conversation she didn't want to have.

"Yes, well, when I find the fool here in the Underworld who said it was better to have tried and failed than to have never tried at all, I'll wring their neck for lying."

Garth cocked his head, a curious look in his eyes. "How could you know this venture of yours will be a failure? To me, it looks like you're just getting started."

"It won't work," Irid muttered.

"Why shouldn't it work?"

Irid sent him an aggravated look. "Look around, there are plenty of florists in Asphodel Meadows. Hells, *Persephone herself* has a floristry chain."

"So?"

"What do you mean, 'so'? They already have someone to go to. Why would they even come over here and ask about mine?"

"If I'd had that thought myself when I was opening a restaurant, I would have never gotten started. It sounds like you're scared."

"Food is different. It's a necessity."

Garth quirked an eyebrow. "Not in the Underworld, it's not."

Irid waved a dismissive hand in front of him. "You know what I mean. The mortal Souls who come here still believe it is, and we perpetuate the myth so it keeps places like yours in business."

"Just like if they knew flowers could still have a scent they'd be buying yours over the others, no?"

Irid tried – and failed – to find a way to disprove Garth's logic.

"I suppose you're right," she eventually conceded.

"So, practise on me."

"Practise what?"

"Selling."

Irid scrunched up her nose. "How?"

"How do you do it in the shop, when they come looking for one of Hecate's things? It's no different."

Irid pinned him with a look of surprise. "I didn't think you knew where I worked."

"Surprisingly, I do ask my staff about their lives. I don't just drive them into the ground like workhorses, despite what it looks like or what others might think."

Garth gave her a look under thick dark eyebrows, one lick of his slick black hair falling over his forehead.

Irid blew out a breath. "Fine."

She gestured to the table. "These flowers are imbued with elemental potions. They'll exist forever, and they'll never stop giving off the essence they've been infused with. That one you're looking at right there, that will ensure a date goes as well as it possibly can if the feelings of attraction are already there. That cinnamon one beside it ensures baked goods always rise just perfectly, even if a baker forgets to set a timer, because it will trigger their memory. I tested that one out on Mel."

"Really?" Garth bent over the table, observing the flower bowls more closely.

"You don't have to mock me while we do this."

He looked up at her in earnest. "I'm not. Go on."

Irid's eyes widened. "Oh, um, okay then. Well, there's one for everything, really: some for insomnia or nightmares, things to ward off bad thoughts and omens, ones to calm you, some to improve digestion, others to aid cramps. Some can even encourage you to dance, which I think would be mighty popular at a wedding or a festival."

"And this one? The one that smells like apples?"

"Oh, the green hellebore?"

"Yes, what does this do?"

"It makes whomever owns it feel like they're unstoppable. Like the Gods themselves could not stop them in their quest."

Irid knew that, because to gain its essence, she had used the peel of one of the Golden Apples of Hesperides she had bought on the black market for Rae a couple of years ago. It had been a slightly different process than working with the floral nectar, but she'd eventually found the right chemical balance. It had just taken a mixture of five other nectars, including frankincense, to get it to work.

"Sold."

Irid stood stock still. "I'm sorry?!"

"You heard me – I'd like to buy it off you. How many tokens do you want for it?"

Garth was already reaching for his pocket.

"But, I haven't sold anything all morning. The market's almost over."

"So?"

"So, why are you buying this from me? Is this a pity sale? Do you feel sorry enough for me that you're just going to take it off my hands? Because I assure you, after how hard I worked on getting that one right, I'm certainly not just going to give it away."

"No, you're going to sell it to me because I want it."

"Whatever for?"

Garth laughed. "My, Mel wasn't wrong when she said you didn't have a filter, was she?"

"Sorry. I just don't get it."

"And at the store, are you in the habit of asking customers why they want to buy something?"

"To be honest, they usually tell me of their own volition before I even sell them anything."

Garth gave a conceding nod. "Well, I don't think your future customers will. But, in this instance, I'll humour you."

It was Garth's turn to take a nervous breath. "There's this ... female. Completely and utterly too good for me. And I know that, and for the life of me I cannot find the courage to ask her out, because if she says 'no', it will devastate me. I am not a daemon used to having problems in such areas, you understand?"

Irid didn't say anything, sensing Garth needed to get something off his chest.

He continued. "She is all that is good and pure in this world, in my life, and I would like to not muck it up. Do you think this will help with that?"

"Just make sure it's in the room with you when you ask her, and it will give you the confidence you need," Irid said quietly.

"How much do you want for it?"

"Ten tokens."

"Only ten?" Garth pulled them out of his wallet and handed them over, each scroll worth a different favour Irid could collect from him at any time. She pocketed them and began wrapping the flower bowl in a small wooden box, the slightly lighter beige ribbon folding over it of its own intention. When that was done, Irid placed the box in Garth's outstretched hand.

He chuckled. "You know, I always wondered how Sunshine had gotten those apples for that dish. Now I know, you were her secret weapon. Perhaps this time, you'll be mine."

"Is the female you speak of, Rae? The one who's 'all that is good in your world'?" Irid cocked her head, her eyes assessing him.

Garth looked at Irid then, his face unreadable as he regarded her, before he smiled.

"Thanks for this. Tell Mel I said 'hi', won't you?"

5

IRID

– AND WHILE YOU WAIT –

Irid came home to the sound of pots and pans banging about. As soon as she opened the door to the hallway, Haymitch jumped off the armchair and wandered towards the noise in the kitchen, undoubtedly to let Mel know Irid had arrived home.

Though it was somewhat of a mystery that Mel was home when she should be at The Watering Hole getting ready for tonight's service. Irid, though exhausted and depleted from the day, decided to follow Haymitch into the kitchen and find out.

"You're home!" Mel exclaimed, putting down the wooden spoon and flying across the kitchen to give Irid a hug. Mel was so short that her head fit perfectly under Irid's chin, which meant Irid could see over top and notice the saucepan of caramel on the stove bubbling over. She made a flicking motion with her wrist, and the wooden spoon began stirring on its own.

Why Mel insisted on cooking without magic was beyond Irid.

"You better get back to that caramel or it's going to boil

over and burn," she murmured against the top of Mel's head, before pressing a kiss to it.

"Oh, you're right!" Mel stepped back and sent Irid a shining smile before turning to the multitude of pots on the stove.

"What are you making this time?"

"Why don't you guess?" Mel smiled playfully. "You didn't when you came in the door like you usually do."

"I wasn't expecting you to be home."

Mel offered a one-shoulder shrug. "Garth offered me the night off. I thought I'd take him up on it, cook you your favourite after a long day."

"That caramel's for your sticky pudding?"

"It is, and simmering away there in the blue ceramic pot is your favourite bisque. I added a little extra saffron and some Cognac this time. Plus, I managed to swipe a few scallops from the markets today, so I'm going to sear them in butter and have them sit in the dish rather than any fish meat, but don't worry – it shouldn't change the balance of the dish – I don't think." Mel frowned.

"So, you went to the markets?"

"Just the fish market. I was going to prepare coq au vin, too; I know how much you love it, but I ran out of time. Good thing, I suppose, or we'd be eating all this for a week!"

"Why are you going out of your way to prepare such an extravagant three-course meal for us? Is there something I'm forgetting? An anniversary of some kind?" Irid asked suspiciously, eyeing Mel as she took a seat at the small table.

"No ... I just thought it might be nice to do something, seeing as it's so rare we get an evening to ourselves together. And two evenings off in two weeks! I must have done something to impress Garth. I can't think why else he's being so generous with the roster."

Irid made a humming noise in the back of her throat.

"Anyway, you never said how your day was," Mel continued.

"Oh, you know, just a day."

"Really?" Mel turned and looked at her. "So, the shop did okay today?"

There was something in her tone that had Irid suspecting Mel knew more than she was letting on. Perhaps Garth had told Mel he had seen her at the markets, or perhaps Mel had been the one to tell him where to find her … if she'd somehow figured it out, or lied about where she'd been today.

There was only one way to find out.

"Actually, I wasn't at the shop today." Irid blew out a deep breath. "I went to the markets instead."

"Oh, so the shop was dead?" Mel pulled a sympathetic face at her.

"No, I chose to go to the markets."

"What for?"

"To try and sell my flowers," Irid said between gritted teeth.

"Oh!"

Now she had Mel's full attention.

"How did it go?"

Mel was so bright and shiny about everything, Irid didn't want to tell her the truth: that sitting there watching hundreds walk past her, uninterested, had been so demoralising and painful that Irid wasn't sure she could put herself through it again; and that she'd actually lost money by closing the store and attempting to sell her flowers today.

"I sold one," Irid shrugged.

"That's incredible! You did it!" Mel went to drop everything and hug her again. "Wait ... why don't you look happy about it?"

"Because I didn't 'do it'. I didn't sell a single thing apart from the one Garth bought."

"But, you sold something," Mel replied without skipping a beat.

"It's not enough. It won't give us the tokens we need to live the life we want here."

"I think you're being a little hard on yourself – it's a start. What's that rule? The first customer is the hardest to get."

"You don't understand," Irid said.

"Yes, well, I'm trying to support you, to encourage you. It would be nice if just *once* you would let me, instead of trying to bite the hand that feeds you," Mel snapped back, clearly at the end of her tether.

Usually, Irid would try to logic her way out of the sour atmosphere that now brewed between them, but tonight she didn't have it in her.

"It doesn't count as a real sale when you send your boss to buy flowers off me! I told you, you have to let me try and do this on my own!"

"I didn't send Garth to the markets, Irid."

"Well, you didn't seem particularly surprised when I said Garth bought something off me."

"Because your flowers are incredible! I'm more surprised you didn't sell more, truth be told, but if this is how you treated customers then perhaps that's why."

The fact that Garth had said something similar had Irid wincing again.

"So, you're saying Garth came of his own choosing? Truly?"

"Yes, obviously."

"Oh."

A beat of silence passed between them, the only sounds the sizzling of burning caramel and the bubbling of the blue crockery pot that belched when it was ready to be taken off the heat.

"I warned you," Mel said quietly, as she turned the burner off.

"Warned me about what?"

"That doing something you love would feel like this. When it becomes more than a job, it's your heart on your sleeve. It will be in every flower you touch, in every sale you don't make. It will hurt sometimes, in a way running a shop for another can't. I warned you that you may not want to do this."

Irid sniffed. "I thought you were being insensitive."

Mel shook her head. "I was sharing a different perspective. I feel the same about the dishes I make. When a dish doesn't turn out perfectly, I feel like I let myself down. When Garth doesn't pick a new dish I've been tinkering with for weeks, I get so deflated that I don't want to eat for weeks. And when a customer returns a dish I create, for whatever reason, I'm absolutely devastated."

"But, you cook wonderful food."

"I know I do, and the good usually far outweighs the bad, but for some reason it's the negative experiences that stick the most. Tell me, now you know I didn't send Garth, how does it feel to have made your first sale for your very own flower creation?"

Irid sat there a moment, replaying the exchange with Garth in her head. She remembered her surprise at him being genuinely interested, her shock at him wanting to buy it, and the bubble of joy that had burst in her throat and sent tears to her eyes as she'd watched him walk away with one of her creations.

"Happy. It makes me truly happy," she whispered.

"Worth all the other feelings?"

Irid didn't even have to consider her answer. "A thousand times over."

Mel nodded. "Well then, you're just going to have to go back to that market and sell some more, aren't you?"

The reality of Mel's words felt like an ear-ringing slap.

"Oh Gods, what if he doesn't like it? What if it doesn't work? What if he returns it?"

Mel smiled as she began ladling the bisque into small white ceramic bowls decorated with trims of blue waves.

"You're just going to have to wait and see."

6

MEL

... THERE'S A SECRET IN EVERY BUD.

"I'm so sorry, Mel. If I had known that Garth was going to go down to the markets I would never have told him about Irid being there," Rae said, as the pair of them sat on one of the staff benches out the back overlooking their pub's small garden area, while they waited for the rush hour to begin.

Two hours to go.

Daylight was fading, and given how many hours they both spent inside that hot, stuffy kitchen, the slightly cooler breeze was welcome as Helios began his descent and Selene her climb, the sun and moon nodding in acknowledgement as they passed one another.

"It's alright. I told Irid I didn't send Garth there myself, and that's not a lie." Mel grinned at her friend.

The truth was, the night after the witches book club, Mel had padded down the stairs in her striped flannel pyjama top and matching fluffy bed socks to make Irid breakfast – to say sorry for pushing her. Mel figured she'd call them 'pushy pancakes' and layer them with strawberries, freshly whipped cream, and lashings of maple syrup.

Maybe put a maniacal smiley face on one to show Irid she could have a sense of humour about it all.

But, something flickering in the corner of her eye as she walked down the stairs stopped her from strolling straight into the kitchen. A tiny corner of a cream envelope was crookedly waving at her. Mel recognised Irid's bag – still the same one she'd had slung over her shoulder the first time Mel had seen her. Looking up the stairs to check there was no sign of Irid coming, Mel had peeked into the unsealed envelope, seen Irid's request for the market stall, smiled, and then slipped it right back where she found it.

Then she'd made Irid the pancakes anyway.

"Still, I feel bad. That could have gone horribly wrong if Garth had mentioned it had all been a case of Watering Hole whispers."

"Don't be. It really helped Irid see she *does* have a valid idea. I've been trying to tell her, but I guess no one believes loved ones are genuine when they give critiques like that."

"Exactly," Rae pointed out, as they watched a rabbit poke out from a burrowed hole beneath a lemon tree and look directly at them before scurrying on. "Even I don't believe it when—"

Rae snapped her small bow-like mouth shut to stop herself, but it was too late. Mel knew exactly the name Rae had been about to say. She'd never pushed their "Sunshine" to reveal how she felt about the boss, especially because Nika teased Rae so mercilessly about it, but even a blind daemon would be able to see the tension and chemistry between them.

Instead, Mel had decided to befriend the small-statured Arae, who was similar to her in so many ways. They both shared a love of baking that no one else in the kitchen team really cared for, which had allowed Mel the odd night off.

They were both quiet creatures, content to work in the silence of the kitchen rather than have music blaring – as both Lexie and Yani, the meat and fish station chefs, preferred. And Mel could always count on Rae to make the best hot chocolate when they arrived in the early hours of the morning to begin prep for the long day ahead, seeing as Mel didn't like tea or coffee. It was a friendship built on small, personal quirks each had noticed in the other, and beyond her relationships with Irid and Garth, Mel considered her friendship with Rae one of her most precious.

So, she knew she had to wait (just as Irid had to wait for flowers to bloom) before Rae would be comfortable talking to anyone about her feelings.

Still, that didn't mean she wasn't going to try.

"When *who* critiques you, *Sunshine*?" Mel teased.

A blush spread from Rae's neck all the way up to her cheekbones. Unfortunately for her, given her pale skin, it was very obvious.

"You better fan yourself, or the nymphs around here are going to think I gave you the secret walnut souffle recipe."

Rae snorted with laughter until finally the blush receded from her cheeks.

"So, this ... critique partner of yours – been shopping for any flowers recently?" Mel nudged Rae.

"He might have," Rae whispered in confession, which was more than Mel had been expecting. She tried not to jump up, shake Rae by the shoulders, and demand she tell her everything. But, Rae was like the rabbit they'd just watched. If there was any hint of movement, she could bolt and shut down again. Rae was a *very* private creature.

"And?"

Nika, of course, chose that moment to open the back patio door, the squeak of the hinges pulling their attention.

"Someone's out the front looking for you," she barked at Mel.

"Irid?"

"Nope, some witch. Hurry up, before she puts a spell on this place. Please."

"I'm coming."

Nika walked away, muttering something under her breath about "damn witches and their witch friends."

"Well, look who's practising her manners, finally," Mel joked.

She exchanged a knowing smile with Rae, before standing up and smoothing out the wrinkles in her apron. She was about to head towards the door when she felt Rae's hand tug on the apron.

Mel turned and looked down, thinking Rae had seen something askew with her uniform. When she saw nothing there, she looked to Rae and saw nervousness flitting across her heart-shaped face.

"What is it?"

"I'm not ready to talk about it yet, but Irid deserves to know. Tell her ... tell her." Rae shook her head. "I don't know what she does to those flowers, but something in them works."

Mel smiled a grin so wide she felt it would crack her face in two. Rae stood, and Mel immediately hugged her.

"Thank you, and I swear, your secret is safe with me." Mel began to walk away. "Until you're ready to tell me, that is!" she yelled over her shoulder, grinning, before she stepped inside and headed towards the bar area to greet her mystery guest.

She almost stumbled into a bar stool when she saw who it was. For, to her surprise, she found Isolde, the witch from the book club with her raven-dark hair on display as she lowered the hood on her cloak, waiting for Mel.

"Isolde, to what do I owe the pleasure?"

As far as Mel remembered Irid saying, her friend did not like to go out in public places in broad daylight. Being exposed to that many emotions at once was taxing for such an empath, Irid had explained.

"I have come to talk about Irid."

Worry squeezed Mel's heart.

"Stop that," Isolde scolded, and Mel felt a ghost hand reach around her heart and gently decompress it. "Irid's fine."

Mel tried to breathe without vomiting as she made her request. "Please get your hand out of my chest."

Immediately, the ghost fingers disappeared. "Others' worry is agitating," Isolde said, as if that justified that she'd literally just reached in with her powers and wrapped figurative hands around Mel's heart.

"Why don't you just tell me what exactly about Irid you want to talk about?" Mel rubbed at her chest trying to ease the sensation that lingered.

"I want to invest in her business."

"Her ... ? Do you mean the floristry?" Mel asked, hopefully.

Isolde gave a sharp nod. "One of my ravens was at the markets the other day. They overheard her talking to that agathodaemon that runs this place, explaining how her flower creations work. Had she told us at the book club what she told him, she would have had no need to go to the markets. I could have told her exactly where to sell her flowers."

"I think she needed to prove the validity of her idea to herself first," Mel offered.

"What a silly notion, when it is not she who will be buying them."

"If she can't believe in it herself, how can she get others to believe in it?"

Isolde balanced a long, coffin-shaped nail, shimmering in midnight blue, against her lip. "I suppose you have a point." She hummed as she continued to think. "What if we were to host a party of sorts? To celebrate the validity of her idea – would that work?"

"You'd be willing to host a party?"

"No, what do they call it in the mortal realms? A baby shower?"

"Irid isn't having a baby."

"Business or baby," Isolde shrugged. "They both take work."

"Okay, so we host a party or shower to show her our support. Where? Here?"

"Oh no, if we want Hecate's blessing, then we must host it at the next Crossroads Supper. Will you and your team be free to cater for the Harvest Moon?"

7

MEL
HECATE'S OFFER OF HOPE

The invitations had gone out immediately, thanks to Isolde's ravens and some fancy calligraphy skills on Nika's part.

"Don't ask," she'd snapped when Mel had simply raised an eyebrow at her penmanship while she watched Nika work at the bar, peering over her shoulder at the message written across the smooth cream parchments. Apparently, Nika's past concealed many talents. The penmanship was exquisite, and the invitation clear: everyone was to bring a guest to the Crossroads Supper who would be interested in Irid's flowers, or someone who they knew could promote them in some form.

The result, Mel decided as she looked around at the event, was spectacular.

Of course, to be invited to a Crossroads Supper was unheard of. So, naturally, everyone had turned up. They may have originally thought the invitation was a hoax, but curiosity appeared to have gotten the better of most, if not all, who would have rather turned up than find out they had missed out on seeing the legendary Thessilian witches in the flesh.

The Crossroads they had chosen were surprisingly close, Isolde having selected the place where the paths crossed between Irid's home and Hecate's Herbs Apothecary. The patch of grass the witches had chosen was spongy and green, as if particular care had been taken to nurture it over the last couple of weeks. Isolde's elemental work at play, Mel suspected. Fireflies buzzed in drunken loops, until it looked like a string of permanent fairy lights enveloped the area. On the ground was a long wooden plank laden with the fruits of The Watering Hole's labour, and an assortment of colourful silk cushions for guests to sit on.

Of course, the piece de resistance were Irid's Feeling Flowers, deliberately placed at different points of the table according to the food. The plan, as Mel had explained it to Irid when they were setting up, was that the menu had been created around the feeling that each flower embodied.

The starters were designed to excite, a range of chicken marinated three different ways: in lemon, lime, and an orange glaze, with just enough heat to have guests' mouths opening and exclaiming their delight as they ate around the orange lilies placed amongst them.

Then, like a buffet, a round of guests moved down to the second area and helped themselves to the main course – Rae's new grape and gorgonzola risotto. With hints of Savvas' golden wine, pine nuts, and fresh basil, it was the perfect complement to Irid's 'inspiration' blend that bloomed from the blue forget-me-nots decorated in a swirl on that part of the table. As Mel walked past, she could hear the diners exclaim that they must remember to get the recipe from the "little Arae with a big future."

Mel smiled.

Of course, the third part of the table had been Mel's domain, and she could think of nothing more fitting than to serve her Snowballs and Brioche Butter Puddings; both the pudding she created to embody Irid, and Irid's own favourite dessert. Mel had finally achieved the perfect light and fluffy consistency for her Snowball, but the brioche-and-butter was a heavier, more substantial dish for those who wanted it. Both paired with Irid's peonies, whose auras made one feel they were basking in indulgence simply by breathing in the air around them. That, Mel knew, was going to be the scent that high-end inns across the Underworld would be clamouring for.

Mel looked around to see if she could spot any hotel investors here. Her eyes landed on Irid, who was off to the side, chatting easily with a group of three smaller ash-tree nymphs. Each appeared to have different flowers cupped in their hands, which they offered to Irid to inspect. Mel couldn't hear what her love was saying, but knowing Irid, she was giving away the secrets of her business for free.

Mel wandered over.

"Yes, I think we should be able to create a custom aura around this. I'll have to be careful, as wildflowers can be a bit temperamental. The clue is in the name, you see. But, barring no complications, I don't see why I shouldn't be able to put the medicinal elements into here. Especially if it's an airborne infection your mother is dealing with. Come by Hecate's Herbs sometime next week and I should have a sample ready for you. Is it okay if I take this to use?" Irid nodded to the white flower she was holding in her hand and one of the ash-tree nymphs smiled encouragingly.

"Thank you for this! Thank you. I didn't know anything like this existed."

"You're very welcome," Irid smiled gently. "My own father was sick once. I know how hard I tried to get anything to work. It's particularly hard when they refuse to accept they are sick." Irid's hand reached out to lightly grasp the ash-tree nymph's arm, who instead fell into Irid's arms and hugged her tightly.

"Sorry," she said, pulling back eventually. "I've just been looking for something that could help for so long – I can't tell you the relief I feel."

Irid was about to answer when a hush descended on the crowd. At the head of the table, the three witches of Thessaly – Eupheme, Isolde, and Phillis, dressed in flowing robes of the deepest green – stood up to address them all. Their faces were illuminated by soft flickering candlelight, the fireflies having dispersed around them.

"We thank you all for coming tonight to celebrate our dear friend, Irid," they uttered in unison. A nod towards Mel and Irid's direction had all eyes swinging towards them. Mel felt Irid's body lock under everyone's gaze. She ran her knuckles down Irid's spine to ground her and felt Irid's hand close over her wrist and squeeze once, then twice. Finally, she heard Irid release a breath and felt her body relax against her own.

"We think you'll agree," the witches continued, "that having such wonder introduced to our Underworld flora is a slice of magic that deserves celebration."

There was a murmur of agreement from the crowd, who were either seated on the cushions still enjoying the feast, or milling around the lawn with cups of wine and mead in their hands.

"Which is why, we would now like to invite the Protectress of Witchcraft to bless this endeavour, so that all may benefit from the good Irid's work brings."

One by one, each of the witches raised their arms, beckoning to the night sky, and all three began to chant an invocation.

"Goddess Hecate, oh ancient one, our guardian of boundaries and thresholds, we call upon you tonight at the crossroads of Irid's destiny. Guide us, wise one, on how we may best serve those who need this gift you have bestowed as a seed in Irid's heart."

The chant grew in intensity, their voices harmonising, as the wind around everyone seemed to pick up. Glasses clinked, the table rattled ... it was as if everything in the wild sensed something coming.

Suddenly, the chanting stopped.

With a flourish from within the pocket of her robe, Eupheme produced a small silver knife, and one by one, the witches began to offer tokens of their devotion to Hecate. Eupheme cut off the resin from an incense stick and scattered it around the base of a silver chalice Mel hadn't noticed at the head of the table in front of the witches. Isolde then used the knife to cut blades of grass and sprinkle them, as Eupheme had, around the chalice. Finally, Phillis used the knife to draw what appeared to be a pentacle around the cup. It was clear, to Mel, that each offering was a personal declaration to Hecate that the witches would continue to use the gifts they'd been given, regardless of the slights and misunderstanding of their craft; that they would continue to treasure them. It was a gesture of respect, a way of acknowledging the crossroads that were their lives, both individually and as a coven.

With the offerings in place, Eupheme filled the cup with an elixir – a blend of herbs and wine that symbolised the union of the spirit realms and the very real earth beneath their feet.

Eupheme raised the goblet high and declared loudly, "To Hecate, we offer our hearts and souls, our hopes and fears, our dreams and desires. May she grant us clarity and strength at this sacred crossroads."

She took a sip before she passed it to Isolde, who made the same declaration, and then Phillis, who followed. Then they all turned and looked to Irid. Isolde made a motion with her hand for Irid to join them. With a slight push from Mel, she stumbled forward so had no choice but to continue walking, all eyes on her.

It was only when she was standing in front of the Thessilian witches that an eerie nothingness descended upon them all. A true nothingness. The wind didn't move; there were no sounds at all, not even those of nature. And then, as if a fog no one knew was there had lifted, Hecate stood before Irid, the witches behind her.

"So," the Goddess said, a slight smile on her face. "You wish to claim the gifts you're offered by Gaia."

Mel watched as Irid gave a robotic nod to the omnipotent being standing before her. Hecate held a fire torch in one hand, illuminating the path for others, a set of keys jangling from a chain on her hips where her other hand sat. A matching gold chain sat around her neck in the shape of a three-headed serpent, and a small diadem the shape of a crescent moon adorned the top of her flowing locks of auburn hair. Her eyes were rimmed with kohl and shadows, the rest of her features surprisingly dainty for such a voluptuous goddess.

"And you know the importance of the task set before you?"

Again, Irid nodded.

"You must say it, child."

"To bring magic back to the Underworld."

"No," Hecate shook her head. "That is the byproduct of what you will do. Choosing this task, choosing to infuse magic back into the world has a much larger ripple effect. Your dream will spur others to dream. Your success will show them that it is safe to follow their own. That is why there is a new realm of witches being born – because of all the work my witches here continue to do. Even when they are misunderstood. Even when they are treated as no more than myth and legend. They continue with their tasks diligently."

Irid nodded. "I understand."

"My child, there will come times when others will not understand you, nor your process. For it is new, and therefore foreign. There will be those who laugh and mock, for they are scared of change. There will be those who offer you unsolicited advice, which is often best ignored – unless heard thrice from three different sets of lips. And, there will be those who wait and watch, to see if you fall or fly. Regardless, they will burden you with expectations, unknown and unseen to them, but felt on your shoulders. When you can see such disillusionment, you can banish it. Your hardships will not be their hardships, but this does not mean you are alone. This does not mean that they do not care or that they do not wish to know. They know not what they need, until it is given to them.

"Remember to see disconnection as the opportunity to build a bridge; to see indifference as a means of education; and any perceived insensitivity as your chance to create something good in this world – opportunity. The shell of hope.

"Do you still wish to claim this gift?"

"Yes." Irid's answer was no more than a whisper as she glanced up at the goddess who stood before her.

Hecate nodded, taking the chalice from the witches behind her and offering it to Irid. As Irid sipped, Hecate spoke now to the crowd.

"I thank Irid for being brave enough to venture into the unknown and create something where previously there was nothing. Even when it looks as if all hope is lost, we must remember that the real magic is that life is cyclic, and so we once again welcome in something new and full of hope."

"We welcome in something new and full of hope," the witches chanted. The crowd followed. And somehow, there was a renewed sense of purpose and unity in the air.

"Now," Hecate clapped her hands. "Let us celebrate! Is that brioche butter pudding, I see?"

YOU ARE WHAT YOU EAT IN THE UNDERWORLD

AUTHOR'S NOTE

When it comes to Greek myths, there are so many stories to choose from. For this novella, I chose Lamia (myth one) and the story of Arethusa (myth two). The two myths aren't connected, but the characters I've chosen to enrich their history are.

Lexie, our grill chef, is a Lamia: a vampiric daemon. In the original Greek myth, Lamia was a queen of Libya who caught the eye of Zeus (who didn't at this point?!). He had an affair with her, fathered children with her, and obviously, Hera (Zeus' wife) wasn't too happy about the matter. She punished Lamia by killing her children. In some versions of the tale, Hera forced Lamia to eat her own children, which, naturally, turned her quite mad. As a result of her suffering, Lamia became a beautiful seductive monster with the upper body of a woman and the lower body of a serpent, who out of envy and bitterness, used her charms to lure and devour young children.

In this story, you'll see I've taken it one step further. Lamia no longer refers to one woman, but has become a whole category of creature unto itself. The original Lamia may have had the lower body of a serpent, but as with human genealogy, Lamias might only pass on certain traits to their surviving offspring. I'll leave you to learn more about that as the novella develops.

As for the story of Arethusa ... this is for our Nereid, Yani.

Arethusa was a beautiful water nymph, known for her love of bathing in a crystal clear spring in Arcadia. Naturally, there was a Greek god watching her, though to our surprise, this time it's not Zeus. It was Alpheus, a river god who fell deeply in love with Arethusa at first sight (such typical god behaviour). In traditional Greek myth fashion, he pursued her relentlessly – because this is always the way to get a woman to feel safe enough to return affection.

Arethusa fled. Artemis, Goddess of the Hunt, heard Arethusa's pleas for refuge and transformed her into a spring of water. As soon as the transformation was complete, Arethusa's waters dove into the earth and beneath the ground, creating a subterranean river.

Alpheus followed.

According to the myth, their waters eventually merged beneath the island of Sicily, yet they still emerge as separate springs today. At heart, it's a tale of unrequited love.

But, I wanted to pull on the other string, the one where creatures can be so similar and yet so different in a myriad of ways; where they can be both beautiful and monstrous, crossing paths and yet never wishing to. I wanted to ask my characters, will the history of who you are define you? Or, will you carve your own new paths if I give you the space on the page?

Let's find out.

Please note the chapters alternate between Yani and Lexie's perspectives.

1

YANI
ARETHUSA'S WELL

They had been children when they met. Though 'childhood' was a relative term for nymphs, who tended to live so long Souls thought them immortal. But, Yani was a mere two hundred years old when Lexie had stumbled upon his grandmother's wishing well.

Some Souls – those newly-dead mortals who would arrive from earthside – would call it a grave, but who had need of a grave in the Underworld? No; graves were for the grievers left behind. Here in the Underworld, places that *caused* the death of another were marked. That way, in the long march of life in death, any creature, Soul, or deity could return to where it all began for them.

No one should have known the wishing well was here, except Yani.

According to family legend, his grandmother, the great Arethusa, had been transformed (thanks to Artemis) into an underground spring that ran beneath the island of Sicily. It was here, in one of the underwater caves, Grotta dei Cordari, that she had emerged at the entrance to the Underworld.

Yani's mother had always whispered that last part when she told him the story at night, as if entering the Underworld was some great prestige bestowed upon his grandmother, and not a realm they all ended up in. Then, Yani's mother would flare her hands out with a sudden flourish as she told the part of the story that Yani had come to loathe.

His grandmother had been about to step into the Underworld, when Alpheus whisked her away, back up earthside, to the island of Sicily. Along the way, their forms intertwined until Arethusa had found herself, to her dismay, pregnant with several Naiad and Nereid children. As punishment for trying to evade him for so long, Alpheus had sent each of their nymph children down here after their births, to the Underworld she had tried to use as an escape.

Yani's mother told him if he listened closely to the well erected in her honour by her children, he would still be able to hear her wailing.

Yani hated his grandfather.

But, no one should have known how to get into the cave. Its entrance from earthside was blocked by unimaginable depths of dark blue seawater. Even if a Soul were to reach that depth, they would have then had to chip away at a spiky coral bed that had grown and formed over the cave mouth for millenia.

This meant the intruder he had heard had to have come from the Underworld entrance. Though, that entrance was no easier to get to. One would have to take the winding tunnels between the rivers of Styx and Acheron.

The tunnels were a labyrinth of dark, damp, dense black rock, with nothing to light the path along the way. Then there was the constant *drip-drip-dripping* of the water trickling through the cracks in the rocks above. It was said that many had gone mad trying to find their way out, the *drip-drip-dripping* convincing them the rock tunnels were about to collapse and the river would crash down upon them, eventually sweeping them out to the Lethe where they'd forget everything.

But, the rocks had held for millenia. Yani reminded himself of that every time he took the journey to Arethusa's death space, his hands tracing the walls of the tunnels lined with moss as they guided him along the route he had memorised.

Three lefts and a right. Then, five crossroads, all of which he must continue straight through, apart from the third one where he had to turn right. Then, three forks in the road – two rights and a left; and then he just had to keep heading straight. And remember to breathe.

The damp vegetation gave the maze a musty smell that made even the darkest of creatures retch. But, Yani had found that as long as he breathed in through the gills behind his ears and out through his mouth, he could keep the stench of decay at bay.

He was more worried about the sharp stalactites he knew hung above his head. Each time he took the journey, as his eyes adjusted to the darkness he could eventually make out the shape of them above: large dagger-like icicles infused with all sorts of minerals that had eroded from the rock over time. If one of them fell on him, well, he wouldn't die, but it would hurt.

Still, it wasn't enough to stop him coming to visit Arethusa's Well. It was his duty to come here to upkeep the well, just as his uncles and aunties had, and as his mother had, until they all stopped coming back to the Underworld altogether. His mother had always sworn she would return, not once breaking her promise, until Yani's one hundredth year. Then, she was gone.

The well was the only connection Yani had to his heritage. He had to maintain its prestige. That way, when his family eventually came back, they'd be proud to see how well he'd kept it; that he'd honoured them all.

Was the intruder he'd heard fumbling through the final tunnel one of them? Had they finally returned? *No, surely it couldn't be, with all that cussing and blinding ...*

"For Hades' hound dogs, please gods, I will take Cyclops' eye if you will just let me—"

Suddenly, there she was, standing in front of Yani, the most beautiful creature he'd ever seen. She uncurled herself from the tunnel mouth and rose to her full height, a good few inches taller than he. She looked about his age. There were streaks of dirt across her cheekbones, which jutted out just sharply enough that her long red hair fell in waves around her face. It was matted with dirt and water from the tunnels, but it was still pretty. At least, Yani thought so.

"Who are you?"

Her tone made it sound like she was accusing him of simply existing.

"Well, who are you?" he retorted.

The female in front of him hesitated, glancing back at the tunnel mouth before she turned to look at him again. He noticed her take a large gulp. Swallowing her pride, he suspected, nodding to himself at his cleverness.

"It doesn't matter who I am. I just need to find a way out of here. Do you know if there's another way out of those tunnels?" She shuddered.

"Only if you want to swim to the earthly realm," Yani said, shrugging and throwing his thumb to the other entrance on the opposite side of the cave.

Apparently, it was the wrong answer, because the female's face fell as she slid down the back wall of the cave, pulled her knees up into her, and began rocking. As she did so, she muttered something Yani couldn't quite make out.

He stepped closer.

"Please don't find me here. Please don't find me here. Please don't find me here."

"Who don't you want to find you?"

The young female startled in surprise as she looked up at him, as if she'd already forgotten he were there. She shook her head. "I don't want to say."

"It's okay, you're safe here. You can trust me."

"How do you know it's safe here?" She looked at him sharply.

"Because this is my family's ... crypt, I guess."

"You *guess*?"

"Well, I've been coming here for a hundred years and you're the only other creature I've seen here in all that time. Maybe I should be asking you how *you* even found this place." Yani crossed his arms defensively and tried his best to scowl at her.

It was difficult; she was *really* pretty.

"I don't know," she said frankly. "I was just trying to get away from ... "

She glanced again towards the tunnels, as if saying who it was would summon them through the labyrinth.

"Well, you must be the luckiest being I've ever met. You're more likely to die in those tunnels than manage to make it here," he told her.

"Really?"

When she said that, her eyes widened in such a way that she looked even more beautiful, even though her eyes were red-rimmed. She must have been crying in those tunnels. Yani couldn't blame her. The first time he'd navigated his way through them, the only thing that had stopped him from crying in fear was reciting his mother's instructions over and over in his head.

Yani sucked in a breath thinking of his mother, and pretended he was puffing his chest out to protect the girl in front of him from the big bad creature she wouldn't name. "Yup."

Slowly, she rose to her feet, only somewhat shakily.

"I promise you, you're safe here. I'm Yani." He stretched out his hand.

She nodded but didn't take it, her hands remaining behind her against the cavern, while she looked at his hand until he dropped it. Then he watched her take in her surroundings from her safe space against the wall.

"Why is this your family's crypt?" From what Yani could tell, there was no judgement in her tone; only curiosity.

"Because this is where my grandmother first came to, when she entered Hades' realm. That, over there, is her wishing well. I mean, it's just a well, but I call it a wishing well. What's your name?"

She glanced at him again, as if sizing him up. "Lexie," she eventually said, as she slowly walked towards the wishing well and peered down into it, her hands still clasped behind her.

"What's down there?"

Yani quirked his lips to one side and shrugged half-heartedly, not wanting to share his family's secret, but at the same time desperately wanting to impress her. "Nothing, I guess. But, my mum used to tell me she could hear my grandma if she listened closely enough."

Lexie immediately cocked her head and turned her ear

towards the well. It sent her long fire-red hair cascading down to the ground. Yani couldn't take his eyes off it – he'd never seen hair so long before. Eventually, she straightened up, and Yani pretended he'd been peering over the well's lip.

"I can't hear anything," she told him.

"Maybe my mum was making it up."

Lexie walked back towards her corner of the cave, kicking at the white pebbled dirt floor. "Yeah, mums like making stuff up."

"What stories did your mum tell you?"

"That one day she would try to eat me."

Lexie said it so matter-of-factly that Yani took a few seconds to register what she'd said.

"That doesn't sound like a very good story at all." He bent to pick up a particular pebble he thought would make for a good wish in the well, then began to search for a second one ... for Lexie.

"It wasn't. Especially when it turned out to be true."

Yani wrinkled his nose. "Why would your mum try to eat you?"

"She said it was the curse of all Lamias, to eat their young."

Suddenly, it dawned on Yani. "Is that who you're running from?" he whispered. "Your mum?"

Lexie nodded.

"She didn't actually try to eat you, did she?"

2

LEXIE

THE QUEEN OF LIBYA AND HER MISSING GEMSTONES

"She didn't used to be all bad," Lexie told him, the strange male with the big black eyes and equally dark curly hair that fell around his face and to the nape of his neck. Lexie couldn't quite tell if his hair was wet or he had put way too much oil in it. He was paler than the other nymphs she had often seen in Tartarus, as if all the colour had been leached out of him.

"When she first told me she'd eat me, I was really little, and she used to nibble on my foot. I thought she was joking, like the other mums that would comment on how cute their little fat cherubs were. Now, I think it might have been a warning."

Yani went to join her. Together they sat against the cavern wall, throwing pebbles towards the well, seeing who could get one in. It felt like they'd been doing it for hours. Eventually, Lexie saw one of her pebbles bounce off the top of the well and down into its depths below. She waited to hear a *plop* as it hit water, but no sound came.

Lexie hadn't answered Yani's original question, instead

opting for silence, and eventually the polite male had moved on to talking about random things – things Lexie didn't understand, like coral and fish, and currents. Between each throw of a pebble, Lexie's eyes would dart back to the tunnel entrance. But, as time continued to drag and her monster of a mother didn't appear, the tight knotted ball in her chest began to loosen and she found herself talking.

"I used to think she was the most beautiful mum in the world. She has long hair like mine, except it's black, and she'd brush it out every morning. It took ages. Then she'd line her eyes with kohl so they were super dark to match her hair, and paint her lips red before she put on all her jewellery. She had a whole trunk by her bed filled with gold crowns and bracelets, pearls, opals, diamonds, and sapphires. She used to put them all on until she was dripping in gemstones. I called it her treasure chest. But, as I got older, it seemed there weren't as many gemstones as I remembered. I could have sworn the chest used to be filled to the brim; that she used to tell me we were descendants of royalty, and that's why she had them."

"Are you? Descended from royalty?" There was a hint of surprise in Yani's tone and Lexie put her pointed nose up in the air.

"Everyone knows opals are a gift from Zeus after he won against the Titans. Didn't you go to school, or have a nanny who taught you anything?"

"So, your dad is Zeus?"

"No," Lexie conceded. "Apparently, all my siblings Mum had with him died. There were a few left when I was born, but I don't remember them, and then they died, too. She always got sad when I asked about them. Sometimes she'd yell, so I stopped asking why they weren't around anymore or why the gemstones kept disappearing. My dad is just a regular Oread."

"What's an Oread?"

Shocked, Lexie turned to stare at him. "You've never met a mountain nymph?"

Yani shrugged. "Never had need to. So, your dad – is he still around?"

"He works in the mountains in Tartarus. He and Mum both said it was better that he stayed there ... "

A brief, sad silence fell between them.

"I never knew my dad," Yani told her. "It was just me and my mum, but that was okay because there were all my uncles and aunties. I was the only kid, though."

"Where are they all?"

"Gone." Yani pointed towards the well, as if they'd fallen down there and never come out.

"Maybe we should get out of here," Lexie found herself saying.

"You ready to go through the tunnels again?"

The knot in her chest constricted with a sudden viciousness. She thought of her mother, slithering along the tunnel floors faster than Lexie could ever possibly run. She imagined her whispering promises of how she'd take Lexie home and keep her warm and safe by the crackling fire, until Lexie could almost feel phantom hands grab her by the legs and pull her towards the flames. She was burning and her mother was hissing, her eyes gleaming as Lexie began to feel tingles crawl up her legs like spiders. Lexie couldn't tell if her mother was shedding tears of pain, or crying with glee.

Suddenly, Lexie found herself back in the cave, the pinprick tingles in her legs the result of the sharp pebbles that had brushed against her skin as she scrambled as far back into the cave wall as she could, curling in on herself.

"Hey, it's okay. We don't have to go anywhere yet."

Yani had moved until he was crouched down in front of her, holding her shoulders in place and blocking her view of the tunnel caves. She desperately tried to look over his shoulder so she could see if her mother was gliding towards them, but he held her firmly in place.

When had he moved? she thought to herself.

"What happened? Where did you go?" he asked her.

"I— I— I ... don't know. One minute I was here, and the next I was back in the tunnels thinking she was coming to get me."

"Is that how you ended up in the tunnels in the first place? She was chasing you?"

Lexie nodded and only then realised her teeth were chattering. She clenched her jaw to make them stop, her canines sinking into the fleshy back part of her lips until she felt blood fill her mouth. She swallowed it. Only when he seemed satisfied that she wasn't going to hurt herself did Yani let go of her shoulders and take a seat beside her again.

"She really can't get me here?"

"I promise, even Theseus himself could not find his way through the tunnels without assistance. Someone wanted you here; wanted you safe. One of the gods must be watching out for you." Yani's face had taken on that serious look of his.

"I'd never seen her without a dress on before," Lexie whispered, admitting it more to herself than to Yani. "I didn't know that underneath, she didn't have legs like me ... that underneath the floor-length dresses was that *tail*."

"A tail?" Yani didn't seem to quiver at the image of a tail, and Lexie had the sneaking suspicion that he was used to being around other creatures that weren't like normal nymphs.

"A snake's tail," she confirmed.

Now, *that* had Yani tensing. "I don't like snakes."

"Me neither."

Lexie had to get this nightmare out of her head. Maybe if it was out in the open, it would be less scary. "She told me she was hungry, that she'd been starving for days, but I didn't understand because we had food in the house. So, I went to make her something, but when I returned to her room she wasn't there. I turned to go check the other rooms in our house, when *something* whipped out and wrapped around my legs. I remember looking down and thinking how odd it was to see a snake's tail. Then, my head hit the floor and I could see my mother's eyes staring at me from under the bed. It was like she was in a trance. Then her forked tongue flicked out, I panicked and tried to scramble away, and she lunged at me.

"I don't know how I got away. I just remember one minute her tail was wrapped around me, and the next it wasn't as she darted towards the door. I remember getting up; I managed to slam the door on her and she wailed. She must have got it open again, because then I could hear her hissing breath behind me getting faster and closer. It felt ... heavier, like she was breathing down my neck.

"I ran towards the mountains, towards Dad and all the other Oread workers. I figured if I could make it through the markets where lots of people could see me, she would stop – but she didn't. She just kept chasing me. Then, I was in the place with all the other miners, and I tripped, and I fell down this little ... track? I think it was a track; rails lined each side, but it seemed abandoned as there was no one down there. So, I kept running and running ... and I ended up here."

"I think you found another entrance to the cave I didn't know about." Yani frowned.

"Is that a bad thing? Should we not be here?"

"No, it's fine. It's just weird that no one in my family told me there was another way to get here before they left. I've always come in through the river entrance."

"You're a water nymph, aren't you?"

"It's called a Nereid. But, yes," said Yani, indignantly.

At Lexie's dubious look, he continued. "We're not as bad as everyone makes out. We're not cold, and we don't make fun of you if you can't swim. We just don't trust a lot of outsiders. They don't understand how we live, nor do they care to, so we end up getting the flack for their ignorance. Maybe that just goes to show that some of the *other* nymphs deserve a reputation for aloofness."

Lexie suspected it was a speech he had heard sometime from another water nymph and simply memorised, because there was no way he fully knew what he was saying. She didn't understand half the words he had used. But, it sounded impressive, so she quirked her eyebrow at him and smiled.

"Still, I can't believe you've never met a mountain nymph."

"Yes, well, have you ever been swimming?"

"I grew up in Tartarus. Who wants to swim in a flame-filled river?"

Yani gave her another serious look down the length of his proud nose, as if he was old before his time. "Tartarus sounds like a horrible place to live."

Lexie didn't know what to say to that, because he wasn't wrong – even if it was her home neighbourhood and she had nothing else to compare it to. She picked up more pebbles and tried to throw them into the well again, one by one.

"Would you like to come back and stay with me for a little bit? Until your mum is gone?"

Lexie dropped the last pebble left in her hand and stared at him.

"What? I told you we're not inhospitable. Not if you're willing to give the water a try. Plus, I can lead you back through the tunnels the way I came. That way, you won't get lost and you know you won't end up back where she is."

"What if she finds us in the tunnels?"

"Well, we might just have to take that risk. We can't stay here forever."

He didn't sound particularly worried, and he had repeatedly said how easy it was to get lost in the labyrinth of tunnels. Plus, he was right, Lexie thought as she looked around. They definitely couldn't stay in the cave forever. There was no food, no water – not even in the well – and nothing to do. They'd go mad if they stayed here. Plus, if Yani had come here more than once, then he'd be able to get them back okay. Surely.

"Okay," she said, standing and wiping her black chiton of the white pebble dust. "Let's go, before I change my mind."

Yani followed her lead, getting up and walking towards the well where he then whispered something Lexie couldn't hear, before heading over to the tunnel entrance. He turned to her and held out his hand.

"You coming?"

3

YANI

NEREIDS AND NAIADS ARE NOT THE SAME
THING

Yani found the tunnels far easier to navigate with company by his side for the journey. He felt Lexie's long elegant fingers with their equally long nails bite into his palm whenever they heard any sound, but otherwise he was surprisingly reassured by her presence. Luckily, there was no serpent mother chasing them, and most of the sounds Yani had heard before – the echo of a step; the water *drip-drip-dripping* down onto the rocks; the occasional slip on slimy moss that made a squelching sound.

Instead, he focused on following the directions in his head in reverse.

Head straight until he reached the fork in the tunnels where the moss met the right side at shoulder height. Then, a left that curled into a right, two rights that curled into lefts, and a left turn at the third crossroads; another left, then three rights. And remember to breathe.

He had forgotten to tell Lexie to breathe before they'd entered the tunnels. He'd been too concerned with getting her in there before she could change her mind. He hoped she wasn't suffocating. He could barely hear her breathing, but that could have been because she was scared her mother would meet them at every corner Yani wound them around.

Eventually, he saw water ahead.

It was a shimmering pool of pinks, purples, and greens, the reflections of the minerals in the cave mouth colouring the water. Yani knew that once they dived in, it would turn a brilliant turquoise blue. He was also aware that the being holding his hand may have genuinely never been swimming before.

He stopped when they were a few feet away from the river entrance, where the water lapped playfully at the edge of the tunnel floor. Even if there was something in the tunnels with them, he'd be able to get Lexie out in time now. He turned to her.

"Right before we enter the water, I want you to take a big deep inhale, okay? You can breathe out while we're underwater, but don't breathe *all* the way out because you can't take another breath until we come up for air again. You understand?"

"Yes."

"Keep hold of my hand. I'll lead you to the air. Don't worry, it will be quick. I know where the currents are. And you can open your eyes if you like, but seeing as they won't be used to it, you might prefer to keep your eyes closed."

"I'll keep them closed," Lexie whispered back.

Yani clasped her hand tightly.

"Okay, here we go."

The second his webbed feet touched the water, Yani felt his whole body begin to relax. As his feet left the ground and his body floated into the embrace of the water, the currents began to tug around him playfully. He yanked Lexie closer, to tell the ocean that she was with him, and to not rip them apart from one another. The ocean could be playful, but dangerous, if Yani didn't make his intentions clear. Luckily, the entity conceded, pushing Lexie further against his side as the water lifted them into a weightless grace.

Lexie's other arm found his bare torso, and soon she had wrapped herself around his back. That was a good thing, as Yani felt his legs start to merge together, until, united, they became a powerful tail propelling them through the water. One arm still cradling Lexie, he used the other to part his way into the current that would shoot them up and out into the Acheron Glade.

Schools of silvery fish joined them, blasting their way through until it came time for them to jump out, like parting waters of a fountain. Yani laughed in delight, the sound coming out in bubbles, and he wondered if Lexie had dared to open her eyes and look at the sensations around her.

But, it was too late, because then they were breaking the surface, and Lexie was sucking in air like her life depended on it. They bobbed there for a moment while Yani let her catch her breath, the water lapping at their chins as they stared towards the entrance of Yani's home.

There was a small patch of land to the left of it, which would lead creatures to the three main neighbourhoods of the Underworld and away from the rest of the land considered 'wild'. Lexie could choose to go that way if she wished, though it would lead her closer to Tartarus and her mother once again.

Yet, something selfish in Yani wanted her to stay.

His home, to the right of the small patch of land, was carved out of a large boulder. The boulder was draped in a cascading wall of seaweed that Yani had carefully woven and hung, so that it looked just like any other rock lapped at by the water.

"Come on," he said to Lexie. "Let's get you dry."

He tugged her back under his arm and used the other to slice through the water, his strong tail propelling them forward with each flick until they were at the entrance. Yani peeled back the seaweed to reveal another cavern, similar in size to the one they'd just left, but undoubtedly more beautiful.

Two of the walls were crafted from the shimmering white scales of fish that caught colours and reflected them back. It looked like an ever-changing, living, breathing wall. The ceiling, made of intricately woven strands of kelp and coral, added a bit of colour to the place, making it feel less clinical. On the third wall, Yani had used every kind of fish scale he could to create a mosaic of him and his mother swimming through the glade towards the well, through the current he'd just swam with Lexie. The mosaic showed a vibrant coral reef at the bottom, schools of fish in every hue imaginable, and him and his mum swimming through it all, laughing at each other. The piece had taken a painstakingly long time, but Yani'd had the time to create it.

A hundred years alone, even for an immortal, was a very long time.

Yani wondered what Lexie would make of it all.

The floor was made of the finest sand, layers upon layers of it, that it felt sturdy enough to stand on as Yani tried to survey the place through a newcomer's eyes.

There were two clamshells, one larger and one small, which had been for Yani and his mother. Their interiors were lined with silk-like seaweed, smoother than the type on the boulder across the entrance, and a plush bed of the softest anemone. He'd taken to sleeping in his mother's shell after she'd gone, but he'd give that up for Lexie if she wanted to stay.

Between the two clamshells was a collection of conch shells that played a gentle melody of the ocean. And in the centre of the chamber was a freshwater spring enclosed by a collection of pearls, creating a small, crystal-clear pool on which floated a magnificent water lily.

"How did you manage to make that pool in the centre like that?" Lexie finally asked, having looked around for long enough.

"Oh, that's spring water, not seawater. My mother made that."

"Huh?"

Yani moved to sit in one of the shells, his legs unpeeling from each other now that he was in an air pocket of dry space. He leant forward towards the spring and moved the water lily slightly with his hand. Immediately, it began bubbling to life. As if they'd heard the spring come alive, the marine fireworms encapsulated in seashells around the cave began to glow.

"My mother was a Naiad – a freshwater nymph, like my grandmother. But, when she met my father, a Nereid, she moved here. Then they had me. I have no idea where he went, but she'd stayed here with me. So, she created this little water feature. It was her way of staying sane while I was given a chance to thrive."

"I don't get it."

"Freshwater nymphs like my mother aren't so close to seawater all the time. The glade offered her a bit of respite as it's not a vast ocean; but it's still saltwater. She needed to be around freshwater. That's why she created this piece of water magic in our home."

"So, Naiads and Nereids aren't the same thing?"

"No way."

"And you're a Nereid? Like your dad?"

Yani nodded. "Turned out to be. We prefer being closer to vast, deep waters. Our lineage is Nereus and Doris. You probably haven't heard of them."

At Lexie's shake of the head, he continued.

"Nereus is an ancient sea god and Doris is a sea nymph. Together they had fifty daughters, then those daughters went on to have nymphs, and so on and so on, until you get to me."

"So, which ones are the evil ones? You know, that sing souls to their deaths. Do any of you work for Hades?"

Yani scowled. "That's Sirens. We are *protectors* of those at sea, not like those nasty creatures that like to eat you."

He realised as soon as he'd said it, it was the wrong thing to say.

"Sorry, I didn't mean—"

"It's okay," Lexie waved him off, crossing her arms and walking up to the mural wall to examine it in more detail.

Panic began to bubble in Yani's chest. Until Lexie had turned up in the cave, he hadn't realised just how lonely he'd been.

"You can stay as long as you like. Then, when you're sure your mum has stopped looking for you, I can show you how to get back through the shoreline," he offered.

"I don't think she'll ever stop looking for me," Lexie replied, not breaking her gaze from the mural.

"So, you'll stay?" Yani tried to hide his smile as Lexie turned towards him.

"I don't have to eat raw fish, do I?"

4

LEXIE
FISHES REALLY ARE FIENDS (APART FROM YANI)

She had tried raw fish, but the way Yani would precisely cut and slurp on the pale flesh had made Lexie's stomach turn. She'd hurled, twice, and refused all offers of fish since. She managed to survive on the vegetation he gathered for her on his outings into the glade. They had enough salt that seemed to satisfy her constitution, but after she found herself hungry only a few hours later, they had agreed that Lexie would go hunting on dry land for meat she could stomach.

She had been nervous at first about stepping onto dry land again, as if somehow her mother would sense her and immediately slither across the Underworld to reclaim her daughter by swallowing her whole. So, Lexie had started looking as close to the water and the marshes as she could, but after trying a particularly slimy frog and retching rather loudly, she'd decided to brave the deeper bush.

Ducks, it turned out, were pretty good. As were the herons. When she gathered even more confidence, she ventured even further into the bush and secured three raccoons, five sparrows, and on her best day – a deer. That had lasted her a whole season.

Lexie enjoyed hunting with Yani in the ocean, too, though. He had taught her how to swim and open her eyes under the water, how to move with the currents, how to use a spear and where to aim it in order to catch and kill the fish for dinner.

Life in the shell, as she called the cavern that was Yani's – and now her – home, was good. As one decade blurred into the next, suddenly the pair found themselves celebrating their centenaries together.

It was as if she had known Yani her whole life, she thought, as she waded out from the glade and onto dry land, her long wet hair pulled back into a plait so she could use it as a tail in the water, as Yani did with his legs.

They visited the well every decade or so. It was only after the fourth visit that Lexie realised just how lucky she was to have run into Yani that time; that perhaps a Fate or a god had been watching out for her after all. Yani had been right, even as a youngling. She would have been more likely to die down there by Arethusa's Well, or in the tunnels, than have her mother ever find her.

Life was good.

Until it wasn't.

There was nothing to tell them that this trip to Arethusa's Well would be any different than the last eleven or so they'd embarked on. Nothing different about the day. Nothing different about the sounds. The current sucked them in, down to that low ocean bed where the entrance to the tunnels lay. The rocks were no wetter than they usually were as they slid their hands across them. The *drip-drip-dripping* was consistent. There was nothing at all to suggest that it was all about to end.

Yani entered the cave first. Lexie always liked to give him a moment of privacy before she followed. She'd become accustomed to the tunnels now, and knew the route well enough to be sure she could beat an intruder – not that anyone was ever down here. So, she'd wait in the tunnel mouth while Yani would fix up anything that seemed out of place and talk to his grandmother. Lexie knew he talked to his mother as well, hoping for a sign, any sign, that one of his family might just return for him. But, when they did come, Lexie knew it wouldn't be what Yani had expected.

Suddenly, she heard a roar so loud it caused the ground beneath her feet to shake. She looked into the tunnels, but the pressure wasn't coming from there. It was coming from the cave.

Turning, she saw the strangest thing. A tidal wave, rising like a spherical current out of the well and hovering menacingly over Yani, who stared up at it in wonder. Lexie wanted to tell him to get out of there, to run, but some instinct in the back of her mind told her to stop, to wait, to watch.

The water fell with a deafening crash across the cave and when Lexie opened her eyes, there was an ancient river god standing in front of Yani. She only knew he was a river god because of the time Yani had taken to explain to her the different schools of nymphs. River gods' skins and scales were always more brown-tinged than the others, as if they had been exposed to too many toxins over the years.

"So," she heard the elder say. "You must be my grandson."

Lexie's head snapped to look at Yani. The river god's back was to her, so she couldn't make out any of his features beyond the brown hue and hair as he towered over

Yani, much as he had in his water form. But, she could see the wonder in Yani's eyes fade, replaced by a narrowing hardness.

"You're not welcome here, Alpheus," Yani said, crossing his arms as he did so.

The old god sniggered. "I've been here longer than you've been alive, *boy*."

Yani apparently didn't have an answer for that. Lexie willed him to say something, *anything*, but his grandfather beat him to it.

"Do you know what happened to all the others before you? Do you know why none of them ever returned?" The way he said it was eerie; mocking. "Do you know why your mummy didn't come back for you?"

"You leave my mother out of this!"

"Because *I* made sure they never interfered with my Arethusa again. Do you know where the well goes, young grandson?"

"To the mortal realm, to Sicily." Yani barely spoke above a whisper, but his voice didn't falter.

Alpheus threw his head back and laughed. "Yes, quite right, boy. That is where your grandmother went, but that's not where the well goes now. Why don't you have a peek over the edge and you can see?" he offered slyly.

"I've already seen it, thanks. There's nothing down there."

"Ah, but do you know where *nothing* goes?"

Something pinged in the back of Lexie's head. Those words, that saying ... her mother had said it to her once. "*Do you know where nothing goes, where nothing grows, where nothing grows? Do you know what nothing loathes, along the river Lethe?*"

It was one of those lullabies that had always made

Lexie shiver. Over the past few decades, late at night when she was alone with her thoughts, she had wondered if the words had actually been warnings from her mother. But, she didn't have time to think of that right now; she had to stop Alpheus from throwing her friend into that well.

That was why none of Yani's family had returned. If his grandfather threw him down the well, somehow he'd end up in the river Lethe, the river of forgetfulness where nothing happened because everyone who drank from it forgot everything anyway. And because Yani was a nymph with gills, his body would automatically breathe in the water. He'd have no way of stopping it if his grandfather had figured out a way to make sure the well led straight there.

Lexie wasn't going to gamble on there being a way out, like there was with the tunnels. Before she knew it, she had crossed the space between the tunnel mouth and where the two of them stood. Between one blink and the next, she was dragging Yani against her before whipping back to the beginning of the labyrinth. She didn't think she'd even taken a breath between one move and the next, and then they were heading through the tunnels.

Straight until there was a fork where the moss met the right side just below shoulder height. Then, a left that curled into a right, two rights that curled into lefts, and a left turn at the third crossroads; another left, then three rights. Damn, remember to breathe; she had to get them out of there.

Lexie had debated for less than a millisecond which way to go. If Alpheus had been in that cave visiting that well longer than the pair of them had been alive, then who was to say he didn't know the tunnels intimately? No; her best hope was to get them back to the Acheron Glade, and from there make their way to the driest land where the river god couldn't get them.

She didn't know if he was behind them. She could hear a roaring, but that same instinct that had dinged in alarm in the back of her head when it had all kicked off told her it was actually her blood making that noise in her ears. So, she just kept running, pulling on Yani to keep up.

Lexie wasn't entirely certain his arm was still in its socket.

5

YANI
ARE YOU SURE ABOUT THE SHORE?

His arm was definitely not in its socket. Yani was certain of that much, as they exited the current and their heads emerged from the skin of the glade.

He looked at Lexie.

"C'mon," she said. "We have to keep going."

She didn't need to drag him anymore, as he was faster than her in the water. But, with one arm out of its socket he was slower than usual, and they both reached the shoreline – not his home – at the same time. Dredging themselves up the bank, Yani lay there while he waited for his tail to unweb into legs before Lexie hauled him to his feet by his good arm.

"If we could just go back to my cave, I can get a seaweed wrap for this shoulder. It will heal itself," he said.

"We can't risk it, we don't have the time."

"I don't think you realise how fast you were going through those tunnels. It was like ... superspeed. No water nymph could keep up with that. You must be as fast as—"

"A Lamia, courtesy of my monster mother," Lexie

finished as she stepped towards him, grabbing the hand at the end of his bung arm and assessing it. "But, your granddaddy isn't any old water nymph; he's a river god. We *don't* have the time."

Snap.

Yani yelped as a blinding white pain shot up through his arm, across his chest, and then radiated all the way down his spine until he could feel it in his phantom tail.

"Sorry," Lexie made an apologetic face at him. "It's better that you didn't know it was going to happen."

"Your mother teach you that, too?" Yani muttered.

Immediately, he regretted it. He saw the stiffness in Lexie's shoulders, felt her spirit recoil into herself.

"Sorry."

"I hurt you, you hurt me. It's normal biology," Lexie shrugged. "But, I'd still rather not let your granddaddy come and chuck us both in the Lethe, so can we please get a move on?"

"Sure, sure, let's go."

Lexie led him through the marsh and out into the forest beyond, weaving them through trees and occasionally using puddles, mud, and leaves to cover their tracks. Yani didn't know if a river god could track them on land, but he thought it smart of Lexie that she didn't want to risk it all the same. Eventually, the forest spat them out and they found themselves standing at the edge of an open brown plain. On the horizon there appeared to be another forest, but strangely there was one lone tree between this forest and the next.

"We want to avoid that," Lexie told him, as she began trudging along the edge of the field.

"Why?"

"That's the Elm of False Dreams."

"The what?"

"Phantasos and his Oneiroi live there. They weave deceptive dreams and then carry them to the mortal realm, trying to convince Souls of things that aren't real."

"Why would anyone want to do that?"

Lexie shrugged, looking towards the tree as they continued on. "Apparently, some of the dreams are messages sent by the Fates — it depends which gate they flock through. If it's ivory, it's false; if it's the gate of horn, it's true. But, my mother said it didn't matter. I suppose when your reality isn't what you want it to be, a dream that convinces you otherwise would be a welcome respite."

At that moment, the dark-winged spirits took flight, a flock of bat-winged creatures against a sky that had begun to turn a hue of lavender as night blanketed them. They swooped and circled together, like the fish did in the currents, and Yani thought he might begin to understand what it would be like to live on air rather than in water.

They kept walking until they reached what Yani had originally believed to be the next forest. It wasn't. It was a hoard of gathered Souls.

"Mortals, waiting to cross," Lexie told him, at his quizzical look.

He hadn't seen many mortals before. He'd never swum earthside and very few visited the glade. These ones all looked much more ... washed out, he decided. Like their life had been leached out of them. But, Yani knew that couldn't be true, because they'd live an equally fulfilling life here if they wanted to. Perhaps only then would their colour return.

"They're waiting for Charon to help them cross Styx.

Then they'll go to the Palace of Hades where Lord Hades and Lady Persephone will welcome them. Do you have any coins?" Lexie whispered, as they began to move closer to the crowd.

The question threw him. "No, why would I have coins?"

"Because we need coins to pay Charon to cross."

"Why are *we* crossing?"

"To get to Asphodel Meadows, of course. It's the fastest way to get to the Lethe by land. That is – if you want to find your mother and family."

Yani stopped in his tracks. He hadn't thought about that. He hadn't thought about anything. It had all happened so fast – his grandfather appearing, Lexie whisking them away, his arm, leaving the glade – he hadn't considered where they were going, except *away*. He marvelled at how Lexie had been able to think so far ahead.

"I'm not sure I want to go there. I don't want to risk him finding me there," Yani eventually said, as they continued to move through the throng of Souls.

Lexie nodded in understanding.

"Plus, it won't really be her, my mother, you know? Once they drink from the Lethe, they're ... other."

"I thought you might say that, but I thought we should head this way anyway. Asphodel Meadows is known for its plumbing. All the water and sewage and everything is kept civilised. It'll be the best place for us to hide and regroup, make a new plan."

"Lexie, we only have the wet chitons on our skins. How are we going to regroup in the most civilised place in the Underworld?"

"I have a friend there who might be able to help us. I knew her when I was a youngling, back in Tartarus. She got out. I'm hoping she's still there."

"A friend, Lexie? Who?"

"Her name's Nika."

"And she's not going to report back to your mother where you are? I know we're worried about my grandfather at the moment, but let's not forget she did try to eat you."

"Nika won't tell my mother; she always hated her own. She gets it."

"Do all mothers like to eat their young in Tartarus?" Yani muttered.

Lexie threw him a wry look before grabbing an unsuspecting Soul by the hand and turning them towards her. Yani watched as she cocked her head and her eyes appeared to narrow into tiny slits as she asked them if they had any spare coins.

To Yani's shock, the Soul placed two large brass coins into Lexie's outstretched palm.

She turned to him and her eyes returned to normal.

"Two coins down, two to go!"

"How did you do that?" Yani whispered as they continued to make their way through the crowd towards the embankment, though he wasn't sure how wise it was to get so close to the water again so soon.

"Do what?"

"Get that Soul to give you those coins."

"You saw me. I asked him."

"No," Yani gravely said, putting his hand out onto Lexie's forearm to stop her pushing any further forward. "I saw you hypnotise him with some weird eye trick you did."

"I didn't do a weird eye trick," Lexie scoffed. "Quit playing."

She tried to shrug him off.

"Yes, Lexie, you did."

Something in his tone must have registered, because Lexie stopped. "Oh."

"You didn't know you could do that?"

"I had no idea."

She tried again to ask Souls for spare coins, this time without cocking her head, but even the ones who clearly had them turned her down. In the end, sighing, they both admitted she should try the weird snake hypnotism again. When Lexie came back with another two coins in her hand, Yani thought she looked sad.

"Did it feel weird? Doing it? Now that you know what you were doing?"

"Yeah, I didn't like it."

"It's okay, you don't have to do it again." Yani squeezed her hand as together, they made their way to the front of the crowd and to the bank where Charon's boat was pulling in.

ASPHODEL MEADOWS WAS AS CIVILISED as Lexie had made out. Her friend, Nika, not so much. It turned out Nika worked at one of the up-and-coming pubs, Zeus' Watering Hole.

"Look, kitchen work won't be easy for either of you. Especially not if you're used to frolicking around the glade or wherever the Hades-hell you've been. And I can't guarantee that Garth will keep either of you on. It's just lucky for you that we haven't been able to find a poissonnier or rôtisseur that's lasted longer than two months before Garth practically eats them alive.

"But," she continued, as she moved efficiently around the guest bed, fitting it with fresh linen, "Garth seemed to like that you came as a pair. And I can vouch for Lexie. If she vouches for you, I trust her."

They'd met Garth earlier that day, after they'd crossed the river Styx in Charon's boat that held a hundred Souls at a time. Lexie had led them off the crossing, grabbed Yani's hand, and marched them assuredly in the direction of Asphodel Meadows. They wound up at that pub that Lexie remembered Nika mentioning when she'd last sent a raven to Lexie, letting her know she had just gotten a job and was 'out' of Tartarus for good. All this Lexie had told Yani as she continued to march them at a punishing pace.

Lexie's brain was as good with memory as it was with making quick decisions, something – Yani suspected – to do with her biological heritage as a Lamia. He just didn't tell her that while she was busy weaving them through cobble-stoned streets with huge trees so big that awnings of leaves hung over their heads.

When they eventually reached the pub, with its big black studded door and neon purple sign, the Fates played ball with them once again. Nika was there as a hostess to greet them, and she recognised Lexie on sight. She'd sat them at a table by the bar, heard their story of everything that had happened, then hurried off to have a conversation with a burly daemon that appeared to have snake-like skin from his neck down. Nika spoke to him animatedly for a minute or two, pointing at the pair of them, before he slinked over.

"So, I hear you two are in need of livelihoods."

Yani and Lexie looked at each other. Yani had never had a *livelihood* before. He hadn't known he'd needed one.

"I guess we are," Lexie answered for both of them.

"Can either of you cook?"

"Cook ... " Lexie said slowly.

Yani never cooked the fish, and Lexie never cooked her meat. They knew how to hunt; they knew how to fillet; they knew how to make the most of their food. That's what Lexie ended up telling Garth, who brushed the dark five o'clock shadow on his chin with his hand.

"Well, the filleting skill will come in useful." He addressed Lexie directly. "You'll probably save us on butchery costs.

"Look, here's what we'll do. We'll take you on as apprentices. You can do the filleting and butchering, and the two chefs we've got now can teach you how to cook the meat and seafood the way our customers like it. Your meals will be included here and Nika will put you up. After six months, we'll assess how you're getting on, and if we like you as part of the team then you'll start to be paid in tokens – enough to find your own place and set up shop here in the neighbourhood. If it doesn't work out, then you'll leave with a new skill set and I'll give you a good reference for another place. How does that sound?"

"Will Nika really be okay with us staying with her for six months?" Lexie asked.

Garth shrugged, the scales across his shoulders shimmering under the lights that swung back and forth playfully overhead. Yani felt Lexie tense at the movement, so he placed his hand on her thigh under the table to steady her nerves. It secretly helped him steady his own nerves, too.

"She was the one who suggested it," Garth told her. "I think she wants to pay it forward." Garth chuckled to himself. It was clearly an inside joke because by the look on

Lexie's face, she had no idea what he was talking about either, Yani thought.

So, that was how they found themselves with jobs, of a sort, and a place to stay.

At least for now.

Nika brought them food and drinks. The pomegranate beer tasted so sweet that each of them had choked on one sip and asked Nika for water instead. The food was also … interesting. Apparently, cooking took all the delicacy out of food, but that, it appeared, was what the majority of the population liked. There were lamb meatballs, made of minced meat of a lamb and a bunch of flavours Yani's tongue had never tasted, and they'd cooked it until it was an unsightly brown. Lexie had complained she could barely taste the slaughtered lamb. Their fish dish didn't appear much better. Yani couldn't understand why they had taken parts of a squid's legs and made it into rings. Apparently, they dipped the legs in a thing called 'batter', which made the outside crunchy while making the squid flesh even chewier than it already was. In the end, they both snacked on cherry tomatoes, cucumber, and olives, doing their best to brush off all the additional herbs and spices that took away from the original freshness of the food.

As they ate and drank, they watched how the place worked. It didn't seem particularly busy, but there were still more nymphs and Souls and deities moving in and out of one place than Yani had ever seen.

When Nika finally finished her shift close to the midnight hour, she walked them back to her small apartment, showed them around, and offered them showers. Yani had found the whole experience of the shower comical. It amazed him that others thought tiny pellets of water hitting them at high speed could clean them. Why did they not just bathe in a river?

Yani was going to ask Nika after he got out, but then remembered that he himself would have to avoid rivers for the foreseeable future, lest he run into his grandfather again. Showers were to become a regular thing in his life, now. Yani held the towel Nika had provided and looked down at it. He felt so lost, so unsure what to do with it, that he was grateful when the charcoal-coloured towel sprung to life of its own accord and began blotting him dry.

Of course, here on land they didn't like to remain wet, he thought.

Once that was all done, he padded back into the lounge to find Nika and Lexie staring at him.

"What took you so long?" Nika asked.

Yani immediately frowned. "It was lots of little water droplets, how was I supposed to be any quicker?"

Nika scoffed, while Lexie smiled at him. "You'll get used to it," Lexie promised.

"Nika here was just asking if we'll be okay sharing the guest room. I told her it wouldn't be a problem."

Yani nodded.

"It's not much, but you should have seen the first place I was in. Paper-thin walls and mould. Luckily, it only took me six months of working at the pub to be able to move into a place like this. Made a good deal with a local land-lord. You'll be able to do the same," Nika told them as she led them to the guest room. They were going to have to get up early for their first day at the restaurant tomorrow.

"And you're sure you don't mind us staying this long?" Lexie asked.

Nika laughed. "You're apprentices who work in the hospitality industry now. You'll barely be here. We all work at least twelve-hour shifts. As apprentices, you'll work longer. I'll scarcely see you, and I'm always at the pub, anyway. Don't even worry about it. Six months is a blink of an eye."

Then Nika left them to it, returning to her own room. Lexie and Yani both lay on either side of the bed. It was softer than the clamshells had been. Yani felt like he was endlessly sinking into algae, but it would be okay, so long as he had Lexie with him.

They were used to sleeping in close proximity to one another. They held hands as they lay down, just as they had when they were staying in the glade. It was a comfort more than anything to each other, Yani often reminded himself. A reminder that, although they were abandoned by their families for different reasons, they had each other. They always had each other.

"Are you sure you're okay with Garth?" Yani asked into the darkness.

"What do you mean?"

"I saw the way you tensed when Nika said Garth ate alive employees he didn't like. And, well, given what he is … "

"An agathodaemon?"

"Well, it's similar to your mother, isn't it? The fact he's part snake. You have to wonder what other traits he's picked up … "

Lexie said nothing.

"I mean, you know I'm not a fan of snakes, so it's going to take some getting used to. I just wondered if you felt the same."

"I don't really want to talk about it," Lexie told him. "Besides, he's not really a snake. He just has … scales."

Yani decided not to point out that Lexie wasn't a snake

and didn't have scales, and yet she could still hypnotise Souls. It seemed, to Yani, like her mother's traits had manifested differently in Lexie, making her a vampiric daemon of some sort unto herself.

He knew she was smart enough to know it, but just not ready to acknowledge it yet, so it sat between them, in the silence.

And, in the darkness, he reached for her hand.

6

LEXIE
MYTHICALS AND MORTALS

Nika was right. Six months had passed in a flash and they were very rarely home. Instead, Zeus' Watering Hole had begun to feel like their second home. Both she and Yani had taken to the kitchen, well, she didn't want to say like fish to water, but …

It filled their days and occupied their minds, much as living in the glade had. There was always something to be done. In fact, *more* than enough to be done. It kept their minds off their families who wanted to hunt them down and snuff out their spirits, and it kept them hidden. Being out back in the kitchen for hours on end felt like the safest place in the Underworld. And they were always so exhausted by the end of the day that both she and Yani would fall back on the bed at the same time, sigh, and proceed to fall fast asleep.

They'd even both gotten used to cooking meat and fish; though their mentors – both old oak nymphs that Lexie knew Garth didn't like – still seemed to over-season every-thing because "that's the way it's supposed to taste." Still, both Yani and herself had proved in the last six months that they could prep for a dinner service, they'd learnt how to cook, and how to balance the flavours to the liking of their chefs. They didn't have to do anything else. It was a routine, a set of instructions, at a brutal pace that Lexie liked.

She didn't miss the slowness of life in the glade, but she knew Yani did. She saw him struggling with the bustle and the number of creatures around him. He'd always been quiet, but he seemed to retreat further into himself. She knew Yani joked that water nymphs weren't aloof, but he was finding it hard to trust the others. Every time she caught him staring woefully at the fish in front of him, she reminded herself to ask him about it when they got back to Nika's, but every time they did, she was too tired and forgot as promptly as her head hit the pillow.

He'd been brilliant with her. He'd always checked in on her to see how she was managing being around an agatho-daemon like Garth. Initially, she just hadn't wanted to acknowledge it, but as she got more and more used to her boss' presence, she realised it wasn't his biology that made him what he was. Garth was simply hardwired to provide the best service he could. That part of his heritage drove him more than anything else, and Lexie could start to imagine a life for herself where her fate wasn't to be eaten or to become some unfathomable monster. Instead, she could use her drive *not* to become that, and forge a name for herself.

She had, in her own time, started experimenting with flavours. Now that their six-month apprenticeships were up, Garth told them to present either what they considered the best dish on the menu, or one of their own creations. If he deemed them up to the standard he expected, they'd be allowed to fill in for the official team whenever they needed a day off. Then, from there, who knew?

"Are you going with a new dish?" she asked Yani as they walked back to Nika's following their last official shift as apprentices. They were due in earlier than usual tomorrow, well before the dinner service was to be prepped, to showcase to Garth what they'd learnt.

"You bet I am. I'm sick of the battered crap Lycus keeps serving up," Yani said.

Lexie grinned. "Oh yeah? What are you going with?"

"Okay, hear me out. I'm going for a taco."

"A taco? You think that's going to impress Garth enough to keep you?"

"I said hear me out! This isn't going to be any old taco. This is going to be a royal ceviche fish taco."

This was the Yani that Lexie knew best – the one so excited by the new, by introducing his way of being into the world. He didn't often come out of his shell around others, but she loved that he did for her when it was just the two of them.

"Oh, excuse me, Mr Fancy Fish," she teased.

Yani gave her one of his grave looks for her sarcasm. "I've already picked out the fish and left it to marinate overnight in an elixir of citrus juices. That combined with the original salt of the fish is going to make it taste like the sun meets the sea in your mouth. Then, I'm going to crown it with ripe, diced mango and place it on a bed of creamy avocado that's been smothered on those artisan corn flatbreads we have. Drizzle it with a lime and cilantro aioli, and there you have it. The freshest fish dish they'll ever have in that joint."

"Do you think Garth will go for it, given it's raw?"

"They should all learn the nature of eating fresh. That's my philosophy. Besides, the acid in the citrus juice effectively cooks the seafood. It's still stripping it of proteins, just like heat would. And it will still have that firm texture and opaque appearance that makes it look cooked."

"Fair enough. I hope it works and he loves it," Lexie told him sincerely.

"Me, too. Anyway, what about you? You settled on which one you're going with?"

"I have," Lexie nodded.

"Well?"

"At first, I was also thinking I would make a raw dish. A carpaccio, with the thinnest slices of prime, ruby-red beef you've ever seen. That marbled kind. I was going to delicately marinate it in that old extra virgin olive oil we have, and some of the dried herbs I know you detest," she teased.

Yani pulled a face that told her again what he thought of dried herbs.

"Then I was going to scatter it with parmigiano-reggiano cheese, arugula leaves, and season."

"Well, apart from the herbs, that sounds delicious. What could be better than that?"

"I wanted to show Garth I could cook, so I'm going to make lamb tagine instead. Even though I have to cook it, I like the fact that the meat remains the star of the show and stays succulent and tender, and that the meat juices stay in the dish. Of course, I'll add in saffron and a medley of spices in the traditional earthenware pot, sweet apricots, and toasted almonds."

"Ah, so your plan is to do something so opposite to what you would want to do, so that you prove you have the range," Yani said, a frown on his face.

"Exactly. Why do you look so worried? Do you not like the idea?"

"No, no, I do! It's just now you have me second-guessing my dish. Maybe I'd be better off doing a traditionally cooked dish, too."

"No," Lexie said, grabbing his shoulder. "I think what you are doing is far braver, and Garth loves ingenuity. Besides, if he really wants to make the place the best it can be, he is going to need a range of dishes – including raw – to lure in all the nymphs, like us who prefer to eat the way nature intended."

"I guess you're right," Yani said as they continued walking and came up to Nika's door.

It wouldn't be long now before they could move out together and find a place of their own. Members of the team had each given them tokens at different points for favours both of them had done over the past six months, which they could then trade for places to stay. That was how the token barter system worked in the more civilised parts of the Underworld. In the glade, there had been no need for such a system – everyone worked the land and there was always plenty to go around. But, members of the team had begun to recognise their hard work and thank them for it with these tiny scraps of paper, with different favours written on them. Lexie thought they might have a dozen or so already between them. If they got Garth's nod of approval tomorrow, then they'd start to be paid tokens regularly.

Yani hesitated at the door.

"You know, I might just go down to the local swimming hole. Just to wash the day off," he told her.

Lexie gave him a knowing look. "Okay, I'll see you when you're back."

Yani nodded, turning and heading back the way they came. Lexie watched him until he was just a silhouette against the sky.

The local swimming hole was a spring that a Naiad had set up in one of the park areas for younglings and others of her kind to enjoy. If it had been anywhere near the rivers, Lexie knew that Yani would have vetoed it immediately, but given it was surrounded by luscious green parkland, it was the closest he'd come to finding an oasis since they'd moved here. She remembered what he had said to her all those years ago – that Nereids and Naiads liked different forms of water. She hoped, even though the local swimming hole was a freshwater pool, it was giving him some respite.

Sighing, Lexie let herself into the house. Immediately, she was accosted by Nika who was spread out on the three-seater, black-studded sofa, snacking on salty black olives by the jar.

"Just you? Where's Yani?"

"Gone swimming."

"*Godsdamn* fishes."

"Cut him a break. This isn't his environment," Lexie sighed. She dropped her bag in the guest room before wandering back into the living area and heading to the open kitchen. The fridge door opened for her, as if it was an old friend looking to embrace her, and a beer fizzed in delight when she picked it up and popped the top off it before joining Nika on the couch.

"How was your day off?"

"Delightful. I've been watching this show about mortal Souls, *Mythicals and Mortals*. You heard of it?"

Lexie shook her head.

"Hermes acts as master of ceremonies between the living and the dead realms. Sometimes, it's an historical episode and you'll even get the likes of Lord Hades and Lady Persephone commenting on those Souls who have come through and what they are up to now. Those are pretty good; you get some pretty funny commentary and reflections. Sometimes, Hermes goes back to visit the ancestors of the great mortal heroes, to see what they amounted to. Then he sets them a task, which they all inevitably fail – mortals these days are far too likely to rely on technology and themselves; none of them even think to invoke the help of the gods! Those episodes are funny, too. But, the best ones are when Hermes convinces a god to agree to grant their powers to an unsuspecting mortal. It's only ever a drop, and you're always waiting to see if the mortal will even notice it and use it before it leaves their bloodstream."

"What happens if they do?"

"Oh, most of them go on to become world-famous artists of some kind, influential in a way the others simply can't be. Talent meets hard work, and that drop of what they think is luck." Nika chuckled. "If only they knew."

"Sounds sort of barbaric, that we prey on them this way and then watch."

Nika shrugged. "It's a good way for us to understand how their world evolves. Their world inevitably affects ours when they come here. Better we watch them in their environment and learn from them now, than be at their mercy later."

Lexie snorted. "No wonder you're turning into one of the most notorious hostesses in the neighbourhood."

Nika pinned her with a look. "I watch you and Yani in this environment."

Lexie's shoulders tensed, and when Nika didn't continue immediately, she had to know. "And?"

"I know you don't like it when he goes swimming in that Naiad's pool without you."

Lexie read between the lines and knew what Nika was saying. "It's not like that."

"No? So, why don't you tell me what's going on, before I come home to a fight I don't want any part of?"

"You're not going to come home to a fight. We're not ... that will never be ... Yani and I will never be romantically entangled."

"You sound very certain."

"You knew my mother. She was cursed for loving Zeus, and even when she found love with one of her kind – *even* when she thought that would break the curse, that she wouldn't try to eat *me* – it didn't work. Love turned her into a monster. I don't want the same thing to happen to me. I certainly wouldn't want it to happen to Yani. He doesn't deserve that."

"You don't know that the curse would be passed down to you."

"I've exhibited enough traits to suspect it already has been, even if I don't have all of them," Lexie said quietly. The weird eye trick had happened again multiple times. Lexie hadn't meant it to, but under the pressures of the kitchen she found herself snapping at her mentor, Elowen, who caved to her demands. Lexie had tried it again at after-work drinks, just to see if it only happened under extreme stress and pressure. But, even relaxed, it happened. In fact, she had to consciously *not* do it.

"Well, that's just shit, isn't it," Nika said.

"Tell me about it."

Nika got up to fetch them two more beers. There was a satisfying pop after she cracked the tops of both of them with her long black nails and handed one to Lexie, who accepted with a nod of her head before taking an exceedingly long gulp down her throat.

"So, what's that look you get on your face about when Yani goes off without you, then?"

Lexie sighed. "I'm just worried about him. I remember what life was like when I was trying to settle into the glade. Learning how to do everything that's the opposite of your nature is hard enough, but trying to 'make it' in a more civilised world has got to be even harder. At least in the glade, there was no hurry. I only had to move at nature's pace. He has the added pressure of the job, and I'm worried he's going to crack. I'm worried those swims are the only way he is staying alive out here."

YANI
WELL WORTH FIGHTING FOR

The next day, when they had to present their dishes to Garth, Yani felt understandably nervous. Lexie had placed her dish in front of Garth first. Yani had originally intended to go first, what with his being a fish dish, but after adding a last-minute element, he'd needed more time. Lexie had offered it to him.

From his position in the kitchen, Yani couldn't hear what Garth was saying to her, and Lexie's expression when she walked back gave nothing away. She was always good at keeping her cards close to her chest.

Perhaps, Yani thought as he walked forward with his dish, she was just waiting to see what Garth said about his dish before celebrating. Or, maybe she didn't want him to get his hopes up. Either way, nerves skittered across his skin in a way that unsettled him, like the air tickling his gills first did when he'd spent too long out of the water. Thank the gods for that local swimming hole he'd found.

Yani placed the dish in front of Garth, at the same table they had both sat at six months ago, and tried to see the dish through his boss' eyes.

On the turquoise plate sat a golden-brown taco, a beautifully cut, opaque, thin fillet of fish, decorated with bright mango and a maroon beetroot garnish. The dish was colourful; perhaps more colourful than anything else they currently had on the menu. It brought Yani joy, but he couldn't quite tell by the look on Garth's face if the agathodaemon felt the same.

Yani still might not like snakes, but Garth had proved himself a very different character. Though the skin from his head down shimmered, and while he could definitely slide behind Yani silently in the kitchen and scare the *be-zeus* out of him, he was a kind creature at heart. It was clear to Yani that Garth liked to help people where he could, to give them chances. He understood that everyone was just trying their best to get by. Plus, when he caught Yani outside of service hours, he would talk to him about anything and everything, and his interest seemed genuine every time they had talked.

After looking at the plate and taking it all in, Garth picked up the fork, used the side of it to slice through the fish effortlessly, nodded, and put the fork back down. Then, he wrapped the entire taco up and slid it into his mouth. Yani watched as Garth clearly assessed the flavour palette in his mouth, and proceeded to swallow the rest.

"Well?"

Garth grinned. "That's the best damn fish I've ever had here."

Yani's chest swelled with pride, but quickly deflated like a burst balloon at Garth's next words.

"If I could only take you, would you accept?"

Yani didn't even have to think about it. "No. It's me and Lexie, or I go with her."

Garth raised both of his dark bushy eyebrows in surprise.

"I didn't realise you felt so strongly about her. I thought you Nereids and Naiads were all cold, aloof types."

Yani knew his face was pulling what Lexie called his 'grave look'.

"It's not like that. It's … don't get me wrong, Lexie is a stunning female. In fact, I used to have a bit of a crush on her when we first met over a century ago," Yani chuckled and rubbed the back of his neck. "And I do love her, but not like that. She's my best friend. We're each other's sounding boards; each other's port in a storm. She's … the only family I've got left. I won't leave her."

"Sometimes, it can be good for us to part ways with those we've grown up with, in order to become who we can be," Garth countered.

Now, Yani placed his hands behind his back, his stance wide, his legs now used to not being in their tail form as often.

"I have my flaws, chef, but I still won't leave Lexie."

Garth leaned forward, about to say something, but Yani continued.

"She is who she is, and I am who I am. I love her for it. She loves me. Our biology and genealogy has dictated a lot of who we've had to become, so we've grown up knowing what is best for each other more often than we know what is best for ourselves. No one just *gets* us like we do. You take us both, or we both walk. We'll be very grateful for all you've done for us, of course, and we'll tell everyone where we were trained, but I won't change my mind on this."

Garth thought about it for a moment, then nodded. "Very well, go and get Lexie for me."

"Does that mean we're staying, or we're going?"

"I'll tell you together."

THEY WERE STAYING.

As Garth announced the news, Yani breathed out a sigh of relief as quietly as he could manage and looked at Lexie with a wide grin on his face. She was smiling back at him just as ferociously.

He had no idea if Garth had said the same thing to Lexie and made the same offering, just to see if they would really stick together. Perhaps he'd never know and Garth would keep that close to his chest. Yani certainly wasn't going to ask Lexie, and by the look on Garth's face, he wasn't going to tell either of them.

"Go on then, you two," Garth said, flashing that sly smile of his that only quirked one corner of his mouth. "You better go and clean that kitchen before the other chefs arrive for service prep. I'll talk to your superiors later. I'm sure they'll be grateful for a day off here and there."

"Yes, Chef," Yani and Lexie chorused.

"Do you think our dishes will go on the menu now?" Yani asked Lexie in hushed tones as they turned and walked back from the galley bar, through the bistro section, and back into the kitchen.

"I don't know," Lexie shrugged at him, a small smile on her face.

Yani went to ask her what Garth's feedback had been on her dish, but Lexie was immediately pulled into prep the minute they returned to the kitchen. Then, the service prep began in earnest with pots and pans whizzing overhead, knives furiously chopping, and ovens sizzling with heat as they prepared for their busiest night yet. The reputation of this place was growing – fast.

Yani felt like he blinked once and the dinner service had begun, blinked again and it was the middle of the rush, and then the third time …

"Last orders: one blackened sea bass, one ragu. Yani, Lexie, you're up!" Garth called out.

Usually, they were just assistants when their superiors were on duty, but seeing as they had all the other dishes in hand, it looked like Garth was giving them their first shot at the pass. Although Yani loathed cooking the bass until it was charred beyond redemption, he knew the methodology and timings off by heart.

"How long?" he called to Lexie.

"Five minutes out. You?"

"Six."

"Gives me more time to make it look pretty, then," Lexie grinned with a flash of her canines.

But, given that Yani's six minutes included the resting time on the plate, they both came to the pass together. Yani brushed against Lexie's shoulder as they stood side by side, plating. She didn't take her eyes off the ribbons of pasta she was carefully shaping around the beef in its rich sauce. Turning back to his own plate, Yani placed the blackened bass on a bed of creamy mash, drizzled the saffron sauce (quickly becoming a restaurant signature) across the crispy skin, allowing it to sink into the depths of the mash, and finished the plate off with microgreens for a pop of colour.

"Good job, you two," Garth nodded, wiping away an

escaped drop of sauce from Yani's plate and three from Lexie's. "You can start the breakdown now."

As apprentices, they'd gotten used to this part – scrubbing the kitchen until it may as well have been brand new again. But, instead of their usual camaraderie, Lexie seemed sullen and silent. When they were done, she immediately took off.

No doubt with another young Dryad she'd picked up after one of their shifts, Yani thought.

He knew why she did it. Lexie was convinced she was going to turn out like her mother, and in an effort to get the others to stop pestering them about when he and Lexie would get together, she made a show of flaunting other males. At first, it had hurt Yani that he wasn't good enough to be the only male she needed in her life. But then, after Nika had quite rightly pointed out that he had found comfort in having other friendships, like the Naiads he had met at the pool, he realised how foolish he was being.

Now, the thought that she was pulling away from him because Garth might *not* have made her the same offer he did Yani, had a stone forming in Yani's gut.

The silent treatment continued for another five days. Yani barely saw Lexie, and whenever they finished a shift together, she would scarper off before he got a chance to talk to her.

Until, on the sixth day, their day off, when she stood in the doorway of Nika's guest bedroom, watching him as he roused from his sleep.

"Lexie? What's going on? Why are you watching me?"

"Get up, sleepyhead. I have something to show you."

"Now?"

"Yes, now! Come on!"

Yani laughed, delighted she was talking to him again. "Alright, alright, I'm coming!"

It reminded him of when they'd lived in the glade and Lexie had been loath to learn how to swim at first. Then, it had been Yani who'd excitedly tried to get her out of bed. Shrugging on a dark blue lounge toga, and slipping into sandals that accommodate his webbed toes, Yani wriggled his feet (shoes were still something he was getting used to, even now) and followed Lexie out into the living room.

Nika was already at the pub, on shift.

"So, what are we doing today that has me getting up so early on the only day we get lie-ins?"

Lexie grinned. "I'll show you."

Grabbing his hand, she tugged Yani out the door and down the street, following the cobblestoned laneways that were a labyrinth of their own. Yani was used to them now, with their large ash and oak trees evenly planted every few feet from one another on either side of the streets. The season had just begun to change – Lady Persephone was due back from the mortal realm any day now – meaning the blossoms falling to the ground around them were a brilliant, light pink, and Yani could almost imagine a fragrant smell of wildflowers in the air.

"Where are you taking me?"

"Come on," Lexie tugged.

Suddenly, Yani was tugged back into what felt like a lifetime ago, when Lexie had been dragging them through the streets, desperately searching for shelter from family members they'd not seen hide nor hair of since. It was one of her uncanny abilities Yani had learnt over time. Alongside hypnotising others, Lexie had the ability to transport others – including herself – into the past.

Eventually, she stopped in a part of the neighbourhood Yani didn't think he'd been to. He certainly didn't recognise it, but then, he didn't get many days off to go exploring. In front of them was a narrow path that appeared to wind its way through two large hedges, and there was the distant murmur of laughter and water splashing.

"Are we near a river?" Yani asked, suddenly alarmed.

While part of his Nereid heart longed to be back in the depths of a vast ocean, to taste that saltwater against his skin, the skittish fear of running into the omnipresence that was his grandfather and the horror of being forced into the Lethe were enough to quash that longing.

"You really think I'd bring you to a river? Now? After we've just spent six months busting our asses to call this place home?"

"Then what is ... "

"I'm surprised you don't recognise where you are, to be honest. We're only three minutes away from the swimming hole."

"Oh!" Yani looked around him. "I've never come this way. I just make a straight beeline for it and then back to ours. I don't *meander* like you do."

"Well, you're lucky I do *meander*, or I wouldn't have found this place."

"And what exactly *is* this place?"

"Let me show you," she said, offering her arm out, suggesting Yani walk down the narrow path first.

It was only due to his unwavering faith in her that he did so.

As he walked along the path, the tall hedges parted gradually, revealing a small cottage built into the base of a weeping tree, and a perfectly adequate pond. A path of smooth stones led around the pond and to the green door.

Lexie's face burst into the widest grin he'd ever seen. "It's ours."

Yani stood there looking at her, dumbfounded.

"What? How?"

"I'll explain how I sorted the tokens later," Lexie replied. "Come, there's something else I want to show you."

She guided Yani towards the cottage and around the pond, to the side of the weeping tree, where a well stood in the dappled sunlight. Its stone walls were weathered by time, and a simple bucket dangled from its sturdy frame.

"There's water in it, if you're wondering. Pure and refreshing. Not saltwater, and I checked with the owner. The water comes from a standalone lake somewhere past the Elysium border."

Yani walked over to it and peered into its depths as a cool breeze carried the faint aroma of earth and moss.

"This is what you've been doing all that time with the other Dryads. Swapping tokens, so you could get this place?"

Lexie nodded. "I came looking for you once when you'd gone swimming. Being back on land has been great, but I kind of missed it – swimming."

Yani felt his face light up at Lexie's confession, as she continued.

"Anyway, I stumbled on this place and when I saw the well, that's when I knew we had to have it. I wanted to get it sorted by the time Garth gave us our jobs. I was gutted when I didn't manage it, but determined to get it as soon as possible. That's where I've been all this week – sorting this. So? Do you like it?"

Yani looked between Lexie and the well, then doubled back when he saw her face painted with a shy look he'd never seen before.

"Lex, this is incredible."

"I just thought, I know how hard you've worked to make a life here ... away from the only one you've ever known. I wanted you – us – to have a place that marks the start of our new lives together."

"And the death of our old ones," Yani murmured.

Lexie nodded. "Exactly. You get it."

"You did the same thing when you came and stayed in the glade."

"And you gave me a home, and let me be part of your tradition. Now this way, we can start our own tradition. Together."

Yani hadn't realised how deeply he was missing the presence of his old life. He had told himself that being close to a freshwater pool had been enough of a reminder of his mother, but it hadn't; not really. It wasn't until he had seen this well, the one Lexie had found for him, that Yani realised he'd needed to mark the passage of time. It was a grounding that finally made him feel like he had one foot planted in the past and the other in the future. For some reason, it allowed him to be fully present.

"This means ... *everything* to me."

They stood there for a minute together, shoulder to shoulder, looking into the well. An object that had defined his life, then tainted it, with the one friend who had been by his side through it all. Now it was a gift, to mark how far he'd come, from his favourite being in the world.

"I don't know how to repay you."

"You already have."

Yani shot her a puzzled look and Lexie poked her tongue out in faux annoyance in return.

"I know you told Garth that we came as a team."

"How did you ... ?"

"I have the hearing of a vampiric creature, remember?"

"Oh."

"Plus, I totally fudged the tagine."

Yani laughed and pulled Lexie's frame into his. She looped an arm across his shoulders and rested her cheek on the top of his head as they looked again at the well.

Just the two of them against the Underworld.

THE RESTAURATEUR IN THE UNDERWORLD

PROLOGUE: GOODBYE GARDEN
OF EDEN

Garth had been a baby agathodaemon, his youngling scales shedding and giving way for his adult ones, when his family had been kicked out of the Garden of Eden.

"But, why do we have to leave, Mummy?"

"Because your great-great-grandmother did something stupid."

"I did not!" remarked the old crone, sitting in the corner of the kitchen in a creaky rocking chair, knitting Garth a chiton that would cover his arms while his scales shed. "It was a bloomin' apple and the young woman was clearly starved! A flat stomach like that, on a woman – imagine! How was I to know she wasn't supposed to eat it? What new god decides to hang a ripe, juicy apple right there and *not* let the mortals eat it?"

"That's not for us to say," Garth's mother retorted. "Thanks to you, great-granddaddy had to plead our case to Zeus. We're lucky he's just condemning us to Hades' realm in the Underworld and not making us live here permanently in snakeform."

"Oh, pish."

Garth watched as his great-great-grandmother, Gigi, whose scales had turned grey, waved off the remark with one of her hands, while his mother continued to move around the kitchen. Garth spent most of his time in this room, sitting at this large wooden dining table. Usually, he would watch his mother potter, measuring ingredients on the magical blue scales that tipped themselves without weights to let her know when she'd got the right amount of something. Occasionally, when he was on really good behaviour, she would even let him do the pouring or use the spatula.

He wasn't big enough to use the knives yet.

Today, she was hurriedly packing those instruments into boxes.

"But, why do we have to leave now? Where are we going?"

His mother flicked a curl of dark black hair from her forehead with the back of her hand. Her scales were tinted with lots of different purples. *Pretty*. His mother was pretty. Still, Garth hoped his adult scales came in a masculine colour; maybe midnight blue.

As the only current child of the agathodaemon family, his scales had been a rainbow of colours growing up. Everyone in the family had cooed over him, but now he wanted to be a grown-up daemon, especially if they were to go somewhere new where no one else knew him. He didn't want those new creatures, whoever they were, to think he was still a baby. He scratched at the scales on his forearm, trying to rub them off more quickly to see what colour he'd end up with.

"Don't scratch. Alora, tell him not to scratch." Gigi barked from the corner.

His mother sighed as she decided to answer Garth's

question. "Because, that was the deal with Zeus. We would leave immediately, he would smooth it over with the Abrahamic god, and all would be well."

"Fat chance of that," Gigi scoffed.

"For the love of the gods, will you stop?" his mother snapped. Turning back to Garth, she dropped to his height. "To answer your second question, we're going to the Underworld."

"Where's that?"

"Imagine a hidden magical realm beneath the ground." His mother's eyes went wide with amazement and Garth found his mouth forming into a little 'o'. "It's filled with mortals who have passed over, they're known as Souls there, and other creatures that are just like us, all with their own magic and talents. It'll be like a brand new secret playground for you to explore."

"Will I make friends there?"

His mother sighed as she stood and ruffled his hair. "I hope so."

"Oh. Are they afraid of snakes there, too?"

"You're not a snake, Garthriel. You're an agathodaemon. You should be proud of it," Gigi grumbled.

But, even before all that trouble in the garden, Garth knew they weren't well-liked. His mum did lots of baking in the kitchen and tried to sell it at the creature school for his bake sales, but no one ever bought anything off her. Garth couldn't figure out why, because his mum's baking was the best.

Maybe it would be different in the Underworld.

Maybe his mum was just being cautious.

1

THE EVE OF DISASTER

Garth sighed, folding his arms across his body, the scales on his biceps shimmering a brilliant spectrum of greens and blues, and the occasional silver, that eventually faded into that deep midnight blue he'd always wanted as a child ... only it wasn't where anyone else could see, down past the vee of his pelvic line.

He knew the females wondered about what they'd find down there if their hands went wandering. Not that he let most of them near him now. Not since he'd seen her.

He'd learned the hard way that down here in the Underworld, creatures either had their own secrets or were looking to use others' against them.

It hadn't been so bad in the beginning when they'd moved here. He had just been a young agathodaemon. His family had taken the brunt of scrutiny. Garth's mother had tried to keep him busy by throwing him in the back kitchen, sifting flour into large buckets, buttering loaf after loaf of bread for the sandwiches of the day. Those were the days when self-buttering knives hadn't yet been imbued with any magical intelligence and Zeus' Watering Hole had been a bakery, not a pub.

Garth's great-great-granddaddy may have done a libation deal with Zeus, which meant that in exchange for fifty percent of their profits for eternity, Zeus would bestow upon the agathodaemon family accolades and acknowledgement that they were the family that gave the gift of food and drink; but, it was really his mother's baking that solidified that belief.

One particularly busy day, his mother had to pull him out from the back kitchen and ask him to help out front with service. Garth's eyes had widened as he'd stepped on through – the place was *heaving*. He could see lots of Souls, those mortals who appeared a little more translucent than they had in the earthly realm and arrived at whichever age they'd died, all dressed in a myriad of coloured chitons. Then there were the nymphs that flitted in between them. The ash-tree and oak-tree ones were the most plentiful. The water nymphs were often tall and gangly, their hair and bodies reminding Garth of seaweed as a few of them swayed through the throng of creatures. Then there were the big, burly mountain nymphs that seemed to bring the chill in the air with them wherever they went. Plenty of other creatures were giving them a wide berth. Garth blinked and swore he could have seen a Satyr in their bakery, too.

That day, Garth learnt that most customers didn't know what they wanted, though they *did* like direction – but, if you pointed that out to them they'd bite your head off. Some of them literally, he imagined. He watched his mother as she packaged up the goods a customer had asked for in brown paper packaging. She was usually so well put-together with her curled hair slicked back in a bun, but with the incessant demands of others she'd become frazzled and bit retorts back to several of the customers who complained she was out of lattice bites – small, coiled pastries filled with a sinfully sweet blend of dark chocolate, crushed nuts, and a spice blend his mother would not reveal, no matter how many people begged or made her great offers.

The rest of his family were no better, he realised. All of them were grouchy with the customers, sick of being on their feet all day, and in desperate need of a break.

"Excuse me, sir, can I recommend the karamela cake?" Garth piped up, his small frame only just putting him at counter height.

The pencil-thin nymph stared down at him with unrelenting blue eyes. *Definitely a water nymph*, Garth thought to himself, before he made sure to plaster a wide smile across his face.

He'd always been told he had a nice smile. With a strong jaw, a round face, and baby black curls that held hints of green in them under certain light, Gigi said he'd have been mistaken for a cherub if it weren't for the scales.

"What is karamela cake? A caramel slice of some kind?"

"Oh no, sir. It's a malt and coconut slice with a hidden surprise inside."

"I don't like surprises."

"Do you like frozen marshmallows?"

"I've never had one."

Garth reached under the counter for the glass jar that held the frozen marshmallow chocolate balls his mother often liked to serve to complement warm drinks. It took all his might to unscrew the lid, but when he did, he gestured for the nymph to hold out his large hand and then popped the candy onto it.

"This one is covered in chocolate, but you'll get the gist."

The man popped it into his mouth, his gaze not breaking Garth's. Garth watched him as he moved it around in his mouth, narrowed his eyes as he assessed the flavour profiles, bit into the treat, and swallowed.

"It is ... different," the water nymph told him. "But," he said after a beat, "really rather good."

Garth's brilliant grin spread out across his face again. "Then you'll like the surprise in the karamela cake."

The nymph nodded to him. "Then I'll take one of those please, young one."

Garth, delighted at his first *official* sale, had practically bounced on the balls of his feet as he went about using the silver tongs to grab the slice and wrestle it into a brown paper package.

He'd never forgotten the feeling of it.

After that day, Garth had bounced around the front shop every day, jovially helping anyone and everyone. Many of the customers didn't take him seriously at first, but when he pointed to the large curved glass cabinet and began to explain how each pastry was painstakingly made – having watched his mother make quite a lot of them – they all eventually came around.

And that was how Garth learnt how to disarm those who might dislike his kind. *Take an interest in what they're showing interest in, talk to them, prove you know what you're talking about, and then ask for their input. Then be excited by what they're excited by.* It never failed to work like a charm.

Even though most factions seemed to stick to their own kind in the Underworld, they weren't cruel to his family, and they didn't dismiss them immediately as snake monsters. They were willing to try the food, and the reputation of his family's small place grew from there.

Until *she* had come to the Underworld, of course.

The tension had grown slowly, like the rumbling of thunder sneaking up behind them, somehow missed until it let out a large growl overhead . That's what it felt like had happened to his family. Even now, when Garth thought about it, he couldn't pinpoint when the exact change had occurred – only that it had.

More and more Souls who made the journey to the Underworld from the mortal Western continents seemed to be distrusting of the agathodaemon family. And while food wasn't a necessity in the Underworld, that wasn't something actively advertised, and so the Souls begrudgingly accepted their food from the family cafe and bakery, named Zeus' Watering Hole.

Except, other creatures (ones that had been in Hades' realm far longer), had begun to see how their small family bakery had performed and chose to open up small cafes, bakeries, and restaurants of their own.

Eventually, as Garth matured into a full agathodaemon, there was competition. So much competition, in fact, that soon there was a whole cobblestone avenue in Asphodel Meadows dedicated to food and drink: Philoxenía Lane. Either side of it held inviting facades to a number of whimsical cafes and snug bars with quaint chalkboard and hand-painted signs announcing their specialties, from foraged vegetarian and vegan-friendly cafes to potion-brewed cocktails. Wooden lattice chairs with small round tables for two or four patrons spilled out onto the sidewalk. Some tables had chequered tablecloths that blew where the wind nymphs went. Others had bright yellow umbrellas hanging overhead during the day that were replaced with tealight candles in the evening hours. Whatever their attire, the places were packed and the laughter of happy customers floated on the air and continued into the night when the lampposts, adorned with wrought-iron scrolls and powered by fireflies, cast a gentle glow over the lane.

Garth had seen her on one of those nights. Her chestnut-coloured hair cascaded over her shoulders and down her breasts in waves. Her body was lithe but curvy; she walked with purpose and yet, as if she had all the time in the world. Her attitude screamed 'no nonsense', even as her dress sense spoke of a soft Soul in a flowery dress. She was a walking contradiction, and she was perfect.

Then, her amber eyes had landed on him.

She'd continued walking along the cobblestones, reading the menus of some places, stopping to smell the flowers at others. When she arrived at Garth's table along the sidewalk, she'd simply looked at him, a question in her eyes.

He'd smiled, a smaller smile than when he'd been that tiny youngling, this one more suave with a hint of confidence, and nodded for her to take a seat opposite him.

"Evie," she introduced herself, as she swept her dress out and took a seat not opposite but beside him. Even her voice sounded like melted butter.

"Garth."

"A pleasure."

Garth chuckled. "Oh, I suspect that will be all mine."

They'd talked about all manner of things – the food, the wine, the street. They'd creature-watched and made up stories about passersby. He asked which part of the neighbourhood she was visiting. It turned out she was one of the latest shipments of Charon's Souls and was staying at a local inn, finding her feet.

He didn't ask how she came to find herself in the Underworld. That wasn't a question creatures brought up in polite conversation down here. But, he had asked her if she wanted to visit his family bakery the next morning – early, so she could get her pick of the goods – and Evie had agreed.

Once she'd shown up the following day, he'd invited her to dinner at his favourite place along the lane: a small red restaurant with a tiny door that sold the best pasta in the Meadows.

Again, she'd agreed.

It became a ritual of theirs, until they had tried every cafe, restaurant, bakery, and cocktail joint along that avenue, and then some that had started sprouting up in other areas of Asphodel. Each time, Evie would point out what was working, and what wasn't. Garth would focus on the food and service, but Evie's piercing eyes missed nothing. From whether the owner used warm or cool colours in their space to if the menu complemented the music – she was able to pinpoint every little detail that was right or wrong about a place.

She pinpointed what wasn't working in Zeus' Watering Hole, too. The space was too large to be a bakery and cafe, but too small to be anything more than a lunchtime restaurant. They needed to expand, they needed to change the colours, they needed to get rid of the creaky floorboards ... her list grew and grew. Garth could see her points, and they were reflected in the sales. Even with the libations, the competition was starting to erode their profit margins and his family was getting grumpier and grumpier by the day.

"The mortal realm has grown more cutthroat since you were there last. Everything is bigger, better, bolder. It was only a matter of time until that attitude descended into the Underworld," she told him one night over dinner.

He reiterated this sentiment to his family when they were having one of their Sunday family dinners. The warm aroma of freshly baked bread wafted through the air as his mother placed it on the cafe tables they had pressed together to form one long family table, adorned with a white linen table cloth. Everyone at the table had contributed a dish. There was flaky spanakopita, savoury moussaka, fresh bread to dip in warm oil, and plump olives. They'd barely begun eating when Garth raised the same point Evie had with him.

Yiorgos, his great-great-grandfather; Gigi, his great-great-grandmother; and his grandfather Papou all regarded him from the other side of the table. Next to him, his mother, Alora, stilled. No one ever talked about what had happened to his grandmother or father, but it was just the four of them, and always had been for as long as Garth could remember.

"You are too young, you don't know what you're talking about," Yiorgos grumbled.

"I am five hundred and twenty years old. I'm not a youngling anymore." He wouldn't say it, not out of respect for Yiorgos, but they all knew who ran the place, who the customers actually liked and trusted. "The neighbourhood is changing; we have to change with it."

"What would you suggest we do, my son?" came the quiet voice from beside him.

"Hire someone with the vision to turn this place around. Someone who knows what the mortal Souls are used to, what they like, what their appetites are."

He could feel the concern buzz between his elders, but he continued speaking passionately about introducing new flavours and engaging the Meadow community in new, innovative ways. They must have heard the determination in his voice, or perhaps they were simply tired of working themselves into the ground, but – eventually – they agreed, and Evie was hired to help them evolve their image and preserve their legacy.

FORCED IN THE FIRE

2

___

FORGED IN THE FIRE

With every change they made, more and more dissent had grown amongst their customers. Evie had completely rebranded the restaurant, turning it from a light and airy bakery into a rich and exotic – albeit small – restaurant. She assured Garth that the exclusivity meant they could put their prices up.

The walls were draped in rich, dark fabrics that slinked down the walls like snake scales. Even the tables were arranged with a sleek, serpentine elegance. She'd demanded they use more spices in the menu, as well as introduce a signature dish. Apples, she recommended to them. They were all the rage in the mortal realm right now.

And Garth, like a fool, had followed her every word.

The problem was, everything she suggested sounded so convincing at first. The new decor *did* add a touch of mystique and allure. The new menu *did* showcase that his family could do more than just bake. The introduction of a bar stocked with alcohol was appealing. Once all those changes had been made, Garth had even (at Evie's request) hired a waitress outside of the family to change their image from family-only – to make them look more professional.

Yet, slowly but surely and day by day, fewer customers came.

He hadn't known the story that was playing out in the Western mortal realm. He hadn't known the Abrahamic god had made his mark; that some had turned from the Greek gods already. He hadn't known snakes and apples were not a good look.

The changes had happened so quickly, the loyal customers they *did* have at Zeus' Watering Hole were bewildered and dissatisfied. Evie had helped Garth inadvertently turn this place into a spectacle, showcasing all the worst things people believed about his kind, when the original concept had had plenty of familiar charm.

It was only once the change was complete that Garth saw it.

The fire of 250 BC had been the end of it.

There had been a chill in the air that night, as if Hades was angry his Perspehone had been away so long. Frost had glinted off the blades of grass outside and fog had misted on the windows of Zeus' Watering Hole.

It had been a dumb name, but one the God of Gods had insisted on. Garth had also insisted it be kept when Evie had petulantly stomped her foot demanding it be changed. Perhaps that was when Garth had known the beginning of the end was coming. Keeping the name was also probably the only good marketing decision he had made. Garth had eventually realised that the initial driver for all the customers was the rumour that Zeus had come to eat and drink here.

The fog on the windows had stopped him seeing the flickering torches of the frustrated Souls barrelling towards the pub. If there hadn't been fog, he would have seen that there were some disgruntled patrons in the crowd, but that it was largely made up of new Souls, and led by ... Evie.

The murmurs and rumblings grew until Garth had stepped towards the door to see what all the commotion was outside of their empty restaurant. That's when something had been thrown through the window. Garth looked down and saw on the floor a stone with something etched into it. He bent down to pick it up for a closer look.

The etching was an apple, with one word written in it – *coercers*.

"Slither away to shadows, return to your unseen burrows! Slither away to shadows, return to your unseen burrows! Slither away to shadows, return to your unseen burrows!"

Windows began to rattle as the mob pounded on the door. Garth turned to look at his family behind him. His mother had lost all the colouring in her scales, and his grandfather looked visibly frightened. Both Gigi and Yiorgos had their lips thinned, but even Garth noticed their limbs trembling as they held each other's hands. They had lived too long to be strong enough to put up with a full-on ambush.

It was all his fault. He had done this; convinced them they needed to change, all because he'd been blindly in love with a pretty Soul. His attempt to modernise the business, to help his family, had alienated the community that had supported them for decades. And now, it made them easy game for the Souls at the door that clearly didn't want them here.

The banging got increasingly louder until one of the torches turned into a projectile and crashed through another window, setting an upholstered chair ablaze. The heavy wall drapings caught next. It wasn't long before the whole place was filled with the scent of burning wood and smoke.

Ushering his family out through the back kitchen, they stood and watched from the back courtyard as the whole place lit up the night sky.

At least his newest recruit, that waitress Nika, wasn't on shift tonight, Garth thought to himself. They could deal with this as a family.

But, by the time the water nymphs' fire unit arrived, it was too late to salvage the once charming establishment that had been theirs. The burnt remnants of the bakery and the look in each family member's eyes said life was never going to be the same. When Garth looked around at the mob who had stayed to watch and caught Evie's eyes, she'd winked at him before turning back to the crowd who had quietened to murmurs now that their anger had been alleviated. Garth knew he'd never trust another female Soul again.

HIS WHOLE FAMILY had decided to drink from the river Lethe.

"You don't have to do this," Garth said.

"We have already been chased from our home once, my darling boy. We do not want to do it again," his mother told him, cupping his face, her eyes shining with tears.

"You can't leave me here alone," he tried again.

It had been a conversation – an argument – they'd had several times over the past month. But, no matter which tactic Garth tried, none of his family members would budge on their stance.

"You can come with us."

Already, Garth was shaking his head. "I'm not *done*. I can't leave my life like ... that."

"I understand."

"Then why won't you stay?"

"For the same reason you must."

His mother was the spokesperson for all of them, who one by one came to kiss him goodbye outside the charred remains of their hopes and dreams. They'd not been able to live in this place since the fire, but now had come back with Garth to say goodbye one last time. Even his Gigi, who as a youngling he thought had an uncrackable shell, shed a tear as she held his face and said nothing and pressed a gentle kiss to his lips.

The only one who stayed by his side was Nika.

Once his family's retreating forms were out of sight, and his heaving sobs that Nika had politely ignored had eventually subsided, Garth took three deep breaths and squared his shoulders. Together, they then both turned to survey the wreckage.

"So, what now?"

Garth crossed his arms. "Now, we rebuild."

It took an entire year of work to rebuild the restaurant from the ground up, and every token he'd earned and his family had given him, but eventually Zeus' Watering Hole stood proudly again, at one of the crossroads of Philoxenía Lane and Móuro Avenue.

The fire had been a blessing in some ways. It had allowed Garth to build from the foundations up, adding the conservatory for Meliae tree nymphs, the upstairs for private parties, and the nook for lovers. He'd even extended the bar so that it moved all the way to the door with proper hardwood flooring this time, not the engineered wood flooring they had before. All of Evie's – if that was her real name – changes had been replaced. To his own surprise, Garth didn't just recreate the bakery, either. Instead he made the restaurant his own design, one that he knew would appeal to every faction of creature. He worked on it day and night, for a year, to crush the voice in his head that said it had all been for nothing.

He knew what had worked in the past: get to know what the customers want and show them you can give it to them. *This time, just don't listen to a snake-in-the-grass disguised as a Soul woman pretending to give a damn*, he told himself.

"Hello? Hades' hellhounds to Garth! Are you even listening to a word I'm saying? No, of course you're not! Have you even thought about how you are going to handle the véα backlash when the theme and signature dish of this Vraveío Astéri is The Kallistē Clash?"

"Huh?"

Present-day Nika scowled across the table at him, though there was no ageing for creatures like her, no extra wrinkles in the furrow of her perfectly manicured brows or at the turned-down corners of her lips as she scowled at him once again.

They were at one of those little cafes still open along the avenue. There weren't as many food joints as there had been when he'd last sat at this exact table (when he'd first seen Evie), but he was pleased this place had lasted through the centuries. It served the best duck ragu in Asphodel.

Now roused from his thoughts by Nika's voice, he looked at her face. "What are you scowling at me for?"

"You do know what The Kallistē Clash is, right?"

Garth rubbed the back of his neck, his scales shimmering in the sunlight. "Should I?"

"It's apples, you absolute cretin. How are we going to win with apples after what happened five centuries ago?"

"Five centuries is a long time, Nika. Even here in the Underworld," Garth murmured as something caught his eye.

Nika scoffed. "Five centuries pass in the blink of an eye for us. What are you—?" She turned her head sharply to see what he was looking at. "Oh no, don't you even think about it, Garth. What is *wrong* with you?"

Garth tore his gaze away and looked into Nika's narrowed eyes which she'd turned back on him.

Immediately, a pang of guilt washed over him, as it always did when it came to Nika. At first, he'd thought it was because she was an Arae. He'd never come into contact with one before her, and after she'd explained why creatures cowered in her presence, he figured the guilt must have been a consequence of some promise he had broken as a youngling in the mortal realm.

But, then he realised it wasn't that, as he'd never broken a promise. Hell, he'd spent the past centuries proving that by putting all his blood, sweat, and tears into the rebuilding of his family's legacy, and with every movement he had promised that he would never let them down again.

No; the guilt he felt towards Nika was because he hadn't hired her for the right reasons. He'd hired her because Evie had told him to hire *someone* – *anyone* – that wasn't a family member. He'd seen Nika the first night she'd entered the place, watching him serve the customers with a yearning in her eye, like she wanted to try it, like she'd be good at it. And she had been. But, to Garth, she was just another thing

Evie had requested. That was why Garth felt guilty, because that was always the first thought he had of Nika, even though she had stuck by his side through it all.

Nika had even warned him – several times – that Evie wasn't who she said she was; that there were shadows in her eyes that haunted her. If he'd known more about Araes then, that the tug to get her to confess to her crimes Nika talked about wasn't just hyperbolic or jealousy, he'd have heeded Nika's warning.

In the aftermath, however, not only had Nika helped him rebuild from the smoulders and then stayed out of loyalty to him for giving her a chance, she herself had chased that horrible viper of a female Soul to the Plains of Judgement like a banshee. Garth wouldn't be at all surprised to learn that Nika had driven Evie into a garden and locked her in there. She had despised Evie in the same way he did. Perhaps moreso.

Yet, here he was, sitting at the exact same table he had when he'd seen Evie, ignoring Nika's warning once again. Instead, he was enamoured with the small, curvy little creature across the lane who was sniffing flowers outside one of Queen Persephone's florists teeming with flowers spilling out the door. He was captivated by the way she laughed as the shop assistant said something to her; at the way her whole body seemed to ripple as she took a deep inhale of the flower's scent.

"Fuck," Garth muttered under his breath.

"What was that?" Nika shot back.

"Nothing."

Still, Garth continued watching the little Arae that looked like sunshine. He knew who she was – the baker Geras had hired her at his grubby bistro the year after the fire. He knew too that she must be good at her job, because

Zeus' Watering Hole had been losing its Sunday lunch customers to her ever since. It was the only day of the week he held a lunch service – in honour of his family. He was desperate to see her work in action after tasting her food, and equally loath to find himself interested in pursuing another female after he swore he would never do so again. At least, he thought, the sunshiney baker wasn't a Soul but an Arae, which meant somewhere along the way she was the same bloodline as Nika. And Nika had always been good for business.

3

ONE YEAR LATER

Garth and Nika had had their share of fights, but — admittedly — the one where he had threatened to fire her had been particularly bad. Cutting Zeus out of the libation tax deal had been stressful on all of the team, but Nika had borne the brunt of it from Garth simply because he knew she could.

Thank the gods that Nika came up with that plan of hers. Okay, so now her mother, Nyx, was attached to The Watering Hole, but the only thing she had asked for was Nika's share of the tokens in the restaurant to increase significantly and for her daughter to never know that her mother had arranged it. Oh, and the name change. Given that Garth was going to offer that to Nika anyway for saving his hide *again*, and he was more than happy to remove Zeus' name from the establishment, it had been the easiest thing in the Underworld to agree to.

In saying that, during the time Nika had been away finding a solution to their problems, life at The Watering Hole had been *cheerful*. Sure, they were certainly all overworked and tired, but they were all family. They made a game out of stressful night shifts by passing corks between each other's aprons. One cork had 'winner' written on it, the other 'loser'. Whoever had the winning cork in their apron at the end of the night got to get the loser to do whatever they wanted. More often than not, the loser ended up dancing on the tables once all the patrons were gone, singing horrible renditions of bard favourites.

Also, Rae had seemed to come out of her shell a little more while Nika had been away. Sure, she still wasn't comfortable enough around the team to get up on the tables and dance, but Garth watched the way she had little interactions with everyone. She and Savvas had bonded over his wine, the Head Bartender grateful that anyone cared enough to ask about his process. Obviously, Melamene and Rae had forged a friendship over pastry already. Even Yani and Lexie, who tended to stick to themselves, gave Rae a gentle ribbing in the kitchen when she seemed stressed, until they had her bending over with bellyful laughter.

During the past year, Garth had alternated between giving Rae her space in the kitchen and not being able to stay away from her. Sometimes, his loathing for females (informed by past experience, of course) would rear its ugly head. When that happened, his sense of self-preservation would kick in and he'd run the kitchen like a tight ship, then grumble his way upstairs to manage the books. But, the minute he saw any one of the team getting Rae to smile that sunshine smile of hers, he found himself right back by her side, desperate to know what had put it there, how he could do it himself, and offering to walk her home to keep her safe. She'd smile a smaller, shyer smile at him or roll her eyes – depending on her mood and his behaviour earlier in the day – but would often take him up on his offer, until eventually, they found themselves in a little rhythm of their own.

He'd even let Rae change the menu on Sundays and incorporated some of the dishes that had made her bakery so famous: the fritters, the fig and goat filo pastries, the sweet and savoury sausage rolls, the lavender meringues, and, of course, the ambrosia dish. When Nika found out about it before she left, she blew a valve, ranting and raving at Garth as he sat back in his office chair while she gestured around him wildly, throwing her hands about to reiterate her point. She didn't need to, though; Garth knew why Nika was worried. She saw the change as the first sign of trouble, that he was going to do the same thing with Rae that he had done with Evie, but Garth knew he wasn't doing that. Rae's changes had lunch services on Sundays back up and running. It made his cold heart swell with pride. Then he'd think of his mother, his grandfather, and his great-great-grandparents, and the sadness of their existence would deflate it.

His mother would have loved Sunshine's dishes.

He told Rae as much one night while they were walking home.

The air was cool, the wind nymphs tired but still slowly making their way through the branches overhead as the leaves rustled and fell, the edges of them a burnished orange as if the trees lamented that Queen Persephone had returned to the mortal realm once again. Conkers littered the cobblestone streets and Garth kicked one that bounced down the path in front of them as Rae spoke.

Rae continued wringing her hands. "But, if Nika still isn't happy with the changes, even though we've been doing them for three months now ... she *is* the one who sells the menu to the customer ... we should really get her on board. She already doesn't like me and I'd really rather not upset the balance any further."

"Customers come because they want to try the food, *all* the food. Having new things on the menu is good for business, no matter what Nika thinks."

"But—"

Garth stopped them in their tracks, and turned Rae towards him with his hands on her shoulders. He used the crook of his index finger to tip her chin up towards him so he could look at her in those big, beautiful, pale blue eyes.

"You don't need to worry about Nika, Sunshine. She's just trying to protect me."

Rae's expression morphed into puzzlement.

"Why would a daemon like you need protection?"

He wasn't ready to tell her the whole truth, not yet, so he settled on a smaller one. "Because you cook like my mother used to, and we weren't exactly profitable back then." It was a tiny lie, just to hide his shame a little bit longer. "Nika doesn't want us to go back to that, that's all."

"Well, *I* don't want you to go backwards, either! I don't want you to risk it on me!"

Garth laughed. "Sunshine, you put us out of lunch business when you were working at the bistro, remember? Having your stuff on our menu is one of the surest bets I can make. Nika will drop her defensive attitude eventually, just you wait and see."

Garth was grateful that Rae was concentrating on Nika's defensiveness, for he found himself needing to protect *his* heart when it came to her. After Nika had returned with Orpheus and Eurydice in tow, when they had begun to play at the pub regularly, Garth felt a tug to just go and be around his Sunshine, who the whole team (sans Nika) adored.

It wasn't hard to adore her. The last sous chef had been a drill sergeant with three heads – one of the Chimera family – and the team had hated him for his lazy, entitled arrogance until Garth had threatened to dispose of one of those heads. The chef had been one of the only hires out of necessity since Lexie and Yani had replaced their counterparts, and it showed. The rest of the team were a family, something Garth had been incredibly proud to cultivate. They had all come to him with no family to rely on, just like he had, with sadness in their eyes that said they just needed another chance, just *one* more chance to make it. That's why he took them in. That's why they never left.

It's why those hired out of necessity never lasted in their family.

It's why Rae was such a perfect fit for him; for them.

She seemed to love everyone in the team, too. All except Garth, that was, and despite his best preservation instincts, he wanted to find out why. Dionysus' party seemed like a perfect time to ask.

The desserts had been served along the tables that were currently placed together to make long banquet-like trestles and covered in thick cream tablecloths, decorated with gold cutlery and wine goblets that had a band of gold across the lips of them. Vines were the centrepieces running along the tables, occasionally broken up with clusters of long-stemmed candles. Alternating along the table were Rae's Ambrosia Crème Brûlée bowls and dainty spoons of Pomegranate Delight. If one were to look at the tables from a birds eye view, the desserts would look like grape clusters running along the vine centrepieces – jewels of the evening to accompany Savvas' Wine of Old.

Through the gauze of whites and all hues of purple that hung from the rafters, Garth spotted Rae heading back out to the doorstep of the garden conservatory, sipping away at one of the frothy pink drinks that Savvas had made.

Smiling, Garth made his way through Dinoysus' guests mingling around the tables, and the merry dancers, before knocking on the back of the glass door.

Startled, Rae turned to him and then shifted forward slightly so he could open the door. She hiccuped as he sat down on the stone step beside her.

"How are Savvas' cocktails?" Garth grinned.

Rae pulled a face as she took another sip from the martini glass. "Not as good as his wine, I'm afraid. They're sweet ... and that's coming from me."

"It sure is."

Rae blushed and looked away, much to Garth's relief. He hadn't intended to say that out loud.

"Can I try it?"

Rae offered him a small smile and handed the glass over. Garth practically choked on the cloying flavours that attacked the slits that were his nostrils *and* his taste buds.

"Dear gods, what was he thinking?"

Rae laughed then, one of those tinkling laughs that sounded like a thousand different little bells, one that always made Garth whip his head round to look at her when he heard it on any given day.

"I think he was more concerned about the wine," she answered.

"He should leave the sweets to you and Melamene," Garth grumbled as he handed the glass back over and Rae drained the rest of it, much to his surprise. "Although it looks like you might like them after all ..."

It was then that he saw the two other empty glasses by Rae's feet. Raising an eyebrow, Garth knew this was it. This was his chance to get Rae's honest thoughts on him. It was cunning, to use such an opportunity, but Garth had always been that way. He wasn't ashamed of it.

"Personally, the only sweet thing I've enjoyed tonight has been your new ambrosia," he continued.

"Yeah?"

"Yeah," he said softly, and was rewarded with one of her smiles. The one that made her eyes twinkle, and the receiver feel a warm glow spread throughout their body like honey.

Garth realised in that moment that he didn't want anyone else to have that feeling. He wanted to bottle it and selfishly keep it for himself.

"Are you happy with how the crème brûlée version turned out?" he asked.

Rae sighed, and Garth felt that warm honey glow flush right out of him. It was he who'd suggested they tinker with the recipe. If she didn't like it ...

"Don't get me wrong – I am happy. It's great.. I just—"

"What?"

"I miss my bakery sometimes. I miss the simplicity of it compared to the extravagance we bring to the dishes now. Every time I feel like I've just got to grips with the job, an event like this comes along," Rae waved to the carnage behind them, the sound of the revellers at least tempered by the thick glass of the conservatory, "and all over again, I feel like I'm barely treading water."

Garth took a deep breath, steeling himself for the question he was about to ask, and for the answers it might bring.

"Is that why you don't like me? Because I took you away from your bakery? Or because I push the team too hard?"

"Oh, no!" Rae's hand flew out to rest on his scaled forearm, the cords of his veins bulging at the *zing* that flew through him again at her touch. "I didn't mean for you to think that I'm not grateful, or that I don't like you. I agreed to join, and I don't regret it. It's just, well … sometimes I don't feel good enough to be here. It's intimidating – the history of it all."

It wasn't him she had a problem with, Garth realised. It was everything that came with him.

He gingerly put his other hand on top of hers, letting it rest there gently. "It's just a pub, Rae. Just a place. It's the people that make it. But, in the end, even people leave." Garth swallowed the lump forming in his throat. "And this could all cease to exist."

He watched her stare at their hands for a moment, his teal scales above her translucent skin, before she pulled her hand back and sandwiched it with her other between her thighs.

"I know you're right," she sighed. "Did you know my original goal was to buy Geras out of the bakery when I won the competition? That's what I was going to use the tokens for. But, Geras went back on our bargain and sold it before I had so much as a chance to put in a counter offer. Now, it's sitting there, at the end of the lane with a damn Olympic investor not doing anything with it, because they don't know tipota about how to run a bakery down here!"

"You really miss it, huh?"

To Garth's surprise, Rae considered her response. This was as honest and open, as raw and vulnerable, as he had seen her since the first time she had yelled at him two years ago at the last cook-off. He found himself craving more. She was just like her food – a sweetness he couldn't get enough of.

"I don't miss how lonely it was, but I do miss having something that I could control. In a way, it was mine."

Garth didn't know if it was the statement itself, or the way Rae had said it, but it had some sort of determination settling in his bones. It felt as it had when his family had left – that he had to do *something* to right the injustice of everything Rae had been through, just like them. For the first time since then, he felt the feeling again. For Rae. For what she felt she was missing.

"I used to be so cross with you," she admitted. "I would threaten curses under my breath when I was rolling out pastry or doing a particularly complicated lattice, that you didn't appreciate what the libations tax got you, how much easier it was for you, how privileged you were winning those competitions every century. But, then I came here, and I saw how hard you work – for this place, for the team – and now I feel guilty I ever had those thoughts. I don't think you push the team too hard. I think I was too harsh on you, and so now I avoid you, because you don't deserve that."

He hadn't been expecting an answer to his original question after her first revelation, but the fact that his Sunshine seemed so grumpy with herself was almost comical. For such a sweet, tiny creature, her anger was like a pent-up rubber bouncy ball that he just wanted to play with. The fact that she had acknowledged how hard he worked and that he was deserving of his success made him realise how unlike Evie she really was. Even Rae's anger would never be an insidious thing, but a multi-coloured explosion that would probably make him laugh *and* want to strive to be even better than they currently were.

Garth really wanted to kiss her.

Then Rae hiccuped again, and he remembered that he had only received the unvarnished, impolite truth from his Sunshine because she'd had one too many once her shift had ended. He wanted to find a way to get that unvarnished, pure version of her every time they spoke.

He wanted the real Sunshine, so he was going to find a way to give her what she wanted – something of her own. Maybe then, she'd give him what he wanted in turn.

4

GIGI'S SPECIAL SOUP

"I want you to run the Sunday lunchtime shift."

Rae stared at him, her mouth agape like the fish on Yani's workbench currently being filleted with precision by the water nymph as they all prepared for said lunch service. "You can't be serious."

"As a snake in the Garden of Eden," Garth winked.

Rae went to whack him with a tea towel. "That is *not* a funny joke."

She didn't know his history, of course. No one in the team but Nika knew.

"That's why I'm not joking," he reasoned with her, leaning against the workbench by the pass, his hands braced on the metal frame behind him. He knew she liked it when he *leaned* – the tips of her ears went pink.

"You're telling me, two hours before we open the doors, that you want *me* to run the service?"

Garth shrugged. "What's the big deal? You used to run all the services by yourself at Geras' Grub less than two years ago."

"But, that was a cafe, a bakery – most people just

ordered to-go!" Rae blustered.

"Practically half the menu we have today is yours, we've done the dishes a thousand times, you know how a service runs here like clockwork, and I'll be here if you absolutely need me," Garth responded calmly. Then, he leaned toward her and whispered the next part so no one else in the kitchen would hear.

Well, perhaps Lexie would, but he was counting on her discretion.

"It's time for you to own it, Sunshine. To have something that is yours again."

Garth didn't know if she remembered their conversation from a fortnight past, about her wanting something of her own, but he figured this was the best place to start. Last Sunday he had done a sneaky trial run, giving Yani an extra day off (claiming he was sick) and cooking in his stead, while leaving Rae to navigate most of the pass by herself.

She'd pulled herself up by the bootstraps – as new Souls were heard saying now – and ran the service perfectly with no hiccups at all. The only other creature who had known it was a test was Lexie. Given how close she and Yani were, she knew he wasn't sick, but hadn't said anything when Garth announced they'd be a chef down for the day. Lexie hadn't pulled any punches either, leaving Rae to serve and dish up the precious cuts of meat as she saw fit. To his surprise, Garth swore he'd seen Lexie watching over Rae's shoulder and raised a thin eyebrow in approval.

She was ready, even if she didn't think she was.

"Fine," his Rae-of-Sunshine said, blowing at her pearl-white curls that had escaped her plait and stuck to the side of her face as the kitchen temperature began to climb. "I'll do it. But if this goes wrong, Garth!" She held up a finger threateningly.

"You'll what? Poke me with that tiny finger of yours?"

To his surprise, again – and to be surprised twice in two weeks was startlingly rare for him – Rae stepped forward and poked him in the chest with her tiny, ineffectual finger.

"I will hound you across Asphodel Meadows until every last Soul, daemon, and deity knows that you are a horrible boss!"

Garth simply smiled.

OF COURSE, the Sunday lunch service had gone off without a hitch.

So, he had Rae run another one; then another. Then, he moved her to weekday lunches at least three times a week *and* the Sunday service. After that, he moved her to running early-week dinner services. She'd panicked a little again at that one, but he'd been in the kitchen the entire time. He'd been working on the books on the server's bench because she hadn't needed him at all, but he was still there – just in case.

She was ready.

The entire team agreed she was ready. Hell, Lexie had even told Garth in front of all the kitchen staff that she preferred when Rae led the pass, and they had all agreed. If it hadn't put the biggest bounce in Sunshine's step, he would have scowled at them all for being traitors. As it was, he had never seen Rae so happy, so confident, so free.

So, that was the reason he'd invited Rae around for dinner. The pub was closed on Sundays after the lunch shift, so it didn't seem suspicious that they were both off work. He had lured her to his place under the pretence that he wanted to try out a new dish and was in need of her expertise.

Garth had found that flattering a female over things she cared about could get a male a lot of places.

But, as he'd looked around his small apartment housed above the pub and adjacent to the small staff room and office on the second floor, separated from the upstairs dining area only by doors that said 'No entry' and a lock on what could be considered his front door, Garth knew he was going to have to spruce the place up.

It was all dark greens and blues and blacks – perfect for a bachelor pad. Not so good, though, if he was trying to build up the courage to ask the sweetest creature he'd ever seen to take a chance on him; on herself; on them. He was, however, particularly proud of the kitchen with its green tile splashback, black marble flooring, and white marble countertops. He hoped Rae would enjoy cooking in it.

As for the rest of the place ... well, that's how Garth had found himself at the farmers' market the day before, while the rest of the team were prepping for the busiest dinner service of the week.

He'd taken the opportunity to look at all the flowers he knew Rae would like: posies, bunches of daisies, three pink peonies that were about to bloom. They were all from Queen Persephone's stand, but none of them really stood out to him. He'd then wandered over to the stand selling exotic plants and wildflowers ... but again, hadn't found anything that could convey the feeling he was trying to capture.

Then, as if the Fates themselves had had a hand in it, he found Irid and her admittedly pathetic-looking stand, and those intriguing flowers that floated in water bowls that *smelled* like ... *something*. Garth just couldn't tell what.

After Irid had stopped being her prickly, defensive self (Garth had witnessed this tactic all too often in up-and-coming chefs who treated their dishes as the most precious creations, which was why he took no offence) and actually explained what the flowers did, Garth was enraptured.

To his further surprise, he found himself drawn to the one that smelled like apples.

Curious.

"And this one?" he had asked Irid. "The one that smells like apples?"

"Oh, the green hellebore?"

"Yes, what does this do?"

"It makes whomever owns it feel like they're unstoppable. Like the gods themselves could not stop them in their quest."

That was what Garth needed – not only to boost his own courage, but also to help convince Rae to agree to take on the final challenge of running a nighttime dinner shift on Saturday, the busiest night of the week, every week. If she could do that (a task he had never given any of his staff since he rebuilt The Watering Hole), then he could name her his successor if there was ever any cause or reason he couldn't do his duties.

It was as close to giving her something of her own as he could manage, without sacrificing everything he'd worked for, as he once had before.

"Sold."

Now, the plant sat on the dark, square, wooden coffee table in the middle of the small living room, tealight candles scattered all around it. Rae was due any minute.

Simmering on the stove was Garth's Avgolemono soup,

something he remembered Gigi making for him once as a youngling – a delicious and comforting lemony chicken soup, thickened with eggs. Except, Garth could never get the egg and lemon mixture right. The first time he tried, he had added it all at once and the eggs had curdled. The following time, he had forgotten to skim off the foam that had risen to the top of the broth and it had made the mixture do a strange thing. One time, he hadn't whisked constantly but sparingly, and again, the egg mixture hadn't taken. Frustrated after the third failed attempt, he'd given up making it. He was not often guilty of quitting, but there was something about not being able to turn to his Gigi and ask her to show him how, that had been too painful to consciously address.

But, his Sunshine had a temperance that could temper anything, and with her pastry skills, he bet she'd be able to read Gigi's scrawled writing in the battered orange cookbook he had opened on the bench, and be able to make a go of it.

There was a knock on the door.

In three short strides, he was swinging the door open to see Rae in a lilac-coloured dress toga decorated with daisies along the edges. It flattered her fuller figure, whilst a white cardigan curled over her shoulders.

He should have gone with the daisies.

Her hair was artfully swished over one shoulder and she'd put kohl across her eyelashes, which emphasised a sprinkling of freckles over her cheekbones. She blinked up at him, a friendly smile on her small lips.

She was beautiful.

"I brought dessert," she said, holding up a container made of clear palladium. Inside were pomegranate tarts and individual soft lemon sponges.

"Oh, uh, come in. You can put them on the bench or there's room in the fridge. Whichever you prefer," Garth offered, eventually managing to find two brain cells to rub together.

Rae stepped inside, glancing around at the kitchen behind him, the living room to her right. He saw her spy the flower and found himself holding in a breath, waiting for her reaction. But, Rae's attention had already turned back to the kitchen.

"Wow," she breathed, almost gliding towards it as she passed him, placed the container against the splashback away from the heat, and then ran her hands along the bench. "Why do you ever bother to come downstairs and cook with us when you have this space up here?"

Garth thought she was joking, until she turned to look at him.

He chuckled, moving through the open-plan space to join her in the kitchen. "Because, I like cooking for others more than I like cooking for myself."

"Me too," Rae admitted, as she stood on tiptoes and peered at the soup bubbling away on the stove.

The lid let out a burp.

"Well, pardon you," Rae admonished.

If he wasn't already infatuated with her, the way Sunshine spoke to the sentient utensils and needed to go on her tippy-toes to see over the whole stove would have done it. A grin, as wide as the one he used to have when he was a youngling wrapping treats in brown paper beside his mother, broke out across his face.

"What?" Rae asked him with a questioning look when she'd turned over her shoulder to glance at him.

"Nothing."

The curious look remained on her face for a moment

before Rae turned back to the pot. "So, then, where exactly are you having trouble with this recipe?"

"It's the egg and lemon mixture." Garth pointed to the bowl which held the mixture he'd already made, and then at the recipe. "Gigi said to add it into the soup mix, consistently whisking as you add in the mixture. But, she doesn't say if it's a ladle at a time, or slowly and steadily, whether to add it before or after the orzo, and I just can't get it right. Any ideas?"

Rae shrugged off her cardigan, placing it over one of the chairs against the small, round dining table that was neatly set for dinner for two. Then, she turned and examined Gigi's cookbook, following each line of scrawled instruction with her index finger.

"I'd say add the orzo after you remove the chicken, but before the egg and lemon mixture. Then add the mixture one ladle at a time, but reduce the heat so it doesn't start to boil. Egg mixes need to be warm rather than hot, in my experience."

Garth nodded. His mother would despair at his baking skills now, but it had been centuries of focusing on restaurant-quality dishes. Those little tricks that only pastry chefs and bakers seemed to know had eroded from somewhere in the recesses of his mind.

"You want to give it a go, while I pour us a couple of glasses of Savvas' wine?" Garth asked.

"You managed to get some of the latest batch from him?"

Garth shrugged. "He wanted a taste-tester."

Rae pinned him with a look and desperately tried not to smile, as she stood over the stove holding a wooden spoon poised in the air. She knew it wasn't true; he could see it on her face.

"You threatened to take his job away, didn't you?"

Garth scoffed. If only she knew his history. "I'd never do that."

"You did something."

"I may have threatened to offer Dionysus a deal on all future parties he hosts at The Watering Hole."

Rae gasped. "Knowing how they ended things? You are the worst, Garthriel."

Garth stopped mid-pour and stared at her. No one had called him that in the longest time.

"How did you know my full name?" He cocked his head at her, suddenly wary.

But, this was his Sunshine, and one of the things he'd always loved about her – even before they were colleagues – was that her brightness had always held a bite to it.

"You're not the only one that can get things they want out of others," she shrugged.

"Who told you?" Garth asked quietly, a wry smile on his face as he stepped to fill the space between them. Rae had to tip her head back to maintain eye contact, a playful glint in her eye.

"Nika," she whispered.

"In exchange for?"

"Wanting to know what we were doing tonight."

She'd sought out personal information about him, and she'd come here tonight looking like a godsdamn fairytale. Perhaps, Irid's flower was already working. Or, perhaps – just perhaps – Rae felt the same way he did.

Slowly, Garth lowered his head, his neck uncoiling until his lips were an inch from Sunshine's. Then, slowly, so slowly – mainly so as not to spook her, or to move away if Rae showed any sign of pulling back – Garth sunk his pointed canine teeth into her lips and bit, gently.

Rae jumped, clearly startled.

"That, my Rae-of-Sunshine, was for ever thinking you needed to exchange information in order to get to know me better. You can do that all by yourself. And this ..." The second kiss he pressed to her plump lips was softer, more delicate. "Is to thank you for agreeing to come tonight."

Gods, that feeling-flower bobbing away on the other side of the room really was overwhelming.

Rae stood there blinking for a few moments, that blush he loved spread across her cheeks. "Wel— ... you— ... you're welcome."

Then, she turned back to the stove, put the wooden spoon in the pot, stirred once, picked up the bowl of egg and lemon mixture, realised she needed a whisk, put the bowl down again, took the wooden spoon out of the pot, looked around for a whisk (which Garth provided by smoothly opening the utensil drawer), and began furiously whisking the mixture into the soup.

"Anything I can do to help?" he asked, unsure at her sudden change in demeanour.

"You can chop the parsley and shred the chicken that made this stock."

"Here?" He gestured to the clean bench beside her. "Or there?" he asked, pointing to the far end of the bench.

"Here is just fine," she said softly.

Garth felt that warm honey glow he could only ever associate with Sunshine pool in his stomach. She wasn't mad that he had kissed her, he realised. She just needed a moment to process. That was all.

Together, they worked in companionable silence, their arms occasionally brushing as Rae finished thickening the soup and Garth chopped the parsley and shredded the chicken.

5

THE ONLY WAY IS THROUGH IT

She'd kissed him next, once they'd finished with dinner, done the dishes together in quiet harmony, and were sitting on his couch with her desserts. They'd kept to quiet conversation, mainly around the food and restaurant, and Garth was just about to compliment Rae on the fact the lemon sponges weren't dry at all, and try to push – in that way of his – for her to reveal the secret of how she did it, when she'd darted forward and kissed him with the softest lips he'd ever known.

He'd groaned in the back of his throat and it had taken him all of two seconds to grip her around the thighs and shift her onto his lap.

She pulled back. "I'm too heavy!" she protested, pushing her hands against his shoulders.

Garth had scoffed and muttered, "No, you're not," and slid his hands into her hair for another kiss.

He had always loved Sunshine's curves. Where his body was all scales and sinewy muscle, she was soft and warm. Her breasts – pressed against his chest – were full, and her hips curved perfectly to the shape of his hands.

Eventually, she pulled back again.

"We can't do this! We're ... colleagues!"

"We've been many things over the centuries, Sunshine. Neighbours, rivals ... but we've never been just colleagues." He touched his forehead to hers.

He knew immediately when Rae went to shake her head, and interrupted before he could hear the rebuttal on her lips.

"I want you to run next Saturday night's service in my sted," Garth whispered, his hands still resting underneath the edge of her dress, on her warm thighs.

Rae sat back, audibly gulped, and slid off his lap. "But, you never let anyone run a Saturday night shift."

"Except you." *Because they were more than colleagues. She had to know that.*

Garth's eyes flickered over Rae's shoulder, to the hellebore sitting on the table, floating in its pool of Irid's magic. *Please don't let it only work just once*, he thought to himself.

At that moment, it seemed to glow just a little bit brighter as he heard Rae say, "Alright, then. I'll do it."

"You will?"

The bolstered confidence with which she'd agreed flickered, casting doubt across her face.

"That's not to say I'm not nervous about it, but you'll be there if I need you, won't you?"

"Of course, but you're going to do great."

THEY HAD two hundred and seventy 'covers' that night, meaning that two hundred and seventy Souls, creatures, daemons, and a few deities would walk through those doors and sit for their dinner. Not all of them at once, of course. The Watering Hole could only hold one hundred and fifty at a time, but Nika and Tomas, along with the rest of the wait staff, would 'turn' the tables, meaning there was one sitting at six o'clock and another at eight o'clock, with each table assigned a party of creatures. Some would come earlier, some would come later, but Nika was a whizz at making sure any early or late arrivals were accommodated. Often, she was able to squeeze in some walk-ins, too.

Two hundred and seventy covers wasn't the most they had ever served in one night, but one thing was for certain: Rae was going to be busy until the very last order.

As promised, Garth was her right-hand, her sous chef for the evening, and there was something delightfully novel about taking on the supporting role that had Garth feeling calm about tonight.

Rae, on the other hand, was a tense ball of nerves. She had snapped at Melamene – her best friend in and out of the kitchen – when they were preparing for service earlier, and everyone had given her a wide berth for the rest of the afternoon. Eventually, Garth had taken Rae outside.

"You're going to have to give a briefing before service starts, get the team onside."

Rae's eyes widened in panic. "I thought you were going to do that."

"I do – when I'm running the show. But, tonight it's your turn, and all of them in there are already treating you with youngling gloves." He nodded towards the staff door that led into the back entrance of the kitchen.

"But, I don't know how to—"

"Yes, you do." Garth turned Rae gently by her shoulders and pushed her towards the door. He considered tapping her bum – the cheekiness of it would undoubtedly spur Rae into action (even if that action was to be furiously indignant with him) – but decided against it at the last minute as Rae took a deep breath, squared her shoulders, and marched back into the kitchen.

"Everyone, can I get your attention, please?" Garth heard her say as he followed inside.

"I, uh, I just want to thank you for sticking with me tonight ... and thank Garth for this opportunity. It's a huge responsibility and I'm honoured. Actually, I'm a little bit nervous – if you couldn't tell. I don't know if I'm supposed to say that, probably not if I'm supposed to be leading you ..."

A few chuckles sang out from the team at that confession.

"I apologise if I've been a bit on edge today," Rae continued, aiming a pointed look in Melamene's direction, who smiled and gave her a nod of encouragement in return.

"But, stick with me, and let's just do what we always do – create stunning food that makes our guests 'ooh' and 'ahh'."

"Ooh-ahh-ahh," Yani joked.

"Ooh-ahh-ahh," they all chorused in jest.

"Yes, ooh-ahh-ahh," Rae smiled at all of them. "Let's get to it."

Personally, Garth would never have admitted his nerves or apologised. He found that creatures needed a strong, sure, confident leader, but the team had seemed to respond well to it, 'ooh-ahh-ahh' rallying cries and all.

It became the running joke of the evening. Every time Rae called out the items on a ticket that had spluttered through the machine, they replied with "ooh-ahh-ahh" to acknowledge they'd heard her, instead of the usual, "Yes, Chef."

The first round of entrees rolled out, no problem, followed by the first round of mains. Then, the second round of entrees started.

And that's when it all began to fall apart.

It began with a daemon returning their steak. No biggie, it happened. Rae simply asked Lexie for another one and sent it right out. They have a contingency budget in place every night for this exact reason.

The next complained that the oysters weren't fresh enough.

Yani had rolled his eyes at that, muttering under his breath. Garth could see their poissonnier getting more and more visibly annoyed, cursing under his breath, but Rae handled it perfectly, touching the back of Yani's arm gently and murmuring that she agreed with him that the customer was a snob who didn't actually know their ass from their elbow.

The problem with oysters being sent back was, if one customer spotted it, others tended to panic about the quality of the dish, especially if they weren't well-acquainted with fresh seafood. So, a second tray of oysters came back, then a third. It was only three in a dozen dishes, but it was still enough that Yani had to shuck and prepare more oysters – an oversight on his preparation part that then threw off the timings of one of the entrees heading to the pass.

"How long on the ceviche tacos, Yani?" Rae called.

"Two minutes, Chef!" Yani bit back. He was racing now, one of his wet curls of hair having escaped his hat. Garth could feel the stress emanating off him.

"I needed it two minutes ago, Yani!" Rae replied.

"It's coming, *for Hades' sake!*"

When Yani approached the bench, Garth muttered to him, "Watch your language."

The domino effect of waiting for one entree dish to join the rest of them so Rae could send out four tables' worth of orders had a catastrophic impact. From then on, they were all on the back foot, desperately trying to make up time on the entrees while maintaining the constant delivery of mains. Worse, was that desserts from the first round of seating had begun, so Melamene wasn't even able to help them pick up speed on the starters.

"I have table twenty complaining that they've been waiting half an hour for their mains. I cleared their dishes myself. What's going on back there?" Nika said, as she glanced across the pass at Rae and Garth.

"It's coming up now," Rae said sharply, reading the line of tickets that just appeared to be getting longer.

"They aren't happy," Nika warned.

"Well, then, charm them!"

Nika raised an eyebrow at Garth and glided away.

But, as the night went on, even Nika struggled to maintain her composure. It was the most important, and most difficult, part of being the front-of-house go-between. She had to look like she was busy, but not so busy that she was stressed. If she was too calm while guests were impatiently waiting, they'd get annoyed with her. If she was too stressed, they'd feel like a burden and become sheepish.

But, Nika couldn't control the speed at which plates came out of the kitchen. None of them could. It took as long as it took to get the food ready from preparation and onto the plate. Though talented multi-taskers they all were, the team couldn't make up time.

"Are you going to step in?" Rae turned and asked Garth,

when Nika had come back to the pass for the fifth time to say customers were complaining.

Rae's eyes were pleading with him.

He almost caved right then and there. But, that part of him that had always kept his eyes on the long-term goal steeled his spine.

"No, Sunshine. This is yours to handle."

She looked like she was about to cry and it took everything in him not to take the words back, not to hold her, not to take charge and tell her that everything was going to be alright. Because, it would be alright. They would get through it; they always did.

"We've had bad nights like this before, and you've seen what I do. You can do this," he told her.

The tears that had been shimmering on the lips of Rae's eyelids disappeared with furious blinking. *Well*, he thought, *she being mad at him was better than her falling apart here and now.*

And, he wasn't wrong. They did get through it. One by one, each of the remaining entrees, final mains, and two rounds of desserts were dealt with. Nika had comped what she'd needed to, in order to appease the Souls who'd taken the brunt of the evening's wait through no fault of their own or the team's; they'd just arrived at that perfect time between disaster and despair, and had to wait the longest. It happened. Garth had no doubt there would be a disgruntled complaint or two in the νέα the next day, but it wasn't a storm The Watering Hole hadn't weathered before. He'd ask Orpheus and Eurydice nicely if they had any new ballads coming up, to make use of them on one of their performing nights sooner rather than later, and all would be well again.

It wasn't the end of the Underworld.

Still, he wasn't surprised when Rae fled for the back door the minute they were done with cleaning down the kitchen. He followed her into the fresh night air.

"Why?" She rounded on him as soon as he appeared. "Why would you put me through that? Why would you do that to me?"

"It was just a bad night, Sunshine. They happen."

"*Don't* call me that! You don't have the right to call me that. Not after tonight."

"You handled it just fine."

"Handled it?! I wouldn't have had to *handle* it, if you'd stepped in like you promised you would!"

"I said I would be there for you, and I was. I was right beside you. You didn't need me taking the reins. Tonight was about proving yourself."

Rae suddenly eyed him with suspicion. "Proving myself for what?"

He hadn't meant to let it slip. He wasn't going to tell her for a long time. But, given the anger emanating off her in waves, he had no choice.

"If something happens to me, I want you to have this place. I want you to run it – to own it. I want it to be yours."

The beat of silence between them seemed to last for an eternity. When Rae eventually spoke, it wasn't the reaction Garth had been hoping for.

"Don't you think that's something you should have asked me if I *wanted*, first?"

"You said you missed having something that was yours. I was trying to find a way to give it to you."

"I'm not one of your customers, Garth! You can't just dish up dreams you've concocted and say, 'Here you go, this is what you want'."

In that moment, he wished she'd called him Garthriel,

to know that he still had her onside. To know that she could at least see that his intentions had been pure, even if he had gone about it the wrong way and she was presently annoyed with him.

"If we'd had a good night, you would be floating on clouds right now. I've seen how your confidence has grown over the past weeks, how free and happy you've become," he tried to reason.

"It doesn't change the fact you can't give me a dream that isn't mine and mould me into wanting it!"

And that was the crux of the matter. Garth realised a moment too late, as Rae stormed past him and back into the kitchen.

6

AIN'T NO SUNSHINE WHEN
RAE'S AWAY

Not one of the team members would tell him where Rae was. She had told Nika after that disastrous night that she was going home, and had then called in sick every day for a week. Garth had been by her house every night to visit, to make his apologies, but the lights were always out. She wasn't home.

Even if his Sunshine was home, she wouldn't see him. She didn't even call Garth to tell him she was sick. She called Nika instead.

It wouldn't have bothered Garth, if only anyone in the team would just tell him where she was. At first, he had assumed that Rae would be staying with Melamene and her girlfriend in that little cottage of theirs, but when Mel had pointed out that Rae was allergic to cats and couldn't spend more than an afternoon around Haymitch, he'd nixed that idea.

Garth asked Savvas next. He knew the Satyr had a soft spot for Sunshine. But, Savvas only shook his head.

"She's not staying on my vineyard. And even if she was, do you think I would tell you?"

Once they realised what Garth had tried to do, the team had all rallied behind Rae. Even Yani and Lexie, who tended not to give a skíouros' ass unless it affected their relationship, had in no uncertain terms told Garth what a fool he'd been for at least not sharing his plan with her first. Garth was almost desperate enough to ask their dishwasher, Ross, but he didn't speak; and Garth doubted he'd have known her whereabouts, anyway.

The only person he hadn't asked was Nika, who was currently standing in the doorway of his office.

"What do you want?" Garth asked grumpily.

"Are you coming down to run service, or would you like Lexie to run it for you? Or perhaps Ross should? Myself? Tomas?"

"Don't you start."

"I have every right to call you out on your behaviour when you're going down a path that isn't good for this place. I saw it once before, remember?"

"Rae is nothing like Evie."

"I'm not talking about Evie."

Garth looked at her in despair. "Then what are you berating me for? I was trying to make sure there was a failsafe for this place and give her something she could own. I was trying to do what was *right*. Why can nobody see that?"

Nika shut the door and leaned back against his desk, her arms folded as she stared at Garth in his chair.

"That's the problem – don't you get it? In your desperation to get it right, you push too hard. You pushed your family too hard, too fast, and they walked away, too. You're bullish and headstrong. The problem is, you're also so cunningly charming you can convince anyone into anything you think is the right thing. But, you don't stop to consider the impact of those actions on other people; you only focus on the outcomes."

"Good outcomes," Garth grumbled.

"I'm not saying you don't have a good heart or that you don't do it for the right reasons." Nika sighed and offered him a knowing smile, an event so rare that Garth could count on both scaled hands how often he had seen it.

"I'm saying you can't solve all our problems on your own. You have to let us in on the grand plans you have. If we really are a family, you have to let us have a say. I thought you would have learnt that after the libation hooplah we all just went through."

Garth went to rebut, but Nika held up a long, elegant hand. "I know why you don't let anyone in. I *know*. I know how Evie did a number on you when you shared your plans with her, when you let her see your hopes and dreams, and then morph them into that nightmare. And I was there when your family left, one by one, remember? But, we aren't her. Rae isn't her. None of us are *her*.

"And, what's more," Nika continued, "you aren't the same agathodaemon, either. You don't blindly follow what someone else says will work. You do your due diligence, you research, you weigh up the risks — I've seen your spreadsheets. Gods, remember when you were thinking about hiring Rae and making changes to the menu? I think those were the first two times in half a millennium I've seen you make a rash move without a pros and cons list."

"Why are you saying this to me, when you were against those decisions?"

"Because, you've got a broken-hearted Sunshine sobbing at home, thinking she let everyone down, and she doesn't deserve that. She's not the one who let you down."

Realisation dawned on Garth as he scrambled to stand and move towards the door. "She's at yours."

Nika moved to block him.

"What in seven hells is she doing at yours? You two don't even like each other."

"I like Sunshine just fine."

"No, you don't."

"I have," Nika countered. "Ever since I saw how much she also cares about this place."

"But, she doesn't want this place."

The unsaid hung heavily between them as Nika eyed him.

"Heed my warning, Garth. If you aren't going to let her in, you'll end up having to let her go."

ONCE NIKA HAD MOVED out of the doorway, Garth had stormed past with every intention of heading straight to hers, banging down the door, and begging Rae to forgive him.

The thought of her crying physically hurt him.

He hadn't meant to make her cry. He hadn't meant for her to think she had let everyone down. That hadn't been his intention at all. And he damn well wasn't letting her go.

He had heeded Nika's warning. Still, he couldn't find it within himself to not come up with *some* sort of plan, which was ultimately why he hadn't gone straight over there. It had been in his nature for so long now that the thought of not having a plan left him feeling unprepared, and acutely uncomfortable about it.

He couldn't do it.

This time, though, he'd run his plan past Rae before he went ahead with it. First, he had to make sure all the numbers and components were in place, so that it wasn't just a dream for her anymore; so that he could apologise, properly, for what he'd asked of her *and* for what he'd put her through.

A knock on his office door.

"Come in."

And there she was, a light of joy in the doorway.

"You wanted to see me?"

Her voice was an octave higher than usual. She was stressed, and Garth realised Rae was probably worried about why he had called her up here on the day she'd returned to work. So, he didn't wait until she was in the room or tell her to sit down on the small two-seater beside the door before launching into what he had to say.

"I owe you an apology."

Rae folded her arms over her chest, pushing up her cleavage, but this wasn't the time for Garth to focus on that.

"Yes," she sniffed. "I suppose you do."

Nika had clearly been schooling her.

Garth nodded. "I'm sorry. You were right. I was trying to mould what you wanted and what I wanted, and I didn't even ask you beforehand if taking over this place was something you wanted to consider. That was a mistake."

"I appreciate that."

It wasn't an acceptance of the apology, but it was a start. He ran both his scaled hands through his thick hair as he leaned back in his office chair.

"So, how would you feel if I said we could get Geras' Grub back instead?"

"What do you mean?"

Garth gestured for her to shut the door behind her and take a seat. He didn't want others in the team possibly coming up the stairs, walking past and overhearing. Not until Sunshine gave her agreement.

"I asked Nyx to find out who the Olympic investor of the place is now. Turns out, the daemon you saw asking Geras for it was actually Plutus, and he got it on behalf of Demeter. Seeing as she's the Goddess of Harvest and her daughter is down here as our ruling Queen, well, I gather it has something to do with wanting to be closer to her. Anyway, Demeter and Nyx have spoken and shared how our arrangement works here at the pub, and how it could work for Demeter if we wanted to expand The Watering Hole into a restaurant *and* a cafe with a bakery. Turns out, she was pissed when you and Geras upped and left anyway; and she didn't know what to do with it, seeing as she doesn't know how the neighbourhood runs down here. She's interested in our help, but I wanted to check with you first before we went ahead with it."

"Why?"

"Because if we do go down this path, and if you wanted it, it would be yours to run. I went the wrong way about giving you something that could be yours, and you once told me that what you actually wanted was Geras' Grub. So, I'm trying to find a way to give it to you – the right way."

An awkward silence filled the air and Garth winced, worried he'd bunged it up with Rae again.

"You want to give me Geras' Grub? Why do you keep trying to give me things?"

"I want to give you all your dreams, Sunshine."

"But, what about here? What about the team? Do you

not want me working with you anymore?" Again, that panic in her voice.

Garth leaned forward and took her hands in his. "Sunshine, you can work here as long as you want. Of course I want you here. You did an *incredible* job running the kitchen, much better than I did the first time I ever had a bad evening. I was trying to show you how good you are, how incredible you are, and instead I made you feel worse. I'm still beating myself up over that, and I will for a while yet. If you want to stay, then of course I want you to. But, if you want this dream more ... then I want you to have that."

"Why?" Rae whispered it this time.

"Because, I care more about your dreams than this place, than what I – what *we* and the team – have built here."

A tear slipped down Rae's cheek. Garth leaned forward and swiped it away with his thumb.

"You shouldn't say such things," she whispered.

"I mean it. You've all helped me realise the dream of The Watering Hole, but it was you that made me realise this place isn't my dream anymore. It hasn't been ever since the day I first saw you in Asphodel Meadows, and then every day since. Every cook-off, every moment I got a glimpse of you, everything I've learnt about you since, has just made me more and more certain of that. I'm head-over-heels in love with you, Sunshine. Can't you see that?"

She was full-on blubbering now.

"Do you remember how this all started? How we got here, when you did me that favour and came to work with us?"

"Then you offered me a job and forfeited the competition so I could have the winnings," she countered between the tears.

"I wanted you close and I was doing anything I could to make it happen. I was strong-arming you, again. I'm not going to do that anymore. I'm going to help you make your own dreams come true, instead."

"What if I don't want to leave you? Leave the team?"

Garth smiled through tears of his own. He'd been hoping Rae would say that.

"I haven't got all the details figured out yet" – and gods did that terrify him – "but, I was thinking we could each split our time between the two places. We can get Mel over there to help you out initially, get it up and running, get some extra hands in, and then we'll figure out how to coordinate the rosters. What do you think?"

"I don't think anyone has ever ... I've never had anyone ... you really love me?" she whispered.

"I love you, Sunshine." Each time he said it, Garth could feel his heart expand, a golden light filling the space that he had closed off for so long. It was an energy that felt intrinsically of her.

Rae hiccuped as she smiled. "I think I've been falling in love with you ever since you stood in the bistro in that flour-bombed apron when you decided to help me make sweets before the cook-off. I think that's why I was *so* mad when your dish was better than mine – because I'd started falling for you."

His heart almost stopped at her quiet confession.

"Oh, yeah?" Garth could feel more tears running down his cheeks as they cracked from the grin that spread across his face, his chest puffed out in pride. He took her hand and led them both to stand, pulling her close. He felt like he couldn't get her close enough. "I want to spend every day cooking with you, Sunshine."

"I'd like that." She snuggled her face into his chest and

wrapped her arms around his waist. They stood there like that in the silence, just holding each other, the divide between them now mended with a love that had been there all along. Garth relished in Rae's touch, in how tiny her hands were at his back. But, eventually, he had to know.

"So, what do you want to do about the bistro?"

She tipped her head back and looked up at him. "I think we should do it, but we should do it together."

"You sure?"

"I am."

Garth leaned down to press a light kiss to her lips. "Okay."

"But, right now, we need to get down there and help the team with tonight's service," Rae admonished. Garth took the chance to dip his head and steal another kiss.

"Lead the way, Sunshine."

A BONUS "TOPPING"
GARTH & RAE'S FIRST OFFICIAL DATE

"A pizza-making competition?" Rae wrinkled her nose at Garth.

"Come on, it'll be fun," he cajoled her, donning a blue-and-white striped apron. Rae eyed him suspiciously, yet there was a playful smile on that little bow-like mouth of hers.

"What's the apron for?"

"Well, you might not be taking this seriously, but I am. I'm going to make you the best pizzas you've ever tasted, and then you're going to realise you can't be without me because you need my pizzas."

Rae laughed that tinkling laugh that had butterflies erupting in his lower belly.

"You really think you're going to win me over with pizzas? Hand me that." Rae reached out for the second apron Garth was holding out for her – this one lilac with white stripes, one he'd brought for her especially.

They were in Garth's kitchen above The Watering Hole, the place below them quiet on a Sunday evening – their only evening off together this week. The green-tiled splash-back was sparkling, the white marble countertops clear.

"So where are the ingredients?" she asked him.

"Right this way, Sunshine." Garth extended one scaled arm and led her to a small walk-in pantry where Rae stood in the doorway, and Garth leaned on the door jam, watching her face light up as she spotted everything in neatly organised containers. He knew she'd like it.

"How did I not know this was here last time?"

Garth came in behind her and bent down to press a kiss between Rae's neck and her shoulder. "Because I was too busy distracting you with other things."

"That's right," Rae sighed before batting him away. "Don't think you'll get away with it this time."

Garth smiled at the bite in her tone.

"May the best chef win, Sunshine."

Together, they gathered the ingredients they would need for the bases and headed back into the kitchen. They were soon both covered in flour when Garth looked over at Rae.

"No peeking!"

"It's hardly called peeking when we're both making pizza dough," Garth drawled. He worked the dough with his hands and was pleasantly surprised to catch Rae watching him back as he worked.

"I thought you said no peeking?" he teased.

A blush spread across the top of her cheekbones, all the way to the tip of her cute pixie ears that poked out beyond her pearl-white hair, neatly tied back in a plait as it always was when they were in a kitchen. Garth couldn't wait to see it down again.

"I wasn't— I was looking at ... never mind."

Garth's grin grew wider.

"What were you looking at, Sunshine?"

"Just, get back to your pizza dough."

He obliged her, but when he grabbed the timer, he wished he hadn't.

Sunshine was up to something.

"I'm setting the timer for an hour; is that okay with you?"

They'd both just placed their doughs in resting bowls and covered them with damp tea towels, though now Garth looked, Rae's dough looked ... heavier to his trained eye.

"Actually, I'll need forty-five minutes, please."

Garth narrowed his eyes. "What are you up to?"

"You'll see," Rae smiled.

The pair of them spent the remaining time preparing their sauces and their toppings. Garth would have expected that they'd have to share the stovetop to create their sauces, but when he saw Rae make a move for the food processor, he knew she wasn't doing a traditional pizza.

"A new creation?" he questioned, as he moved into her space near the stove and grabbed a wooden spoon to stir the marinara sauce that had begun to bubble and thicken in the pot.

Rae sent him a dazzling smile as she strained chickpeas.

"Oh no. You think I was going to try out something new when this is a competition? I know how it goes against you, Garthrial. I'm not bringing anything less than my A-game, and I happen to know this pizza is a fan favourite."

A fan favourite.

"Sunshine?"

"Hmm?"

"Did you ever serve pizza at the bistro for lunch?"

He'd never seen it on the menu before, but he couldn't be certain. He'd known of her for five centuries; it was likely she'd changed the menu during that time. It wasn't like he'd gone into the bistro every day. Even though he'd wanted to.

"It was known to happen on the odd occasion," she teased him.

Garth upped his game then, adding herbs and spices, testing the sauce until it had a hint of sweet chilli that would provide a kick and the perfect amount of seasoning. He expertly chopped artichoke hearts into quarters, roasted red peppers while the oven was warming for their pizza doughs, de-pipped and sliced black olives, and shredded basil leaves.

The timer went off.

He watched as Rae rolled out her dough to a quarter-inch thickness and reset the timer for nine minutes.

"You don't mind, do you?" she looked up at him with wide, round eyes, all fake innocence.

Garth knew what she was doing, and for the Underlife of him wasn't going to stop it. He had the timer he needed in his head. Still, this was a competition, and he wasn't just going to roll over.

"It will cost you," he murmured as he leaned down, his lips inches from hers.

She pressed a quick peck to his lips and darted away. "Thanks!"

He grimaced. "Not what I had in mind, Sunshine."

"Oh, I know."

When the timer went off again, and Rae produced a puffed-up, golden-brown Turkish flatbread, Garth knew she'd won on ingenuity alone. He used the free oven opportunity to remove the roasted peppers from the other tray in the oven and cut them in preparation for his toppings. It was the only thing he had left to organise. He watched as

Rae layered the bread with a generous layer of hummus, scattered cherry tomatoes, red onion slices, and Kalamata olives.

Garth tried to stop himself from moaning out loud, but when she sprinkled crumbled feta over the top, he couldn't help himself. She didn't turn to look at him, but he noticed the side of Rae's mouth quirk up into a smile. She finished her work with a drizzle of olive oil and cracked salt and black pepper, dusted her hands off on her apron, and turned to him.

"Ready when you are."

Garth quickly worked to pour a thin layer of his sauce over the pizza dough, sprinkled a generous helping of shredded mozzarella cheese, and arranged the rest of his toppings in a swirl.

"Let's do this."

They both slid their pizzas into the oven, their cheeks practically pressed side to side as they did so.

"Timer?" he asked her.

"Twelve minutes please. You?"

"Twelve minutes, too."

They spent the time cleaning down their bench areas and putting excess ingredients either away or in the compost bin. Only then did they both take off their aprons. Garth grabbed the glasses from the overhead cupboard, seeing as Rae was too short to reach, and poured them each a glass of wine.

"To the best pizza," Rae toasted.

"To the best first date," Garth amended as their glasses clinked together.

When the timer went off and both of them slid their pizzas out onto wooden chopping boards, Garth finished his with fresh basil leaves, capers, and a drizzle of balsamic glaze. Rae sprinkled chopped fresh mint leaves over hers.

"Ta-da! Mediterranean Delight!" she announced, the smile on her face one of pure joy and delight.

As they sat down to try each other's dish, Garth knew he'd never want to win another competition against Sunshine again.

WANT MORE?

If you would to follow more of Gwen's work, sign up for her newsletter at www.gwynethlesley.com.

A special thanks to Kimberly, Charlie, Aleena, Shamera, Erin and George for taking a chance on this series before anyone else did. It has turned out to be an absolute gem to write and a refreshingly cozy* experience against some of my heavier, more heartbreaking books. I think I shall return to these again and again and read them myself when I need a pick-me-up. I make no promises about whether I will ever return to this version of the Underworld with these creatures. The door is always open, but I think, for now, it's best to leave them to get on with their immortal lives.

*While all of these tales have been written in British English, I chose the American spelling of 'cozy' purely for search term, metadata, and marketing purposes.

RECIPES FROM THE UNDERWORLD

RAE'S SWEET & SAVOURY SAUSAGE ROLLS

*Some recipes are modified for mortal enjoyment from Rae, who, despite lacking professional culinary training, disclaims any responsibility for kitchen mishaps or recipe misfortunes.

Ingredients:

- 1 1/2 lbs (680 g) lean ground pork
- 1/3 cup (80 mL) hoisin sauce (to replace Rae's caramelised burnt bits)
- 1/2 cup (125 mL) bread crumbs
- 1 tbsp (15 mL) honey
- 1 tsp (5 mL) salt
- 1 tbsp (15 mL) sriracha
- 4 cloves garlic, finely chopped or grated
- Freshly ground black pepper
- 1 sheet pre-rolled frozen puff pastry, thawed
- Flour as needed
- 1 egg yolk, lightly beaten
- 3 tbsp (45 mL) sesame seeds

Instructions:

In a large bowl, combine pork, hoisin, bread crumbs, honey, salt, sriracha and garlic. Add a few grindings of coarsely ground black pepper. Mix with your hands until evenly combined.

Cut a piece of parchment paper roughly the size of a baking sheet. Lightly sprinkle with flour and unroll your puff pastry overtop. Sprinkle pastry with a bit more flour and gently roll out with a rolling pin to lengthen into a 10 x 12-inch (25 x 30-cm) rectangle.

Working lengthwise, leave a 1-inch (2.5-cm) border on one side and arrange the sausage mixture in a log-like roll parallel to the border. Brush the border with egg yolk. Using the parchment, lift the pastry from the other side and bring it into contact with the egg-washed border to enclose meat (the ends of the sausage roll will remain open). Use a fork to seal the long edge. Carefully transfer parchment and roll to baking sheet and refrigerate for 30 minutes.

Preheat the oven to 400°F (204°C).

Score three short slashes on top of the roll to vent, brush with remaining egg yolk and sprinkle with sesame seeds. Bake on the centre rack for 45 to 50 minutes or until the top has developed a deep golden colour. Let cool to room temperature, wrap in wax paper and refrigerate until ready to pack up.

To serve, cut into 12 equal-sized slices.

RAE'S FIG & GOAT FILO PARCELS

Ingredients:

- 6 figs, large
- 125g goat's cheese, soft, rind removed
- 2 tsp black peppercorns, ground
- 50g butter, melted
- 6 filo pastry, large sheets
- a few chives, snipped

Instructions:

Heat the oven to 200C/fan 180C/gas 6. Slice the stems off the figs, then score a deep cross shape into each, cutting two-thirds of the way through. Squeeze each fig a little at the base to open them out a bit.

In a small bowl, mix together the goat's cheese and black pepper, then divide equally into the middle of each fig. Press the sides back up a little so the cheese is snugly inside.

Take the sheets of filo and slice into quarters. Stack 4 quarters and brush lightly with butter. Put the stuffed fig in the middle of the filo squares and draw up the sides around it.

You want the fig to be surrounded but not covered on top so simply fold and press the pastry so it fits. Repeat with the other figs. Bake on a baking-paper-lined tray for 12-15 minutes until the pastry is crisp and golden.

Allow to cool a little before eating as the figs will be tongue-burningly hot straight from the oven. Sprinkle with the snipped chives just before serving.

RAE'S BLISS BALLS
(FOR WHEN AGGRAVATING AGATHODAEMONS GET UNDER YOUR SKIN)

Ingredients:

- 1 grapefruit, pitted
- 1 tbsp honey
- 1 tsp ground cinnamon
- 1/2 cup cashew meal
- 1/4 cup shredded coconut
- 2 tbsp white chia seeds

Instructions:

Place grapefruit, honey, cinnamon, cashew meal, and chia seeds in a food processor. Process until well combined and mixture forms a thick paste-like consistency.

Roll level tablespoons of mixture into balls. Roll in shredded coconut to lightly coat. Place balls on a plate. Refrigerate for 20 minutes or until firm.

RAE'S PAN FRIED FISH

Ingredients:

- 1 cup thick Greek yoghurt
- 2 tbsp tahini
- 300g white fish of your choice
- 1 tbsp olive oil, plus extra, to drizzle
- 4 eggs (don't have to be quail like Rae's!)
- 4 wholemeal flatbread
- 1 lemon (in place of lotus flowers)
- 1/2 bunch of fresh dill, chopped
- 80g feta
- 60g baby rocket

Instructions:

Heat a 25cm frying pan over medium-high heat.

While the pan heats up, combine the yoghurt and tahini in a bowl. Season.

Pour the oil into the pan and crack in the eggs. Cover the pan with a lid and cook for 2 minutes or until the egg whites are set but the yolks are still runny.

Meanwhile, spread the yoghurt mixture over the flatbreads. Cut the lemon into wedges.

Divide the fried eggs among the flatbreads.

Pan-fry the fish until cooked, then flake and add to the flatbreads.

Crumble over the feta and sprinkle with dukkah. Top with the rocket and dill. Serve with the lemon wedges.

GARTH'S HOMEMADE SAFFRON BUTTER & ARTISANAL LOAF

*This recipe (and others like it) has been modified for mortal enjoyment by Garth, who disclaims any responsibility for kitchen mishaps or recipe misfortunes.

Artisanal Loaf Ingredients:

- 4 cups all-purpose flour
- 1 tablespoon sugar
- 1 tablespoon active dry yeast
- 1 1/2 teaspoons salt
- 1 1/2 cups warm water (about 110°F/43°C)
- Olive oil (for greasing)

Instructions:

In a bowl, dissolve sugar in warm water and add yeast. Allow it to sit for about 5-10 minutes until it becomes frothy.

In a large mixing bowl, combine flour and salt. Make a well in the centre and pour in the yeast mixture. Mix until it forms a dough.

Turn the dough onto a floured surface and knead for about 8-10 minutes, or until it becomes smooth and elastic.

Place the dough in a greased bowl, cover it with a damp cloth, and let it rise in a warm place for 1-1.5 hours, or until it doubles in size.

Punch down the risen dough, shape it into a loaf, and place it in a greased loaf pan. Cover it again and let it rise for another 30-45 minutes.

Preheat your oven to 375°F (190°C). Bake the loaf for 25-30 minutes or until it sounds hollow when tapped. Allow it to cool on a wire rack.

Homemade Saffron Butter Ingredients:

- 1 cup unsalted butter, softened
- 1/4 teaspoon saffron threads
- 1 tablespoon boiling water
- 1/2 teaspoon honey
- 1/4 teaspoon salt

Instructions:

In a small bowl, pour boiling water over saffron threads. Let it steep for about 10-15 minutes until the water turns golden yellow.

In a separate bowl, combine softened butter, honey, and salt. Pour in the saffron-infused water (make sure to include the saffron threads).

Whip the ingredients together until well combined. Adjust salt or honey according to taste. Refrigerate for at least 30 minutes to allow the flavours to meld.

Slice the artisanal loaf, and serve with generous slathers of homemade saffron butter. Enjoy the rich, golden-hued butter paired with the warm, freshly baked bread.

RAE'S FIG & SPIKENARD
SALAD WRAP

Ingredients:

- 2 figs
- 1 cup of rocket salad
- 1 wholemeal tortilla wrap
- 1 tsp spikenard root (crushed)
- 1 pomegranate

Instructions:

Crush the spikenard root in a mortar and pestle.

Cut the pomegranate in half and scoop out the insides into the mortar and pestle. Mix together.

Spread the sauce from the mortar and pestle across the circumference of the tortilla wrap.

Add rocket salad and sliced figs placed evenly throughout the wrap.

Fold and serve.

Note from Rae: *Spikenard can be slightly sweet and slightly pungent — a little like what you mortals call liquorice. Crushing the root will make sure you keep that aromatic spicy taste. Mixed with the sweet pomegranate and you've got the perfect spicy & sweet blend!*

GARTH'S STYX SEAFOOD CHOWDER

Ingredients:

- 1 lb mixed seafood (shrimp, squid, scallops), cleaned and diced
- 1/4 cup squid ink
- 4 slices bacon, diced
- 1 onion, finely chopped
- 2 cloves garlic, minced
- 2 medium potatoes, peeled and diced
- 1 cup corn kernels (fresh or frozen)
- 1 cup leeks, thinly sliced
- 4 cups fish or vegetable broth
- 1 cup heavy cream
- 1/2 cup dry white wine
- 2 tablespoons butter
- 2 tablespoons all-purpose flour
- 1 bay leaf
- Salt and pepper to taste
- Fresh parsley for garnish

Instructions:

In a bowl, season the mixed seafood with salt, pepper, and half of the squid ink. Toss to coat evenly and let it marinate while you prepare the chowder.

In a large pot over medium heat, cook the diced bacon until crispy. Add chopped onions and minced garlic, and sauté until softened.

Melt butter in the pot, sprinkle in flour, and stir continuously to create a roux. Cook for 2-3 minutes until it turns a light golden colour.

Pour in the white wine to deglaze the pot, scraping up any browned bits. Add the fish or vegetable broth gradually, stirring to avoid lumps. Add the remaining squid ink for that deep Styx-like colour.

Toss in diced potatoes, sliced leeks, corn, and the bay leaf. Simmer until the potatoes are tender, usually 15-20 minutes.

Stir in the marinated seafood and let it cook for about 5 minutes until the seafood is just cooked through.

Pour in the heavy cream, stirring gently. Season with salt and pepper to taste. Let the chowder simmer for an additional 5 minutes.

Ladle the chowder into bowls, garnish with fresh parsley, and serve hot. Enjoy the smoky illusion and fresh seawater flavours that blend seamlessly in this mythical culinary creation.

RAE'S AMBROSIA

Ingredients:

- 1 kg yoghurt (choose your favourite flavour rather than goat's milk)
- 500 ml cream
- 250 g of milk chocolate digestive biscuits
- 1 packet marshmallows (sorry, Rae won't give up her secrets there!)
- 2 tbsp honey

Instructions:

Cut marshmallows into quarters.

Crush the biscuits until they are in bite-sized pieces with a rolling pin.

Whip cream till you get soft peaks, then add the yoghurt and mix until it's well combined.

Add the honey, marshmallows, and biscuits and fold them into the mixture.

Move the mixture into a cake tin, and leave overnight in the fridge to set, before slicing and serving.

NOTES FROM RAE: *Do not underestimate the power of this dish! Now, it sets into cake slices for the Underworld ... but we have different temperatures there. You might want to spoon this instead into glasses and then serve.*

MEL'S POMEGRANATE TART

*This recipe (and others like it) has been modified for
mortal enjoyment by Mel, who disclaims any responsibility
for kitchen mishaps or recipe misfortunes.

Ingredients For the Tart Crust:

- 1 1/4 cups all-purpose flour
- 1/4 cup granulated sugar
- 1/2 cup unsalted butter, cold and cut into small
  cubes
- 1 large egg yolk
- 2 tablespoons ice water

For the Pomegranate Filling:

- 2 cups pomegranate juice (about 4-5 large
  pomegranates)
- 1 cup granulated sugar
- 1/4 cup cornstarch
- 1/4 teaspoon salt

For the Pomegranate Glaze:

- 1/2 cup pomegranate arils (seeds)
- 1/4 cup apricot preserves

Instructions:

Tart Crust: In a food processor, combine the flour, sugar, and cold butter. Pulse until the mixture resembles coarse crumbs. Add the egg yolk and ice water, pulsing just until the dough starts to come together.

Turn the dough out onto a lightly floured surface. Knead it a few times until it forms a cohesive ball. Flatten the dough into a disk, wrap it in plastic wrap, and refrigerate for at least 30 minutes.

Preheat Oven: Preheat your oven to 375°F (190°C).

On a floured surface, roll out the chilled dough into a circle large enough to fit your tart pan. Gently press the dough into the pan, trimming any excess. Prick the bottom with a fork to prevent it from puffing up during baking.

Line the tart shell with parchment paper and fill it with pie weights or dried beans. Bake for 15 minutes. Remove the weights and parchment, then bake for an additional 10-12 minutes or until the crust is golden brown. Allow it to cool completely.

Pomegranate Filling: Cut the pomegranates in half and juice them to obtain approximately 2 cups of fresh pomegranate juice.

In a saucepan, combine the pomegranate juice, sugar, cornstarch, and salt. Whisk continuously over medium heat until the mixture thickens to a custard-like consistency. Remove from heat and let it cool slightly.

Pour the pomegranate filling into the cooled tart crust, spreading it evenly.

Pomegranate Glaze: In a small saucepan, heat the apricot preserves until they become liquid. Strain out any fruit pieces.

Mix the strained apricot preserves with the pomegranate arils.

Gently brush the pomegranate glaze over the top of the tart.

Refrigerate the tart for at least 2 hours or until the filling is set. Slice and serve chilled. Enjoy your delightful home-made pomegranate tart!

RAE'S COCONUT ICE
(EASIER THAN APPLE ICE IN THE
UNDERWORLD REALM)

Ingredients:

- 200 g icing sugar 2 cups
- 300 g desiccated coconut 3.5 cups (in place of Garden of Hesperides apples)
- 400 ml condensed milk one tin
- 3 drops red food colouring

Instructions:

Pour the icing sugar, desiccated coconut and condensed milk into a large mixing bowl. Mix with a spoon, then with your hands, into a firm dough.

Transfer half the dough into a square tin lined with baking paper and press out with your hands or a spatula until flat and even.

Add red food colouring to the remaining dough and use your hands to knead until you achieve an even pink colour.

Spoon out portions of the pink mixture over the white layer, and use a fork to lightly scrape and even out first. Then use your hands or spatula to press out and flatten. This helps you achieve more even layers.

Chill for 1-2 hours in the fridge until set. Slice into small 2.5 cm / 1 inch squares as they are quite a sweet treat!

GARTH'S FIG SORBET (ΣΟΡΜΠΈ)

Ingredients:

- 2 cups fresh figs, stemmed and quartered
- 1 cup water
- 3/4 cup granulated sugar (adjust to taste)
- 2 tablespoons lemon juice
- 1 teaspoon lemon zest
- 1/2 teaspoon vanilla extract (optional)

Instructions:

Wash and quarter the fresh figs, removing any stems. If desired, peel the figs for a smoother sorbet texture.

In a saucepan, combine water and granulated sugar. Heat over medium heat, stirring until the sugar completely dissolves. Bring the mixture to a gentle simmer, then remove it from heat and let it cool to room temperature.

In a blender or food processor, combine the quartered figs, simple syrup, lemon juice, lemon zest, and vanilla extract. Blend until you achieve a smooth and homogeneous mixture.

For a smoother sorbet, you can strain the mixture using a fine-mesh sieve to remove any fig seeds or pulp. Press the mixture through the sieve using a spatula.

Refrigerate the sorbet mixture for at least 2 hours or until it's thoroughly chilled. This step is crucial for optimal sorbet texture.

Pour the chilled mixture into an ice cream maker and churn according to the manufacturer's instructions. This usually takes about 20-30 minutes.

Once the sorbet reaches a soft-serve consistency, transfer it to a lidded container. Smooth the top with a spatula and cover the surface with parchment paper or plastic wrap to prevent ice crystals from forming.

Freeze the sorbet for an additional 3-4 hours or until it firms up to your liking.

Scoop the fig sorbet into bowls or cones. Garnish with fresh fig slices or mint leaves if desired. Enjoy the refreshing and delightful taste of homemade fig sorbet (σορμπέ)!

NYX'S LAGANON PASTA

*This recipe (and others like it) has been begrudgingly
modified for mortal enjoyment by Nika, at Rae's insistence.
They both disclaim any responsibility for kitchen mishaps
or recipe misfortunes.

Ingredients For the Pasta Dough:

- 2 cups all-purpose flour
- 2 large eggs
- 1/2 teaspoon salt
- Water, as needed

For the Laganon Sauce:

- 3 tablespoons olive oil
- 4 cloves garlic, minced
- 1 can (14 oz) diced tomatoes
- 1 teaspoon dried oregano
- 1 teaspoon dried basil
- Salt and pepper, to taste

- Red pepper flakes (optional)
- Grated Pecorino Romano or Parmesan cheese, for serving

Instructions:

Prepare the Pasta Dough: On a clean surface, mound the flour and create a well in the centre. Crack the eggs into the well, add salt, and gradually incorporate the flour into the eggs until a dough forms.

Knead the dough for about 8-10 minutes until it becomes smooth and elastic. If the dough is too dry, add water, a tablespoon at a time.

Wrap the dough in plastic wrap and let it rest at room temperature for at least 30 minutes.

Using a pasta machine or a rolling pin, roll out the dough to your desired thickness. Dust with flour to prevent sticking. Cut the rolled-out dough into rectangular or square pieces to resemble laganon pasta.

Bring a large pot of salted water to a boil. Cook the laganon pasta for 2-3 minutes or until al dente. Drain and set aside.

Make the Laganon Sauce: In a large skillet, heat olive oil over medium heat. Add minced garlic and sauté until fragrant.

Pour in the diced tomatoes and their juice. Stir in dried oregano, dried basil, salt, pepper, and red pepper flakes if you like a bit of heat. Simmer for about 10-15 minutes, allowing the flavours to meld.

Toss the cooked laganon pasta into the tomato sauce, ensuring the pasta is well-coated.

Plate the laganon pasta, drizzle with a bit of olive oil, and sprinkle with grated Pecorino Romano or Parmesan cheese. Serve immediately and enjoy your homemade laganon pasta with a flavourful tomato sauce!

RAE'S LAVENDER MERINGUES

Ingredients:

- 2 large egg whites, at room temperature
- 1/8 a teaspoon of cream of tartar
- 1/2 cup of sugar
- 1/4 teaspoon of vanilla extract
- 2-3 teaspoons of culinary lavender
- Purple food colouring, if desired

Instructions:

Place an oven rack in the middle position and preheat your oven to 200 degrees Fahrenheit.

Use an electric mixer (I used my stand mixer with the whisk attachment), beat the egg whites on medium-low until they become slightly opaque and frothy. This should take 20-60 seconds.

Add the cream of tartar and increase the mixer's speed to medium high. Beat the egg whites until they become white and thick. They'll actually look and act sort of like shaving cream! This usually takes 90-120 seconds.

Slowly add in 1/4 cup of the sugar and continue mixing. Once it is fully incorporated, reduce the mixer speed to low.

Add in the remaining sugar, vanilla extract, and lavender. With an electric mixer, beat until just combined.

Transfer the meringue to a piping bag fitted with a 3/4"-1" tip or a ziplock bag, as discussed above.

Pipe the meringues onto a baking sheet, trying to make them each about the size of an unshelled walnut and spacing them an inch apart.

Bake without opening the door for 90 minutes, turn off the oven, and allow the meringues to cool without opening the door. Keep the meringues in the oven for as long as possible - several hours to overnight!

Store the cooled meringues in an airtight container. They keep very well and, if allowed to fully cool in the oven, should keep for at least two weeks.

NIKA'S SPANAKORIZO

Ingredients:

- 1 cup long-grain white rice
- 2 tablespoons olive oil
- 1 large onion, finely chopped
- 2 cloves garlic, minced
- 1 bunch fresh spinach, washed and chopped
- 1 cup vegetable or chicken broth
- 1/2 cup water
- 1/2 cup fresh dill, chopped
- 1/4 cup fresh parsley, chopped
- Juice of 1 lemon
- Salt and pepper, to taste
- Crumbled feta cheese for garnish (optional)
- Lemon wedges for serving

Instructions:

Rinse the rice under cold water until the water runs clear. Set aside.

In a large, deep skillet or pot, heat olive oil over medium heat. Add the chopped onion and sauté until it becomes translucent. Add minced garlic and cook for an additional 1-2 minutes until fragrant.

Add the chopped spinach to the pot and stir well. Allow the spinach to wilt down, cooking for about 3-5 minutes.

Stir in the rinsed rice, ensuring it's well-coated with the onion and spinach mixture.

Pour in the vegetable or chicken broth and water. Bring the mixture to a gentle boil, then reduce the heat to low. Cover the pot and let it simmer for about 15-20 minutes, or until the rice is tender and has absorbed the liquid.

Season the spanakorizo with salt and pepper to taste. Stir in the chopped dill and parsley, ensuring the herbs are evenly distributed.

Squeeze the juice of one lemon over the spanakorizo and give it a final stir. Adjust the seasoning if needed.

Spoon the spanakorizo onto serving plates. If desired, garnish with crumbled feta cheese and serve with lemon wedges on the side.

Spanakorizo is delicious served warm as a main dish or a side. Enjoy the vibrant flavours of this classic Greek spinach and rice dish!

RAE'S CURRY PUFF BOMBS

Ingredients For the Pastry:

- 2 cups all-purpose flour
- 1/2 cup unsalted butter, cold and cubed
- 1/2 cup cold water
- 1/2 teaspoon salt

For the Filling:

- 2 tablespoons vegetable oil
- 1 onion, finely chopped
- 2 cloves garlic, minced
- 1 tablespoon curry powder
- 1 teaspoon ground cumin
- 1 teaspoon ground coriander
- 1/2 teaspoon turmeric powder
- 1 lb (450g) potatoes, peeled and diced
- 1/2 lb (225g) ground meat (chicken, beef, or lamb)
- Salt and pepper to taste

- 1 cup frozen peas

Instructions:

Make the Pastry: In a large bowl, mix the flour and salt. Add the cold, cubed butter, and use your fingers to rub it into the flour until the mixture resembles breadcrumbs.

Gradually add cold water, stirring with a fork, until the dough comes together. Knead briefly on a floured surface until smooth. Wrap in plastic wrap and refrigerate for at least 30 minutes.

Prepare the Filling: Boil or steam the diced potatoes until just tender. Drain and set aside.

In a pan, heat vegetable oil over medium heat.

Add chopped onion and garlic and sauté until softened.

Add curry powder, cumin, coriander, and turmeric to the pan. Stir well to combine.

Add ground meat to the pan and cook until browned. Season with salt and pepper.

Add the cooked potatoes and frozen peas to the pan. Stir to combine and cook for a few more minutes until the peas are heated through. Remove from heat and let the filling cool.

Assemble the Curry Puff Bombs: Heat vegetable oil in a deep fryer or a deep, heavy-bottomed pan to 350°F (180°C).

Roll out the chilled pastry on a floured surface to about 1/8-inch thickness.

Using a round cutter or a glass, cut out circles from the pastry.

Place a spoonful of the cooled filling in the centre of each pastry circle.

Fold the pastry over the filling to create a half-moon shape. Press the edges to seal, and use a fork to crimp the edges.

Carefully place the assembled puffs into the hot oil and fry until golden brown, about 5-6 minutes.

Remove the curry puff bombs from the oil and drain on paper towels. Serve them warm and enjoy!

RAE'S DARK CHOCOLATE CARAMEL HONEYCOMB SLICES

Ingredients For the Biscuit Base:

- 2 cups digestive biscuits, crushed
- 1/2 cup unsalted butter, melted
- 2 tablespoons brown sugar
- Pinch of salt

For the Caramel Layer:

- 1 can (14 oz) sweetened condensed milk
- 1/2 cup unsalted butter
- 1/2 cup brown sugar
- 1/4 cup dark corn syrup or golden syrup
- 1 teaspoon vanilla extract
- Pinch of salt

For the Honeycomb Layer:

- 1/2 cup honey

- 1 cup granulated sugar
- 1 tablespoon baking soda

For the Chocolate Topping:

- 8 oz dark chocolate (70% cocoa or higher), chopped
- 1/2 cup heavy cream
- 1 tablespoon unsalted butter

Instructions:

Preheat your oven to 350°F (175°C). Line a square baking pan (9x9 inches) with parchment paper, leaving some overhang for easy removal.

In a food processor or by placing the biscuits in a plastic bag and using a rolling pin, crush the digestive biscuits until they resemble fine crumbs.

In a bowl, combine the crushed biscuits, melted butter, brown sugar, and a pinch of salt. Mix until the crumbs are evenly coated.

Press the biscuit mixture firmly into the bottom of the prepared pan. Bake in the preheated oven for about 10 minutes or until the base is set. Allow it to cool while you prepare the caramel layer.

Prepare Caramel Sauce: In a saucepan over medium heat, combine sweetened condensed milk, butter, brown sugar, dark corn syrup (or golden syrup), vanilla extract, and a pinch of salt. Stir continuously until the mixture thickens and becomes a rich caramel colour. This may take about 8-10 minutes.

Pour the caramel sauce over the cooled biscuit base, spreading it evenly. Place it in the refrigerator to set while you prepare the honeycomb layer.

Prepare Honeycomb: In a saucepan, combine honey and granulated sugar. Heat over medium-high heat, stirring constantly until the mixture reaches 300°F (150°C) on a candy thermometer. This is the hard crack stage.

Remove the saucepan from heat, quickly stir in baking soda, and watch the mixture foam up. Immediately pour the honeycomb mixture over the set caramel layer. Allow it to cool and harden.

Make the Chocolate Topping: In a heatproof bowl, melt the dark chocolate over a double boiler or in short bursts in the microwave. Stir until smooth.

In a small saucepan, heat the heavy cream until it just starts to simmer.

Pour the hot cream over the melted chocolate and stir until well combined. Add the butter and continue stirring until smooth and glossy.

Pour the chocolate ganache over the honeycomb layer, ensuring an even coating. Smooth the top with a spatula.

Place the pan back in the refrigerator and chill for at least 4 hours or until the chocolate is set.

Once fully set, use the parchment paper overhang to lift the caramel honeycomb slices from the pan. Cut into squares or bars. Serve and enjoy these indulgent dark chocolate caramel honeycomb slices!

RAE'S SUMMERY LEMON POPPY SEED MUFFINS

Ingredients:

- 2 cups (254 grams) all-purpose flour
- 3/4 cup (150 grams) granulated sugar
- 2 tablespoons poppyseeds
- 1 tablespoon baking powder
- 1/2 teaspoon baking soda
- 1/2 teaspoon fine salt
- 1 cup whole milk, at room temperature
- 1 stick (113 grams) unsalted butter, melted and cooled
- 1 large egg, at room temperature
- 2 tablespoons fresh lemon juice
- 1 1/2 tablespoons fresh lemon zest

Instructions:

Preheat the oven to 400°F. Line a standard muffin tin with paper liners.

In a large bowl whisk together the flour, sugar, poppyseeds, baking powder, baking soda, and salt.

In a small bowl whisk together the milk, butter, egg, juice, and zest. Pour into the dry ingredients and stir with a rubber spatula until just combined. Do not overmix, there should be a couple streaks of flour remaining. Divide evenly among the muffin tin cups.

If time permits, cover and refrigerate the batter overnight for taller, more tender muffins.

Bake until golden brown and a toothpick inserted in the centre comes out clean and the edges are golden, about 20 minutes. Let cool until barely warm.

Serve or store in an airtight container at room temperature for 3 days. Muffins can also be frozen in an airtight container for up to 3 months.

MEL'S PISTACHIO SORBET

Ingredients:

- 1 cup unsalted pistachios, shelled
- 1 cup granulated sugar
- 2 cups water
- 1/2 cup light corn syrup
- 1 teaspoon pure vanilla extract
- 1 tablespoon fresh lemon juice
- Pinch of salt

Instructions:

In a food processor, pulse the shelled pistachios until finely ground. Be careful not to over-process, or you may end up with pistachio butter.

In a small saucepan, combine the ground pistachios, sugar, and water. Heat the mixture over medium heat, stirring until the sugar dissolves. Bring it to a simmer, then remove from heat. Let the mixture cool.

Transfer the cooled pistachio mixture to a blender and blend until you get a smooth pistachio paste.

Strain the pistachio paste through a fine-mesh sieve or cheesecloth to remove any coarse bits. Press down on the solids to extract as much flavour as possible.

In a bowl, combine the strained pistachio paste with light corn syrup, vanilla extract, fresh lemon juice, and a pinch of salt. Mix well until the ingredients are thoroughly combined.

Refrigerate the sorbet base for at least 4 hours or, preferably, overnight. This allows the flavours to meld and the mixture to thoroughly chill.

Pour the chilled pistachio sorbet base into an ice cream maker and churn according to the manufacturer's instructions. This usually takes about 20-30 minutes.

Transfer the churned sorbet into a lidded container and freeze for an additional 4 hours, or until firm.

Scoop the pistachio sorbet into bowls or cones. Garnish with chopped pistachios if desired. Enjoy the rich and nutty flavour of this delightful pistachio sorbet!

RAE'S CORN FRITTERS
(AN EXCELLENT BRUNCH ITEM IF YOU DON'T HAVE BLACK PUDDING TO HAND)

Ingredients:

- 3 cups fresh corn kernels
- 1 cup all-purpose flour
- 1 Tablespoon sugar
- 1 teaspoon baking powder
- 2 large eggs, lightly beaten
- 3/4 cup heavy cream
- Vegetable oil, for frying
- Pomegranates and balsamic vinegar, for serving

Instructions:

In a large bowl, stir together the corn kernels, flour, sugar, baking powder, ½ teaspoon salt and ¼ teaspoon pepper.

Stir in the eggs and heavy cream until the batter is well-combined.

Line a plate with paper towels. Coat the bottom of a large sauté pan with vegetable oil and place it over medium-high heat. Once the oil is hot, scoop 2- to 3-tablespoon mounds of the corn batter into the pan, spreading it lightly into a flat, circular shape.

Cook the fritters for 2 to 3 minutes, then flip them once and cook them an additional 3 minutes until they're golden brown and cooked through. Transfer the fritters to the paper towel-lined plate, season them immediately with salt and repeat the cooking process with the remaining batter, adding more oil to the pan as needed.

Garnish the corn fritters with a tablespoon of balsamic vinegar and a pomegranate cut in half.

NYX'S SAVOURY CURD
(AS GOOD AS A TONIC, IF YOU ASK NIKA.)

Ingredients:

- 2 cups plain yoghurt or Greek yoghurt
- 1/4 cup fresh mint leaves, finely chopped
- Zest of 1 citrus fruit (lemon, lime, or orange)
- 1-2 tablespoons citrus juice (from the same fruit)
- Salt and black pepper to taste
- Olive oil for drizzling (optional)
- Fresh mint leaves for garnish

Instructions:

If using regular yoghurt, strain it in a fine-mesh sieve or cheesecloth over a bowl for a few hours to achieve a thicker consistency. Skip this step if using Greek yoghurt.

In a mixing bowl, combine the strained or Greek yoghurt with finely chopped mint leaves and the zest of the citrus fruit.

Squeeze the juice from the citrus fruit and add it to the yoghurt mixture. Adjust the amount of juice based on your preference for citrus flavour.

Season the savoury curd with salt and black pepper to taste. Mix well to ensure even distribution of flavours.

For enhanced flavour, refrigerate the savoury curd for at least 30 minutes to allow the ingredients to meld. This step is optional, and you can serve it immediately if preferred.

Before serving, drizzle a bit of olive oil over the top for added richness and a smooth texture. This step is optional but highly recommended.

Garnish the savoury curd with additional mint leaves for freshness. Serve chilled or at room temperature.

Enjoy the refreshing and tangy flavour of the savoury curd sprinkled with mint and a dash of citrus juice. This dish makes a delightful appetiser or a flavourful accompaniment to a variety of dishes.

GARTH'S CAULDRON SOUP
(AN OLD RECIPE REVAMPED FOR DIONYSUS' SOIREE)

Ingredients:

- 1 medium-sized pumpkin (about 4-5 lbs), peeled, seeded, and cut into chunks
- 1 large onion, chopped
- 2 cloves garlic, minced
- 2 tablespoons olive oil
- 4 cups vegetable or chicken broth
- 1 teaspoon nutmeg, freshly grated
- Salt and black pepper to taste
- 1 tablespoon truffle oil
- 1/2 cup heavy cream (optional, for extra richness)
- Fresh sage leaves for garnish
- Croutons (optional, for serving)

Instructions:

Preheat the oven to 400°F (200°C). Place the pumpkin chunks on a baking sheet. Drizzle with olive oil, season with salt and pepper, and toss to coat. Roast in the oven for about 30-40 minutes or until the pumpkin is tender and lightly caramelised.

In a large pot, heat 2 tablespoons of olive oil over medium heat. Add chopped onions and minced garlic. Sauté until the onions are translucent and fragrant.

Add the roasted pumpkin chunks to the pot, stirring well with the onions and garlic.

Pour in the vegetable or chicken broth, ensuring it covers the pumpkin. Bring the mixture to a simmer.

Add freshly grated nutmeg to the pot. Start with 1 teaspoon and adjust according to your taste preferences. Season with salt and black pepper.

Allow the soup to simmer for about 15-20 minutes to let the flavours meld. Use an immersion blender or transfer the soup to a blender in batches to puree until smooth.

Stir in truffle oil to the velvety soup. If desired, add heavy cream for extra richness.

In a separate pan, heat a little oil over medium heat. Add fresh sage leaves and fry until they become crispy. Remove and set aside.

Ladle the roasted pumpkin cauldron soup into bowls. Garnish each bowl with crispy sage leaves. Optionally, add croutons for a delightful crunch.

GARTH'S GOAT CURRY
(SAVVAS' FAVOURITE)

Ingredients

- 2 lbs goat meat, cut into chunks
- 2 large onions, finely chopped
- 4 cloves garlic, minced
- 1-inch ginger, grated
- 2 large tomatoes, chopped
- 2 green chilies, sliced (adjust to taste)
- 1/4 cup cooking oil
- 1 cup plain yoghurt
- 1 tablespoon tomato paste
- 2 teaspoons ground coriander
- 2 teaspoons ground cumin
- 1 teaspoon turmeric powder
- 1 teaspoon chilli powder (adjust to taste)
- 1 teaspoon ground cinnamon
- 1 teaspoon ground cardamom
- 1 teaspoon ground cloves
- 1 teaspoon garam masala
- Salt to taste

- Fresh cilantro, chopped (for garnish)
- Cooked rice or naan (for serving)

Instructions:

In a large bowl, combine the goat meat, yoghurt, half of the chopped onions, minced garlic, grated ginger, and a pinch of salt. Mix well, cover, and let it marinate for at least 2 hours or overnight in the refrigerator.

Heat cooking oil in a large, heavy-bottomed pot over medium heat. Add the remaining chopped onions and cook until they become golden brown.

Add ground coriander, ground cumin, turmeric powder, chilli powder, ground cinnamon, ground cardamom, and ground cloves. Stir well and cook for 2-3 minutes until the spices release their aroma.

Add chopped tomatoes and tomato paste to the pot. Cook until the tomatoes break down and the mixture forms a thick, aromatic paste.

Add the marinated goat meat to the pot, ensuring all pieces are well coated in the spice mixture. Cook for 10-15 minutes until the meat is browned.

Pour in enough water to cover the meat, bring it to a boil, then reduce the heat to a simmer. Cover the pot and let it cook for 1.5 to 2 hours, or until the meat is tender and the flavours meld.

Season with salt and add garam masala. Stir well and let it simmer for an additional 10-15 minutes until the curry reaches your desired consistency.

Garnish with chopped cilantro and sliced green chillies. Serve the goat curry over steamed rice or with naan bread.

MEL'S BRIOCHE BURGERS WITH MUSHROOM PATTIES

Ingredients For the Mushroom Patties:

- 2 cups finely chopped mushrooms (blend in a food processor for a finer texture)
- 1 cup cooked quinoa
- 1/2 cup breadcrumbs
- 1/4 cup grated Parmesan cheese
- 1 clove garlic, minced
- 1 tablespoon soy sauce
- 1 teaspoon dried thyme
- Salt and black pepper to taste
- Olive oil for cooking

For the Brioche Burgers:

- Brioche burger buns
- Mayonnaise
- Blue cheese, sliced
- Beetroot, thinly sliced
- Black pepper, freshly cracked

- Lettuce leaves
- Caramelised red onions
- Olive oil for toasting buns

Instructions:

Cook quinoa according to package instructions. Let it cool.

In a bowl, mix together the finely chopped mushrooms, cooked quinoa, breadcrumbs, grated Parmesan, minced garlic, soy sauce, dried thyme, salt, and black pepper. Form the mixture into patties.

Heat olive oil in a pan over medium heat. Cook the mushroom patties for 4-5 minutes on each side or until golden brown. Set aside.

Cut the brioche burger buns in half. Toast them lightly in a pan with a touch of olive oil until golden.

Spread a thin layer of mayonnaise on the base of each bun.

Place the cooked mushroom patties on the mayo-covered buns.

Add slices of blue cheese on top of the mushroom patties.

Use a kitchen torch to gently torch the blue cheese until it melts slightly.

Layer the bright red beetroot slices and lettuce leaves on top of the melted blue cheese.

Crack black pepper over the beetroot and lettuce layers for added flavour.

Place a small dollop of caramelised red onions on top of the lettuce.

Finish by placing the top bun on the assembled ingredients with a slight crunch.

MEL'S RICE PUDDING WITH RASPBERRY JAM

Ingredients For the Rice Pudding:

- 1 cup Arborio rice
- 4 cups whole milk
- 1/2 cup granulated sugar
- 1 teaspoon vanilla extract
- 1/4 teaspoon ground cinnamon
- Pinch of salt
- 1/2 cup heavy cream

For the Raspberry Jam:

- 2 cups fresh or frozen raspberries
- 1 cup granulated sugar
- 1 tablespoon lemon juice
- 1 tablespoon water
- 1 teaspoon cornstarch (optional, for thickening)

Instructions:

Rinse the Arborio rice under cold water until the water runs clear.

In a medium-sized saucepan, combine the rinsed rice, whole milk, sugar, vanilla extract, ground cinnamon, and a pinch of salt. Bring to a simmer over medium heat.

Reduce the heat to low and simmer the rice mixture, stirring frequently to prevent sticking, for about 25-30 minutes or until the rice is cooked and the mixture has thickened.

Stir in the heavy cream and continue cooking for an additional 5 minutes until the rice pudding reaches a creamy consistency.

Remove the rice pudding from the heat and let it cool slightly. It will continue to thicken as it cools.

In a separate saucepan, combine raspberries, sugar, lemon juice, and water. Bring the mixture to a boil over medium-high heat.

Reduce the heat to low and let the mixture simmer for about 15-20 minutes, stirring occasionally. If you want a thicker jam, mix cornstarch with a little water to create a slurry and stir it into the raspberry mixture. Cook for an additional 2-3 minutes.

Mash the raspberries with a spoon or fork to achieve your desired consistency. Allow the raspberry jam to cool.

Spoon the rice pudding into individual serving bowls.

Spoon a generous dollop of homemade raspberry jam over each serving of rice pudding.

Optionally, you can garnish with fresh raspberries or a mint sprig for a decorative touch.

Serve the rice pudding with raspberry jam warm or chill it in the refrigerator for a few hours before serving.

MEL'S GRAPE GALLETTES

Ingredients For the Galette Dough:

- 2 cups all-purpose flour
- 1 tablespoon granulated sugar
- 1/2 teaspoon salt
- 1 cup unsalted butter, cold and cubed
- 1/2 cup ice water

For the Filling:

- Red seedless grapes, stems removed
- Creamy Brie cheese, sliced
- Fresh thyme leaves
- Balsamic reduction or glaze

For Assembly:

- Flour (for dusting)
- Egg wash (1 egg beaten with 1 tablespoon water)

- Granulated sugar (for sprinkling)

Instructions:

In a large bowl, combine the all-purpose flour, granulated sugar, and salt.

Add the cold, cubed butter to the flour mixture. Use a pastry cutter or your fingertips to quickly incorporate the butter until the mixture resembles coarse crumbs.

Gradually add the ice water, one tablespoon at a time, while gently mixing with a fork. Stop adding water when the dough starts to come together.

Turn the dough out onto a floured surface and knead it a few times until it forms a rough ball. Flatten into a disc, wrap in plastic wrap, and refrigerate for at least 30 minutes.

Preheat your oven to 375°F (190°C).

While the dough is chilling, prepare the grapes by removing the stems, slice the Brie cheese, and gather fresh thyme leaves.

On a floured surface, roll out the chilled galette dough into individual circles or one large circle, depending on your preference.

Place the rolled-out dough on a parchment-lined baking sheet. Arrange slices of creamy Brie cheese in the centre of each galette. Add a generous amount of red seedless grapes on top. Sprinkle fresh thyme leaves over the filling.

Carefully fold the edges of the dough over the filling, creating a rustic border. Press gently to seal the edges.

Brush the edges of the galette with the egg wash for a golden finish.

Bake in the preheated oven for 25-30 minutes or until the galettes are golden brown and the filling is bubbly.

Remove the galettes from the oven and let them cool slightly. Drizzle each galette with balsamic reduction or glaze.

Optional: Sprinkle the galettes with a little granulated sugar for extra sweetness.

Serve the grape galettes warm or at room temperature. They can be enjoyed as a delightful dessert or a unique appetiser.

MEL'S POMEGRANATE SURPRISE SNOWBALLS

Ingredients For the Coconut Marshmallow Base:

- 2 cups desiccated coconut
- 1 cup sweetened condensed milk
- 1 teaspoon vanilla extract
- Pinch of salt

For the Pomegranate Coulis Filling:

- 1 cup pomegranate seeds (from fresh pomegranate or store-bought)
- 2 tablespoons sugar
- 1 tablespoon lemon juice

For the Icing:

- 2 cups powdered sugar
- 2 tablespoons water
- 1/2 teaspoon vanilla extract
- Extra desiccated coconut

Instructions:

In a large mixing bowl, combine desiccated coconut, sweetened condensed milk, vanilla extract, and a pinch of salt. Mix until well combined.

Take small portions of the mixture and shape them into spherical balls. Place them on a parchment-lined tray and refrigerate for about 30 minutes to set.

Prepare the Pomegranate Coulis Filling: Extract the seeds from a fresh pomegranate or use store-bought pomegranate seeds.

In a blender, combine pomegranate seeds, sugar, and lemon juice. Blend until you have a smooth coulis. Strain the mixture to remove seeds if desired.

Once the coconut marshmallow snowballs are chilled, use a small spoon to create a well in the centre of each snowball. Fill the well with the pomegranate coulis, then rework the coconut marshmallow over the well.

In a bowl, whisk together powdered sugar, water, and vanilla extract until you have a smooth icing consistency.

Dip each filled snowball into the icing, ensuring they are evenly coated. Allow excess icing to drip off.

Roll the coated snowballs in extra desiccated coconut until they are fully covered. Place them back on the parchment-lined tray.

Refrigerate the pomegranate surprise snowballs for at least 1-2 hours to set the icing and coconut coating.

Share these delightful treats with friends and family, and watch their faces light up with the surprise of the hidden pomegranate goodness in each snowball.

MEL'S SCALLOP BISQUE

Ingredients:

- 1 pound fresh scallops, cleaned and patted dry
- 1 onion, finely chopped
- 2 carrots, peeled and diced
- 2 celery stalks, diced
- 3 cloves garlic, minced
- 4 tablespoons unsalted butter
- 1/4 cup all-purpose flour
- 1/2 cup cognac
- 1/2 teaspoon saffron threads
- 4 cups seafood or vegetable broth
- 1 cup heavy cream
- 1 bay leaf
- Salt and black pepper to taste
- Fresh chives or parsley for garnish

Instructions:

In a large skillet, heat 2 tablespoons of butter over medium-high heat. Sear the scallops for about 1-2 minutes on each side until golden brown. Remove from the skillet and set aside.

In the same skillet, add the remaining butter. Sauté the chopped onion, carrots, celery, and garlic until softened.

Sprinkle the flour over the vegetables and stir continuously for 2-3 minutes to create a roux.

Pour in the cognac, scraping the bottom of the skillet to deglaze and incorporate the flavours.

Add saffron threads to the skillet, allowing them to infuse the mixture with their aromatic flavour.

Transfer the vegetable mixture to a large pot. Pour in the seafood or vegetable broth, add the bay leaf, and bring the mixture to a gentle simmer. Let it simmer for about 15-20 minutes to allow the flavours to meld.

Use an immersion blender or transfer the soup in batches to a blender to puree until smooth.

Return the bisque to the pot. Stir in the heavy cream and season with salt and black pepper to taste.

Chop half of the seared scallops into small pieces and add them to the bisque. Reserve the remaining whole scallops for garnish.

Allow the bisque to simmer for an additional 10-15 minutes to heat through and let the flavours meld.

If the bisque is too thick, you can adjust the consistency by adding more broth or cream. Taste and adjust the seasoning as needed.

Ladle the scallop bisque into bowls. Garnish each serving with a whole seared scallop and sprinkle fresh chives or parsley on top.

MEL'S SECRET WALNUT SOUFFLÉ

Ingredients:

- 1 cup finely ground walnuts
- 1 cup whole milk
- 4 tablespoons unsalted butter
- 1/2 cup all-purpose flour
- 1/2 cup granulated sugar
- 4 large egg yolks
- 1 teaspoon vanilla extract
- Pinch of salt
- 5 large egg whites
- 1/4 cup granulated sugar (for meringue)
- Powdered sugar (for dusting)

Instructions:

Preheat your oven to 375°F (190°C). Butter and sugar the inside of a soufflé dish or individual ramekins.

In a saucepan, heat the milk until it's warm but not boiling. Add the finely ground walnuts and let them soak in the warm milk for about 30 minutes. After soaking, blend the mixture until it forms a smooth walnut paste.

In another saucepan, melt the butter over medium heat. Add the flour and cook, stirring constantly, until it forms a smooth paste (roux).

Gradually add the walnut paste to the roux, whisking continuously to avoid lumps. Cook for a few minutes until the mixture thickens.

Stir in the granulated sugar, vanilla extract, and a pinch of salt. Mix until the sugar is fully dissolved.

Beat the egg yolks in a separate bowl. Gradually add a small amount of the walnut mixture to the beaten yolks, whisking constantly. This helps to temper the yolks and prevent curdling.

Combine with Walnut Mixture: Pour the tempered egg yolk mixture back into the saucepan with the walnut mixture. Mix well and cook for a few more minutes until it thickens to a custard-like consistency.

In a clean, dry bowl, beat the egg whites until soft peaks form. Gradually add 1/4 cup of granulated sugar while continuing to beat until glossy stiff peaks form.

Gently fold a third of the whipped egg whites into the walnut mixture to lighten it. Then, carefully fold in the remaining egg whites until just combined.

Pour the soufflé mixture into the prepared dish or ramekins, filling them almost to the top.

Place the soufflé dish or ramekins in the preheated oven and bake for 25-30 minutes or until the top is golden brown, and the soufflé has risen.

Remove from the oven, dust with powdered sugar, and serve immediately. The soufflé will start to deflate quickly, so enjoy it while it's at its lightest and fluffiest.

RAE'S BACON-WRAPPED HONEY GLAZED PRAWNS

Ingredients:

- 1 lb (about 450g) large prawns, peeled and deveined
- 10-12 slices of bacon, cut in half
- 1/4 cup honey
- 2 tablespoons soy sauce
- 1 tablespoon Dijon mustard
- 1 tablespoon olive oil
- 1 teaspoon smoked paprika
- 1/2 teaspoon garlic powder
- Freshly ground black pepper, to taste
- Wooden toothpicks, soaked in water

Instructions:

Preheat your oven to 400°F (200°C).

In a bowl, whisk together honey, soy sauce, Dijon mustard, olive oil, smoked paprika, garlic powder, and black pepper. This will be the marinade for the prawns.

Toss the peeled and deveined prawns in the marinade, ensuring they are well-coated. Allow them to marinate for at least 15-20 minutes to absorb the flavours.

Take each marinated prawn and wrap it with a half-slice of bacon. Secure the bacon with a soaked wooden toothpick, piercing through the bacon and prawn.

Place the bacon-wrapped prawns on a baking sheet lined with parchment paper or aluminium foil, ensuring they are not touching each other.

Bake in the preheated oven for about 15-20 minutes or until the bacon is crispy and the prawns are cooked through. You can also broil for the last couple of minutes to get the bacon extra crispy.

In the last 5 minutes of cooking, brush the bacon-wrapped prawns with additional honey for a sweet glaze. This step enhances the flavour and gives the prawns a beautiful caramelisation.

Remove the bacon-wrapped prawns from the oven. Carefully transfer them to a serving platter. Discard the toothpicks before serving.

Garnish with chopped fresh parsley or a sprinkle of smoked paprika.

NYX'S BLACKENED FISH & ROASTED MARROW

*This recipe (and others like it) has been modified for mortal enjoyment by a begrudging Nika who passed it onto Garth for the restaurant. They both disclaim any responsibility for kitchen mishaps or recipe misfortunes.

Ingredients For the Blackened Fish:

- 4 fish fillets (such as red snapper, grouper, or catfish)
- 2 tablespoons paprika
- 1 tablespoon dried thyme
- 1 tablespoon onion powder
- 1 tablespoon garlic powder
- 1 teaspoon cayenne pepper (adjust to taste)
- 1 teaspoon dried oregano
- 1 teaspoon ground black pepper
- 1 teaspoon salt
- 1/2 cup unsalted butter, melted
- Lemon wedges for serving

For the Roasted Marrow:

- 2 large beef marrow bones, halved lengthwise
- Olive oil for drizzling
- Salt and black pepper to taste

For the Melted Cheeses:

- 1 cup shredded cheddar cheese
- 1 cup shredded mozzarella cheese
- 1/2 cup grated Parmesan cheese

Instructions:

Preheat a heavy skillet over high heat until smoking hot.

In a bowl, mix paprika, dried thyme, onion powder, garlic powder, cayenne pepper, dried oregano, black pepper, and salt to create the blackening seasoning.

Brush each fish fillet with melted butter, then generously coat both sides with the blackening seasoning.

Place the fish fillets in the hot skillet and cook for 2-3 minutes per side or until the exterior is blackened and the fish is cooked through. Adjust the cooking time based on the thickness of the fillets.

Squeeze fresh lemon juice over the blackened fish fillets before serving.

Roasted Marrow: Preheat your oven to 400°F (204°C).

Place the halved marrow bones on a baking sheet. Drizzle with olive oil and season with salt and black pepper.

Roast in the preheated oven for about 20-25 minutes or until the marrow is soft and easily scooped out with a spoon.

Prepare Cheeses: In a bowl, combine the shredded cheddar, mozzarella, and grated Parmesan cheeses.

Once the fish and marrow are ready, top each fish fillet with roasted marrow, then generously sprinkle the melted cheese mixture over the top. Place the assembled dishes under the broiler for 2-3 minutes or until the cheese is bubbly and golden.

LEXIE'S ROASTED GOAT
(NOT HER FAVOURITE ON THE WATERING HOLE MENU, BUT BETTER THAN RAW FISH.)

*This recipe (and others like it) has been modified for mortal enjoyment by Lexie, who, despite lacking official professional culinary credentials, disclaims any responsibility for kitchen mishaps or recipe misfortunes.

Ingredients For the Marinade:

- 4-5 lbs goat meat, cut into large chunks
- 1 cup plain yoghurt
- 1/4 cup olive oil
- 4 cloves garlic, minced
- 1 tablespoon ginger, grated
- 1 tablespoon ground coriander
- 1 tablespoon ground cumin
- 1 tablespoon paprika
- 1 teaspoon turmeric
- 1 teaspoon cayenne pepper (adjust to taste)
- Salt and black pepper to taste

For Roasting:

- 2 large onions, sliced
- 2 lemons, sliced
- Fresh herbs (rosemary, thyme, or oregano)
- Olive oil for drizzling

Instructions:

In a large bowl, combine all the marinade ingredients: yoghurt, olive oil, minced garlic, grated ginger, ground coriander, ground cumin, paprika, turmeric, cayenne pepper, salt, and black pepper.

Add the chunks of goat meat to the marinade, ensuring each piece is well-coated. Cover the bowl and refrigerate for at least 4 hours or preferably overnight for the flavours to infuse.

Preheat your oven to 325°F (163°C).

Place the sliced onions, lemon slices, and fresh herbs in the bottom of a roasting pan. This will create a flavourful bed for the goat meat.

Arrange the marinated goat chunks on top of the onion and lemon bed in the roasting pan. Drizzle with a little olive oil.

Cover the roasting pan with aluminium foil and roast in the preheated oven for 2.5 to 3 hours. The goat meat should become tender and easily pull apart.

Remove the foil and increase the oven temperature to 400°F (204°C). Roast for an additional 20-30 minutes or until the goat meat develops a nice golden-brown crust.

Allow the roasted goat to rest for a few minutes before serving. Garnish with fresh herbs and lemon slices.

Serve the roasted goat with your favourite sides, such as rice, couscous, or roasted vegetables.

LEXIE'S BEEF CARPACCIO
(ORIGINALLY DONE WITH DEER, BUT SHE HEARS MORTALS PREFER BEEF.)

Ingredients:

- 8 ounces (225g) beef tenderloin, trimmed and thinly sliced
- 1 cup arugula, washed and dried
- 1/4 cup shaved Parmesan cheese
- 2 tablespoons capers, drained
- Extra virgin olive oil, for drizzling
- Lemon wedges, for serving
- Salt and black pepper, to taste

For the Marinade:

- 2 tablespoons extra virgin olive oil
- 1 tablespoon Dijon mustard
- 1 tablespoon Worcestershire sauce
- 1 clove garlic, minced
- 1 teaspoon balsamic vinegar
- Salt and black pepper, to taste

Instructions:

In a small bowl, whisk together the extra virgin olive oil, Dijon mustard, Worcestershire sauce, minced garlic, balsamic vinegar, salt, and black pepper.

Place the thinly sliced beef tenderloin in a shallow dish. Pour the marinade over the beef, ensuring each slice is well coated. Cover and refrigerate for at least 30 minutes to let the flavours meld.

Arrange the marinated beef slices on a serving platter, slightly overlapping.

Scatter arugula over the beef slices. Sprinkle shaved Parmesan cheese and capers evenly.

Drizzle extra virgin olive oil over the beef carpaccio for added richness.

Season the dish with salt and black pepper to taste.

Serve the beef carpaccio immediately, accompanied by lemon wedges on the side.

GARTH'S LAMB TAGINE
(WITH SOME OF LEXIE'S AMENDS)

*This recipe has been modified for mortal enjoyment by Garth & Lexie, who both disclaim any responsibility for kitchen mishaps or recipe misfortunes.

Ingredients:

- 2 pounds (about 1 kg) boneless lamb shoulder, cut into 1.5-inch cubes
- 2 tablespoons olive oil
- 1 large onion, finely chopped
- 3 cloves garlic, minced
- 1 teaspoon ground cumin
- 1 teaspoon ground coriander
- 1 teaspoon ground cinnamon
- 1 teaspoon paprika
- 1/2 teaspoon ground ginger
- 1/2 teaspoon ground saffron
- 1/4 teaspoon cayenne pepper (adjust to taste)
- Salt and black pepper, to taste
- 1 can (14 ounces) diced tomatoes, undrained

- 1/2 cup dried apricots, chopped
- 1/2 cup golden raisins
- 2 tablespoons tomato paste
- 2 cups chicken or vegetable broth
- 1 cinnamon stick
- 1 bay leaf
- 1/4 cup chopped fresh cilantro, for garnish
- 1/3 cup toasted almonds, chopped
- Cooked couscous or rice, for serving

Instructions:

Pat the lamb cubes dry with paper towels and season them with salt and black pepper.

In a large tagine or a heavy-bottomed pot, heat olive oil over medium-high heat. Brown the lamb cubes on all sides until they develop a golden crust. Work in batches to avoid overcrowding the pot. Remove the browned lamb and set it aside.

In the same pot, add chopped onions and sauté until softened. Add minced garlic and cook for an additional minute.

Stir in ground cumin, ground coriander, ground cinnamon, paprika, ground ginger, ground turmeric, cayenne pepper, and cook for 1-2 minutes until fragrant.

Return the browned lamb to the pot. Add diced tomatoes (with their juice), chopped dried apricots, golden raisins, and tomato paste. Mix well.

Pour in chicken or vegetable broth, ensuring that the ingredients are well submerged.

Toss in a cinnamon stick and a bay leaf for additional flavour. Bring the mixture to a gentle simmer.

Reduce the heat to low, cover the pot, and let the lamb tagine simmer for 2 to 2.5 hours or until the lamb is tender and the flavours meld.

Taste and adjust the seasoning if necessary. Remove the cinnamon stick and bay leaf.

Before serving, garnish the lamb tagine with chopped fresh cilantro and toasted almonds.

Serve the lamb tagine over cooked couscous or rice.

YANI'S CROWNING GLORY
(OTHERWISE KNOWN AS THE CEVICHE FISH TACO)

*This recipe (and others like it) has been modified for mortal enjoyment by Yani, who, despite lacking official professional culinary accreditation, disclaims any responsibility for kitchen mishaps or recipe misfortunes.

Ingredients:

- 1 pound fresh white fish fillets (snapper, tilapia, or halibut), diced
- Juice of 4-5 limes
- 1 ripe mango, diced
- 2 ripe avocados, mashed
- 1/2 red onion, finely chopped
- 1 jalapeño, seeds removed and finely chopped
- 1/4 cup fresh cilantro, chopped
- Salt and black pepper, to taste
- Artisan corn flatbreads

Instructions:

In a glass or non-reactive bowl, combine the diced fish and lime juice. Ensure that the fish is well-coated. Let it marinate for about 15-20 minutes until the fish turns opaque.

While the fish is marinating, mash the ripe avocados in a bowl. Season with salt and black pepper to taste.

Spread a generous layer of the mashed avocado onto each artisan corn flatbread.

Place the marinated fish on top of the creamy avocado layer.

Sprinkle the diced ripe mango over the fish, creating a vibrant and sweet contrast.

Scatter finely chopped red onion, jalapeño, and fresh cilantro over the ceviche.

Season the ceviche with additional salt and black pepper according to your taste preferences.

Serve immediately to enjoy the freshness of the ingredients.

ALORA'S SNAKE LATTICE BITES

*This recipe has been modified for mortal enjoyment by Garth from his mother's original recipe. He (once again) disclaims any responsibility for kitchen mishaps or recipe misfortunes.

Ingredients For the Filling:

- 1 cup dark chocolate, finely chopped
- 1/2 cup mixed nuts (walnuts, almonds, or pistachios), finely crushed
- 1/4 cup brown sugar
- 1 teaspoon ground cinnamon
- 1/2 teaspoon ground nutmeg
- 1/4 teaspoon salt

For the Pastry:

- 1 package (17.3 ounces) puff pastry, thawed
- All-purpose flour (for dusting)

For Egg Wash:

- 1 egg, beaten
- 1 tablespoon water

Instructions:

In a bowl, combine the finely chopped dark chocolate, crushed mixed nuts, brown sugar, ground cinnamon, ground nutmeg, and salt. Mix well to create a sweet and nutty filling.

Preheat the oven to the temperature specified on the puff pastry package.

On a lightly floured surface, roll out the puff pastry into a large rectangle.

Spread the chocolate and nut filling evenly over the puff pastry.

Carefully roll the pastry into a log, creating a spiral effect with the filling.

Slice the rolled pastry into bite-sized pieces, about 1 inch wide.

Place the coiled pastries on a baking sheet lined with parchment paper, leaving space between each piece.

In a small bowl, whisk together the beaten egg and water to create an egg wash.

Brush the tops of the lattice bites with the egg wash for a golden finish during baking.

Bake in the preheated oven according to the puff pastry package instructions or until the lattice bites are golden brown and puffed.

Allow the lattice bites to cool slightly before dusting with powdered sugar if desired.

Serve these delectable chocolate and nut lattice bites as a delightful treat with a cup of coffee or tea.

DUCK RAGU FROM THAT LITTLE PLACE IN ASPHODEL MEADOWS

Ingredients:

- 2 duck legs, skin-on
- Salt and black pepper, to taste
- 2 tablespoons olive oil
- 1 onion, finely chopped
- 2 carrots, finely chopped
- 2 celery stalks, finely chopped
- 4 cloves garlic, minced
- 1 cup red wine
- 1 can (28 ounces) crushed tomatoes
- 2 tablespoons tomato paste
- 2 bay leaves
- 1 teaspoon dried thyme
- 1 teaspoon dried rosemary
- 1 teaspoon dried oregano
- 1/2 teaspoon red pepper flakes (optional)
- 1 cup chicken or vegetable broth
- 1/2 cup whole milk

- Grated Parmesan cheese, for serving
- Fresh parsley, chopped, for garnish
- Cooked pasta or polenta, for serving

Instructions:

Season duck legs with salt and black pepper. In a large Dutch oven or heavy-bottomed pot, heat olive oil over medium-high heat. Sear the duck legs until golden brown on both sides. Remove from the pot and set aside.

In the same pot, add chopped onion, carrots, celery, and garlic. Sauté until the vegetables are softened.

Pour in red wine to deglaze the pot, scraping any flavourful bits from the bottom.

Stir in crushed tomatoes, tomato paste, bay leaves, thyme, rosemary, oregano, and red pepper flakes (if using).

Place the seared duck legs back into the pot, nestling them into the sauce.

Add chicken or vegetable broth and pour in the milk. Stir to combine.

Bring the mixture to a simmer, then reduce the heat to low. Cover and let it simmer for 2-3 hours until the duck is tender and the flavours meld.

Once the duck is cooked, remove the legs from the pot. Shred the meat, discarding the bones and skin.

Allow the sauce to simmer uncovered to thicken. Adjust the seasoning with salt and pepper as needed.

Serve the duck ragu over cooked pasta or polenta. Garnish with grated Parmesan cheese and chopped fresh parsley.

SAVVAS' SICKLY SWEET PINK COCKTAIL

*This recipe has been modified for mortal enjoyment by Savvas, who, despite lacking professional winemaking training (unless being trained by Dionysus counts), disclaims any responsibility for kitchen mishaps or recipe misfortunes.

Ingredients:

- 2 oz raspberry-flavoured vodka
- 1 oz strawberry liqueur
- 1 oz cranberry juice
- 1 oz pink lemonade
- 1/2 oz simple syrup (adjust to taste)
- Splash of club soda
- Ice cubes
- Fresh berries for garnish
- Pink sugar (for rimming, optional)

Instructions:

If desired, rim a chilled cocktail glass with pink sugar. To do this, moisten the rim with a slice of lemon or water, then dip the rim into pink sugar.

Fill the prepared glass with ice cubes.

In a cocktail shaker, combine raspberry-flavoured vodka, strawberry liqueur, cranberry juice, pink lemonade, and simple syrup.

Shake the ingredients well to chill the mixture.

Strain the shaken mixture into the prepared glass over the ice.

Top the cocktail with a splash of club soda for a fizzy finish. Gently stir to combine.

Garnish the cocktail with fresh berries like raspberries or strawberries for a burst of colour and flavour.

Serve this super sweet and vibrant pink bliss cocktail immediately.

GIGI'S AVGOLEMONO SOUP

Ingredients:

- 8 cups of chicken broth
- 1 cup orzo or rice
- 3 eggs
- Juice of 2-3 lemons (about 1/2 to 3/4 cup) Salt and pepper, to taste
- 1 cup cooked and shredded chicken (optional) Fresh dill, chopped, for garnish

Instructions:

Cook the orzo or rice according to the package instructions. Drain and set aside.

In a large pot, bring the chicken broth to a simmer. If using cooked and shredded chicken, add it to the broth.

In a separate bowl, whisk together the eggs until well beaten. Gradually add the lemon juice to the beaten eggs, whisking constantly. This helps prevent the eggs from curdling when added to the hot broth.

Take a ladle of hot broth from the pot and slowly pour it into the egg-lemon mixture, whisking continuously. This process helps temper the eggs

Pour the tempered egg-lemon mixture back into the pot with the simmering broth, stirring constantly.

Stir in the cooked orzo or rice into the broth and egg- lemon mixture.

Season the soup with salt and pepper to taste. Adjust the lemon juice according to your preference.

Allow the soup to simmer for an additional 5-10 minutes, ensuring it is heated through.

Garnish with chopped fresh dill for added flavour and freshness.

Ladle the avgolemono soup into bowls and serve immediately.

YANI'S CLASSIC FRESH OYSTERS

*Recipes are modified for mortal enjoyment. This one is from Yani, who does not believe you should eat oysters in any other way whatsoever. Still, he disclaims any responsibility if you have a mishap with this recipe or simply don't like them.

Ingredients:

- 12 fresh oysters, in the shell
- Crushed ice or rock salt (for serving)
- Lemon wedges
- Freshly ground black pepper
- Cocktail sauce (optional)
- Mignonette sauce (optional)

Instructions:

Ensure you buy fresh, high-quality oysters from a reputable source.

Scrub the oyster shells under cold running water to remove any dirt or debris.

Using an oyster knife, carefully shuck the oysters by inserting the knife into the hinge of the shell and twisting to pop it open. Be cautious to avoid any shell fragments falling into the oyster.

Arrange the freshly shucked oysters on a bed of crushed ice or rock salt on a serving platter.

Place lemon wedges on the platter to squeeze over the oysters before consuming.

Provide freshly ground black pepper for those who enjoy a bit of extra spice.

Serve with cocktail sauce and/or mignonette sauce on the side for dipping. Cocktail sauce typically includes horse-radish, ketchup, and Worcestershire sauce, while mignonette sauce consists of shallots, vinegar, and pepper.

Present the platter in a visually appealing way, making sure the oysters are easy to access.

ABOUT THE AUTHOR

Gwyneth Lesley loves to write modern-day Greek myth retellings. Her first collection, the Femme Fatale series, is a mixture of heartbreaking, steamy, standalone books, following the archetypes of seven different women with untold ties to Greek mythology.

The first three in the Femme Fatale series are:
Prometheus' Priestess
A Lifetime Kind of Love
Madonna: Medusa's retelling

What Gwen is working on next:
Odette's Vow (Book 1 in her *Iliad* & *Odyssey* duet)
Apollo's Oracle (Femme Fatale Book 4)
Odysseus' Promise (Book 2 in her *I&O* duet)

As reviewers say, her work is: "Definitely recommend[ed] to people who have never read any Greek mythology and are looking to expand their reading palette."

Learn more at: https://www.gwynethlesley.com

www.ingramcontent.com/pod-product-compliance
Lightning Source LLC
Chambersburg PA
CBHW011112100726

47898CB00011B/3050

RAE'S SUBLIME HOT CHOCOLATE

Ingredients:

- 2 cups whole milk
- 1/2 cup heavy cream
- 1/4 cup granulated sugar (adjust to taste)
- 1 teaspoon vanilla extract
- 1/4 cup unsweetened cocoa powder
- Pinch of salt
- 4 ounces high-quality dark chocolate, finely chopped
- Marshmallows (for melting)
- Whipped cream
- Chocolate sauce
- Grated chocolate or cocoa powder (for garnish)

Instructions:

In a saucepan over medium heat, combine the whole milk and heavy cream. Heat until it starts to simmer but avoid boiling.

Whisk in the granulated sugar, vanilla extract, unsweetened cocoa powder, and a pinch of salt. Continue whisking until the mixture is smooth and well-combined.

Add the finely chopped dark chocolate to the milk mixture. Stir continuously until the chocolate is completely melted, and the hot chocolate becomes rich and velvety.

Allow the hot chocolate to simmer gently for a few minutes, ensuring it reaches your desired consistency. If it's too thick, you can add more milk.

Pour the decadent hot chocolate into mugs, leaving some space at the top for toppings.

Place marshmallows on top of the hot chocolate and use a kitchen torch to gently melt and brown them. Alternatively, you can place the mugs under the broiler for a brief moment, but watch carefully to avoid burning.

Generously top each mug with a dollop of whipped cream.

Drizzle rich chocolate sauce over the whipped cream, creating a decadent and visually pleasing pattern.

Finish by grating some chocolate or dusting with cocoa powder for an extra touch of indulgence.